"YOU ARROGANT BASTARD!"

She hit him a resounding slap with every ounce of her weight behind it.

Gordon put a hand to his flaming cheek. "You will pay for that, wench." He lunged after her as she scrambled up the slope on hands and knees. His hand caught her ankle and dragged her back down. Then he straddled her hips and pinned her arms to the ground. She writhed and thrashed desperately, but her strength was no match for his.

"Let me go, or I'll kill you!" she screamed, her eyes burning with hatred.

He ripped at the buttons of her blouse. She gasped as he bared her flesh and appraised her nude body with undisguised hunger. He bent himself to her and smothered her face and neck with wet kisses.

"Oh, God!" she moaned as he teased her with his tongue.

SECRET SINS

STEPHANIE BLAKE

PLAYBOY PRESS
PAPERBACKS

To my faithful friend and muse without peer, Samantha J. Katz, without whose encouragement and support my six best-selling novels could never have been written.

Stephanie Blake

Published simultaneously in the United States and Canada by Playboy Paperbacks, New York, New York. Printed in the United States of America. Library of Congress Catalog Card Number: 80-80982. First edition.

Books are available at quantity discounts for promotional and industrial use. For further information, write to Premium Sales, Playboy Paperbacks, 747 Third Avenue. New York, New York 10017.

ISBI: 0-872-16719-4

First printing August 1980.

MARA
THE
FIRST

CHAPTER ONE

On the morning of November 8, 1960, Mara Rodgers Tate woke up with a tingling sense of excitement and anticipation.

"Today is the day," she soliloquized. "In just a matter of hours the entire course of American history will take on new direction."

Now, after twenty years of bleak darkness, there was the promise of new and brighter horizons, a radiant dawn. The most savage and costly war in history, waged against the maniacal, inhuman Nazis and the warlords of the Rising Sun; the precarious cold war with the Soviet Union; the infamous civil war within instigated by witch-hunter Senator Joseph McCarthy; the tragedy of Korea, wherein the United States—naïve giant—after 160 years of "invincibility," learned the bitter lesson of the futility of fighting for lost causes, tilting at windmills; followed by the tranquil do-nothing eight years in which Ike quite literally sat in the White House, an intermission between the acts—these were past history now.

Mara would never forget that milestone day when she sat in the Los Angeles Memorial Sports Arena, listening with bated breath to the votes being tallied, state by state, and then to the momentous announcement: "One thousand, five hundred twenty-one votes. John Fitzgerald Kennedy is hereby nominated for President of the United States by the Democratic Party. . . ."

It swept over Mara with the intense ecstasy of an

7

orgasm. She smiled and closed her eyes, hearing the clash of cymbals, the roll of drums, celestial strings, all playing the grand overture. The curtain was about to go up on the finale, the *pièce de résistance*. After twenty years, the light at the end of the tunnel shone like the evening star.

Here was America the beautiful on the brink of a new manifest destiny, an era of unprecedented national glory, prosperity, and harmony with all the nations of the world unmatched since the Founding Fathers put their signatures to the Declaration of Independence back in 1776.

Mara threw back the coverlet and got out of the enormous bed, which one of her lovers, upon seeing it for the first time, described thusly: "The headboard looks like the instrument panel of a 707!"

It was no exaggeration: four rows of buttons, dials, levers, and switches, plus a miniature telephone switchboard, that controlled a combination hi-fi record player/ radio, five television sets banked on a wide shelf at the far end of the room, and a movie projector set in the wall behind the bed. A green lever that reminded her of the ones in voting booths operated a sliding partition that exposed a fully stocked bar and an ice machine.

Mara idly laid a hand on the lever and gently stroked its erect plastic length. In another few hours she would step inside a booth in her district and cast her ballot for "Johnny" and the rest of the Democrats. There was not a hint of a doubt in her mind about the outcome. When the final tally was completed, John Fitzgerald Kennedy would be elected the thirty-fifth president of the United States.

Tempering the immense pride and exultation she was experiencing from his impending victory was a minuscule pang of regret, a sense of personal loss. The indelible, exquisite idylls they had shared in the past were forever gone. Never again would she know the joy and bliss of his hands on her vibrant flesh and her fingers caressing his hard, muscular, sweet male form.

Her hand clenched hard for an instant on the plastic-covered handle, and an expletive, a short gasp, escaped between her gritted teeth. She shuddered and laughed dryly; shook herself like an animal shedding water from its hide.

Above all, Mara Rodgers Tate was a realist, hers a pragmatic philosophy. One could not hope to win every hand or every roll of the dice; and nothing endured forever. "Give 'em, hell, Johnny," she said aloud and padded barefoot and naked into the bathroom.

Mara was a Tate through and through, one of the third generation of the penniless Welsh-English immigrant family who had disembarked from steerage of a fourth-class merchant ship at Ellis Island, port of New York, on a dreary day in April 1876—Drew and Gwenn Tate and their progeny: Emlyn, Allan, Gilbert, Dylan, and Mara (Mara the first).

As soon as they had been cleared for entry into the United States, Drew invested the family savings in two horse-drawn wagons and all the supplies they could afford, and headed west for the territory of Arizona. He wanted to satisfy an obsession that had been festering inside him for two years after he'd read an item in the Cardiff *Herald* about the scarcity of experienced miners to work the silver, gold, and copper lodes of barren Arizona.

"The blighters can't abide the extreme heat," he told his sons, all of whom had followed their father down into the Cardiff coal pits, as had been the Tate family tradition for generations: "Bet we could teach them a thing or two about digging. Compared with these damned Welsh hellholes we labor in twelve hours a day, seven days a week, Arizona would be like a week-end at Brighton beach shoveling sand."

And on New Year's Day of 1876 the patriarch had announced, "I booked us passage to America. We sail in the spring." He swept thirteen-year-old Mara onto his broad lap and hugged her to his bosom. "And what do you think about that, light of my life? Will you be eager to go to America?"

Deceptively frail in appearance, Mara's slim, wiry body had the tensile strength of drawn steel. Thick black hair hung down her back to her waist, framing an oval face with flawless olive skin and dominated by enormous dark eyes that glowed with a feverish bright-ness when she was excited, as she was now.

"I can't wait, Da. Ever since you first spoke of it, I've been reading everything I can get my hands on about the United States and especially about the ter-ritory of Arizona. Did you know it was discovered by a Spanish priest back in 1539? And the following year another priest was the first white man to set eyes on the Grand Canyon?"

"The Grand Canyon?" Her father was perplexed.

"One of the great wonders of the world, that's all it is—over one mile deep and up to fourteen miles wide and over two hundred miles long. Can you picture a gorge such as that?"

The entire family gathered around the girl as she recited an explicit history, spanning a period of more than 200 years, of the land that was to be their new home: "The first real mining commenced in Arizona in 1854 when an army captain came upon a rich silver-copper-ore deposit. . . ."

Drew Tate listened in wide-eyed amazement as his young daughter completed her erudite and informative recitation. Mara was the pride of his existence. Later that night in bed, he confided to his wife, "That child, she's got more inside her head than all the other children put together." His mouth twisted in a wry grin. "And mine and your head as well."

Just before she entered the bathroom, Mara the third's eyes were drawn to the oil painting of her grandmother that hung on a wall opposite her bed. Frequently, in the dark hours of the night when she was harassed by insomnia, her mind working like a runaway computer trying to absorb and resolve the infinite problems that confronted her each day as the chief executive of a multibillion-dollar international conglomerate, Mara would switch on the light and look to Mara the first for advice and moral support.

All the while she was describing her dilemmas, the old woman in the painting would hear her out with what she imagined was an expression of understanding and concentration, the eyes coming alive, it seemed; and rarely would she disappoint Mara:

Well, that's no problem at all, my girl. Offer them a package of cash, warrants, and debentures. How can they refuse such an offer?

An answer like that was sure to elicit a warm chuckle from the younger woman. "Now, why didn't that occur to me, Granny?"

Oh, it would have sooner or later, my child.

And Mara the third would swear her grandmother had winked at her. *Mara the third*—no affectation in it at all; she wore the title like a badge of honor, as her mother, Mara the second, had worn hers. Her grandfather's name had been Gordon Ewing, her father's Samuel Rodgers; but both she and her mother had preferred to employ "Tate" as a surname: Mara Ewing Tate; Mara Rodgers Tate.

A Tate is a Tate is a Tate, as Gertrude Stein might have phrased it, Mara reflected as she stepped into the shower and turned the solid-gold faucets.

In less than five minutes—as much time—as she

would ever relegate to such a trivial necessity—she was showered and already wrapped in a voluminous terry-cloth towel. With a corner of it she wiped the steam from the full-length mirror on the back of the door and surveyed herself in the glass. It was an impassive, objective appraisal: high patrician forehead; high cheekbones with the hollows beneath them still intact; slim, slightly aquiline nose with just the right flare to the nostrils; wide-set blue-gray eyes, clear as crystal despite the fact that she had worked in her apartment office until four this morning. Mara tested the flesh under her chin with the back of one hand— no dewlap; and not a strand of gray in the thick, long black hair that had body even though sopping wet.

One final part to her morning ritual: She removed the towel and examined her naked reflection front side, in profile, and peering over her shoulder, from the rear: flat belly, firm buttocks, no trace of cellulite in her rounded thighs. She lifted her breasts with her hands and frowned.

"Think you're developing some sag, my girl," she said.

Purposefully she opened the medicine chest and took out a toothbrush. Lifting her left breast, she tucked the toothbrush snugly beneath the pear-shaped mound and let the breast down gently. To her satisfaction, the implement promptly fell to the tile floor. If the muscle tone of mammary tissue betrayed any sign of deterioration, the breast would have held the brush fast to the chest wall. She repeated the procedure on the right breast, with identical results. Smiling, she replaced the toothbrush in the cabinet.

She finished drying her body, wrapped a towel turbanlike around her gathered-up hair, slipped her feet into red-velvet mules, and went back into the bedroom. Opening the sliding doors of a thirty-foot wardrobe closet she chose a robe from a varied assortment

—a flowing velvet hostess gown gathered at the yoke and bordered with flowers. She closed it loosely with a sash and left the bedroom.

When she was in New York City, which was at least six months a year, Mara Rodgers Tate the third resided in a spacious eight-room duplex penthouse overlooking Central Park and flanked on two sides by an open patio garden landscaped with a variety of exotic plants and shrubs, predominantly strains native to Arizona. There was saguaro cactus—a grotesque caricature of a deformed human being, all accordion pleats and sharp spines, its ugliness mitigated by creamy white blossoms and plump red fruit —and century plants, prickly poppies, desert mariposa, verbena, marigolds, blue dicks, lavender pentstemon, golden columbine, and a patch of earth containing scores of tiny "stomach plants," so called because one could admire them properly only by lying prone with a magnifying glass. The sliding glass doors overlooking the garden were shut against the brisk November gale assaulting the high-tower apartment complex.

Humming the Kennedy victory song, Mara went to the recessed bar against one wall of the living room and pressed the button set in the mahogany panel that concealed it. The panel slid aside silently, revealing a service bar the equal of any in New York's most fashionable cafés and restaurants. From behind her came a stern admonition:

"Before breakfast, hon? Over my dead body!"

Mara turned and smiled at Francine Watkins, the slender, pretty black woman who served as her pesonal maid and companion. Francine was wearing a tailored suit of gray velour, the softness of the material moderating the severity of the design.

"I thought I might have a split of champagne with my orange juice—you know, to celebrate the happy occasion."

Francine grunted. "He's not elected yet. You'd better be careful you don't jinx him."

Mara laughed. "Oh, it's definite, take my word. You know my instincts are never wrong."

The black woman's eyes shifted uneasily. It was true that Mara possessed foresight denied to *normal* mortals. (The word was italicized in Francine's mind.) Mara's attorney, and occasional lover, declared emphatically that her foresight was a rare and genuine case of extrasensory perception, mundanely referred to as "second sight." In Jamaica, where Francine's parents had been born, they called it "voodoo."

"Miss Castle called, but I told her you left orders not to be disturbed." Jean Castle was Mara's chief assistant and a vice-president of Tate International Industries.

"Anyone else? Sara?" Sara Cohen was her executive secretary and girl Friday supreme.

"She's still alive, isn't she? Of course Sara called —five times. She says there are ten command decisions awaiting your decision. Come to think about it, you sort of do remind me of General MacArthur."

"And you remind me of Red Foxx."

Francine whooped "Low blow!" and slipped into her Uncle Tom routine: "Li'l white missy ready for her breakfas' now? Hilde done cooked you up a right mess of grits, corn pone, and fatback."

"Yuk! Tell Hilde I'll have two eggs over light, dry toast, and black coffee, but first my orange juice and champagne." She removed a split of Dom Perignon that had been cooling overnight in an insulated ice bucket and handed it to Francine. "Tell Hilde to hold breakfast until I give the word. Is Mr. O'Toole up yet?"

"He's been working in the study since eight."

Mara shook her head. "He couldn't have had more

than three hours' sleep. We stayed up past three going over the company books."

Lewis O'Toole was chief accountant for TII and Mara's current lover.

As Mara headed down the hall to the study, Francine called after her, "Don't be long, hon. Hilde wants to go to the market early, and I think I'll go with her. Need some things from the drugstore. Can I get you anything?"

"No thanks. And tell Hilde to forget about my breakfast. You two go on. I'll whip up something myself after I talk with Lewis."

The study in Mara's apartment was more like a company boardroom. A long polished mahogany table with four chairs on each side and one at the head dominated the decor, belittling the small desk by the picture window and the brick fireplace on one wall.

Lewis O'Toole sat at the head of the table, only his curly red hair visible as he pored over a ledger, one of many scattered about the table.

"Good morning, darling," she called to him.

He looked up, glassy-eyed from his intense concentration, his expression vacuous, as if he did not immediately recognize her. "Oh, Mara," he said finally. "What time is it?"

"Almost eleven." She took in his disheveled appearance, gym pants, and sweat shirt. "You had better shower, shave, and dress. I want to stop and vote before we go to the office. I want to phone Jack and tell him we're all rooting for him at TII."

"Speak for yourself, Miss Tate." He stood up and stretched full length; tall, lean, and sinewy; Irish blue eyes set deep in a craggy face that was masculine yet sensitive.

"I know you never liked Jack Kennedy, but you can't deny he's got it all over that weasel Nixon."

"No contest," he conceded. "I'm just annoyed that you're still carrying a torch for the guy."

She laughed, showing white teeth that were nearly perfect, but for a tiny gap between the two upper front teeth. Her father had wanted to have the problem rectified by an orthodontist when she was a child, but Mara had stubbornly refused.

"I like it," she'd said; "it's different. All those girls at school with their braces and retainers so that all their smiles will be identical. When I smile, people will recognize sincerity and character."

And she was right. All of her adult life, men adored Mara's pixyish grin, and women envied her for her uniqueness.

"Me carry a torch? How droll you are, Lewis. Carrying a burned-out torch is my idea of nothing to do. It's like masturbation—pure self-gratification of one's masochistic tendencies."

His grin was crooked, and he scratched his head. "I never thought of masturbation as being masochistic. Come to think of it, though, I went through considerable agonizing as a youth, dreading the growth of hair on the palm of my hand and premature baldness and the inevitable shriveling up of my testicles."

She chuckled and moved closer to him, slipping one hand up under his sweat shirt and splaying it across his flat, hard chest. "Poor lamb. Too bad I didn't know you then. We would have played doctor-nursie together and worked out your sexual kinks in short order." She cast a sly glance at the front of his pants. "Then again, I never was a girl for 'short orders,' and this is most definitely *not* one." Her hand traveled down and under the waistband of his trousers. "Most definitely *not* a short order."

He gasped, and the muscles in his thighs and stomach rippled. "Wanton wench."

"Horny Mick."

"You want it right here on the desk?"

"Not particularly—not when a comfortable bed awaits us."

"Francine and Hilde?"

"They're off shopping. Stop looking for excuses. You bombed out on me last night. If you don't cut the mustard now, you're fired."

"Yes, ma'am, Miss Tate." He pulled the bow of her sash and the robe fell open. His large hands cupped her breasts as he bent to kiss her lips.

Mara put her arms around his neck and molded her body to his. "Let us dally no longer," she whispered. "I can't wait much longer. . . . No!" she gasped as he ran a hand down her body and squeezed her mons Veneris. "You want me to come in my pants?"

O'Toole laughed. "No pants that I can detect."

She took his hand and practically dragged him out of the study and along the hall to her bedroom. There she flung off her robe and stretched out languidly on the big bed, watching him undress with bright, avaricious eyes.

Her eyes turned deep indigo when she was excited, and the sight of his ready manhood excited her to a state of lewd frenzy. She reached out for him with both hands as he kneeled on the bed, singing the words of the old Gershwin tune—"Gimmee, gimmee, gimmee, gimmee what I sigh for, you know you got the kind of kisses that I die for—" ad-libbing obscenities as she swung into the second chorus.

He smothered her right breast with kisses, rolling the nipple between his lips the way she liked her sex partners to stimulate her in foreplay. Physically and mentally, Mara was more sensitive on her right side.

She teased him with her fingertips, stroking, gently pinching, until his erection was rigid and unbending as steel. Her thighs were already wet with her own juices, and in an urgent voice she pleaded, "Now, Lewis, now, my darling. I can't wait a moment longer."

He entered her slowly and easily, a sheath of hot, damp velvet, and she commenced her contractions even before he had made full penetration. Their bodies began the torrid dance of love, the tempo increasing with every rhythmic stroke. It was a mindless act, sex, Mara often reflected after the fact—pure animal passion that betrayed the acquired refinements and culture of evolution. Even in the high delirium of orgasm, a small part of her remained aloof from the panting, heaving woman on the bed, a detached witness to the ageless primitive ritual of the act of procreation. Basically that is what sex was: nature's foolproof mechanism to safeguard the preservation of the species.

She had a recurrent dream: her soul, or whatever it was that made each individual unique and precious, cast back in time and entering the body of a grotesque apelike female spread-eagled on a bed of furry hides on the rocky floor of a cave, and crouched over her, ready to mount, her Neanderthal male counterpart, their coupling more a physical battle of the sexes, accompanied by mauling, biting, growling.

Not all that different, she mused as she sank her teeth into O'Toole's shoulder.

"Jesus Christ! That hurts like hell!" he complained when they were through making love. He rubbed the tender spot, fiery red and bearing the clear imprint of her teeth in his flesh.

"My savage instincts got the better of me," she said, only half in jest. "Light me a butt, will you?"

He reached back on the headboard's shelf, took two cigarettes from a lacquered box, lit them, and gave one to her.

She lay back, legs crossed at the ankles, one arm propping up her head. "You want to use the shower first?"

"I'd better use the one in my room. Francine and Hilde might come back sooner than we expect."

Mara laughed. "You imagine they don't suspect we do the two-backed beast together?"

"Of course, but I still like to be discreet."

"You can't shake off your Northern Irish Protestant puritan ethic, can you?"

"I suppose not," he admitted sheepishly.

A speaker on the headboard emitted a soft chiming alert, and one of a dozen banks of lights above the phone switchboard commenced flashing.

Mara frowned. "The red phone; that's my private wire." She sat up, reached back, and pushed two buttons, one to activate the red phone, the other to switch on the amplifier.

"Mara Tate here."

"Good morning, Miss Tate," a woman's voice said. "Mr. Joseph Kennedy wishes to speak with you."

"I'd be delighted to speak with Mr. Kennedy." Her face was animated.

After a pause, the distinctive voice came on: "How are you, Mara?"

"Just great, and I don't have to ask you how you are. It's a red-letter day for sure. I'm on cloud nine myself."

"Pretty confident, aren't you?" He sounded amused.

"A shoo-in."

"I feel the same way." A note of concern inserted itself into his voice. "Actually, though, I'm not calling about Jack. It's about your cousin Sean."

"Sean?" she said tersely, and flashed her eyes at O'Toole.

He looked very concerned indeed. "Damn!" he said in an undertone. "Ten to one it's that Coppertone business."

Joe Kennedy was suddenly wary. "Is there anyone there with you, Mara?"

"Yes . . . Lewis O'Toole."

"Oh. Good man. How are you, Lewis?"

"Fine, sir, and you?"

"I'll feel better when this night is done."

"No sweat. You heard Mara guarantee Jack's election."

The two men laughed; then abruptly O'Toole was very somber. "What's this about Sean Tate?"

"Coppertone Cookware."

"I was afraid of that."

Coppertone Cookware, a subsidiary of Tate International Industries, produced high-quality, expensive copper cooking utensils and an assortment of other household items. Sean Tate was president of the firm.

Kennedy took a deep breath. "I hate to spoil your day, Mara, but I have it on unimpeachable authority that before the week is out, the Securities and Exchange Commission is going to file a civil suit against TII, naming you and Sean and Harvey Sayer as co-defendants.

"On what grounds, Joe?"

"The specific charge will be that the three of you siphoned off and mishandled more than five million dollars in Coppertone funds through private transactions between the company and yourselves. And the SEC will request the court to appoint a receiver for Coppertone Cookware."

"The whole thing is absurd," Mara scoffed irritably. "Why, for the past two days Lewis and I have been going over all of TII's books, a complete inventory. Five million dollars indeed! That would be quite an item to sweep under the rug!"

O'Toole winced visibly. "Mara, I'm not through with the Coppertone books yet, but there is a memo from Stevens, whose team did the preliminary auditing. It bears minute scrutiny. I was in the midst of it when you——" He halted, aware that Joe Kennedy was hearing every word they said.

Mara winked and dropped a hand on his thigh, groping him with lascivious relish. "Joe," she said, "I really appreciate your letting me know about this development, not that we have anything to concern ourselves with seriously; but it may be messy. Adverse publicity never helped anybody, with the exception of actors and politicians. Speaking of politicians, do I detect the fine machiavellian hand of Senator Manning behind this move by the SEC against TII?"

Mark Manning was the chairman of a Senate task force appointed by the Ways and Means Committee to play the role of watchdog over big business, to investigate dubious corporation procedure—vertical mergers, reciprocity agreements, and the like—and advise the Justice Department of alleged violations of the federal antitrust laws.

"No doubt about it, Mara. The Mannings and the Tates have been rivals ever since copper was discovered in Arizona and Montana."

Mara chewed her underlip and nodded grimly. In a fifty-year competition for supremacy in the copper-mining enterprise, TII had eventually seized control of Manning Montana Limited. The Mannings were still one of the state's wealthiest and most prestigious families, but their animosity toward the Tates remained unabated.

"Jilting Mark back when he was the young dandy of the Harvard social whirl didn't do anything to improve his disposition toward the Tates, either," Kennedy reminded her, tongue in cheek.

Mara grimaced. "Mark was a pri—"—she caught herself— "a prig then and he still is."

"You were right the first time," was Joe's laconic comment: "*prick*. Well, look, dear, I have twenty more calls to make before lunch, so I'll have to sign off.

Maybe we'll phone you tonight after election results are final." He hesitated and went on self-consciously, "Of course, you know you're welcome to join the family festivities and——"

"Thank you, Joe," she cut him off tensely. "I don't think that would be good politics at all. You phone and we'll drink a champagne toast together."

"As you say, dear. Good-by, now, and stay on your toes with the SEC."

"Will do, and thank you again, Joe. You're a helluva man."

"And you are one helluva woman."

"Thanks and good-by." She hit the switch and broke the connection. Then, lighting another cigarette, she lay back on the pillows, deep in thought. "What were you saying about the Coppertone books, Lewis?"

"I'd prefer to shelf it until I digest the total picture later this afternoon."

"All right. Meanwhile . . ." She turned and ran an index finger along a row of buttons on a panel that represented three dozen phone numbers of close business associates and friends registered in a computer. She found Sean Tate's Florida residence and hit the button.

The maid answered; then Barbara, Sean's wife, got on, her voice oozing honey: "Why, Mara darling, what a wonderful surprise. Don't tell me: You're going to pay us a surprise visit."

"Not this time, Barbara," was the cool reply.

You phony bitch. We hate each other's guts and we both know it!

"How's the weather in New York?"

Mara ignored the question. "Barbara, is Sean home? This is extremely urgent."

"Afraid not. He was up at dawn to play golf, and I don't expect to see him again till after six."

Mara's next words had the staccato impact of

machine-gun bullets. "You get on the phone and have him paged at once! Tell him to haul his ass home and start packing. I want him here in New York by six o'clock, at my office!"

"Oh, I couldn't do that. He'd be *furious!*" Barbara's voice kept rising higher and higher.

"He'll be more furious if he finds himself out of a job. I'm deadly earnest, Barbara. Six o'clock, New York!" She broke the connection.

O'Toole smiled. "You never were one to mince words, were you?"

"I have very bad vibrations about this Coppertone mess. You know Murphy's first law?"

"Anything that can go wrong will go wrong."

"And it goes double wherever Sean is concerned —he and that tinhorn vice-president of his, Harvey Sayer. A couple of riverboat gamblers, that's what the two of them remind me of. All they need is black string ties and pearl-handled derringers." She shook her head. "I warned Sean after I bailed him out of that toy-manufacturing deal: 'If I ever catch you dealing off the bottom of the deck again, you're through for good—forever—and don't ask for any references, either, cousin!' "

O'Toole grimaced. "I keep forgetting he's your cousin. What is he, a second or a third?"

"I never can keep trivia like that straight. Christ! The farther he's removed from me, the better! Come on, lover, put on your pants and go home. We have a busy afternoon ahead of us."

"One . . . two . . . three . . . four . . . five."

...his began, and Mam Tate opened her eyes.

CHAPTER TWO

The Drew Tate building on Third Avenue was sixty stories high, eight floors of which were occupied by TII and its affiliates.

The confrontation between Mara Tate and her cousin Sean Tate took place in the executive boardroom. Also present were Lewis O'Toole; Robert Hunter, chief of TII's legal staff; Jean Castle; Wendell Holmes, president of TII and second in command to Mara; and Sara Cohen, who took minutes of the conference on a stenotype machine.

All of the women on Mara's staff had physical and mental characteristics in common. They were *good-looking*, not pretty and tinsel-slender, somewhat large-boned—and dressed fashionably and expensively without ostentatious frills. Jean had short sandy hair and freckles. Sara was dark and olive-skinned, the one feature Mara disapproved of was her snub, upturned nose, the product of plastic surgery; it did not go with the rest of the face—most nose jobs do not—giving her an artificial expression.

Mara was wearing a navy and white striped cardigan suit with a sleeveless top and neatly pleated skirt of bouclé knit. It achieved the calculated effect that distinguished all of her wearing apparel: an air of authority without sacrificing femininity.

The meeting had been in session for only a quarter of an hour when Harvey Sayer arrived unexpectedly. He was perspiring profusely and reeked of bourbon.

"Sorry I'm late," he apologized. "Big traffic jam

25

coming out of Kennedy, in addition to which we got a late start from Bloomington." Bloomington, Illinois, was the site of the Coppertone Cookware plant.

Mara had a difficult time hiding her contempt for Sayer. At the time TII took over the factory, Mara had wanted to let Sayer go, but Sean had insisted that Sayer would be invaluable as an aide to him because he knew the business from the ground up. Now more than ever. Mara was sorry that she had relented.

"Mutt and Jeff," the employees of Coppertone called them behind their backs. There was a likeness to those comic-strip characters. Sean was a large, beefy man with curly red hair and watery blue eyes. Sayer was small and dapper, also with short reddish hair but small, beady black eyes. The two men shared many of the same habits; the most opprobrious, to Mara's sensibilities, was the tendency to laugh too boisterously and too frequently—extreme self-consciousness influenced by an innate sense of guilt.

"Sean would laugh while he was putting a slug in your belly," Mara appraised the trait.

On this evening there would be an abundance of such artificial hilarity.

"Shall we review what we've been discussing for Harvey's benefit?" Wendell Holmes inquired wearily.

"No need." Sayer said, waving a hand. "The entire allegation is preposterous. Sean has filled me in on what's been happening." He and Sean joined in a chorus of braying laughter.

The two men maintained an attitude of injured indignation and brash indifference, though it was obvious to all present that both were badly frightened. Sayer took a cigarette from a gold case, but it remained unlit in his mouth because his hands were trembling too much to light it.

With a gleam of malice, Holmes leaned across the table and flicked his lighter under Sayer's nose. "Allow me, Harvey." TII's president had been named after the famous Justice, and now, in his early sixties, he bore a remarkable resemblance to his namesake.

"Let them indict us," Sean said belligerently. "The case will be thrown out of court." He slammed a big hand down on a stack of Coppertone ledgers in front of O'Toole. "Our records are unimpeachable to the last detail. The SEC can't prove a thing!"

Mara stared at him coldly: Sean Tate true to form, always protesting innocence too vociferously even before he had been accused.

"Sean is right about one thing," O'Toole told them. "Coppertone's books balance up very neatly, not a decimal point out of place."

"There you are!" Sean said triumphantly, and he and Sayer laughed at the absurdity of it all.

O'Toole impaled them with a contemptuous glare. *"Very* neatly. The books provide an itemized record of how Coppertone plunged $5 million into the red less than six months after TII acquired ownership."

"Of course we lost money!" Sean was full of self-righteous bluster. "Coppertone has just come through a complete reorganization. A year from now, our profit margin will have the stockholders chortling with glee."

Mara was unimpressed. She lit a fresh cigarette from a finger-singeing butt, chain-smoking throughout the conference. "What happened to the $5 million, Sean? How did you and Sayer manage to lose that much money in so short a time?"

"Now, see here, Mara," Sayer shrilled, "I resent your implication that I——"

"Shut up, Harvey!" She picked up a memo that O'Toole had handed her, tapping it with a spiked fingernail painted blood red. "Like this $90,000 retainer to the law firm of Blandings and Olson."

"That was an honest fee," Sayer stated defensively.

Mara nodded at O'Toole, indicating that he had the honor of dropping the bomb.

"In reality, it is *your* law firm, Mr. Sayer, isn't that so? I mean, you took your name off the door, but you're still calling the shots at Blandings and Olson," O'Toole said.

Sayer winced at the ominous address from TII's chief accountant—*Mr. Sayer*. He glanced at Sean, his eyes and voice desperate, pleading. "Sean . . ." He strangled briefly, then cleared his throat. "Are you going to sit here and put up with this disgraceful inquisition? I have been reviled, insulted; *both* of us have."

"Nobody's reviling or insulting either one of you," Mara snapped. "All we're asking is that you account for this $90,000. That's a lot of money for a little legal advice—advice that has not as yet, to my knowledge, been solicited."

"And that is merely the tip of the iceberg," O'Toole added. He shuffled through his papers and picked up a yellow sheet. "By *coincidence*, the same day that Coppertone's $90,000 check cleared the bank, Blandings and Olson delivered a check to Harvey Sayer in the sum of $50,000, which was subsequently split fifty-fifty between Harvey and Sean."

"Total fabrication!" Sean's ruddy complexion became scarlet. "That money was the repayment of a personal loan Harvey and I had made to John Blandings over a year ago to bail him out of a stock-market jam."

Mara's lip curled in a sneer. "You're a damned liar, Sean! You've never had $25,000 to play Lord Bountiful with in your whole life! And, as I recall, just about the same time, you borrowed $100,000 from me to bail yourself out of the sporting-goods business."

Lewis O'Toole looked as somber as a pallbearer

at his best friend's funeral. "There's something else, Mara. I dug it up just before we convened this meeting." He took a deep breath. "On the same day that Coppertone delivered the check to Harvey, a messenger delivered a personal check to your office in the amount of $25,000. That check was signed by John Blandings, of Blandings and Olson."

Tense silence settled over the assembly. For one of the few times in her life, Mara Tate was at a loss for words.

A vindictive smile played around the corners of Sean's eyes and mouth. "Well, well, well, did you hear that, Harvey? All the while my dear cousin has been casting slanderous innuendos in our direction about accepting kickbacks, and now it turns out that she's been on the take from Blandings and Olson."

Abruptly the pieces fell into place in Mara's mind. "Hold it, Sean! You know perfectly well what the check from Blandings represented—the first repayment on the $100,000 I loaned to *you*. Blandings and Olson handled the transaction."

"Is that what it says on the check, Mara?" Sean asked slyly.

Mara looked to O'Toole, who shook his head. "Nothing to allude to the transaction with Sean whatsoever, Mara. If it had been through accounting, we would have picked it up and requested another check with specific endorsements as to the nature of the payment."

"But I deposited it in my personal account," Mara said heavily. "It was a personal loan from me to Sean."

Sean was fairly dancing with joy. "I can't accept that my genius cousin, with her computer brain, could have committed such an obvious blunder—no indeed. Still, it *could* have happened the way she says. Then again, maybe it's a case of collusion among the three of us—me, Harvey, and Mara—to line our pockets out of the coffers of Coppertone Cookware."

"There were two more payments to you, Mara," O'Toole pointed out, "both from Blandings and Olson."

"Additional installments on the same loan," she explained in a dull tone.

O'Toole frowned. "The hell of it is, those payments coincided with the exact days that large sums of money changed hands between Coppertone and the law firm. There were other recipients of payments from Coppertone, including a plumbing firm that produces about fifty percent of the copper pipe and tubing used in the United States."

"Pacific Pipe Incorporated," Mara acknowledged. "Coppertone purchased it outright three months ago. She slumped deeper into her chair. "And I thought it was a creative move on Sean's part."

"It would have been if he hadn't paid twice what it was worth," O'Toole said disdainfully, "and if the seller hadn't been his brother-in-law."

"Vito Mosconi," Mara said without emotion. "Did your father-in-law arrange it, Sean, the way he arranged for you to knock up his daughter, threatening to have his goons cut off your nuts if you didn't make an honest woman of her, so that he'd have a direct pipeline into the Tate financial empire?"

Sean's face turned ashen. He stood up, swaying from side to side, and his voice was thin and barely audible. "I don't have to listen to any more of your filthy slander, Mara."

"You're damned right you don't!" she shouted. "Get the hell out of this office, this building, and never show your face here again!" Her bitter laughter had the quality of dry sand rattling on the lid of a coffin about to be interred. "If you do, I might make a deal with Bruno Mosconi myself, better than the one you offered him and Vito. There's no doubt in my mind that for the right price the old don would be only too glad to put out a contract on the likes of you, Sean. Now, get out, and take your lackey faggot with you!"

Without another word, Sean Tate and Harvey Sayer gathered up their hats, topcoats, and briefcases and departed.

No one spoke for a long time until Mara put into words what all of them were thinking: "Sean really put the shaft to us this time, didn't he? Circumstantial evidence, but good enough for the SEC to base a case on." She looked at Robert Hunter: "Well, Bob, you've been conspicuously silent tonight."

He pressed one hand against the other in front of him, palm to palm, fingers splayed, replying without looking at her. "There's not a hell of a lot to be said, Mara—not at this time at least. I mean, it looks bad, no doubt about it, but I think we can show that you were duped by Sean and Sayer. What the hell! An organization such as TII, so sprawling, so diverse, so complex, the SEC can't reasonably expect you to be personally responsible for every one of the million-and-one details in its day-to-day operations. In legal alone, I sign my name every day to documents I've never even glanced at, on the recommendations of the staff."

"In accounting, too," O'Toole agreed hastily. "I've got to depend on a team of other accountants to do the addition and subtraction. In your case, there is no way to circumvent the necessity of delegating authority to your company executives—Sean, for example. If what he does checks out—remember, on paper everything he's done appears reasonable enough—there's no feasible way you can fault him. Your hands are tied."

"Bullshit!" Mara slammed both hands down hard on the table in helpless frustration, a state of mind thoroughly alien to her personality. "I *am* responsible.

That's the name of the game I'm in, and you all know it. As good old Harry T. put it, the buck stops at my desk." A tremor ran through her body and she put a hand to her throat. Her voice was weak and tremulous: "Water . . . will someone give me some water, please?"

She rose hesitantly and would have keeled over sideways if Hunter and O'Toole had not leaped up in time to break her fall.

"Mara, what is it?" the accountant demanded anxiously. "Are you ill?"

She tried to answer him, but the words died in her throat. Then all the blood washed out of her face and her eyes closed, and she went limp as death in their grasp.

"Jean, phone for an ambulance!" Hunter said, on the edge of panic. "I think she's——" He paused and tempered the awful thought: "I think she's fainted."

CHAPTER THREE

The tall liveried doorman looked down his long, thin Irish nose at Max Fiedler. *"Dr.* Fiedler?" he said with a distinct note of incredulity.

"Actually, I'm a lingerie salesman," said Fiedler, blue eyes twinkling merrily, "but I figured a classy joint like this, I stand a better chance of getting in with a title."

The doorman's expression of intolerance hardened. "Are you meeting a member here or not? There are others waiting behind you."

"I'm sorry," a chastened Fiedler said. "Yes, I have a luncheon date with Dr. Leslie Tompkins. And I *am* Dr. Fiedler."

While the doorman got on the phone, Fiedler caught a disturbing glimpse of himself in the mirrored wall just inside the main entrance and winced.

What a slob!

Self-consciously he ran his fingers through his hair, unruly and long overdue for a trim, and straightened and tightened his tie in a vain attempt to hide the fact that the top button of his shirt was missing. His blue serge suit needed pressing, but, fortunately, the too-long trousers concealed his white sweat socks.

"Dr. Tompkins is expecting you at the grill, second floor. The elevators are to your left."

Fiedler felt like an interloper as he scurried across the marble floor of the grand amphitheater beyond the lobby, with its high-vaulted ceiling adorned with Byzantine murals. There were groupings of leather

33

chairs and couches on oriental rugs with ankle-deep nap, calculated to provide an atmosphere of intimacy within the cavernous room. Reading lamps and coffee and end tables completed the appointments. The inhabitants of these cozy nooks had the anonymity of stage props. Tall, short, thin, or fat, they nevertheless exuded the same unmistakable identity—white Anglo-Saxon Protestant. Fiedler was as out of place in this stereotype of *the* university club as one of its members would have been at the Fulton Fish Market.

He breathed easier when he walked into the second-floor grillroom. It was more informal than the rest of the establishment, with highly polished wooden tables and dark paneled walls.

A red-jacketed waiter with a faint British accent bowed stiffly to him: "Dr. Fiedler?"

"The same."

"Come with me, please."

Fiedler followed him across the room, conscious of the cold, curious stares of the other diners. In his last semester at Harvard Medical School, his adviser had told him only half in jest, "Jesus, Max, I just can't see you as a doctor. You look more like a stand-up comedian."

Fiedler's plump, cherubic face had lit up impishly and he'd launched into mimicry of two well-known comics: " 'Now, take my wife, for example. . . . *Please* take my wife. . . .' 'Why is it I don't get *no* respect?' "

His adviser had laughed. "See what I mean?"

"Seriously, Mr. Fleming, that's why I'm going to specialize in psychiatry. God knows, shrinks' patients can use a few laughs."

A broad grin spread across Les Tompkin's face as Fiedler approached their corner table. He stood up and extended his hand. "Max, it's good to see you. How long has it been?"

Fiedler shook his hand, shrugging. "Two, three years; the last seminar down in Miami, wasn't it?"

"Think so." Tompkins tapped his half-empty glass. "Another martini, Bobby, and what are you drinking, Max?"

"Pepsi, like always."

The waiter raised an eyebrow.

"He means it, Bobby." Tompkins shook his head. "Still Pepsi after all these years."

"It's all I could afford in school, and after so much time I got hooked."

"How's the wife?"

Fiedler hunched his shoulders. "Better than nothing, and yours?"

Tompkins let out a loud guffaw. "Still the same old *shtick,* you crazy sonovabitch."

They exchanged amenities for a while, and then Fiedler doffed his buffoon's hat for his professional's. "So what's up, Les? You didn't invite me to this goy temple to go through my comic act."

"I read the paper you did for the psychiatric journal last March; it was brilliant."

"The one on age regression?"

"Yes. I gather you're into that rather heavily?"

"When it lends itself to the general therapy of the patient."

Tompkins lit a Sherman and offered the pack to Fiedler.

"No thanks; Kojak I ain't."

Tompkins chose his words carefully. "I can go along with the theory as far as taking a subject back in time through his childhood—to a point, that is—but I think you're getting into parlor games when you claim you can take him back before his birth to a previous existence. I cannot in all conscience buy that or any part of it."

"Neither can I," Fiedler declared.

Tompkins was perplexed. "I don't understand. What's the point in practicing it, then? You dedicated an extensive section of your paper to the subject of age regression and pre-birth regression."

"I did."

"And you don't believe it?"

"It's not as simple as that, Les. I had an old prof who always slipped a trick question into his tests: 'What is the preferred treatment for hysterical dissociation?' And you know what the right answer was?"

Tompkins shook his head.

"Whatever works—that's the answer. I have patients, it's the only way you can get inside their heads—make them believe they had a life or lives previous to this one, then put them into a deep trance, conventional hypnosis- or drug-induced. Mind you, this isn't accomplished in a single session; it might require five, ten. The point is, once you move them back across the threshold to what they believe is a previous existence completely apart from their present life, you can break down inhibitions that could never be breached by conventional hypnosis or basic age regression alone. They let it all hang out, all their repressed desires and fantasies—things so abhorrent to their conscious minds that they could never admit them to anyone, least of all to themselves. In a sense you're right; it is sort of a parlor game, but a highly effective and productive game nevertheless."

"Whatever works," Tompkins mused, and nodded in comprehension. "All right." He drained his martini glass and signaled the waiter for another. "I've got a patient for you, Max. I'm convinced that you are the one man in the psychiatric field who may be able to help her."

"What's her problem?"

"That's for you to find out. It's way beyond my

depth, I'll tell you that. You've heard of Mara Rodgers Tate the third, of course?"

"Along with the Fords, Rockefellers, and Kennedys. Is she a patient of yours?"

"Has been for eight years. She's always been as healthy as a horse—physically, that is. And I've always thought she was sound as a dollar mentally as well. Oh, she has her share of human eccentricities, like the rest of us."

"Amen," Fiedler muttered. "When that alarm went off this morning, I had all I could do to force myself out of that snug bed of mine. What I wanted to do was curl up with my teddy bear, pull the covers over my head, and suck my thumb."

Tompkins grinned and went on: "Then two days ago something bizarre happened to Mara. As you must know, she's the chairman of the board—chair*woman* —of Tate International Industries."

"That in itself is grounds for at least a nervous breakdown."

"It's an enormous responsibility for a man or a woman, especially one so young; she's only thirty-nine."

"So what happened two days ago?"

"There was a big business meeting Tuesday night, all the company top brass. TII is in some kind of trouble with the government, the SEC. Seems Mara had quite a hassle with the president of one of TII's affiliate companies—her cousin, as a matter of fact, Sean Tate. She literally threw him out of the board-room."

"Sufficient to induce trauma."

"When it was over she collapsed, passed out."

"Was she hospitalized?"

"Harkness Pavilion. It's been almost forty-eight hours and she's still in a coma. We've run every conceivable test on her—EEG, skull X-rays, arteriogram, pneumoencephalogram, even a brain biopsy. Negative all the way."

"Nothing of any significance whatsoever?"

"Well, maybe one thing: Every ten minutes, like clockwork, a highly irregular pattern of brain waves manifests itself."

"Irregular in what way?"

"That's the damnable thing, Max. I've never seen anything quite like this before. You'll have to study the readout yourself."

"And all this while, she's never regained any degree of consciousness at all?"

"No sign at all. It's as though"—he hesitated—"as though she's in a deep trance."

Fiedler leaned forward, acutely attentive, his arms folded on the table. "Mara Tate is beginning to fascinate me very much indeed. You mentioned her eccentricities. Describe them to me."

"I don't think there's anything significant there, Max."

"Don't be too sure, my friend. In my field little things mean a lot, like the song says. . . . For beginners, she practically enshrined her grandfather and grandmother. Drew Tate—he was the founder of the family empire—came over to the States back in 1876 with his wife and five children, a poor family of miners from Wales. The rest is history. The very name 'Tate' has a mystique for Mara, just as it did for her mother and grandmother. Both of them continued to use the family name and to relegate their true surnames to second place—Mara Ewing Tate; Mara Rodgers Tate. Doesn't that strike you as odd?"

Fiedler shrugged. "It's an affectation many of the rich and famous are given to—Henry Ford the third; John D. Rockefeller the third."

"It goes deeper than that with Mara. Perhaps 'mysticism' is a more fitting description than 'mystique' for her preoccupation with her ancestors. She claims that on frequent occasions both her mother and her grandmother come back to lend her support and counsel in times of crisis."

"Come back, like from beyond the grave?"

Tompkins grimaced. "That sounds absurd, I know, but that's her own phrasing: 'come back.' "

"Is she a religious person?"

"That's what makes it eccentric. No, Mara is not religious at all. I'd call her an agnostic. We've had extensive discussions about it. She professes not to believe in a life hereafter; yet she maintains that these materializations by her mother and grandmother are real."

Tompkins frowned. "The first year she was my patient, she came down with a severe case of Rocky Mountain fever. It was a near thing, let me tell you. She was delirious for almost thirty-six hours, and in her delirium she would cast herself in the roles of both Mara the first and Mara the second. She babbled on incessantly concerning experiences each of those women had encountered in her own day and age. It was eerie, frightened her private nurses half to death. Of course, knowing something of her obsession with the Tate family and its proud history, it didn't strike me as all that illogical. I mean, she has a shelf in her library devoted entirely to the Tate family tree and records of the Tate influence on the development of the state of Arizona."

Fiedler nodded. "Most natural thing in the world for her to switch identities with those two much-admired and revered relatives, particularly in times of stress." His eyes were bright with anticipation. "This sounds like a classic case."

"A classic case of what?"

Fiedler winked. "I haven't come up with a definition yet; it may be a first. One thing I can say: Mara

Tate is the perfect subject for age-regression therapy, pre-birth regression. When can I see her?"

"As soon as you like."

Fiedler stood up. "What are we waiting for? I wasn't hungry anyway. Just point me to a phone so I can call my girl and have her cancel my afternoon appointments."

In the cab on the way to Harkness Pavilion, Tompkins remembered something he had neglected to mention to Fiedler: "There's another intriguing circumstance about the three Maras. They share something else in common, aside from their names and that they look uncannily alike."

"Strong family resemblances are not all that unusual. My sister was gray before she was thirty, and even today, at a distance, I can't tell her and my mother apart."

"Admitted, but that's not the similarity I had in mind. The three of them were born on the same day, October twentieth, somewhere within the span of the quarter-hour before midnight. Oh, yes, and in each case it was the night of a full moon."

An uncertain smile formed on Fiedler's face. "Oh, come on now, Les, you're putting me on!"

"It's the truth, Max; you can verify it in the family archives."

"Yeah, I'd like to have a look at those records sometime soon, learn as much about the Tate family as I can so I can deal with Mara Tate on some basis of parity—*if* I decide to take her case. . . . Look, about their all being born on the same day and near the same time, granted it's an improbable coincidence, but it is not impossible. I'm sure it would take a good computer man less than a minute to give you the odds on such an occurrence happening. What I'm driving at is, we are dealing with the real and reasonable world, not something out of the Twilight Zone." He inhaled deeply. "I'm almost afraid to ask this question: Was there any pattern in the deaths of the first two Maras?"

Tompkins was amused. "Do you mean did they both die on the same date? Lord, that would even make a believer out of me! No, the original Mara was aboard the *Titanic*. Both she and her husband, Gordon Ewing, went down with the ship."

"Tragic—and how traumatic for her daughter . . . and her granddaughter. What about the second Mara?"

"She lived to a ripe old age—seventy-two or -three, I'm not sure. Still, her death was equally as tragic as her mother's: She died in a plane crash about four years ago."

"Yes, tragic indeed, and my question was not as foolish as I first thought. There definitely is a pattern to their deaths. A highly sensitive person—what we frequently refer to in the trade as a 'hypersensitive overreactor'—might interpret such violent deaths as 'acts of God.' Do you see what I'm driving at?"

"Yes, a person with close personal ties and who felt intense emotion toward the deceased women might believe that the Tate women were cursed, so to speak. God, I sound like a heathen!"

"There's a little heathen in all of our hearts and souls, a touch of the primitive. . . . Where did the crash occur?"

Tompkins hesitated, almost as if he was reluctant to answer the question. He grimaced, rubbed the back of his neck, and finally said, "It fits the pattern all too neatly, Max. The airliner Mara Rodgers and her husband Sam were passengers on went down somewhere in the so-called Bermuda Triangle. No survivors. No trace of the wreckage."

Fiedler stared at him in disbelief. "No shit?"

"No shit. . . . Now, don't look at me as if I'm some

kind of nut. I don't put a grain of salt in all that mumbo-jumbo about the Bermuda Triangle and flying saucers."

"One helluva lot of perfectly sane people do, though, Les. What about Mara? How did she feel about her mother's death?"

"It hit her extremely hard, naturally. They were very close. It's the only time since I've known her that she took more than a week off from her job at TII. For a full month after the accident she spent every day, from dawn to dusk, flying crisscross over the projected area where the plane went down, seeking some trace. The family was damned worried about her, thought she might be going off the deep end."

"You should have told them not to worry," Fiedler demurred. "So long as she could afford the indulgence, it may have served as preventive therapy, helped her get it out of her system."

"Anything else, Max?"

"Not for now, Les. Just arrange with whoever is taking care of her apartment for me to look over her library and journals."

"I'll alert Francine Watkins; she's Mara's personal maid and companion."

"Is this Mara's only residence, in New York?"

"God no; she has apartments and houses all over the world—London, Paris, Cannes, Rome, San Francisco. And of course there's the big family mansion in the desert outside Tucson. Actually, it's become more of a showpiece in recent years, like Taliesin. I believe Frank Lloyd Wright also designed Glammorgab; that's what they call the old homestead. Mara has played hostess there to a gaggle of world celebrities, kings, shahs, prime ministers, and even our debonair new president."

"Jack Kennedy?" Fiedler was surprised and impressed. "She knows him?"

Tompkins's smile was cryptic. "She knows him very well indeed. I guess you don't read the gossip columns."

"What about that?"

"From the beginning, Mara has been one of JFK's most ardent supporters. She predicted he'd be president even before he won the West Virginia primary."

"It was a near miss; he just scraped by Nixon— what, by a hundred thousand votes?"

"A fraction more, but the irony is, she doesn't even know he's won the election."

The cab pulled up in front of the hospital, and Tompkins took care of the fare. "Come along, doctor; your patient awaits you."

Fiedler grunted as he struggled out of the cab; he was not an agile man. "*If* I take the case."

"Oh, you'll take it; it's as sure a bet as JFK."

mic amazing; they relax together. The only other time

CHAPTER FOUR

Before he saw Mara Tate, Fiedler went over her chart and the reports from cardiology, pathology, virology, endocrinology, neurology, neuropathology, encephalography, and psychology with Tompkins and the hospital's chief of staff, Dr. Werner Kessler.

"In thirty-five years in practice, I've never encountered a case like it," Kessler declared. "What do you make of it, Dr. Fiedler?"

"Total confusion on my part. Could I please see the cardiogram again?" He spread it out full length on the table and compared it with Mara's encephalogram. "If you will note the sporadic succession of waves on the encephalogram"—with the tip of a pencil he described the zigzag tracing, a series of abnormally high peaks and low valleys on the chart—"these spikes correspond to the period of auricular diastole on the cardiogram. Right here, the PQR waves and the QRS waves. See how the ST waves flatten out."

The other two doctors peered intently over his shoulders.

"You're right, Max," Tompkins agreed.

"Yes, but what is the significance of it?" Kessler wanted to know.

"I don't know if there is any significance, except that it would seem to indicate that when the auricles are in a state of relaxation, the brain, for some unexplained reason, is afflicted with frenzied agitation. The thing is, why? Normally the brain and heart enjoy a rhythmic empathy; they relax together. The only other time

45

I observed a similar phenomenon was at a hypnosis seminar in Prague several years ago—a demonstration of deep trance induction by Dr. Anton von Jursik."

"Deep trance!" Tompkins exclaimed. "Remember I said that's what Mara's condition reminded me of?"

"Yes. . . . Anyway, von Jursik's subject was number one on the accepted susceptibility scale of one through five. I've never seen anyone in a deeper state. At the time, it struck me that it was the lowest plateau of life and consciousness, on the very borderline of death."

Fiedler looked perplexed. "There is one radical difference: Mara Tate's vital signs—heartbeat, blood pressure, respiration—are all normal. With von Jursik's subject, as the trance became deeper and deeper, heartbeat and blood pressure decreased, and the encephalogram flattened out dangerously."

"What was the purpose of such an experiment?" Kessler asked.

"It was a demonstration of age regression, one of the most dramatic I have ever witnessed. The subject went back in time one hundred years to a previous life in which he was a world-acclaimed concert pianist and composer"—he cast a mischievous glance at Kessler—"Franz Liszt, to be exact."

"Franz Liszt!" Kessler exclaimed incredulously. "You can't be serious, Dr. Fiedler?"

"It was a very serious experiment, I can assure you."

The chief of staff shook his head. "Surely you don't believe in reincarnation? Franz Liszt indeed!"

"I didn't say I believed in reincarnation, sir. I daresay Dr. von Jursik didn't, either. As I explained to Dr. Tompkins earlier, it does not require the therapist to believe in age regression in order for him to employ it as an effective instrument that will be of benefit to the patient. Our concern is with Mara Tate, so I won't digress too much on this case, only insofar as the implication that this form of therapy *could* be applied to Mara."

Kessler was crimson with hostile indignation. "Dr. Fiedler, *not* in my hospital! Why, I've never heard of anything so ridiculous, so . . . so unprofessional!" He appealed to Tompkins. "Leslie, I ask you——"

Fiedler smiled and held up his hands. "Please hear me out, Dr. Kessler. "As it turned out, von Jursik's patient was the son of a once-famous concert pianist and harpsichordist. The mother gave up her career to marry and raise a family. Karl was the apple of her eye, the sole one of the three children to inherit his mother's musical talent. She set her heart on his carrying on the proud tradition that she had betrayed. 'Betrayed'—it was her precise word. She never was able to absolve herself of the deep guilt she felt over having betrayed her gift, her public, and herself most of all.

"In Karl she saw her salvation. His conquest of the music world would be her absolution. She would be giving back to life what she had taken away from it. There was only one drawback: Although Karl was enormously talented and graduated with honors from the Paris Conservatory, he did not possess the 'gift,' the 'genius,' that is required of a truly great virtuoso of the keyboard.

"To oversimplify it, Karl wanted to believe in reincarnation. He wanted to believe that in a former life, he *had* achieved the greatness that would forever be denied to him in this life. This conviction provided him with the inner sense of self-worth and self-confidence that he needed to lead a normal, healthy, productive existence as a piano teacher. Call it a crutch, a placebo, faith healing, laying on of the hands, witchcraft, exorcism of the devils that haunted him, call it anything you will so long——"

"As it works!" Tompkins finished the idea, grinning

broadly at Kessler's disconcertion." Doctor, Mara Tate is my patient and I will take full responsibility for her care and well-being." He looked at Fiedler. "I am beginning to have a faint and fuzzy notion of what you're driving at, Max. You believe that this coma, trance, whatever her condition is, may have been self-induced?"

"I am almost convinced of it. Such cases are legion, the ultimate form of escapism from the real world. Far more desirable than classic catatonia, I would say. You say she has always been obsessed with her roots, the lives of her forebears. This state she's in may be a desperate effort on her part to find her way back to that cherished world of the past. And, if all goes well, if I can reach her at all, penetrate her deep sleep, I just may be able to provide the 'transportation' she'll need to reach her destination."

Kessler stared at him aghast. He couldn't speak above a whisper. "I can't believe this is happening —black magic at Harkness Pavilion!"

Mara lay still as death on the large bed, not a hospital bed; she had been installed in a private suite reserved for ailing VPs. Her black hair was fanned out across the white pillow; it struck Fiedler that it must have been arranged so by a set designer. There was about the entire scene a theatrical air, all of it staged for photographing a magazine advertisement.

It was the woman herself who set the tone. Her appearance was so striking, so commanding of one's attention. The mole on her cheek emphasized the fine texture of her skin; her nose was a tinge too sharp, yet it complemented her prominent cheekbones and strong chin. There was no one feature to dwell on; rather, the whole was a perfect composition. Fiedler fell in love with her at first sight.

"Just like Sleeping Beauty," he said in a hushed voice.

"Let's hope you will be the prince who awakens her," Tompkins said, not in jest.

Dr. Kessler had declined to be present at this "travesty of mumbo-jumbo," as he scathingly termed it.

Tompkins nodded at the private nurse. "Take a break, Miss Allison." He looked at Fiedler. "How long will you be with her today?"

"No more than half an hour at the beginning."

When the nurse was gone, he sat down on the edge of the bed and motioned Tompkins to a chair. He took her hand and tested it for temperature and texture; then he stroked her forehead, brushing back a lock of hair. He eyed the paraphernalia of stands, bottles, and rubber tubing at the other side of the bed.

"She's being fed intravenously?"

"We just started yesterday. I ordered it discontinued temporarily this afternoon, pending your verdict."

Fiedler turned her hand over and observed the purple bruises where the needles had been inserted into her wrists. "How are the bowel and kidney functions?"

"Satisfactory, under the circumstances." Tompkins took the chart off the peg on the footboard and handed it to Fiedler, who scanned it perfunctorily.

"Nothing new here." He stood up and pulled back the covers, revealing a breathtakingly lovely female body scantily concealed by a gossamer nightgown, a diaphanous frippery of satin and lace purchased at an exorbitant price, Fiedler suspected; but then patients of Mara Tate's renown wore whatever they cared to at Harkness Pavilion.

He felt a flush suffusing his face, and was annoyed at himself for the fleeting guilt he experienced admiring her form with masculine instinct instead of with conventional physician's dispassion. "I want to test her reflexes. Can I borrow some equipment?"

"Of course." Tompkins rang for the floor nurse, and Fiedler gave her a list of the equipment he required.

In the twenty minutes that followed, he examined her from head to foot, kneading, probing with his fingers, pricking her toes and fingertips with sterilized pins, tapping her elbows and knees gently with a rubber hammer. Mara remained as unresponsive as a mannequin; only the gentle rise and fall of her bosom testified that she was alive.

Satisfied, Fiedler sat down on the bed again, took both her hands in his, and commenced speaking to her matter-of-factly, as though she could hear him: "Your grandfather, Drew Tate, certainly would have been proud of you, Mara. All of the Tates would have, especially your——"

Tompkins interrupted him: "Drew was her great-grandfather."

Fiedler smiled. "I know that, Les. I wanted to see if the error elicited any response from her."

"But she's out; she can't hear you."

"She's unconscious, but it doesn't necessarily follow that she can't hear what I'm saying." He continued: "Your grandmother, Mara the first, was a lovely woman—I've seen pictures of her—and your mother as well. Blood tells, and you are the living proof of it—the last of the beautiful Tate women. . . . Then again, of course, you might marry and give birth to Mara the fourth."

He was watching her closely and thought he detected a brief fluttering of her eyelids. Tompkins's hand clasping his shoulder from behind confirmed it.

"I'll be damned!" Tompkins said. "For an instant I thought she was going to open her eyes."

From time to time, Fiedler's rambling monolog

would evoke an almost indiscernible response from the woman: a fluttering eyelid; a tic at the side of the eye or the mouth; a finger or a toe twitching. At last he discontinued this modus operandi. "I'm getting through to her, no doubt about it, but not in any really effectual way. Suppose we call it quits for today. Tomorrow morning at nine I'll administer sodium pentothal. Leave word with the nurse to have the IV set up, ready to go, when I arrive."

"I don't understand," Tompkins objected mildly. "What is the purpose of inducing hypnosis with drugs when she's already in a deep trance?"

"But not under my control. What has to be done is to jar her out of her present state. No, that's not the correct image. What I want to do is like putting a derailed train back onto the tracks so that it can continue running under the engineer's direction. I'm the engineer."

Tompkins looked uncertain. "I'm glad old Kessler decided to stay away from this affair."

Fiedler laughed and clapped him on the shoulder. "Don't worry about her, Les. My intuition tells me that the lady is going to make out just fine. Look, if I hurry, I can still make my last appointment of the day. I'll see you tomorrow morning?"

"Bright and early. I wouldn't miss the show for the world."

Fiedler did not appreciate the humor. "Bad joke, pal," he said. "I assure you, what will take place tomorrow is not a show in any sense of the word. Believe it or not, when I'm working, I am an exceedingly sober and solemn practitioner of the skills of psychiatry." Then he smiled and squeezed Tompkins's bicep. "See you tomorrow, then, Les . . . and thank you for considering me as the psychiatric consultant in this case. I'll do my damnedest for Mara Tate."

He cast one final look at the inert woman on the

bed, and lifting a hand to his lips, he blew her a kiss. "So long, sweetheart."

Tompkins watched him leave the room with a wry grin. "That, Miss Allison, is a very special man," he said to the private nurse as she entered the room.

CHAPTER FIVE

At measured intervals a drop of liquid would be ejected from the IV bottle on the stand beside Mara's bed and trace a sinuous course through the clear plastic tubing until it reached its destination, to be transfused into Mara's vein by the gleaming metal needle.

Fiedler sat on a chair beside the bed, leaning forward with his forearms braced on his thick thighs. He was coatless and tieless, and his sleeves were rolled up, revealing muscular, hairy arms.

The blinds were drawn, and a single soft-white bulb glowed in a bed lamp attached to the headboard. Tompkins sat in the background, out of the penumbra of light, observing with rapt attention.

As the sodium pentothal, combined with a minute amount of a new hallucinogenic drug Fiedler had been experimenting with, spread through her body, Fiedler began to speak softly: "Mara, you are in a very deep sleep . . . deep . . . deep . . . very deep . . . another world that you have regressed into by sheer force of will, but you cannot reach wherever it is you are seeking all alone. Right now you are in a state of suspended animation, a limbo, hung up between this world and the other world. . . . I want to help you, Mara. Please let me help you. . . ."

He talked on and on in a singsong monotone that had a strong hypnotic quality. More than once Tompkins caught himself nodding, and his eyelids felt leaden.

Fiedler cajoled, pleaded, reasoned with the unconscious woman:

"You *will* let me help you, won't you, Mara?" He took her free hand and placed it on the coverlet over her stomach. "If you agree to let me help you, Mara, lift the index finger of your left hand. . . . All right —*now.*"

Holding his breath, he riveted his attention on her slim, graceful hand. Ever so slowly the designated finger moved, a twitch at first; then it began to quiver as if struggling with a ponderous weight and, gradually, lifted into the air.

Fiedler did not let his immense elation intrude into his voice. Matter-of-factly he said, "That's very good, Mara. I'm extremely pleased. Now we can really make some progress. . . . Mara, you must relax completely. Your body and, most important, your mind must relax. Try to imagine yourself floating in the water, weightless, no weight or substance whatsoever. . . . Your mind is a total blank. Wipe every thought out of your mind, Mara. . . . You are looking at a blank blackboard. Now an invisible hand with a piece of chalk commences writing on the blackboard—a number, Mara. The number is one hundred. . . . Do you see the number on the blackboard? . . . Lift your finger if you can see it."

This time the index finger lifted with more purpose.

"Ahhh, that's very good, Mara. . . . All right, now tell me what number you see, Mara. . . . Come along; you promised to let me help you. The number, Mara . . ."

For the first time since she had been stricken, her pale face showed expression: petulance and annoyance.

"Tell me what the number is, Mara," Fiedler said firmly. "We can't afford to waste time. . . . Quickly, what is the number?"

The hair on the nape of Tompkins's neck bristled, and his fingertips tingled. He felt, irrationally, that in this simple demonstration of Fiedler's skill, he was witnessing a miracle of sorts.

Mara's voice shattered the silence of the room like an echo from out of the grave: "One . . . hundred."

"That's it, Mara. . . . All right, now we erase the first number and the chalk is writing once again. Yes, the next number is ninety-nine. Do you see it, Mara? No finger this time. Speak to me. What number do you see?"

"Ninety-nine," she said without hesitation.

"Excellent, and now the hand will continue to write a series of numbers running backward from ninety-nine. . . . All right, Mara, you say the count out loud, all the way back to zero. Do you understand?"

Impassionately, she began the recitation: "Ninety-eight, ninety-seven . . ."

While she was counting, Fiedler turned back to Tompkins: "I've managed to transfer her from her self-induced trance to another state, which I can control. The transformation will be complete when she reaches zero."

"Can she hear us? Will it interrupt the process?"

"No, she will hear only what I want her to hear, what I instruct her to hear and do." He smiled puckishly. "I'm not certain my methods would have the unqualified backing of my psychiatric peers. I've always felt that in any endeavor one tackles, it should be approached with an open mind, a willingness to improvise along the way, rather than confine oneself to an intractable plan. We shall see." He turned back to Mara.

When she said the last digit, "Zero," Fiedler patted her hand. "That's fine, Mara. Thank you for your cooperation. . . . Now let's go back a little ways into your past—not far at this point. . . . Les, what—would be an important date Mara would be likely to remember—a fairly recent date?"

"That's easy: July fourteenth, the day John Kennedy was nominated by the Democrats."

Fiedler nodded and addressed Mara again. "Does the date July fourteenth mean anything to you, Mara? Is it especially memorable?"

Slowly the death mask she had worn for three days dissipated, like a ceiling of storm clouds penetrated by the sun. Her smile was radiant, and her voice rang with enthusiasm: "July fourteenth, 1960—how could I ever forget that marvelous day when Jack was nominated for president by the Democratic Party! Would you like to hear about it?"

"Some other time, Mara. You see, we have a lot of ground to cover. So, for the present, let's move on to another memorable day."

Cued on by Tompkins, Mara's longtime friend and confidant, Fiedler exhumed a succession of important events in Mara's contemporary life, not one of which he pursued to any great depth or dimension. After about an hour, he decided that she had made enough progress for one day. To Tompkins he said, "If my prognosis has been correct, I will now be able to bring her out of the trance and back to full consciousness and comprehension."

"Miraculous!" Tompkins said in awe, and stood up in expectation.

"The human brain concocts its own miracles," said Fiedler. "All you have to do is find a way to direct it. . . . All right, Mara, we've done enough reminiscing for one session. Now, I am going to count to five, and when I say 'five' and snap my fingers, you will regain consciousness. Do you understand?"

"Yes, I understand."

"Okay: One . . . two . . . three . . . four . . . *five*." He snapped his fingers and Mara Tate opened her eyes.

In her facial expressions and her eyes, he read the chain of emotions she was going through: shock; bewilderment; fear; and, at last, a healthy curiosity.

She struggled to sit up. "What's going on here?" Her dilated pupils focused with difficulty on Fiedler. "Who are you?"

"I'm Dr. Fiedler." He put his hands against her shoulders and restrained her gently. "It's all right, Miss Tate. Lie back and relax."

She regarded the IV equipment and the needle in her arm with alarm. "My God, what are you doing to me? Where am I? God damn it!"

Tompkins stepped closer to the bed. "Everything is going to be fine, Mara. You're in Harkness Pavilion."

With relief she recognized Tompkins. "Les? Harkness—the hospital? But why?"

"Don't you remember, Mara? the big meeting at TII? the Coppertone business with Sean?"

"Yes, I . . . I remember." Plainly, the memory was still fuzzy.

"You passed out. You've been unconscious for three days."

"Three days? You can't be serious."

"Don't worry about it, Miss Tate," Fiedler soothed her. "You've been under sedation. When it wears off, your memory will be fine again. Les, call the nurse and have her get the IV out of her arm. I want to talk with Miss Tate for a few more minutes."

Tompkins left the room purposely, rather than summon the nurse by the call button, so that Fiedler could be alone with his patient.

Mara's wide-set, questioning eyes fixed on Fiedler, looking him up and down, appraising him. You said your name . . ." She'd lost it.

"Fiedler—Dr. Max Fiedler."

"You've been treating me?"

"Dr. Tompkins called me in as a consultant."

"Have I really been unconscious for three days? I mean, that has got to be serious. What did I have? a coronary? stroke?"

He shook his head and smiled reassuringly, knowing full well that nothing was going to reassure this dynamic woman short of the truth. Unfortunately, he didn't know the exact truth—not yet. What he had told Tompkins was strictly a hypothetical prognosis. "Miss Tate, you're going to have to be patient with us for a time. The thing of it is——"

"You don't know what's wrong with me?" Her quick mind seized the truth.

"Not positively, no."

"For Christ's sake, doctor! You say I've been unconscious for three days and you have no inkling of what caused it?"

"I didn't say that. I have a fairly good idea of what caused your condition; it's just not my policy to play guessing games with my patients."

Her eyes narrowed shrewdly. "Exactly what kind of a doctor are you?"

"I'm a psychiatrist," he told her quietly.

"Psychiatrist?" The fear was creeping into her voice and expression again. "What do I need with a psychiatrist? So that's what this is all about: You and Les think I'm a candidate for the loony bin!"

"Not so, Miss Tate. There isn't a single person on this earth who is immune to emotional and mental problems, any more than there's anyone who is immune to the common cold—and that goes for psychiatrists. I don't mind telling you that I've been under analysis for three years. I've got some phobias that are dillies, like when I leave here, I'll have to wash my hands ten times before I can relax and stop worrying about germs."

She smiled weakly. "That's not a very good self-recommendation."

He hunched his shoulders. "Got to be honest in my business. If the patients can't trust the shrink, who can they trust?"

"Shrink . . ." She shook her head in blatant disbelief. "It was sheer madness of Les to call in a psychiatrist. I mean, I *was* unconscious; that's a physical symptom, not a psychological hang-up."

He looked at her solemnly and took her free hand in both of his. "Miss Tate, I can see you're not the type of person who will accept evasion, subterfuge, half-truths. I'm going to level with you, not that I expect you to accept what I tell you one hundred percent. You may even come away with the conviction that I am one fat b.s. artist; but let's give it a shot." He winked. "As they say on Madison Avenue, let's run it up the flagpole and see if anybody salutes it. Please hear me out before you come to any conclusions; that's all I ask—your forebearance."

She shook her head affirmatively. "I'm listening, Dr. Fiedler."

He explained it to her pretty much as he had divined it for Tompkins—"divined" as in "divining rod," for that is how the black art of psychiatry appeared to the layman; even to himself sometimes. You covered a section of terrain with this magic stick held in your hands, and when the stick canted downward, it meant you had struck a deep well. A well of water or a well of knowledge—the principle was the same in both cases. The practitioner had chiefly his instincts to rely on; the stick and the couch were stage props to assuage the customer, the client.

Mara was more receptive to his prognosis than he had dared to hope. "My mind fairly reels at all this, Dr. Fiedler," she told him, "although I must confess I've always felt that I was a little different from other people."

"Different in what way?"

Her laughter was self-conscious, even self-mocking. "I don't know exactly how to define it. That I am psychic, clairvoyant, have second sight, as my grandmother would have called it."

He was thoughtful. "Yes, your grandmother, Mara the first. Was she psychic, or whatever this power is you believe you possess?"

"Yes, and my mother had it as well."

"Mara—do you mind if I call you Mara?"

"Certainly not. And I prefer to call you Max."

"Great, because we're going to become good friends before we clear up your little problem."

Amusement lit up her eyes, more gray than blue now. "My 'little problem'? Just what makes you think I have any real problem? I mean, I've attained the good middle age of thirty-nine years and am the head of a multibillion-dollar industry. And what you consider an 'unhealthy preoccupation with my roots' has never interfered with my performance in business, in my social life, or *in bed*." Her eyes flashed impishly.

To his private mortification, Fiedler blushed. His laughter had a false ring to it.

Damn it, Max, you're behaving like a love-sick schoolboy!

There was no denying it: Mara Tate held a strong physical attraction for Fiedler, more so than any other woman he had ever met, including his wife Ruth. He affected his best brusque bedside manner, standing up and letting go of her hand. Flesh-to-flesh contact suddenly seemed indecent. "Now, that is your definition, not mine. I never said that your preoccupation with the Tate family was unhealthy. The Tate tradition is something to be proud of. Not many of us are so fortunate to have such renowned and illustrious forebears. Personally, I find the Tates a fascinating topic of research."

She was obviously pleased. "Then I must let you

read some of my books on the subject. A great deal has been written about the Tates, going all the way back to Gwen and Drew, when he and the boys worked the coal mines in Cardiff."

"I'd like that very much."

"Look, how much longer do I have to stay here?"

"As far as I'm concerned, you can leave whenever you please. Nothing wrong with you physically."

"Only mentally, is that it?" There was a sharp edge to her voice.

He sighed. "Mara, as I told you, no one of us is without hang-ups. You have got to face up to the hard fact that you did pass out. You have been unconscious for three days. Now, that we—least of all you—can't afford to ignore. It could happen to you again, you know, under stress."

"I've lived with stress all my life. Love it. Couldn't live without challenge."

"Be that as it may, there comes along the straw that breaks the camel's back. I strongly advise you—no, I'm *entreating* you—to continue therapy with me."

"What kind of therapy?"

"What I have just described to you: hypnosis and age regression. Do you know, I honestly think you would enjoy it."

"Going back in time," she had her own definition. She looked straight through Fiedler, her vision eclipsed by images in her mind, images of long, long ago. "Well . . . what the hell! I'll humor you, Max. Now, get a nurse to take this damn needle out of my arm and let's get out of this mausoleum!"

As she walked down the steps of Harkness Pavilion to the street with Fiedler and Tompkins on either side of her to lend support in the event she faltered, Mara joked, "God! I feel like an old granny!"

"You've been off your feet for three days," Tompkins

reminded her. "Got to get your sea legs back. Taxi!" He waved at a cruising cab.

"I want to go to the office," Mara said as they settled themselves in the back seat.

"Not a chance," Tompkins said firmly. "You've got to take a few more days to reorient yourself, get your strength back."

"There must be a backlog on my desk up to the ceiling—decisions that only I can make."

"Bullshit!" Tompkins said in exasperation. "It's time you got off the ego trip you've been on ever since I've known you. You'd think the sun rises and sets in your posterior—'the world can't get along without me' syndrome. Listen, Mara, TII was doing just fine when you were still in diapers, and it will continue to prosper long after you're in the grave. Holmes, Castle, and O'Toole have kept your desk clean as a whistle."

She didn't like to hear that. "Now, wait a minute, Les. Who gave them authority to——"

"You did!" he cut her off. "That's why you hired them at the most exorbitant salaries in the field. Hell . . . Wendell Holmes's take-home pay makes the president of the United States' salary look like peanuts."

"The president of the United States!" It came to her with a shock. "The election! Jack won, of course."

"He won, but it was nip and tuck until late Wednesday morning. There are still die-hard Nixonites who are clamoring for a recount. . . . By the way, you received get-well telegrams from both Joe Kennedy and the president."

She giggled. "The *president*—yes, we'll have to get accustomed to that. No more Jack and Johnny. *Mr. President*. Nice ring to it at that." She turned in the seat and smiled at Fiedler. "All right, when do I get my next session on the couch, Mr. Shrink?" She gave it a suggestive connotation.

Oh, how I'd like to get you on the couch, you busty wench, you!

He smiled. "I'd like to see you three times a week for a time. How about the day after tomorrow to begin with?"

"It's a date. Your place or mine?" Again the sly innuendo.

"It will have to be at my office, where my nurse can administer the sodium pentothal."

She regarded him with amused affection. "You want to know something, Max? You are not exactly what I've always considered to be the prototype of a shrink: tall, slender, with a pipe and horn-rimmed glasses—Gregory Peckish."

Fiedler grinned. "One of my patients says I remind her of a big teddy bear, warm and cuddly to snuggle up with at night."

Mara's smile was enigmatic. "I'll bet you are at that."

CHAPTER SIX

On the afternoon of her appointment with Fiedler, Mara stepped out of the cab on Fifth Avenue in the upper sixties and handed the driver a five-dollar bill.

"Two-ten out of five," he said.

"Keep it," she said, and walked briskly into the building, eliciting an admiring stare from the doorman. Her splendid figure was flattered by her form-fitting attire: a black blazer piped in red over a black skirt, narrow and split to show off a modest expanse of silkened thigh, and a red-tie blouse of crepe de chine. Under one arm was a folded copy of *The New York Times*.

She got off the elevator at the tenth floor and, with the aid of a wall directory, found room 1067. A receptionist in a small anteroom directed her through a door into a waiting room that was a radical departure from any other doctor's office she had ever visited. It was appointed in the style of a warm and comfortable parlor, with colonial furniture, wooden pegged floor, and paintings that comprised a montage of the American Revolution. She walked to a large aquarium set in a bay window overlooking the avenue and studied the wide variety of tropical fish tracing lazy designs in the aerated water.

"Miss Tate?" a woman's voice said from behind her.

Mara turned and replied to the uniformed nurse, "Yes, I am."

"Dr. Fiedler will be with you in a few minutes. He's

running behind schedule today. May I get you anything? coffee, tea, ginger ale?"

"No thanks; I'll read my paper."

Ten minutes later she was ushered into Fiedler's office, a medium-sized room with dark wood paneling and dominated by a wide desk strewn with books, papers, and the remains of a box lunch.

Fiedler rose from behind the desk to greet her, taking her extended hand in both of his. "Mara, you look positively lovely. Sorry to keep you waiting."

She smiled. "No sweat, Max. You look lovely, too."

His baggy trousers looked as if he had slept in them. He was coatless, his sleeves rolled up and his tie all askew. And he still needed a haircut, she observed.

"Sit down and I'll make up a case sheet on you. Most physicians leave the paper preliminaries to the receptionist or the nurse, but I prefer to write them up personally. That's it precisely; it's more personal." He nodded at the nurse. "Nancy, is the examination room all set up for Miss Tate?"

"Yes, sir." She disappeared through a side door.

"You have quite a layout here, Max—very, very chic."

"Thanks. It was decorated by one of my patients. Many of my patients are in the art field or allied fields."

"Not many female executives?"

"A fair share." He put on horn-rimmed glasses and winked. "At least I measure up to your concept of shrinks on one count." He tapped the specs and sighed. "Maybe next week I'll go on a diet, join a gym, and try to work up to the Gregory Peck image."

Mara laughed. "I wouldn't hear of it. Stay just the way you are, Max. I don't believe I'd trust myself with Gregory Peck."

His eyes twinkled roguishly. "I'll bet!" Then, seriously: "How have you been feeling since I saw you last?"

"Fit as a fiddle, though I've never understood what that expression means."

"It has to do with tuning, I believe." He placed a blank case-history sheet on the blotter in front of him, brushing aside a mound of debris. "All right now, your name is Mara Rodgers Tate——"

"The third," she said without smiling.

He glanced up at her but made no comment. "And your address is . . ."

Twenty minutes later he made a final notation at the bottom of the sheet on the reverse side. "So much for that. Now, if you will step into the examination room, Nancy will help prepare you."

"Prepare me? You make it sound like I'm a rib roast."

"Bet you'd be tender as butter, too."

"Like hell!" she said wryly. "I'm as tough as cowhide."

He watched her walk through the doorway into the examination room and close the door behind her.

What a beautiful arse she's got! All the rest of her is first-class, too.

He picked up the paper she had left on his desk and scanned it idly. It was open to the financial page, and the article she had been reading caught his eye immediately:

Today the Securities and Exchange Commission filed a request with the U.S. Attorney General's office to indict Mara Rodgers Tate, chairwoman of Tate International Industries, on charges of perjury and filing false reports with the S.E.C. and likewise falsifying statements to T.I.I. stockholders in connection with a T.I.I. subsidiary Coppertone Cookware.

Similar indictments are being sought by the S.E.C. against Sean Tate and Harvey Sayer, the president and the vice-president of Coppertone Cookware. Simultaneously, a group of dissident stockholders of T.I.I. are seeking an injunction from the courts that would compel the Tates and Harvey Sayer to remove themselves from office at T.I.I. and Coppertone until the S.E.C.'s case has been ruled on; and they have asked the court to appoint a receivership to regulate the management of T.I.I.'s diversified holdings. Also pending against the three company officers is a lawsuit filed against the Tates and Sayer by two T.I.I. major stockholders for recovery of $5,000,000, which they allege the defendants "conspired to divert to their own personal use along with other substantial funds and assets."

Fiedler put the paper down without reading any further.

I wouldn't want to be in that lady's shoes for all the money and power in the world!

She claimed to thrive on stress and challenge; but Fiedler had a hunch that in this particular crisis, Mara Tate the third was going to come face to face with her moment of truth. He stood up and walked toward the doorway leading into the examination room.

Mara was lying on her back on a narrow cot against one wall. The nurse had asked her to remove her blouse and brassiere and provided her with a white smock that tied in back. She had already commenced the intravenous injection of sodium pentothal, and Mara was quite drowsy by the time Fiedler arrived.

"You can go now, Nancy," he said. "She's pretty much under, I'd say."

"Almost as soon as the IV was activated, she responded. A good subject, isn't she?"

"Excellent. . . . Before you go, start the tape recorder." He sat down on a metal chair beside the cot and spoke to her: "Mara, can you hear me?"

She opened her eyes and smiled at the ceiling, not looking at him. "Yes, I can hear you . . . Max."

"Good. Now, you're going to do exactly as I tell you. You are beginning to get very sleepy, am I right?"

"Yes." She shut her eyes again.

"You are going into a deep, deep sleep, Mara, but even though you are asleep, you will be able to hear everything I say to you, and you will answer my questions truthfully to the best of your ability. Do you understand?"

"Yes."

"All right. . . . When I say 'start,' you will count backward from one hundred, and each time you mention a number, you will descend deeper into the trance. . . . *Start* counting."

There was a moment of hesitation; then she licked her lips and began: "One hundred . . . ninety-nine . . ."

All the while she was counting, Fiedler was taking her pulse. Her progression into deep trance was uncommonly rapid, and her pulse rate slowed down commensurately. When she had reached the count of fifty, it had fallen to forty-five beats per minute.

"Forty-one . . . forty . . ." Her voice was thick, and she paused a long time between numbers.

Fiedler was filled with mounting anxiety as the pulse plunged to thirty beats per minute. At this rate, her heart might stop altogether before she finished the count. "All right, Mara," he said, "that will be enough. You're at the bottom."

She obeyed. Her pulse remained stable at thirty, and

her respiration was a low five inhalations a minute. Fiedler had never observed a subject in a deeper trance than Mara Tate. She would be a phenomenal subject to display at a seminar.

"We will start off today by letting you pick an area of discussion, Mara. Let's see; you like birthdays, don't you?"

She smiled. "Especially when I was a little girl. Birthdays were always special occasions in our family."

"Let's talk about one of your birthdays that was especially memorable. Can you remember a birthday like that?"

Her brow furrowed as she concentrated; then it smoothed. "Oh, yes, I do remember one very special birthday—my fourteenth."

"What was so special about it?"

"It was the day we arrived in Arizona."

Fiedler frowned. "But I thought you were *born* in Arizona."

She laughed, a queer laugh that disturbed him. "No, you silly willy; I was born in Wales." And, to his astonishment, she rattled off a guttural litany in what he vaguely recognized as the Welsh language. Her voice, all of her mannerisms, were childlike now. She *was* a little girl.

"Where did you learn to speak Welsh?" he asked, still perplexed.

"I spoke Welsh before I spoke English."

"Jesus Christ!" he said under his breath, and the back of his neck felt cold. His own heart leaped like a greyhound breaking out of the starting gate, but his voice, when he spoke, was calm: "Mara, what day were you born? What year?"

"June fifteenth, 1863," she answered without hesitation.

Fiedler was close to a state of shock as the full

implication of what had occurred came clear in his brain. Without any prompting, without the slightest suggestion on his part, Mara Tate had taken the initiative in the complex and controversial mental process of age regression; and she had taken a giant leap backward in time on the Tate family tree!

Impossible! . . . But was it? She possessed near-total recall when it came to family background and history. Undoubtedly she knew nearly as much about the childhood of Mara Tate the first as the original Mara could have related, *had* related to her daughter, Mara the second, in countless vivid anecdotes. Plainly there was a strain of keen, active imagination running through the bloodline. His rational, objective physician's mind refused to accept the explanation that Mara Tate the third *was* the reincarnation of her grandmother.

Her voice jarred him: "Now I'll tell you about my fourteenth birthday. . . ."

CHAPTER SEVEN

The wagon train entered the territory of Arizona at the northeast corner where it bounded Colorado and New Mexico, heading for Monument Valley.

Mara was riding up front in the lead wagon with the wagon-train boss, Sam Pickens, a grizzled veteran of the Southwest. Along the way, she and Sam had become fast friends. He was impressed by her extensive knowledge of Arizona history gleaned from the books and newspaper articles she had pored over so avidly before the Tates embarked from the British Isles for the New World. On her part, Mara listened attentively to the endless stories and anecdotes Sam recited, covering the thirty-odd years he had explored the barren, ruggedly beautiful regions of the Far West.

One of the first wonders of this new land she set awed eyes upon were the dwellings of the ancient cliff dwellers perched atop high mesas and on rambling ledges across precipitous canyon walls. Sheer miracles of engineering and ingenuity, soundly built of adobe, on wooden frames in many cases, these structures were from one to four stories high.

"How did the Indians get up to their houses?" Mara asked Sam.

"Series of ladders, which they pulled up at night so that unfriendly tribes or wild animals couldn't sneak up on 'em while they slept. They were the ancestors of the Pueblo Indians. Great farmers, way ahead of their time. Some of their irrigation canals are still in workable shape today."

73

The clear, dry atmosphere was a dramatic contrast to the dull, damp, foggy climate of England and Wales.

"You can see so far and wide and so clearly, it fairly hurts my eyes," she exclaimed.

The remarkable clarity of the air played tricks on the eyes. Distant mountains stood out so vividly, one had the feeling one could reach out and touch the towering ponderosas and Douglas firs that flourished on their slopes.

Sam chuckled. "Got a saying that the air's so pure, a cowboy can see a gal wink a mile off."

The wagon train's route was to the south, rolling plains and dry desert floor sweeping away to the horizon. To Mara's surprise, the desert was not the ominous, barren, dull wilderness as depicted in the books she had read. There were areas ablaze with cactus plants and other flowering plants and trees—dazzling splashes of gold and crimson, vivid blues and greens and orange: sotol, yucca, and the strange-looking Joshua tree, called the Lord's candle because of its resemblance to a lighted candelabrum with white and purple flames; desert willows that bore orchidlike blossoms; flowering acacia; brilliant yellow brittlebush, the cream-colored cliff rose.

Just before noon, Mara spied a curious phenomenon about a mile ahead of their caravan. It reminded her of a black door in the midst of the sun-drenched atmosphere, stretching from the earth to the heavens.

"That's a rain squall," Sam told her.

She stared at it with disbelieving eyes. "You mean it's just raining where the black oblong is?"

"Yep. If you were standin' up there off to the side, you could reach into it and wash your hands without gettin' your sleeves wet."

"You're having fun with me, Sam," she declared.

"You'll see. Before we get to where we're going, you'll have a chance to test it."

By the time they reached the area, the shower was over and they passed through a patch of saturated scrub bush.

"It smells like hot tar, the way they cooked it back home," she exclaimed.

"Creosote bush," he told her. "Tar comes from it."

When they took a break for lunch, Mara ran back to the Tates' wagon, drawn by two horses. "Isn't it absolutely marvelous here?" she said with excitement.

Drew Tate was a thickset man with brawny arms and legs and a thick neck. He was pleasantly homely, with a knobbed nose and a chin like granite. Mara had inherited only his blue-gray eyes; fortunately, in all other respects, she took after her mother, a tall, buxom woman with a pretty face and dark hair held in a bun at the base of her neck. Her four brothers had the same dark, dour, brooding mien as their father— "black Welsh," as their English brethren referred to them snobbishly.

Drew laughed and hugged the child to his chest. "It's a regular desert rat you're getting to be, my love; though I must say the rustic existence seems to agree with you. You're bronzed as an Indian and there's new flesh on your bones."

"Do you know what day this is, Mara?" her mother called from where she was bringing a pot to boil over the cookfire the boys had built.

Mara skipped over to her mother and put an arm around her waist. "Of course; it's my birthday. Sam says there'll be a party and dance in my honor tonight. Will you be having a birthday cake for me, Mum?"

Her mother's eyes twinkled mischievously. "Now, you know we don't have an oven way out here in this Godforsaken place." She saw the disapproval in the child's face and amended it. "I mean, it's a truly magnificent land, but not at all civilized."

Mara took a deep breath and gazed around her. "I love it. It's not all cramped and cluttered like in Wales. So bright and happy and big. Sam says Arizona is bigger than all outdoors—so big it makes you feel smaller than an ant."

Her brother Emlyn, the eldest, came up and pulled her braids. "You won't think it's so marvelous when we've had our first Indian raid."

"Stop that, Em!" he was admonished. "You'll be scaring her half to death."

"I'm not scared," Mara maintained stoutly. "Sam told me all about the marauding Apaches. They're the fiercest people on all the earth. Even their name means 'the enemy.' They never take prisoners when they make war. They cut them up and mutilate their bodies in the vilest fashion—ears, noses, fingers, and toes. Sometimes they strip their prisoners naked and stake them out on the desert sand to fry in the sun *with their eyelids cut off!*"

Gwen Tate turned white and clutched her throat. "No more of that talk, young lady, or you'll be confined to the wagon for the rest of the day."

After a simple meal of beef jerky softened in hot water and boiled with some dried potatoes and other vegetables, served with tea and hardtack, they cleaned up, stomped out the fires, and resumed their journey to the south.

The rich ore-belt in Arizona ran diagonally from the northwest corner of the territory to the southeast corner. Their destination was the Nogales, Tombstone, and Bisbee area.

They made camp at sunset on high ground just to the east of Monument Valley.

"This ain't Indian country, least not Apaches," Sam

Pickens told his flock. "Just the same, don't pay to take no chances."

The sixteen wagons were arranged in a loose ring with horses tethered in the gaps between the wagons. Each family had its own cookfire built and ready to ignite when darkness fell.

Mara watched breathlessly as the blazing orange ball of the sun set beneath the mountain ranges to the west. The peaks were tipped with fire; plateaus were golden lakes laced with the deep purple windings of the shadowed valleys. Her eyes filled up and she rubbed a lump in her throat. "It's the most gorgeous sight I've ever seen," she said aloud.

"Indeed it is," a male voice concurred from behind her.

Mara started and whirled. It was Gordon Ewing, the son of another wagon family. He was tall, slender, and muscular with a strong, rugged profile, his face all angles and shadows, and piercing blue eyes. His head was a tangle of blond ringlets. The very sound of his voice reduced Mara Tate to quivering jelly. Though he was six years older than she, Mara loved him madly.

"Better get back to camp," he said finally as the display ended with the sun's disappearance. They turned from the bluff and walked silently back to the wagons, each lost in his own thoughts.

Within the perimeter of the wagons, Mara felt snug and secure, warm and bright from the light of sixteen blazing fires. The men, and boys over fifteen, were to take turns standing guard. Two to a shift, they patrolled the ring of wagons on the outside, armed with rifles and pistols.

Mara, wearing the new dress her mother had made for her on the long trek across country—a smocked shirtwaist with puff sleeves, worn with a multicolor print skirt over a crinoline petticoat—fairly glowed with joy and pride. Patent-leather slippers with brass buckles completed her ensemble.

Her euphoria was intoxicating when Gordon Ewing said, "Say, you look much older tonight, somehow."

For the occasion, Mara's long black hair was swept up high on her head and held in place with two mother-of-pearl combs, which Gwen's sister had presented to her on her wedding day. Mara wanted to be grown up so very badly.

Many a night, on her straw mattress in the back of the wagon, Mara would lie sleepless, staring into the darkness, her head swimming with daydreams. Her hands would slip up under her nightgown and examine her budding breasts, already the size of small, hard plums. A sensation of warm lassitude would flow through her body, and she would think of Gordon Ewing, imagine how it would feel to have his hands caressing her breasts, her body. Then she would blush with shame. The very idea of Gordon seeing her gangly, undeveloped body in the nude was humiliating.

Not now, but someday, in two or three years, all that would change. She would have a woman's breasts, a woman's hips and buttocks, a woman's—she had no idea what it was called—"parts"; parts that were quite different from a boy's or a man's parts. A girl with four brothers was not kept in the dark very long about the differences between the sexes. Now she tried to imagine Gordon naked, and the "good feeling" all over made her stir restlessly on her straw bed. And powerless to prevent it, she would hold her breath as her hand, with a will of its own, slid down over her quivering belly, and her trembling fingertips explored the mystery between her thighs.

After the ecstasy subsided, she would be beset with agony:

What type of a wanton, depraved girl are you, Mara

Tate? But, despite her persistent vows *never* to succumb again to that *bad* girl, that other Mara, nothing in the world could stop her from indulging in sweet fantasies of handsome Gordon Ewing, and she would be helpless against the lure of her forbidden delight.

On this, her first night in Arizona, her special birthday, Mara was the center of attraction among the wagon-train people. To a family, they all favored her with small gifts, garnered from their sundry possessions: a comb, a fan, a handkerchief, a stickpin.

The highlight of her party was the birthday cake her mother produced as if by miracle—a fruitcake heavily laced with rum, which she had stored away covertly all the way across the Atlantic and halfway across North America. Tears of gratitude and love welled up in the girl's eyes, and she embraced Gwen while her father and brothers serenaded her with a Welsh birthday song.

When she got into her wagon bed late that night, Mara fell asleep immediately, too tired even to think about her true love, Gordon.

It seemed but an instant later when the sound of rifle shots caused her to bolt upright. Then, through the canvas flap at the front of the wagon, she saw that it was early dawn.

Her father ripped the flap open and yelled, "Come out of there, you two! Indian attack!"

Her mother stirred at the other end of the wagon. "What is it, Drew?" she inquired crossly, still half asleep. "Must you be hunting so early in the day, so none of the rest of us can catch a wink extra?"

"By God, woman, *wake up!*" He leaned inside the wagon and shook her roughly by the shoulder. "The Apaches are attacking us!"

That stirred her adrenaline and she called to her daughter, "Hurry up, child, get your clothes on."

"No time for that!" Drew shouted. "Come along, *now!*"

The women and children were herded into the middle of the circle of wagons, where they huddled behind barricades, erected the previous night, consisting of bales of hay and bags of flour, oats, and other produce. The men and older boys took their assigned places underneath the wagons behind similar barricades and sighted along their rifle barrels.

"Don't shoot at random," Sam Pickens instructed them. "Wait until you have a target."

The wagon master had selected this camping site with a mind to its defensibility. To their north was a sheer bluff, and to the east and west were thick forests; but the enemy would have to cross two hundred feet of open ground on either side to reach the wagons. The greatest threat was posed from the south; tall grass, almost a man's height, grew to within fifty feet of the wagons. Sam picked six men, all crack shots, to defend this position. It was a sound decision, for the first wave of Apaches attacked from this direction.

There was no mistaking that they were Apaches in their distinctive loincloths, leggings, and ornamented moccasins, with their long, straight black hair bound back by strips of red cloth wrapped tightly across their foreheads. The "tigers of the human species," they had been branded by General George Crook, the greatest Indian fighter of them all.

And to Gordon Ewing, fighting with the southern defenders, wild tigers they seemed as they came bounding across the open ground. It had been previously agreed that the Indian leading the attack would be Sam Pickens's target and the brave behind him Lem Owens's. Gordon was assigned the third in the ranks. He found his man and squeezed the trigger. Bull's-eye!

All six defenders had found their mark.

"That's showing 'em, men!" Sam cheered.

A second and a third fusillade echoed across the plateau, and the deadly marksmanship of the defenders sent the Apaches retreating to the tall grass to regroup. With them they carried six of their wounded. Twelve dead lay scattered in front of the wagons.

The attacking Indians carried rifles, but behind them in the high grass was their "bow-and-arrow artillery." From the rear they rained flight after flight of arrows on the new settlers, not very effectively, though, largely due to Sam Pickens's strategy of placing his men beneath rather than between the wagons, where they would be vulnerable to the arrows arcing out of the sky—the more conventional wagon-train tactic in doing battle with marauding Indians.

Next time around, the Apaches attacked from two sides, with no better results than the initial assault. At this point their chieftain patently decided that he had underestimated these particular foes and withdrew from the fray.

The white men emerged from their defenses and yelled and cheered and tossed their hats into the air in a celebration of victory. It turned out to be premature, for, in a typically wily Apache ruse, a force of the bow-and-arrow artillery had remained behind, concealed in the grass, and when the defenders showed themselves, the Indians loosed two savage volleys into their midst, killing two and wounding seven others. Then they rode off to catch up with the main body of Apaches.

"Dirty bastards!" Sam shouted, and the outraged settlers fired after them, but to no avail.

Among the wounded was Gordon Ewing, who had been struck with an arrow in his left shoulder. Mara averted her eyes as Sam kneeled beside the youth with a wicked-looking bowie knife and made a long gash alongside the wound in order to remove the fishhook-like arrowhead.

Later she visited his wagon where he lay recuperating. Timidly, she poked her head inside the flap. Gordon grinned at her:

"Well, hello there, Mara. It's nice of you to pay me a visit."

She gulped. "You were very brave, Gordon. You're a real hero."

"A hero—that's funny!" He threw back his leonine head and laughed, dazzling her with his perfect white teeth. Mara had good teeth herself, except for the gap between the two top front teeth. It didn't bother her, though, and everyone else said it was cute.

"You *are* a hero."

"I was near frightened to death."

"I don't believe it. You'll always be a hero to me."

His blue eyes glinted and he half turned on his mattress and rummaged for something in a box. Turning back, he handed her an Apache arrowhead with an inch of splintered shaft still attached to it. "Here's another birthday gift for you, Mara."

Her eyes went round with wonder. "Is that the one that——" Her gaze was fixed on his bandaged shoulder.

"Yup, one and the same."

"Oh, Gordon, it's . . . it's . . . the best present anyone ever gave me!" she exclaimed, hastily adding, "but I'm sorry to have gotten it this way, you getting wounded."

"Nothing to it." He winked. "Remember, I'm a big hero."

She clutched the arrow to her bosom and her eyes were filled with stars. "I must leave now and show it to everyone. . . . Oh, Gordon, thank you so very much!" Impulsively she climbed on the tailgate of the wagon, leaned toward him, and kissed him on the cheek. Then, blushing to the roots of her hair, she ran off with his affectionate laughter trailing after her.

A day to remember.

CHAPTER EIGHT

"I don't want to bring you back yet, Mara. We may never have a breakthrough like this again. Are you comfortable? Are you relaxed?"

"Oh, yes, I am very, very happy. This is where I want to be. I don't care if I ever go back to where I came from."

"Don't say that, Mara. You will wake up when I choose to wake you, and the dream will be gone."

"No! There is so much more I have to tell you."

"All right, Mara; I am listening."

Mara Tate had never been so happy in her life. Gordon Ewing, whose family had brought along three saddle horses, taught her to ride on the long trek south, and the two of them would ride ahead of the wagon train or to the west, exploring the wonders of this amazing land. There were towering stone spires thrusting into the cloudless blue sky like giant stalagmites.

"As perfect as church steeples," the girl said.

Scattered all about the desert were huge monuments of every size and shape—human, animal, grotesque forms—that might have been sculptured by the hand of the Almighty himself. The land was a montage of spiritual as well as corporeal beauty and grandeur.

One day Sam Pickens rode with them to the Petrified Forest, a wasteland of fallen logs and stunted trees, all solid stone.

"It's spooky!" Mara said in a hushed voice. "Some witch or demon has put a spell on them."

Sam chuckled. "Sure looks that way. Fact is, this forest was covered by glacial soil ages back, and salt and other minerals filled the pores of the wood over the centuries. God only knows how long it took for the soil to erode away, but when it did, this is what it gave back from the grave—the Petrified Forest."

He took them to the Painted Desert, where the dazzling rainbow-colored sands again called to Mara's mind the analogy of the Almighty's hand. *He* did paint this picture for all mankind to gaze upon with the sure conviction that there is a power higher than mere mortal influence, she was convinced.

Nearby was Meteor Crater, a gigantic hole six hundred feet deep and a mile in diameter.

"Sure glad I wasn't in these parts when that fiery monster came tumbling down out of the sky," Gordon said in awe.

On the way back to the wagon train, they took a shortcut, riding along a dried-up riverbed that traced a serpentine course in a northeasterly direction. Suddenly, Sam reined to a stop and signaled for them to stop, too.

"Shhh . . . Listen, do you hear it?"

Gordon and Mara strained their ears. "Sounds like distant thunder," they concurred.

"Maybe so, but we ain't taking chances. Come on, let's get out of here!"

He whipped his mount into a gallop, heading for the nearest bank, with Mara and Gordon on his heels. Sam and Gordon scrambled safely up the steep incline, but Mara's filly stumbled and fell, unseating her, and horse and girl tumbled all the way back down the bank.

As Mara regained her feet, the roaring sound swelled in volume, so loud now that she could not hear what Sam and Gordon were yelling at her. Following the direction of their frantic waving, she saw it—a solid wall of water, twenty or thirty feet high, a tidal wave, sweeping downriver toward her at astonishing speed.

The horse's eyes rolled in terror and it scrambled up the bank and ran off. When the moment of shock had dissipated, Mara climbed up the bank on all fours. She would have fallen except that Sam and Gordon formed a human chain to assist her. She clasped Gordon's hand an instant before the mountain of angry, frothing white water tumbled over the spot where she and the horse had been lying. The flying spume drenched them all.

"Whatever was *that?*" Mara demanded in a tremulous voice.

"Flash flood; it's common in the territory," Sam said. "Must have been a big cloudburst up near the source. Only river around here runs continuously is the Colorado. All the others depend on their flow from rainfall, and the dry sand drinks it up faster than you can say your name. I've seen rivers like this one go from zero to more than a hundred thousand cubic feet per second. Got to keep on your toes or you might get swept to eternity in a flood."

"I came close," the girl said, shivering and wrapping her arms around her body.

Gordon dropped a big hand on her shoulder and massaged her taut muscles. "It's all right, love."

Day after day they went out exploring, and on their return to camp, Mara would recount the new spectacles she had encountered to her friend Marion Murphy, one of three Irish immigrant sisters who had joined the party at Denver. Orphans, they were traveling with their uncle and aunt.

"You should really come with us, Marion," the younger girl suggested.

Marion's expression was one of distaste. "I never was one for exercise. No way to get me on a dirty horse." Her lilting Irish brogue was a source of constant delight to Mara.

The three Murphy sisters, ages sixteen, eighteen, and twenty, were the best-dressed women in the caravan. They spent most of their time primping and preening in the back of their wagon and attending to their wardrobes. The first time they hung out their underwear to dry, it caused a scandal among the other women and gave the men something to daydream about.

"All them fancy frills and satin and lace," Sam said to Gordon. "Wouldn't surprise me if they've come west to open a whorehouse."

Mara idolized Marion, who frequently let the young girl observe when she was attending to her makeup, nails, and hair. The Irish lass was the oldest of the three sisters and, in Mara's estimation, the prettiest, with her long, glistening auburn hair—brushed fifty strokes three times a day—almond-shaped hazel eyes, and pert upturned nose. She had pear-shaped breasts, lifted high by a boned undergarment, a delectable sight peeping out of her daring décolletage. Her skirts were not like the voluminous shapeless garments worn by most of the women. Flounced at the hemline, they fit snugly about the hips and were slit up the side, to reward the men with a teasing glimpse of slender leg when she walked or crossed her legs.

Visiting Marion's wagon after they had camped one afternoon, Mara announced, "Sam says we'll be in Bisbee day after tomorrow. My father and brothers can hardly wait. They expect to get rich on gold as soon as they get there."

Marion laughed. "Sure and begorra and it's damned few gold hunters ever strike it rich." Her eyes sparked.

"Now, as for meself and me sisters, we've got our own gold mine already staked out."

"Do you really?" Mara asked innocently. "Oh, I don't believe you, Marion. You've never been to Arizona before."

Her sisters Bridget and Maggie, sewing at the front of the wagon, began to titter. Bridget was blonde and Maggie was raven-haired; they resembled Marion but had plumper figures.

"Aye, I haven't. But you see, Mara, we're bringing our gold mine along with us."

All three older girls burst into hearty laughter. Mara felt the color rising in her neck and suffusing her cheeks as the light dawned: The Murphy sisters were prostitutes! The revelation left her tongue-tied.

Marion, still guffawing, put an arm around her shoulders. "What a way for me to speak in front of a mere child. Someday you'll come to realize the truth of what I'm saying, darlin'. The men may have the brawn and the brains and the power, but women have, you might say, an *ace in the hole!*"

This produced even greater hilarity—not from Mara, however. Indignantly she pulled herself loose of Marion's grasp.

"Is that all you think of yourselves, Marion? think of women? Well, I have higher ambitions for myself than being a plaything for the male sex."

Marion chucked her under the chin. "Listen to her, girls, and all of fourteen years old. Just wait, me dear. The time will come when you'll be eager to play with the fellers." A sly glint sharpened her eyes. "Fact is, I wouldn't be surprised if you have the itch to play already. I've seen the way you look at that big good-looking Ewing boy. Truthfully, I wouldn't mind playing with that one meself."

"I must go back to my wagon," Mara said stiffly,

striving to keep her temper. "Thank you for your hospitality."

She jumped off the tailgate and walked primly off in the direction of the Tate camp, with the jeers and catcalls of the Murphy girls ringing in her ears.

Later that night in her rough bed, she called to her mother in the dark: "Mum, did you ever want to be anything other than a wife and a mother?"

Gwen was silent a moment; then she answered, "Not really. There's scarcely any other occupation open to a woman than keeping house . . . or being a whore. . . . Incidentally, I don't like you spending so much time with those Murphy girls. Tarts—you can tell it the moment you set eyes on them."

"They're very proper around me," she lied, and thought about what her mother had said—*keeping house or being a whore*. That's terrible, Mum, but it's going to be different over here in America than it was in the old country. Women aren't going to sit back and take it anymore, being treated like inanimate possessions—tables, chairs, dishes—to serve the whim of their 'masters.' The way it is now, we're little better than slaves."

"Listen to the girl," Gwen murmured. "You're too young to be speaking like that. And exactly what new and grand opportunities do you see ahead for yourself in this new land?"

"Unlimited opportunities. You wait and see: I might even become a lawyer or a doctor or even a judge."

"Saints preserve us! I think all that reading you do has gone to your head, child. Now, quiet down and go to sleep."

"Good night, Mum."

Mara lay there listening to the sounds outside the wagon. The men were still talking around the fire, laughing and swapping anecdotes with the men from other wagons and passing around bottles of homemade whiskey. The men customarily slept outside around the fire, wrapped up in blankets.

And Gordon Ewing's handsome face materialized before her on the canvas roof.

You have the itch to play already. . . .

Marion was right; and the "itch" was manifesting itself uncontrollably here and now. Despising herself for her lack of willpower, Mara succumbed to the forbidden delight.

As Sam Pickens had predicted, on Thursday afternoon a mountain range emerged on the horizon at three o'clock.

"There she be, the Mule Mountains," Sam chortled. "Tonight we'll be camping in Mule Pass Gulch."

"And we'll be digging for copper and gold and silver," Emlyn Tate said, and his brothers clapped and let out a chorus of Ayes.

"Not much high-grade gold and silver ore in Arizona," Sam informed them. "What there is is mostly a by-product of copper mining. I thought you boys was gonna work for one of the big operations."

"He's right, boys," Drew Tate said sternly. "We're going to put in a lot of hard work before we can strike out on our own. This trip has taken every cent we own. It's down in the mines for us in the beginning. Think we'll have trouble finding work, Sam?"

"Not if you're the professionals you claim to be. One mine in particular you might try—the Copper Store. Last year they had to close off two tunnels because of fire—a vein of coal or natural gas; I'm not certain. After a year of burning, the rock all around it gets plenty hot. They say the temperature gets as high as one-fifty in parts of the mine that's still being worked. Only men they can get to go down there is a bunch of Chicanos."

"Anything a Mexican can do, a Welshman can do better," Drew Tate said with total confidence.

Sam Pickens smiled and slapped the reins down on the stout backs of the horses. "Enough jawing; let's move on."

CHAPTER NINE

Bisbee—the "mile-high town"—literally hung on canyon walls only slightly less precipitous than those on which the cliff dwellers had built their homes. Row upon row of ragtag huts and bungalows set on steplike terraces ascended to the top of the hillsides on either side of Mule Pass Gulch.

A standing joke was that if a resident were to fall off his front yard, he would land on his neighbor's roof. In truth, anxious mothers tethered their toddlers to the front porch when they were playing outdoors. The height of the level one lived on determined the social pecking order in Bisbee. On the summit, Quality Hill, lived the most affluent and high-ranking company officials.

The town itself was two miles long, stretching up Mule Pass Gulch, but only a few blocks wide. The gulch was lined with saloons, and the farther up the gulch one traveled, the tougher the clientele. At the far end of Bisbee were the whorehouses, rickety shanties built on the hillsides, with concrete steps leading up to the front doors.

"Five thousand feet high, Bisbee is," Sam Pickens informed them. "And that's about as close to heaven as many of its citizens are apt to get!"

Land was plentiful in the Bisbee district, and the new arrivals were readily assimilated into the mining community. As in most pioneer societies, there existed a spirit of camaraderie seldom found in urban settlements. The old-timers welcomed the newcomers with unbounded hospitality. Scores of volunteers formed work squads to help them build houses and clear land. Hard-pressed for money after their long odyssey across country, the latest settlers were dependent on charity for sustenance until they found a means of self-support.

The Tates held a marked advantage over their fellow travelers because of their mining experience in Wales. James Donovan, the superintendent of the Copper Store, hired Drew Tate and his four sons on the spot when they showed up at company field headquarters in the Mule Mountains. And as Drew Tate had vowed, the five Welshmen kept pace with the Mexican miners and then some. Drew solved the problem of the super-high temperatures in the mine, caused by the fires in adjoining shafts, by dousing himself and the lads with water until their clothing was sodden. Every hour they were down in the pits, the watering-down would be repeated. It was still brutal work but tolerable.

In the early months at Bisbee, Gwen and Mara toiled in their new home, scrubbing, washing, sewing, making repairs. All of their furnishings were acquired by salvaging cast-off items from the town dump, and required extensive renovation. Fortunately, the men of the family were handy with tools and were competent carpenters.

The Ewings had been the most prosperous members of the wagon train. The elder Ewing had a degree in mining engineering, and every major mining company in the district bid for his services. He accepted a position with the Copper Store as assistant chief engineer, and before long the Ewings were ensconced on Quality Hill.

Gordon became a full-time prospector in the Mule Mountains. Frequently he would camp out for weeks at a stretch. His long absences from Bisbee depressed

Mara, and she would sulk around the house and be curt to the other family members.

"She's just love-sick," her brothers would tease, which was a sure way to send her flying out of the house to seek the solitude of the hills.

One day, on impulse, Mara walked to the far end of town where the sporting houses were. It was a warm day in late August, and many of the "ladies" were taking the air on their front porches. From a distance, at least, they all looked very elegant to Mara, and a lot healthier and happier than the other women in Bisbee. The majority of the housewives in town looked like washed-out scarecrows in their shapeless, patched, drab clothing, all of the feminine vitality drained out of them by constant drudgery.

"Lookin' for someone, ducks?" a cockney accent called down to her.

Mara looked up at the plump blonde wearing only a camisole and ruffled drawers and cleared her throat nervously. "Yes, ma'am. Do you know where the Murphy sisters are staying?"

"Marion and her bunch got the shack four down. You a friend o' theirs?"

"We came to Bisbee on the same wagon train."

"That so. Well, that Marion is some girl, I can tell you. Been here less than six months and she's got the best business in the gulch. Outbids the rest of us for all the new merchandise comes to town."

"Merchandise?" Mara inquired.

"New girls. . . . Is that what you want to see her about, joining the ranks?"

Mara was mortified. "Certainly *not!* This is a social call."

The blonde laughed. "Don't go putting on airs with me, ducks. We're all sisters under the skin—or should I say the 'sheets'?"

"Thank you very much," Mara said haughtily and walked along stiff-legged and stiff-spined.

At the foot of the cement stairs leading up to the shack the woman had designated as Marion's, she hesitated. Possibly it was not a very good idea after all. She would have turned and retraced her steps if someone hadn't called to her from an open window in the upper story of the dwelling:

"Mara Tate, I don't believe me eyes! And I thought you had forgotten all about us. Come on up here at once so I can see you proper."

She climbed the steps up to the porch and stood at the door with her hands folded primly in front of her. In a short while Marion opened it, her face beaming with pleasure. She threw her arms around Mara, dragged her inside the house, then stepped away to look at her.

"Gor! What's happened to you, child? Child! What am I sayin'? You're practically a woman. Well, I never!"

It was true that within a span of months, Mara Tate had blossomed forth from her young girl's form like a butterfly shedding its cocoon. Her breasts thrust out boldly in her gingham frock, and her hips and buttocks asserted themselves most appealingly, items that had not gone unnoticed by Gordon Ewing. Like a woman, she wore her black hair long down her back and tied with a red ribbon.

"It must have been that fourteenth birthday you had on the trail. It's worked sheer magic. Come along and I'll fix us a cup of tea." She rushed Mara past a parlor where three girls were entertaining prospective customers with wine, song, and provocative glimpses of breasts and thighs revealed by diaphanous garments, and into a fair-sized kitchen, shutting the door behind them.

"Your house is much bigger than it looks from the outside," Mara observed.

"It keeps expanding. Just about ready to add a new wing on the back again. Business is booming." Humming, she spooned tea into a china pot and put up a pan of water to boil on the banked woodstove.

"How are Bridget and Maggie?"

"Thriving like all of us. I've been thinking of opening a branch up at Tombstone. The girls can manage Bisbee well enough. Of course, my place in Tombstone would have real style. There are some very distinguished gents live there. But what about you, dearie? What have you been up to?"

"Helping Mum with the housework and things like that." She sighed. "Mostly I'm bored."

Marion gave her a sharp glance. "Bored? Is that big good-looking fellow still around? What was his name, Gordon?"

"Gordon spends most of his time in the mountains looking for copper or gold."

Marion smiled. "Then you have every right to be bored. Well," she said, a twinkle in her eye, "if you want some excitement, come down here. I can guarantee that you won't be bored."

"Oh, Marion, what a thing to say." Mara was flustered. "See, your tea water is boiling over."

"Jolly ducks and drakes!" Marion ran to the stove. While the tea was steeping, she opened a tin with pictures all over it. "Hand-painted," she said.

"It's beautiful," Mara said admiringly.

"From France. See what's in it." She held out the open tin and showed the contents. "All these cute little cakes."

"Petits fours," Mara said. "I've read about them, though I've never tasted one."

"They're heavenly. Help yourself."

Mara took one of the cakes and bit into it. "Ummm . . . delicious."

Marion cocked her head to one side. "How do you know things like that? *Petits fours* . . . Imagine, you even speak French."

The girl laughed. "I don't speak French, although I would fancy it. There are some expressions that come from the French and become part of the English language."

"See how much you know? I wish I was educated."

"You can be if you really care to. My education came from books mostly. I learned more from them than from all my teachers back in Wales."

"Trouble is, I can't read," Marion said sheepishly.

"Can't read at all?" Mara's eyes were saucers. The idea of not being able to read confounded her. "How wretched for you. Would you like me to teach you how to read and write?"

Marion was overwhelmed. "Do you think you could?"

"Of course. How would it be if I came back next Monday and then on Wednesday and Friday?"

"Marvelous. Will one o'clock till three suit you? That's our slowest time."

"That will be fine. You can ask Bridget and Maggie to come to school as well, if you like."

"I'll ask them. . . . I don't want to be impolite, dear, but I fear there's a ruckus going on in the parlor. Why don't you leave by the back door. There are sights not fit for virginal eyes such as yours."

On the way back down Mule Pass Gulch, Mara ruminated on Marion's last remark. "Damn it! I'm sick and tired of being a virgin!" she said aloud to a horned toad sitting on a rock at the side of the road.

* * *

On September 12, 1877, the Tates were invited to Gordon's birthday party at the big house on Quality Hill. The affair was a milestone in social commerce at Bisbee, the first formal celebration since the rugged mining town's inception.

At first Gwen and Mara refused to accept the invitation. "We don't have finery like those rich women," Gwen told Drew. "And even if there were stores where we could buy it, we couldn't afford it."

"There's a Jew peddler just came to town," Drew said. "I hear he's got bolts of fine fabrics to sell. You might go see him. You two were always good at sewing."

Mara clapped her hands together. "Mum, what a marvelous idea! Let's go right away!"

Reluctantly Gwen allowed her daughter to drag her down the hillside and onto the main street. The traveling peddler had set up his wagon in the village square, and by the time the Tate women arrived, the townspeople were swarming around him, vying to bid for his wares: shoes; simple dresses of cotton gingham and wool and other hard-wearing materials; coarse practical undergarments; footwear; and bolts of cloth to appeal to women who could make their own dresses.

What attracted Mara's eye right off was a stack of how-to booklets containing instructions and patterned diagrams for a variety of enterprises, including how to build one's own house and deep well. Mara fished out a slim book on dressmaking; the cover boasted that the "very latest styles from New York, London, and Paris are included herein."

Mara selected a checked taffeta material for her gown, along with a length of muslin with bright barber-pole stripes for her petticoat. Her mother chose silk-crepe Georgette with a flowered print.

"I feel like a thief," Gwen lamented as they showed

off their acquisitions to Drew. "There goes a whole week's food allowance."

Drew smiled and put an arm around each of them. "You're not to worry, you hear? I've been told there's big things ahead for me in the near future. Those ideas I gave to Donovan last week were received with enthusiasm by the high mucky-mucks in the company."

"But what about you, Drew? What will you wear?"

"John Ewing has already provided for me, ducks. He is lending me a pair of his formal trousers, a black jacket, and a white waistcoat—we're near the same size—so all of our problems are solved." He turned to his dour-looking sons. "Sorry, boys, that you won't be able to join us, but there is just so much expensive attire we can provide for."

"It's all right, Dad," Emlyn assured him. "We all have business in town that night. And, in any case, none of us can abide with those monkey duds you'll be wearing."

Drew winked and clapped Emlyn on his brawny shoulder. In an undertone he said, "I can guess what kind of business you'll all be doing in town that Saturday night. Up the north side of town, is it?"

Emlyn reddened. "You're wrong. I'll be visiting Millicent Baxter at Fort Huachuca."

"Will you, now, lad? Ah, that's splendid." Drew was delighted.

The fact that Emlyn was twenty-seven years old and unmarried was a source of much concern to Drew and Gwen Tate. Emlyn was the least attractive of the Tate sons; he had red hair and the milk-white skin that so often goes with it, a throwback two generations, and a weak chin, which he covered with a scrawny beard.

Millicent Baxter was the daughter of an army major stationed at the nearby fort. The military and the miners saw a good deal of each other in the Bisbee district, where the soldiers were assigned to seek out and destroy Apache marauders. The miners claimed, tongue in cheek, that the army spent more time prospecting for rich ore in the Mule Mountains than they did looking for Indians. It was true that quite a few soldiers had made profitable strikes in the fields.

The other Tate sons were dark-complexioned, ruggedly handsome with an animal sensuality about them that fascinated the young ladies of Bisbee.

Drew addressed Allan, twenty-five, his second son: "And what is your business in town that night, lad?"

Allan, who was constantly being mistaken for a Jew because of his Semitic mouth and nose, did not meet his father's questioning stare. "Meeting some fellows down at the John Peel Inn for a game of cards," he mumbled. He could not tell his father that he was having a torrid affair with a sensuous girl of Mexican-Indian extraction named Maria Beaver.

"And you, sir?" Drew inquired of Gilbert, three years junior to Allan and the most handsome and dashing of all the brothers.

"I'm visiting a young lady. As a matter of fact, I'll be on Quality Hill myself that night."

"Do tell." His mother could not conceal her pleasure. "And who might she be?"

"Jayne Minton. Her father is a New York banker looking for investments for himself and a group of wealthy eastern friends."

"How nice." Gwen glanced at her youngest son with misgiving. "I wish Dylan would find himself a nice girl so he wouldn't have to mope around by himself all the time."

"Oh, Dyl has his poetry," Allan teased. "Nothing better he cares to do than to go off in the wilderness and write. What was your last one, Dyl? 'Ode to a Gila Monster,' wasn't it?"

Crimson with restrained anger, Dylan spun on his heel and walked out of the room. He was the smallest of the Tate sons, a shy, withdrawn youth who made little effort to initiate a social life either with women or with other men his age.

CHAPTER TEN

On the night of the Ewing party, mother and daughter appraised each other critically.

"I think we did pretty well, all things considered," Gwen said. "You look lovely, dear."

Although there was no full-length mirror to afford her a proper examination, Mara could feel that the checked taffeta princess gown fit her body perfectly. It had taken her hours to get the drape of the skirt just right to show off the striped petticoat beneath it.

"You look divine yourself, Mum," Mara returned the compliment.

Gwen ran her hands down her waist and across the flare of her hips. "Do you think this flowered print is too young for me?"

"It's perfect for you."

"The skirt's too short."

"Poo! Stop fretting."

Gwen ran her hands over the padded hip flounces and the boned cage that gave the skirt a saucy flare behind. "My backside is big enough; I don't need this nonsense to exaggerate it."

Drew came into the room, laughing. "Stop bellyaching. Suppose you looked like me? I feel like one of them dandy fops who parade around London with a silk handkerchief tucked into their cuffs."

"You look very handsome, Da. Here, let me fix that cravat for you." Mara went over to him and fussed with his neckpiece.

Gwen regarded her short cloth boots with the patent-leather toe caps dismally. "How on earth are we ever going to walk up the hill in these fripperies?"

"We'll manage, Mum. It's time we got started."

They arrived at the Ewing house promptly at seven. "It's a mansion," Gwen said.

It was an overstatement; the dwelling was basically Georgian design modified to suit the uneven terrain. "American functional," some called the architecture. It was far from "grand" by London or New York standards, but out here in the Far West, where the style of living was spare, fundamental, and humble, the Ewing house radiated an air of grandeur.

John and Susan Ewing greeted them warmly: "We're so glad you could come." Susan embraced Gwen and Mara and admired their gowns. "You both look beautiful. Where did you get such up-to-date dresses out here?"

"We made them," Gwen told her.

Gordon came over to greet them. At the sight of him, Mara almost swooned. He was so handsome in his blue frock coat, fawn trousers, and red ascot knotted casually at the throat of his white silk shirt.

He shook hands with Drew, bowed to Gwen, and took Mara by the hand. "You are the most beautiful girl in the world," he whispered to her.

Her ears tingled. His piercing blue eyes bored into hers, but she refused to blink. "You're beautiful yourself," she said impishly, and was pleased to see him blush.

"I'm glad nobody else heard that." He looked around apprehensively. "Come on, I'll get you a glass of punch. Real rum in it, too."

Mara had never tasted spirits in her life, and the introduction was pleasant, disguised as the alcohol was by fruit juices and chilled to perfection by a small block of ice, an uncommon luxury in the Arizona desert. She drained her cup with relish.

"That's delicious. May I have another?"

Gordon grinned. "Of course." He was thoroughly enjoying her reaction to the rum.

"I feel so giddy . . . so silly." She giggled and clutched his arm. "Am I getting drunk?"

"Not yet, but you're on the way. Here, I better finish that for you." He took the cup and drained it. "Let me take you out back and I'll show you Mother's garden."

He steered her through the cliques of guests talking and laughing in the parlor, down the center hall, through the kitchen, and out onto a flagstone patio. Behind the house was a garden the like of which Mara had never seen before—a dazzling array of nearly every species of cactus native to the region.

Gordon pointed out a saguaro cactus with accordion walls designed to expand as the plant absorbed moisture during heavy rains, a mass of creamy white flowers festooning it. He picked a blood-red fruit from a stem and broke it open to show her a mass of black seeds.

He led her to an immense plant, at least fifteen feet high, decorated with appendages that resembled organ reeds. "This one is an organ-pipe cactus. And here's a barrel cactus"—a roly-poly plant that was bloated with interior water. "The name is obvious. It's saved the lives of many a thirsty traveler in the desert, myself included. "See how it bends to the southwest—an infallible compass."

There were many other varieties: rainbow, hedgehog, fishhook, prickly pear, staghorn, teddy bear.

"The teddy bear can go five years without moisture."

In every case the cactus bore an uncanny resemblance to the object from which it derived its name.

"This century plant grows as much as twelve inches in twenty-four hours."

Mara stroked a velvet leaf with awe. "They're all so beautiful. I wish I had a garden such as this."

"Maybe one day you will," he said. The inflection in his voice made her glow inside as she fantasied a time when she would become Mrs. Gordon Ewing.

"When are you going off prospecting again?" she asked.

"I'm not sure—probably Monday or Tuesday."

"Don't you get discouraged? I mean, all these months you've been tramping through the mountains and you've got nothing to show for it."

"That's where you're wrong," he said. "Every square foot of ground I've been over is recorded on my charts. I know a thousand and one places *not* to look for copper. Each time I go out into the mountains, I narrow the scope. Sooner or later I'm bound to strike it rich. My next trip will be up Tombstone Canyon."

On impulse she declared, "I think I'll come along with you."

Gordon was flabbergasted. "Go with me? Into the mountains? You don't understand, Mara. This isn't an afternoon's jaunt. I may be out in the wilderness for days, weeks."

"Nevertheless, I want to do it." Her dark eyes were adamant, unblinking.

"Impossible! Besides, your parents would never hear of it. A fourteen-year-old girl going off alone with a man? It's absurd."

"We'll see. . . . Don't you want my company?"

"That's not the point. Of course I'd like your company. It gets damned lonely out there with only the coyotes and night creatures to break the monotony."

"I'll make out fine; you'll see. After all, we camped out clear across the country getting to Arizona."

"That was different." He removed a watch from the

pocket of his waistcoat. "We'd better be getting back inside. Dinner will be at eight."

Dinner would be delayed that evening until eight-thirty, owing to an animated discussion taking place in the library that included John Ewing, James Donovan, Drew Tate, and a delegation of three from an eastern investment group headed by one Avery Phelps.

Phelps, chewing on a Havana cigar, addressed Drew Tate on a subject that was of foremost concern to almost everyone who had migrated to Arizona: "Mr. Ewing tells us that you think the boom in copper production is already on the wane, Mr. Tate."

"I do, sir. The way I see it, all the high-grade ore in these parts will be exhausted by the turn of the century. But there's still a fortune in low-grade ore beneath the surface."

"Irrelevant," Phelps said brusquely. "I've consulted some of the best mining engineers in the country, and to a man they agree that low-grade copper cannot be mined profitably."

"Not by the methods in use today, Mr. Phelps," Drew replied evenly. "I've got an idea how it might be done. Learned it from some old-timers back in Cardiff. Their background in the field goes back generations."

"And what method would you suggest, Mr. Tate?"

"Instead of trying to process low-grade ore piecemeal, the way it's done now, you move it raw to a central location and concentrate all the deliveries in a big pit—and I mean a big, *big* pit. I figure that by processing the ore by the mass, it would be possible to extract seven to twelve pounds of pure copper from one ton of ore."

Phelps glanced at one of his associates. "Roberts, how does that strike you? Would such a venture be profitable, seven to twelve pounds of copper from one ton of rock?"

"Absolutely, Mr. Phelps. But what Mr. Tate fails to take into account is that it would require unlimited quantities of water to maintain an open-pit operation. And, as we all know, there is barely enough water to sustain life in this Godforsaken country."

"Begging your pardon, sir," Drew interjected. "My daughter Mara is a serious student, and she knows as much about this country as a native-born Indian. She's reading all the time, everything she can lay her hands on, and she tells me the Indians long ago had irrigation systems that were as efficient as anything you can find around today."

"He's right, Avery," Donovan agreed. "Look what they accomplished at Phoenix, restoring those ancient Hahookam canals to carry water from the Salt River. Within a year they were growing crops on land that had been arid desert."

A visiting English scholar, struck by the analogy between the rebirth of the desert land around the site and the mythical bird the phoenix, which, according to Egyptian legend, burned itself on a funeral pyre every 500 years, only to be resurrected from its own ashes fresh and beautiful, named the city Phoenix.

"There's plenty of water deep underground," Ewing said. "The trick will be to find it and sink artesian wells, as the Australians have done in their desert land."

Phelps drew on his cigar and fixed Drew Tate with a thoughtful and respectful look. "This is all extremely interesting. And I have welcomed hearing your views on the subject of open-pit mining, Mr. Tate. I assure you the matter will be thoroughly investigated by our organization. Also I wish to explore the advisability of bringing over some of these Australian well diggers."

On the way into the dining room, Ewing put a hand on Drew's shoulder and drew him in back of the others. In a low voice he confided, "I'm very impressed with you, Drew, with your ideas. So was Phelps; it was obvious. I wouldn't be surprised if a promotion and a raise is in order for you."

"Rightly the credit should go to Mara," Drew demurred. "Most of what I know comes second-hand from her books."

"Modesty becomes you, old boy. . . . Yes, your daughter Mara has a head on her shoulders—Gordon has been saying it since we first met on the trail—and a pretty head as well. That girl will turn a lot of heads when she grows up."

"Mara is pretty much grown up now," Drew said laconically, "or haven't you noticed?"

Ewing looked at him and smiled. "To be sure." Then, with a hint of irony: "I do believe Gordon has been observing her remarkable flowering with special attention."

"A fine lad, your Gordon, Mr. Ewing."

"I wish you'd call me John. After all, we are friends, Drew."

"As you wish, John."

Neither man would have revealed it to the other, but, by coincidence, the same fleeting idea passed through their minds:

We are friends . . . and someday maybe we will be family.

The Tates did not get home until well after midnight. Even as they were walking up the path to the house, Drew began taking off his clothes: coat, tie, shirt. Inside, he gratefully kicked off his tight shoes and collapsed in an easy chair in front of the potbellied stove.

"Gor, I never thought I'd make it through!" he said. "How about fixing us a pot of tea, mother?"

"Just as soon as I get out of this tight corset," she called on her way into their bedroom.

Mara smoothed down the front of her gown lovingly. "I don't want to take it off, ever. . . . Imagine, there are ladies who dress up like this every day."

"More's the pity for 'em. Well, you certainly had a good time tonight, didn't you, young lady?"

"It was wonderful." Her eyes were sparkling with the memory of the glorious party.

"I must say the Ewings did it up real proper," he admitted, glowing a bit himself at the recollection of the praise he had received from all the eminent company executives for his theories on pit mining.

Mara, sensing he was in a good humor, decided to broach the subject of her impending trip with Gordon Ewing into the Mule Mountains. "Da, would it be all right with you and Mum if I was to go prospecting next week?"

He lit up one of the fine cigars Ewing had sent him home with, not taking her seriously at all. "Prospecting, is it? What ideas you have, child."

"I am *not* a child!" she said heatedly. "And I meant what I said. I am going prospecting with Gordon Ewing!"

"Gordon Ewing!" He was no longer amused. "What the devil's gotten into you, Mara? Prospecting indeed! You must have been drinking that rum punch. Of course you cannot go off into the hills with that boy— that *man!* It would be indecent."

"Gordon Ewing happens to be a very decent young man and very honorable."

Drew's face was beet red as he got up from the chair and approached her menacingly. His voice was ominously calm: "Let me tell you something, young lady. There'll be no more back talk from you. You're still not too big to get a proper tanning, and I'm prepared to give it to you."

She retreated before him, but her voice was steady and firm: "I am going nevertheless."

"That does it!" Drew began to remove his belt.

Gwen burst into the parlor and stepped between them, clad only in her camisole and long drawers. "What's going on here?"

Drew gave her an account of the encounter, punctuated with blasphemous expletives: "I'll not only tan the hide off her, but tomorrow I'll blacken both that young whippersnapper's eyes, that's what!"

"And say good-by to your fine promotion as well. Now, calm down the two of you," she said flatly. The look she gave him was meaningful and calculating; Drew did not fathom it immediately.

"Mum——," Mara began, but Gwen silenced her: "To bed with you, miss. I'm handy at tanning myself. To bed!"

Her tone was a familiar one that none of the children dared ignore, even when they had grown into their late teens and twenties. Gwen meant business, and it was best not to get in her path.

Mara spun around on her heel and stalked off to her bedroom.

"What the devil was that all about?" Drew demanded. "This has to be settled once and for all."

"Not tonight, Drew."

"And why not?" he asked in exasperation. "The very idea of our daughter going off on a camping trip with a man, sleeping away overnight—God only knows how many nights!—and her, only fourteen years old. Glory be, Gwen, I hope she isn't taking after your cousin Agnes. What a hussy *that* one is."

Gwen's half-smile mocked him. "Don't criticize Agnes. After all, there was a bit of it in all of us Thomas women."

"Gwen!" He was shocked.

"You have a bad memory, Drew." She came toward

him, wearing a suggestive glint in her eyes and swaying her hips. He stood speechless as she slipped her arms around his neck and pressed her voluptuous body against him.

She buried her face in his neck and whispered in his ear, "Why was it we left Tydfil, Drew? 'Cause me, a mere slip of a girl, had not the willpower to resist the persuasive fingers and the romantic talk of a certain hot-blooded young hooligan, nor bank the fires of my own hot blood."

"Stop talking like that, Gwen," he said, red and uncomfortable.

She snickered. "Want to forget how you seduced me without benefit of the marriage vow?"

"I married you," he said.

"So you did, and not a day too soon. Even so, there was plenty of suspicion when Emlyn was born six months from the month we took the vows."

"All right," he conceded. "Remember you're the one brought this up, so you, of all people, should blanch at the idea of *your* daughter, your flesh and blood, going off with young Ewing into the wilderness."

She smiled thoughtfully and rubbed her belly against his, exulting in the gradual thrust of his manhood against her soft flesh.

"Mara is sweet on Gordon, and from the way he looks at her, I'm sure the feeling is mutual."

"Aye, and all the more reason why they must be kept apart."

Gwen kissed his ear, nibbling at the lobe. "Suppose my folks had said that about us? We wouldn't be here today with five wonderful children."

Slowly it was dawning on him what her ulterior purpose was. "Can you be meaning what I think you are? that it would be a nice arrangement, Gordon Ewing and our Mara?"

"What would be wrong with it? To me, it would be an ideal match. The Ewings are a fine family."

"More highbrow than the Tates," he said spitefully.

"Only richer; that's what determines the height of the brow. Besides, it would provide you with unlimited opportunities to advance yourself. The Ewings would see to it that the family of their daughter-in-law achieved a place closer to their own level on the social ladder."

Drew was stupefied. "I can't believe my ears, woman! You'd barter away your daughter for social gain?"

"Barter? Me? Never. I'm just being realistic. Why postpone the inevitable? We could lock her in her room until she's of age, but what would it gain? The minute she got out she'd run off with Gordon or some other young stallion. Like I said, there's a bit of cousin Agnes in all the Thomas women, and, to tell the truth, I'm aware of the 'bit' right strong at this moment. Would you be up to a bit of cuddle, Drew darling?" She reached between them and squeezed his taut erection. "Ah, yes, the governor speaks for you. Come along." She led him by the hand to their bedroom and cast off her camisole and drawers.

He devoured her with ardent eyes as he took off his clothes. Gwen had the full, ripe figure of a Rubens nude, too heavy for some tastes, but ideal for Drew's. "I love you more than ever I did," he told her breathlessly as he reached in back of her and cupped her full cheeks in his large, callused hands. Like soft down pillows her buttocks were: her big breasts, too.

She caressed his swollen manhood with eager fingers, his engorged testicles, and laughed softly. "There's certainly a lot more of me to love, ducks."

She lay back on the bed and pulled him down between her wide-spread thighs. Their mating was as natural as breathing, as natural as sight and sound to the eye and the ear.

"I'm coming, Drew."

"Easy does it, love. No rush."

Loins pounding each other frantically, they reached climax together and, spent, lay side by side in blissful exhaustion.

"And this is what you'd be having our daughter doing, is it?"

Gwen sighed. "I only wish it will be as good for her as it is for me. Stop fretting, Drew: Time and tide wait for no man—and neither does sex."

CHAPTER ELEVEN

Gordon had added two sturdy, short-legged geldings to the Ewings' stable to be employed in his forays into the Mule Mountains. Not as handsome as saddle horses, they were better suited to the rugged, rocky terrain than the other mounts.

Gordon rode Black Star, dark as midnight except for his white mane. Mara was aboard Ches, named for his chestnut color. The brawny animals were laden down with overstuffed saddlebags as well as their riders, yet they never faltered even climbing the steepest inclines or plowing across shoulder-high streams.

Gordon carried a rifle in a saddle holster. "Lots of wild animals in the mountains—mountain lions, bears, wild bulls. Not long back, a band of five hunters was attacked by a herd of bulls in a blind canyon. The battle lasted for two hours, and when it was finished, all five were dead along with thirty bulls they'd shot."

"How horrible!" She shivered.

"And then there's the rattlesnakes. Liable to wake up one morning with one of 'em cuddled beside you in your sleeping bag."

"I'm beginning to regret that I came along. But that's why you're telling me all these stories, isn't it, Gordon—so that I might decide to go back."

He laughed. "Not so. I'm damned glad to have the company. I still can't fathom how you pressured your mother and dad into letting you do it, though."

"I am a very determined woman."

"Woman!" he snorted. "You're still not dry behind the ears."

"I'm almost fifteen!" she said haughtily.

"But you look so much younger," he said with sarcasm.

Mara's cheeks flamed. "Go to hell, Gordon Ewing! I think I *will* go back to Bisbee."

"Never make it before dark."

"I'd rather sleep with a grizzly bear than with you!" It was out before she realized how it sounded, as if she actually was contemplating sleeping *with* him.

Gordon sensed her embarrassment and tactfully made no further comment. In spite of his teasing, he was very much aware that Mara was blossoming into a woman—a vivacious, highly sensual female. More than once along the trail he admired, covertly, the flare of her buttocks across the saddle, provocatively displayed by her skintight denim riding trousers, and the thrust of her firm conical breasts shaping the flannel shirt. Her long hair was braided and wrapped around her head underneath the wide-brimmed Mexican sombrero.

They were entering a veritable labyrinth of canyons and guillies twisting their way through the mountains on all sides, intersecting at places, then veering off in contrary directions, only to link up again farther along.

"Got to keep on our toes day and night for cloudbursts," he warned, "and take to high ground at the first rumble of thunder. Remember the time we almost got caught in that flood on our way to Bisbee with Sam Pickens?"

"I've never been so scared in my life."

"A soldier—army officer—was drowned around here last month. They named the canyon after him. Rucker was his name. . . . Keep a lookout for Apaches, too." In truth he was not very concerned about Indians, as the area was infested with army patrols and the Apaches kept to the most remote regions high in the mountains.

"Do you ever prospect anywhere else than in the Mule Mountains?" she asked.

"Not yet, but I intend to look around up near Prescott and Jerome, as far west as Kingman. Things will be a lot better when the Southern Pacific brings the railroad across Arizona. The bridge is already built over the Colorado River at Yuma."

For no reason apparent to Gordon, Mara suddenly declared, "I'll bet you didn't know that those fearsome Apaches are ruled by women chieftains."

"The hell you say!"

"It's true. Oh, there are lesser chieftains, men, who lead war parties, but the tribes are governed by squaws. All property is in their name as well. And when a man and a woman get married, the husband moves into the wife's family."

"You're joshing me, Mara."

"Just like a man. You can't tolerate the idea that women just might be the better sex—brainier, level-headed, more practical. You men, you're just overgrown boys, swaggering around beating your chests like apes, shooting each other up like goes on in Tombstone. You'd never catch women behaving so stupidly. Yes, the Apaches have the right idea: Leave the management of important issues and affairs to the best-qualified members of the tribe."

"God bless the ladies." Gordon rolled his eyes heavenward. "Next thing, you'll be suggesting that the president of the United States should be a woman."

"Oh, that's inevitable. It may take a while, but one day it will come to pass. There will be a woman president, and women leaders in other countries, too. Then we'll stamp out these silly wars you men adore so much. You can play less dangerous games to release your hostility."

He looked at her incredulously. "I think I'm a little afraid of you, Mara Tate."

Her eyes gleamed and darkened. "As well you might be, Gordon Ewing."

I'm out to get you for my very own, Mr. Ewing, and there's nothing you can do to avert it!

At five o'clock that afternoon they found an ideal campsite, an underground spring in a cluster of organ-pipe cactuses. After they had brushed and watered the horses, Mara collapsed on her blanket.

"I must say that prospecting is very dull business," she complained.

Gordon sat cross-legged alongside her and rolled a cigarette. "Once you make a strike, all the hard work and tedium becomes worthwhile."

"Let me have a puff of your cigarette," she said.

He was startled. "Are you daft, girl? Your father would cut off my ears if I did such a thing. Ladies don't smoke."

"Marion Murphy does."

"Marion Murphy!" He raised his eyebrows. "As I said, *ladies* do not smoke."

"Marion is a very nice person . . . and a *lady.*"

"Damn it, Mara; you really shouldn't associate with a notorious woman like her."

"I'm teaching her and her sisters to read and write. And what's wrong with the Murphy girls?"

"You're not naïve, Mara. You know perfectly well what they are."

"Prostitutes. What of it?"

Gordon stood up. It was obvious that the conversation was making him uncomfortable. "Look, let's drop the subject. Do you know what you are, young lady? You are a provocateur. You like to stir up controversy."

"And you don't think that proper young ladies should be controversial, is that it?"

"There are endeavors better suited for women."

She sprang to her feet and confronted him, nose to nose, feet spread, her hands on her hips. "Such as lying on their backs with their legs spread, waiting for their lords and masters to mount them, and bearing children? That's the limit of female endeavor in your piggish male mind!"

His steely blue eyes bored into hers; she did not blink or give an inch. "That will be enough out of you, miss."

"You arrogant bastard!" She hit him a resounding slap with all of her weight behind it.

Gordon staggered back and put a hand to the flaming welt on his left cheek. He was more shocked than hurt. Anger speeded his recovery. He walked toward her purposefully, flexing his fingers. "You deserve a spanking, brat, and that's exactly what I'm going to give you."

"You wouldn't dare!" Her voice registered alarm as she realized he was not bluffing. She backed off. "Don't you touch me, you brute! Just like a man: If you don't have everything your own way, you resort to violence and force."

He lunged at her, but she eluded his grasp and turned and ran. Gordon was in hot pursuit. She raced down a narrow gully that terminated in a dead end, a rocky incline that veered up at a forty-five-degree angle. Mara went scrambling up the slope on hands and knees. She almost reached the top when Gordon's hand clutched at her ankle.

"Bastard!" She kicked at his head with her free leg.

"Bitch!" He caught both her feet and dragged her back. The two of them slid down the slope on their bellies. Gordon straddled her hips and pinned her arms to the ground. Her eyes were midnight blue and bright with anger and defiance.

"Let me go or I'll kill you!"

"Are all Welsh females as ornery as you?"

She writhed and thrashed desperately, but her strength was no match for his. At last she went limp and docile. "That's why you keep us servile," she spat. "Just because you're bigger and more muscular . . . All right, you've rendered me helpless. What will you do now? rape me?"

He blushed to the roots of his hair. "I wouldn't touch you if you were the last female on earth. I'd rather frequent Marion Murphy's cathouse."

"That's no secret. You've been there plenty of times; Marion told me. What's the matter, Gordon? No girl will do it with you unless you pay her?"

The color drained out of his face, and rage numbed his reason. "You nasty bitch!" Almost as if he was in a trance, he let go of her hands and bent over her, one knee on each side of her body. She remained inert, her expression a mixture of anger, fear, and anticipation. Fascinated, she watched his fingers fumbling with the buttons on her plaid shirt.

He spread open the shirt and stared at her heaving breasts under the filmy shirtwaist; no boned undergarments required to support her firm fruits, fruits the size of ripe peaches.

She gasped as he lifted up the shirtwaist and bared her flesh to his avid eyes. Her eyes were riveted on the expanding bulge in his crotch, and her own loins caught fire.

He wants me—in the way that a man wants a woman!

His sexual excitement was proof, and she was filled with pride and elation.

I am a woman—at last! I will not recover from this encounter as a virgin! She was determined.

She held out her arms to him, and he bent his mouth to her eager lips. She clasped her hands behind his neck and pulled him down. He smothered her with wet kisses on her mouth, her eyes, her ears, her throat.

"Oh, God!" she moaned as his tongue teased her turgid nipples. His mouth covered first one areola, then the other.

Her hands were busy undoing the buttons of his fly. His swollen member sprang free, and she cuddled it the way a child reveres a new toy. "Oh, my love, you're so beautiful!"

He peeled off her trousers, then her cotton drawers, and appraised her nude body with undisguised delight. " 'Feast one's eyes'—now I know what it means," he said, a note of awe in his voice.

"Well, I am waiting to feast my eyes, so take off your clothes, please."

He did, and she shivered from sheer pleasure. "I lie awake at night and picture how you would look naked."

"You do?" He laughed self-consciously. "And do I measure up to your expectations?"

She licked her lips. "In every fashion." Her hands were hot and eager on his flesh, exploring, teasing. She took one of his hands and pulled it down between her thighs. "I picture you doing this to me."

Her candor stimulated Gordon as intensely as her plying hands. He bent to kiss her breasts once more. His tongue ran down over the swell of her belly, tickling her navel.

"Oh, God, this is heavenly! Darling, do it to me now; I'm ready and then some."

He moved between her legs and probed with his erection against her lubricious parts.

"Here, let me show you the way." She reached down and guided him.

Penetration was not easy. "I don't want to hurt you."

"I'm not concerned. Push harder." She lifted her hips to meet his thrust, and the membrane parted. The momentary pain Mara felt was soon dispelled by the mounting pleasure. She was giddy with ecstasy. "Oh, my love, my love, my precious darling," she moaned.

He could scarcely believe the high pitch of her ardor. Breasts, belly, loins, flanks—it seemed she was an extension of his own body, molded to him, and they were as one heaving, writhing flesh. The tempo quickened until Mara was wracked by a gigantic spasm and another even more violent and in fast succession an endless series of pleasure pangs so rhapsodic she felt that if the agonizing joy did not cease, she would surely die.

His face above her was contorted with bliss, his eyes closed. She felt his powerful contractions deep inside her and thought she must burst if he persisted.

Afterward they lay hip to hip, holding hands and dozing—a timeless interlude. Finally he raised himself on an elbow and smiled at her. "I love you, Mara Tate."

"I love you, Gordon Ewing." She reached up and stroked the fine angle of his jaw with her fingertips.

"I want to marry you."

She laughed. "Don't you think I'm a little young to be a wife?"

"You're a woman, age regardless. You're *my* woman."

Her smile was bittersweet. "No, Gordon, human beings cannot own each other. I'll be proud to become your wife, but I will never be your woman; that's slavery."

His expression was quixotic. "What an odd girl you are, Mara, so unlike all the other girls I've ever met—hothouse violets who want to be spoiled and pampered and cared for."

"Oh, I want to be cared for, too, and I want to care for you." She smiled coquettishly. "I'll take good care of you for the rest of your life. Do you want to 'care' for me again before we get dressed?"

"Hussy."

"The worst sort of hussy. I want to be on top this time."

He was shocked. "You on top? That isn't proper."

"Any way is proper that feels good. Now, lie back and relax." She swung a leg across his body, straddling his hips, rocking to and fro until Gordon's erection rose up between her thighs like a sturdy shaft.

The novelty of the uncommon posture was highly titillating, and he had to hold back with all of his willpower so as not to climax prematurely. At last he felt her orgasm and let the frantic tide explode.

"It was even better than the first time," Mara exulted when the thrills subsided. On impulse, she lay across his legs with her perky backside in the air. "You can give me that spanking now if you care to."

Gordon laughed and paddled her playfully. "All right, wench, put on your pants."

While they were dressing, Mara looked up at the steep bank she had been climbing when Gordon caught her. They had dislodged a portion of an outcropping in their tumbling descent.

"What is all that green stuff in that rock, Gordon?"

He whistled. "Looks like copper carbonate to me, and lots of it. Wait here while I get my equipment."

He ran back to where the horses were tethered and got a prospector's kit out of his saddlebag. When he returned to Mara, he opened the kit and took out an iron mortar and pestle. Then he clambered up to the outcropping and chipped off several samples of the rock. Placing them in the mortar, he ground them up into a fine powder, poured the powder into a glass jar, and added two ounces of sulphuric acid. "Now we shall see what we have here," he said, and took a hunting knife out of the sheath on his belt.

Mara watched in fascination as he dipped the shiny steel blade into the solution. When he withdrew it, there was a pure copper coating on the section of the blade. "Magic!" she exclaimed.

"Not magic; even better. This must be one of the richest copper veins in Arizona—maybe bigger than the Mercury Mine." He grabbed her in a bear hug and swung her off her feet. "Do you know what this means, Mara? We're going to be rich, and it's all because of you! If you hadn't angered me with your sauciness and led me on the chase down this gully, it would have gone unnoticed."

"What do we do now?"

"Stake out a claim and then go back to Bisbee and register it at the assay office."

It marked the beginning of the Tate copper empire.

CHAPTER TWELVE

In the decade that followed, the Copper King out-stripped every other mine in copper production under the joint ownership of the Tate-Ewing clan; one vein alone was five feet thick.

The Tate-Ewings were a clan in every sense of the word after Gordon Ewing took seventeen-year-old Mara for his wife in the spring of 1880.

In 1883 the Copper King yielded $10 million, and over three quarters of the handsome sum was clear profit. Tragically, that same year John Ewing died of pneumonia. Heartbroken and ailing herself, Susan Ewing moved back to New York to live with her two maiden sisters, selling her shares in the mine to Drew Tate for $4 million. The transaction left Drew with 52 percent of the company's stock, an arrangement that John Ewing had agreed upon when they first set up the corporation. Each man received 26 percent of the Copper King's stock, with the remaining shares divided up among the six children: 23 percent for Gordon; 25 percent for Mara and her four brothers. Their marriage assured Gordon and Mara of a total of 28 percent of the ownership of the mine, second only to the majority shareholder, Drew Tate.

After Ewing's demise, Drew was elevated to president of the Copper King. He made his son-in-law executive vice-president and appointed each of his sons to key posts in the rapidly expanding operation.

Gordon's prime responsibility was to initiate a crash program to explore thoroughly the concept of open-pit mining, with an eye to extracting low-grade ore at a profit before the alluvial deposits were exhausted. In this endeavor he worked very closely with Dr. James Douglas, chief assayer for the Copper Queen and son-in-law to Lewis Williams, one of the firm's partners.

To say that Bisbee was a boom town would be an understatement. Prosperity was not reserved for the miners alone. Shopkeepers and bankers grew wealthy almost overnight at the height of the boom. Within five years of her arrival at Bisbee, Marion Murphy had acquired a reputation throughout the territory with her string of ten "houses" that extended from Bisbee to Tucson, Phoenix, Prescott, Jerome, Tombstone, and Kingman. She became the darling of many rich men, all of whom advised her of investment opportunities that eventually made her a wealthy woman, aside from her income from her sporting houses.

She built a mansion the equal of any manor on Quality Hill or in the Bisbee district, which was the scene of some of the most spectacular and lavish parties in the territory. Bankers, brokers, lawyers, judges, and tycoons vied for invitations to Marion's soirees. Her old friend Mara and husband Gordon were always at the top of her guest lists.

It was customary for Marion, at some point in the festivities, to drag Mara off to a secluded part of the huge house to "kick off our shoes, loosen our corsets, and jabber about old times." The rich brogue was unadulterated by the years she had spent in America.

"I'm opening a fancy restaurant in Tombstone," she told Mara one night. "You and Gordon must come on opening night."

"We'll do our best. And when will it open?"

"I'm shooting for New Year's Eve."

"I'll keep it in mind. How are Bridget and Maggie?"

"They're me troubleshooters on a steady basis now. No more work for them—least not the kind of work they've been accustomed to. They visit from place to place to see that everything is kept orderly and that me high standards are kept up. Would you believe it I've got French girls coming to work here from Paris? Chinese gals, too, from San Francisco and Hawaii."

Mara laughed. "There's no more enterprising woman in this territory than you, Marion. I hear tell that the legislature is considering giving you a special award for your cultural and humanitarian contributions to Arizona society."

Marion threw back her head and laughed heartily. " 'Humanitarian'—I like that. Can't deny that these poor sex-starved fellers who was here when I got here thought of me and the girls as sort of angels of mercy!"

Happily, Marion Murphy never lost the common touch. In the midst of a formal dinner party one night, a constable came to the door to inform her breathlessly, "One of your places is afire, other end of town."

"Jesus Christ! I've got to get down there at once." With a parting expression of regret to her guests, Marion raced upstairs, cast off her finery, and dressed in old denim trousers and a wool shirt. Then it was down to the stable, where a stable hand had a mount saddled and ready for her.

Ten minutes later she reined in at the scene of the conflagration. It was the fanciest establishment in Bisbee, and Marion was altogether disconsolate. A troupe of volunteer firemen were battling the blaze with a bucket brigade, but they appeared to be losing ground.

A fountain of resourcefulness, Marion took a fistful of metal tokens she had had stamped in Tombstone and passed them out among the fire fighters. "Do your best for me, boys. You can cash these in the same day we can open again."

The men paused in their efforts to read the inscription on the tokens: Good for One Screw—Marion Murphy. A resounding cheer went up, and the men resumed fighting the fire with redoubled vigor. Not long after, it was extinguished with a minimum amount of damage to the dwelling.

Marion's tokens turned out to be the brainchild of her "profession," for it eliminated the direct exchange of money between girls and clients, which had always proved a disadvantage at the house. Now the customers had to pay their fees to either the madam or the bartender. At the end of the evening, the girls turned their tokens back and received their percentage of the night's take.

On October 20, 1883, at precisely 11:49 P.M., Mara Tate Ewing gave birth to a baby girl.

"The spitting image of you, Mara!" her mother exclaimed when she and Drew saw the child for the first time.

"Indeed she is," Drew agreed.

Mara cuddled the child to her breasts, swollen with milk. "And that's going to be her name as well—Mara Tate the second.

Drew and Gwen glanced furtively at Gordon, who was standing in the background. A cynical smile played about his pursed lips.

"You mean Mara Ewing," her mother corrected.

"She means Mara Tate," Gordon said tonelessly. "Excuse me, I have an appointment at the assay office." He walked over to the bed, bent and kissed Mara's forehead, and patted the child's head. "I'll see you later."

"Will you tell the nurse it's time for Mara's bath?" his wife called after him.

Drew consulted his pocket watch. "I must leave myself. I'm having lunch with Jim Douglas." He bade his wife and daughter good-by.

When they were alone, Gwen said to Mara, "What is this foolishness, calling the child Mara Tate the second? And in front of Gordon, too. Think how he must feel; it's *his* child."

Mara's eyes shaded—deep, unfathomable pools. "You're wrong, Mum. Gordon may have fathered her, but she is *my* child. You said yourself she was the spitting image of me."

"Yes, but you're his wife. You bear his name, and so does the baby."

"Mother, Gordon and I have been through this before, even before we were married. Just who discerned the universal truth that a woman should adopt the name of her husband? Why not the man taking on the name of his wife?" She smiled. "Like the Apaches do. It's the female's family who dominates everything in the tribe."

"Nonsense! The saints preserve us, you've always had queer ideas, Mara."

"Nothing queer about it. I am a Tate, and in my mind this daughter of mine will always be Mara Tate the second."

"Such vanity! The good Lord will punish you for your way of thinking."

"Naturally, every human being should have the right of self-determination. When she comes of age, Mara the second will have the option of employing her legal name, Ewing, or retaining the name of Tate, which I take great pride in."

"As well you should. The Tates are very special people—better than my own kind, I must admit."

"Descendants of Druid priests. Great philosophers and warriors, they fomented the revolt against the Romans. They practiced magic—real magic, not like that the imposters perform at the music halls. Did you know, Mum, their religion was based on the immortality of the soul?"

Gwen squirmed uncomfortably. "I don't like such talk, Mara—magic, witchcraft, the like."

Mara laughed. "I used to pine to be a witch."

"Mara, stop it at once!"

Mara swung the child back and forth in her arms, cooing to it in Welsh. It gurgled and smiled at her.

Gwen was amazed. "I never saw one so young so bright and responsive."

Mara's eyes glittered with mischief. "Perhaps she's a witch as well."

To Gwen's relief, the nurse came into the room, terminating this foreboding talk. "Time for baby's bath, ma'am?"

"Yes. Here, take her." She handed the child over and the woman, a local midwife, carried it out of the room.

"What's wrong between you and Gordon?" her mother asked intuitively.

Mara did not meet her gaze. "Nothing, Mum, nothing whatsoever."

Her expression belied the denial. Since her third month of pregnancy, there had been widening estrangement between Mara and her husband, not that she took it too seriously: A pregnancy puts uncommon strain on both parties in a marriage, especially in the latter months, when sexual intercourse may become uncomfortable for the woman and ultimately impossible.

"It will pass now that the baby is here," she told herself as well as her mother; yet, deep within her heart, there was doubt. The truth was, now that she had little Mara, Gordon was no longer the prime object of her affections and attention, as he had been for the past three years.

The realization brought her a vague sense of guilt, and that night she turned and tossed restlessly until she heard the grandfather clock in the hallway below chime the hour of three. With abrupt resolve, she got out of bed and walked barefooted into the adjoining room, where Gordon had been sleeping for the last few months of her pregnancy.

She stood over his bed in the pitch blackness, listening to his slow, rhythmic breathing. Gently she pulled the covers off him and placed a hand on his naked chest. He stirred and mumbled in his sleep as she stroked his hard pectorals. Her fingers walked down over his belly, ridged with layers of muscle, and curled around his flaccid penis. His reaction was dramatic; it seemed to explode in her hand, swelling so that her fingers could no longer encircle it. Gordon woke up, startled.

"What the devil!"

"It's me, darling," she whispered, and bent her lips to his.

"Mara?"

"Who else? Were you expecting another lady?"

He shook his head and sat up. "I'm a little foggy. Would you light the candle on the night table? There's matches there."

She found the matches and lit the candle. As the halo of light expanded, he stared at her hand manipulating him.

"My God, Mara, what the devil do you think you're doing?"

"It seems perfectly obvious to me. Don't you like it?"

"I thought we'd never be doing it again. I *love* it." Then he tensed: "Mara . . . it's too soon for us to be doing it, isn't it? The baby is only a week old."

"Don't worry, love; we're not going to be doing it. This is a special treat for you. I've been neglecting you lately. Lie back and relax." She pushed him back on the pillow.

Still in a semicomatose state, he did as she told him. Mara took his rigid staff in two hands and guided it to her mouth. Her eager lips engulfed the head.

"Oh, my God . . . my darling!" He arched his back and lunged upward. His hands clenched in the tangle of her hair, holding her head fast as he rotated his hips in an erotic frenzy.

At last he lay still, spent and placated. Mara went to the washstand in the corner. When she returned to the bed, he took her hand and pulled her down beside him.

"I wish I could make you as happy as you've just made me," he said.

She kissed his cheek. "My time will come in a few more weeks. I have missed you, you know."

His brow furrowed. "Have you really? For the past two months you've seemed totally preoccupied with the baby."

"Maternal instinct," she said lightly.

He held her close and kissed her eyes, ears, and lips. "There is something I must tell you, sweet: Your father wants me to accompany Jim Douglas to Europe."

"Europe? Whatever for?"

"The company has acquired shares in a German mining company—the Saar. He wants us to look things over and make recommendations to increase production."

"The Saar—that would be coal mining. Why doesn't Dad send one of the boys? They know coal mining from the ground up."

He sighed. "Emlyn and Gilbert, both their wives are expecting early this spring. As for Allan . . . well, as you know, your father and he are barely civil to each other because of his alliance with that half-breed. And Dylan, he acts as if he were born with a silver spoon in his mouth. His life's ambition is to become a gentleman poet and philosopher, like that Thoreau fellow, and spend the rest of his life at some sylvan pond contemplating the mysteries of the universe."

Mara knew about the deteriorating relations among the other members of her family all too well. Once they had been so close; now they were drifting apart.

In the case of Emlyn and Gilbert, each had married well. Emlyn had taken for his wife the army colonel's daughter, Millicent Baxter; Gilbert the tycoon's daughter from Quality Hill, Jayne Minton. Both women were overly ambitious and social climbers, and the provincial climate of Arizona bred in them deeper contempt with every passing year. They yearned for the urbane environment of the East—New York, Philadelphia, Boston—where they might infiltrate the ranks of the fledgling American aristocracy.

Allan had been carrying on an affair with Maria Beaver, daughter of a hard-working blacksmith, half Mexican, half American Indian, in defiance of his family's disapproval. He kept threatening to sell out his holdings in the Copper King, marry Maria, and move to San Francisco.

Just before the baby was born, Drew had lamented to Mara, "We all were a lot happier when we were poor and working in the mines, shoulder to shoulder. Money, it's the tool of the devil. Aye, I confess I'm victim to it, too. Never satisfied. I've got to keep expanding, investing in new ventures with an eye to doubling and tripling our assets, even though we've got more wealth now than all of us could spend in our lifetimes."

"It reminds me of a fairy tale," Mara said. "King Midas, he prayed to the gods to bestow upon him the power to turn to gold everything he touched. He soon discovered how destructive his heavenly gift could be. He was threatened with starvation because whatever food he touched turned to inedible gold. At last he lost his most prized and beloved possession, his daughter, because she too was turned into a gold statue."

"Aye, now there's a telling parable. Do you know,

Mara, you have the best head in the family. When I die, the Copper King, all of Tate Industries, will be in your hands—yours and Gordon's. He's a good man, more dependable than any of my own sons."

And that, of course, was why he was sending Gordon to Europe.

"I'll be back by summer," Gordon promised. "Meanwhile, you'll have plenty to occupy your time with a new baby in the house and all."

Yes, dear, and if I get bored, perhaps I can persuade Marion to let me turn a trick or two in one of her establishments!

There was a sense of malicious satisfaction in the absurd idea.

CHAPTER THIRTEEN

Gordon Ewing was due to arrive home for Christmas, but at the end of November a cablegram was delivered to the offices of the Copper King:

REGRET TO INFORM YOU THAT IT IS IMPERATIVE I REMAIN HERE FOR AT LEAST ANOTHER MONTH STOP JAMES AND I HAVE BEEN INVITED TO ATTEND A CONFERENCE OF MINING ENGINEERS TO BE HELD IN VIENNA ON JANUARY FIFTEENTH STOP PLEASE GIVE MY DEEPEST LOVE TO MARA AND LITTLE MARA STOP I WILL MISS THEM SORELY OVER THESE LONG DREARY HOLIDAYS IN MY HOTEL ROOM STOP.

"Damn it anyway!" Mara said when her father showed her the cablegram. "Dreary holidays indeed! I'll wager he and James have chic Parisian mistresses to ease their loneliness."

"That's not fair, Mara," the old man remonstrated. "You should be applauding Gordon's loyalty to the company. He's constantly striving to learn and perfect new techniques."

Her laughter was dry and sarcastic. "I imagine he's learning some revolutionary 'techniques' from those French sporting ladies."

"Mara!" Drew was shocked. "What a thing for a lady to say!"

"I never claimed to be a lady, Da. Truthfully, I feel

more comfortable with Marion Murphy than I do with those insufferable snobs Millicent and Jayne and their ilk. . . . Come to think of it, now would be a perfect time to visit Marion in her new diggings in Tombstone."

"That's no place for a woman to be traveling, particularly a woman alone. I've heard some chilling tales about that town. Every man is a law unto himself."

Her eyes deepened in color and glowed with anticipation. "It sounds very exciting to me. I can hardly wait to get there and see for myself."

Baby Mara was left in good hands with her grandmother and Ruth Reilly, a full-time nurse, the daughter of a village shopkeeper. The night before she left for Tombstone, Mara attended a dinner party hosted by the Emlyn Tates. Also present were her brothers Allan and Gilbert and Gilbert's wife, Jayne. Allan was sullen and rude because Maria Beaver had not been included.

"I don't give a damn what any of you think of her," he said to Emlyn over a private drink in the study. "I love Maria and I intend to marry her and the hell with the family and the company! Do you know that Phelps-Dodge has offered me more than a million dollars for my shares in the Copper King?"

"Is that a fact?" Emlyn ran a hand through his thinning red hair and licked his lips. "As a matter of fact, I've been sounding out several prospective buyers myself. A million dollars . . . hmmm . . . that's a tidy nest egg to have in one's bank account."

"Then you're thinking of leaving Bisbee, too?"

"Well, Millicent has been urging me to make some move. Her father is retired now and chairman of the board of some large banking institution in Philadelphia. He's offered me a very good position. But where will you go if you leave Bisbee?"

"There are fine investment opportunities out in California—real estate, vineyards, farmland; but first Maria and I will get married."

Emlyn started to protest once more, then thought better of it. It is an awkward thing to tell a man, especially one's own brother, that the woman he loves has a reputation of being the village nymphomaniac. "We had better join the others," he said with resignation.

When they walked back into the parlor, the women were discussing Dylan, who had declined the invitation to the party.

"He's becoming more of a loner every day," Gilbert said. "I can't think of one close friend he has."

"Nor female companionship," his wife added, with a glance of sly connivance at Millicent. "Seems abnormal to me that a man his age should shun women the way he does."

"Dylan has always been shy," Mara said, defending him. "I agree that Arizona is thoroughly incompatible with Dylan's temperament and tastes."

At the dinner table, Emlyn related the conversation he had had with Allan in the library.

Jayne placed a hand over Gilbert's on the damask tablecloth. "Gil and I have been seriously discussing a move ourselves. "Father would be delighted if he took charge of the firm's London offices."

Mara was outraged. "I think you're all contemptible for even considering leaving Dad with all of the responsibility of managing the company at his age!"

"The old man could sell out for a bloody raja's fortune, and he and Mum could enjoy life before they die—travel, see the sights, maybe even a trip to Wales to rub it in with the poor relations." Gilbert laughed, and his brothers joined in.

Mara turned crimson with suppressed anger. "You ought to be ashamed to call yourselves Tates! Tates stick together; they're not quitters. I'm a true Tate and proud of it."

"That's a lot of hogwash, dear sister," Allan said. "The Tates battled and worked their bloody balls off for generations because they were poor as dirt. This indomitable quality you attribute to them was simply an instinct for survival. You think Grandfather Tate would have worked in the mines until the day he died with black lung if he had had a shilling to his name? Hell no! He didn't quit because he *couldn't* quit."

Mara stood up and placed her napkin on the table. "If you will excuse me, all, I really must go. I'm catching the early stage to Tombstone tomorrow. . . . Emlyn, Millicent, it's been a very pleasant evening." The flatness of her voice denied it.

"You're quite daring, you know," Jayne told her. "The stories I've heard about that place—another Sodom or Gomorroh. Where will you be staying while you're there, dear? Certainly not with that awful Marion Murphy?"

Mara impaled her with eyes like steel daggers. "Marion Murphy is my good friend—possibly my *best* friend." The implication was clear: Her two sisters-in-law rated well beneath Marion in Mara's estimation.

As Jayne had warned Mara, Tombstone was the Sodom of the plains, a composite of all that was bad in the old West. A drab mining camp perched on a mile-high ledge in the middle of the desert, it came to life in spectacular fashion when a miner named Ed Schieffelin struck a vein of silver assayed at $20,000 a ton of ore. Within a year the population leaped from 500 to 15,000.

Even as the Concord Thoroughbrace stagecoach rumbled down dusty Allen Street, Mara felt her pulse quicken. Excitement hovered in the air like static electricity. Tombstone was a boom town in every sense of the word. At high noon the streets were teeming with people: grizzled miners in muddy boots and dirty shirts and trousers, rubbing shoulders with cowboys in ten-gallon hats; dudes in evening clothes on their way home from all-night gambling sessions; professional dealers clad all in black, like minions of the devil; and ladies of every age, description, and reputation. Men dressed like vagrants staggered drunkenly back to their flophouses with thousands of dollars in bills stuffed in every pocket.

In the middle of the main street was an enormous hole, at least fifty feet in diameter, fenced off like an unfinished monument. Mara addressed the passenger sitting beside her, a tall, lean man with handsome angular features and steely blue eyes. He was immaculately dressed in striped trousers, black frock coat, and polished boots. A black string tie adorned his white silk shirt. "Whatever is that hole? Some sort of monument?"

White teeth flashed under a smartly groomed mustache. "You might say that, ma'am," he drawled. "Awhile back they took a cool million dollars in metal out of that hole. You see, it's more of a shrine to metal. Gold and silver are God Almighty in Tombstone. And for every man who comes here to seek an honest fortune, there are half a dozen more dedicated to stealing it away from him."

They passed a succession of "palaces of pleasure," as they were fondly referred to by Tombstone's residents—the Oriental, the Crystal Palace, the Alhambra, the Taj Mahal.

"That's the place my friend owns," she said, laughing. "I can't believe there are such fashionable places of entertainment in such a rustic town."

"The Taj Mahal?" He looked at her through narrowed eyelids. "You mean to say you're in Tombstone to see Marion Murphy?"

"Yes, we're old friends from Bisbee. Do you know her?"

He slapped dust from his trousers with a wide-brimmed Stetson, avoiding her eyes. "Sure enough. Marion Murphy has a *lot* of friends." He seemed embarrassed. "You coming to work for her?"

Mara laughed as she gleaned his meaning. "You mean work in one of her establishments? No, this is just a social visit. I'm Mrs. Mara Ewing Tate." She extended her hand to him.

He took her hand. "Pleasure to make your acquaintance, Mrs. Tate. My name is Wyatt Earp."

"It sounds familiar somehow. Do you live in Tombstone, Mr. Earp?"

"I did for a time, but I'm just visiting now, seeing some old friends"—he smiled—"including Marion. Where will you be staying, ma'am?"

"Marion made reservations for me at the Russ House."

Earp peered out the window as the coach braked to a stop. "And that's where we are now." He opened the door and leaped to the ground. "Let me help you, Mrs. Tate." He grasped her slender waist in his huge hands and swung her lightly down and out of the coach.

"Thank you, sir." She felt flushed and hoped he did not notice. He was a vitally attractive man, exuding raw masculinity, and she, an equally vital woman, experienced a strong sensual response to his touch.

Earp had sensed a rapport between them the instant their eyes met while she was standing on the platform of the Bisbee coach station—a stunning brunette wearing a tailored suit of lavender velvet with a tight jacket bodice that showed off her magnificent breasts; and a form-fitting skirt with a small basque forming high curves at the back. Her jet-black hair was held in place by a barrette of embroidery silk and ornamented with violets picked fresh that morning.

The driver got down from the seat and unloaded

her luggage from the boot at back. Earp put on his hat and picked up the two suitcases.

"Allow me to help you with these to your room, Mrs. Tate. I don't believe you'll find any bellboys to assist you, like they have in the eastern hotels."

"I've never been to an eastern hotel," she said candidly. "My family was very poor when we passed through New York from Ellis Island. Thank you in any case, Mr. Earp."

The hotel was plain but clean, and her accommodations consisted of a suite with a small bedroom, sitting room, and bath.

The manageress, Mrs. Kurt Schultz, was a stout blonde woman with braids who spoke in a guttural German accent. "If you vant a bath, I vill haf one of my maids fetch der vasser from der vell," she told Mara.

"Thank you, Mrs. Schultz. A bath would be quite refreshing after the long ride in the stage."

Earp tipped his hat. "Then I'll be seeing you around, Mrs. Tate—I hope, at least."

"So do I, Mr. Earp." She offered her hand, and he squeezed it, not letting go. "I expect to be visiting Marion later on this afternoon. Perhaps we will meet there."

"Indeed we shall. I intend to see Marion myself. Tell you what, how about the three of us having supper—that is, if I wouldn't be intruding?"

"Not in the least, Mr.——" She hesitated. "I do believe we can drop the formalities, Wyatt."

His rakish smile warmed Mara like sunshine breaking through clouds. "I'm for that, Mara." He squeezed her hand one more time and departed.

Later, luxuriating in her tepid bath water, Mara thought a good deal about Wyatt Earp, and her flesh glowed as she soaped her belly and loins. Mara had not known the comfort of a man's body since the last night Gordon had been at home, before leaving for New York, where he embarked for Europe. And from the tone of his cablegram, her physical deprivation would go on for an indefinite period in the future.

Anger and frustration welled up inside of her as she visualized her husband languishing in the bed of a voluptuous Parisian coquette all lace and frills.

"Damn it anyway!" she muttered. She put that image out of her mind and lay back in the tub, eyes closed, conjuring up a picture of Wyatt Earp—in the nude. He would be long and lithe, with broad shoulders and a tangle of dark hair on his muscular chest; his belly flat and rippled with muscle as well; his legs long, straight, and sturdy. She gasped as a wave of desire engulfed her.

See here, my girl, what are you thinking of doing? That was all right when you were a child, but a woman needs more tangible pleasure than make-believe.

She stood up abruptly and stepped out of the tub. She toweled herself so briskly that her skin smarted, then went into the bedroom to choose her wardrobe. She discarded several items of plain cotton underclothing, settling on a camisole and French panties of sensuous silk and trimmed in lace. The only other time she had worn these "friskily indecent" garments, as Gordon called them, had been on her last wedding anniversary.

"Where the devil did you get those wicked fripperies?" he had demanded.

"At the Goldwater-Castenada store," she'd told him. "Joe Goldwater brought them back his last trip to New York, straight off the boat from France—he says especially for me."

"I'll have to have a talk with that old lecher," he had said in mock anger. "Bet he wanted you to model them for him."

She had laughed. "I only model for my beloved husband." Then, pirouetting around the bedroom: "Do I pass muster?"

He had caught her in his arms and buried his mouth in the small of her neck beneath her ear. "You look good enough to eat, a delicious confection of pink frosting and whipped cream."

"Be my guest," she had said with ardor, and pulled him over to the bed.

Thinking back, Mara shivered and clasped the frothy underthings to her bare bosom. Her heart beat faster as the notion struck her that she might well be modeling them again for—she strove to quench the hot fantasy but without success—for *Wyatt Earp*.

She dressed carefully, choosing attire quite unconventional in the environment of the western frontier— an intricate border-print caftan in rich, exotic earth shades, also purchased at the Goldwater-Castenada store, one of a lot of items Goldwater had bought from an Oriental peddler passing through Bisbee.

"See, I told you, José," he'd jeered at his partner. "He said I was a schlemiel for taking them, that we'd be stuck with the lot. Do you know, Mrs. Tate, these are handmade one hundred percent? Hand-carved blocks of different designs are dipped in dye and hand-stamped onto the cotton fabric. Beautiful, isn't it?"

It was gorgeous, Mara thought, admiring herself in the bureau mirror. To complement her exotic image, she did up her hair in a chignon snood of copper thread and adorned with minuscule chips of precious and semiprecious stones.

Watch yourself tonight, Mr. Earp!

CHAPTER FOURTEEN

The Taj Mahal was the most impressive café, music hall, dance hall, restaurant, and saloon in Tombstone, Arizona. Its clientele was a melting pot of every ethnic group and social class in the country. As the old nursery rhyme phrased it: "Rich man, poor man, beggarman, thief; lawyer, doctor, Indian chief."

Mara passed through the main entrance to a balcony overlooking the sunken bar and dining room and stared down at the customers: dinner jackets, evening gowns, wool work shirts, leather chaps, town suits and gowns, sombreros, and ponchos mingling in ever-changing patterns like the designs in a kaleidoscope; hobnailed boots grinding dirt and grime into the finest Brussels carpet; drunken cowboys cutting their initials in the hand-carved mahogany bar. Crystal chandeliers imported from Scandinavia dazzled the eye, reflecting the light of thousands of candles. At the far end of the dining room a string quartet, decked out in white tie and tails, alternately played Mozart and western folk tunes.

Mara stood there for a long time savoring the novelty of it all. Out of the corner of her eye she recognized Wyatt Earp, dashing in his dinner jacket, white tie, and white gloves, ascending one of the twin circular staircases that led up to the mezzanine.

He smiled and bowed from the waist. "Mara, you are without a doubt the most enchanting woman in this establishment tonight—for all the nights to come." He took her hand and kissed it.

"And you are the most attractive man, sir."

"The perfect couple." He took her right hand and tucked it into the crook of his left elbow, pressing her forearm against his side. "Your dress is stunning. What is its origin, inspiration?"

"The Far East—India. Have you seen Marion yet?"

"Yes, we're to meet her in a small private dining room at the back."

They wended their way among the crowded dinner tables and through an archway into the gambling rooms. There was every known device and game in progress that could be found at Monte Carlo: cards, dice, the roulette wheel, the gamut. Behind the gambling salon were half a dozen private rooms for special parties, and one small, intimate compartment where Marion Murphy entertained her closest friends.

Marion rushed to embrace Mara as soon as they entered the room. "Ducks, it's marvelous to see you! You get to be more beautiful each time. Oh, this is going to be a special night—Christmas come early! You will stay on for Christmas, won't you? There'll be a bash here the likes of which no social event anywhere in the world can compete with."

"I don't think so, Marion. I really should be home with the family and my daughter. The Welsh know how to give a fine Christmas celebration as well as the Irish. . . . Darling, you look wonderful, the same as when we first met on the trail."

It was true. In spite of the physical and emotional demands of her profession, the Irish lass could hold her own with any group of ladies of quality, beauty, and manners—and she frequently did. Her auburn hair shone like burnished copper, her complexion was peaches and cream, and her almond eyes were clear as crystal, swimming with flecks of green the shade of copper carbonate.

Her gown was breathtaking—white Lyons silk with

a shadow decoration of flowers, trimmed with antique lace and lime ribbon. The neckline was cut modestly high both in front and in back, and the hemline swept the floor, showing no glimpse of her shapely limbs. There was no need for flagrant exposure, for the material had been custom cut to fit her ample form like a second skin, highlighting every protuberance and declivity of her body, and it enhanced her sexuality more so than if she had been nude.

The three of them sat at a round table and were served by a waitress wearing an off-the-shoulder blouse with a plunging V neck that exposed half of her unfettered breasts. Her skirt reached only to mid-thigh, and her plump but attractive legs were encased in black-mesh stockings. It was the uniform of the Taj Mahal.

At the beginning, Wyatt Earp sat silent, sipping his whiskey and smoking his black cheroot, listening to the girls reminisce with a slightly amused air of masculine chauvinism.

"I can't get over this place!" Mara enthused. "It's so . . . so . . . so *grandiose;* that's the only way to describe it. A fit setting for a king to dine——"

"Or to participate in all of the varied diversions that kings, as well as copper miners, like to engage in." Wyatt winked at Marion, and the three of them laughed.

Mara shook her head. "Incredible to think that all of this began with a tumbledown shack at the end of Mule Pass Gulch."

Marion's eyes twinkled. "The just desserts due a high-minded, morally upright daughter of the Old Sod who says her Hail Marys faithfully morning and night and cherishes her purity."

Mara and Wyatt doubled up with laughter, and when Mara caught her breath, she remarked, "From what I can see, this 'pure' daughter of the Old Sod has the wherewithal to make a triumphant return to Ireland and play the lady of the manor in a castle, like the landed English gentry."

"She'd really turn their heads, now, wouldn't she?" Wyatt mused.

Mara became serious. "Truthfully, Marion, what new worlds do you plan to conquer?"

Marion took a gold-tipped cigarette from an ivory case and offered one to Mara, who declined. "I've given it a lot of thought, ducks." She bent to the match that Wyatt proffered, and inhaled deeply. "As you know, I've got a lot of solid investments, so money will never be an object of concern again. Actually, I'm restless. I've given serious consideration to financing an expedition to Mexico or Alaska to look for gold. Then there's a promoter trying to get me to invest in crude-oil wells in Texas."

"That's the coming thing," Wyatt assured her: "oil. I've got a bundle invested in it myself. One day oil will be worth its weight in gold."

Marion laughed. "Well, hardly that, Wyatt."

"You'll see."

Mara had a sudden premonition, so strong she could feel the vibrations all through her body. "Oil . . . Do you know, Wyatt, I believe you. I've done some reading on the subject. There's a man named Rockefeller back east who built a prosperous business supplying the Union army with kerosene and axle grease. I must speak to Gordon and Father about exploring the possibility of investing in oil."

"How is Gordon making out in Europe?" Marion asked.

Mara's eyebrows raised. "How is he making out? What a quaint way to put it, dear. Making out in what respect? Businesswise or romantically?"

Marion was flustered. "I didn't mean it the way it sounded."

Mara's smile was tight. "That's all right, Marion. Gordon is a big boy. He can do as he pleases. And so can I." Wyatt looked at her intently, and she met his stare without blinking.

Over coffee and brandy, Marion steered the conversation to Wyatt Earp. "Did you know, Mara, Wyatt is undoubtedly the most famous celebrity Tombstone has ever produced?"

"Really? I *thought* the name sounded very familiar. What was the source of his fame?"

"His six-guns. Wyatt was sheriff and then U.S. marshal here at Tombstone until he retired. Tombstone is still a tough town, but compared to what it was like when Wyatt took charge, today it's tamer than a Sunday-school picnic."

Wyatt smiled self-consciously. "That's a mite exaggerated, Mara. Now, let's talk about something more interesting. When I hung up my guns, it was for good. And that goes for talking about them, too. . . . Let's talk about you, Mara."

"That's all we've been doing all evening, Marion and me, talking about ourselves."

He leaned forward, folding his arms on the table, the cheroot jutting out of the side of his mouth at a jaunty angle. "I mean before you two met, going back to Wales."

It was Mara's turn to be self-conscious. "I'm afraid there's very little to tell of interest about my childhood."

"I'm listening."

At that moment the waitress came over and bent to whisper something in Marion's ear. The proprietress of the Taj Mahal stood up. "You'll have to excuse me for a while—some trouble with a drunk in one of the rooms upstairs."

Wyatt held up his hands. "Don't look at me, sweetheart. I've thrown my last drunk out of this place or any other place in Tombstone."

When she was gone, Mara began her recitation. "I was born in Cardiff, Wales, the youngest of five children. I've got four brothers. . . ." As she went on, her enthusiasm heightened because of the immense pride she took in her family.

"They sound like quite a bunch, the Tates. I'd like to meet the rest of 'em."

"Why don't you stop over at Bisbee? We have ample room, and I'd be delighted to have you as a houseguest."

He rolled the cigar around in his mouth. It was a disturbingly sensual mouth, Mara thought, and she wondered how it would be to feel his lips against her own. Goose bumps rose on her arms, and the fire in her loins, banked for so long, commenced kindling.

"I just might do that," he said. "But what would your folks and your neighbors think, you having a man in the house with your husband off in Europe?"

"We wouldn't be alone in the house. There's little Mara and the nurse."

"Well, then, you've got yourself a deal." He smiled and put his large tanned hand on top of her slender hand on the damask tablecloth. "I like you, Mara Tate Ewing."

"It's Mara Ewing Tate," she reminded him. "I like you too, Wyatt Earp."

"How cozy," Marion commented as she returned to the room. "Would you two lovebirds care to have some action in the gaming room?"

"By all means," Wyatt said. "I feel lucky tonight. What about you, Mara? Feel lucky?"

"Yes, I do, but I must warn you I've never done any gambling. However, by nature, I am a gambling woman. All of the Tates are born gamblers."

"And winners, from the looks of it," he said.

They rose from the table and followed Marion out into the cavernous gaming salon.

Wyatt Earp's hunch was correct. In less than one hour he had won $2,000 at roulette and at the crap table. Mara was intrigued by the dice, and within a short span of observing the players, she quickly acquired the basic fundamentals of the game. She took five hundred-dollar bills from her gold lamé evening purse and handed them to the croupier. "Chips, please."

When it was her turn to roll the dice, Mara took her place at the head of the long green felt-topped table, with Wyatt standing just behind her. Crowded in by a mob of waiting rollers and bystanders, he was pressed tight against her. She was pleasantly aware of his hard loins pressing into her buttocks, the gentle prodding of his manhood.

She cast the dice with a flair that made Wyatt chuckle. A hundred-dollar chip lay on the betting line.

"Seven!" The stickman retrieved the dice.

"Let it ride," she said in imitation of Wyatt and the other rollers.

The tumbling ivory cubes careened off the backboard and came to rest—a five and a three.

"Eight's your point!"

She rolled again—six and three. And again—two fives. Once more—a double six.

"Boxcars," Wyatt muttered. "Good girl!"

Mara kept the dice for more than fifteen minutes and made eight consecutive points and passes. She walked away from the table with a little over $16,000 in winnings. Wyatt cashed in her chips and they went to the bar.

"Champagne," he told the bartender. "Lucky lady, congratulations!" He bent and kissed her on the mouth.

His mustache tickled her upper lip, and she shivered.

"I've never kissed a man with a mustache," she quipped.

I've never kissed a man other than Gordon!

"Do you like it?" he asked lightly.

She shrugged and rubbed her upper lip with a finger. "It scratches."

"Then I shall shave it off."

"Don't bother. You won't be kissing me again in any case."

He studied her in silence for a moment; then a grin spread slowly across his face. "Care to bet on it, lucky lady? I told you this was my lucky night."

She looked at him saucily. "Lucky at cards, unlucky at love."

"Suppose we discuss it on the way back to your hotel." He signaled the bartender. "Walt, put 'er in a bucket of ice to go, okay?"

Before they departed, they said good-by to Marion. The two women embraced and touched cheeks.

"It's been a marvelous evening," Mara said, "especially seeing you, dear."

Marion laughed dryly. "I should say it's been a wonderful evening for you, ducks. You damned near broke the bank at the crap table. Most expensive dinner party I ever gave anyone." She gave Mara an affectionate pat on the arm. "Don't let it worry you, ducks. I'll make ten times that back before this night is over."

They agreed to meet again the next day, and then Mara and Wyatt left the Taj Mahal. Outside, he hailed a horse-drawn cab and helped her climb in.

"The Russ House," he told the driver.

"We should have walked; it's such a beautiful night," she said.

"I didn't feel like lugging this heavy bucket."

Her eyes gleamed in the moonlight. "And just what do you propose to do about that champagne?"

"Why, drink it, of course."

"And where will you drink it?"

"*We* will drink it, and in your parlor."

"I never entertain strange men in my room."

"We can always leave the door open. That's quite proper behavior back east, I'm told, in fashionable circles."

"Sounds reasonable. All right, then you may come up with me, Mr. Earp."

"My pleasure, Mrs. Tate."

He put his hand on her knee; she slapped it away. "No monkey business, Mr. Earp, or I will retract my invitation. "Now, wait a minute, just what do you——"

The rest of the protest was smothered as he took her roughly in his arms and kissed her hard on the mouth. She struggled to no avail; her strength was no match for his. And both were tacitly aware that her efforts were feeble, to say the least.

He let her go and settled back on the seat, presenting her with his strong profile. Nonchalantly he lit a cheroot. "You were saying, ma'am?" he inquired airily.

Mara took a deep breath; her pulse was pounding in her ears, and her cheeks were aflame. "Mr. Earp, you have rendered me quite speechless!"

When they arrived at the hotel and had climbed the stairs to her floor, she handed him the room key. Once inside, she bustled about, lighting the candles and oil lamps while Wyatt placed the wooden bucket of ice in the bathtub.

"Leaking some," he said. He removed a large pocket-knife from his coat pocket and extracted one of the implements. "Corkscrew," he said. "I always go prepared."

She stood in the doorway and stared at him intently. "I certainly hope so, Mr. Earp."

Still kneeling alongside the tub, he turned and looked

up at her, his head cocked to one side. "You like to play word games, Mrs. Tate. . . . Just what kind of 'preparation' did you have in mind?"

She smiled aloofly. "Wine goblets, for one thing. I detest drinking champagne out of tin cups."

"I can always sip from your slipper, dear lady."

"I think it would be preferable if you went downstairs and rustled up a couple of glasses from the innkeeper."

"As you wish." He left and returned five minutes later with two glass beer mugs. "Best I could do."

"We'll pretend it's crystal."

"I'll open the bottle. You best light the fire; it's cold in here." He handed her a tin of sulphur matches.

The maid had laid firewood on kindling in the fireplace and had turned down Mara's bed in her absence. Mara gathered up the flowing skirt of her caftan and kneeled down to put a flaming match to the rolled-up paper beneath the kindling. It burst into flame immediately; Arizona wood was bone dry. She warmed her hands before the mushrooming blaze until Wyatt returned with two mugs, each half full of sparkling wine.

"I want to propose a toast to the luckiest lady in Tombstone, who also happens to be the loveliest lady in Tombstone."

"Thank you, sir." They touched glasses and drank of the wine. "Delicious," she said, "even without crystal."

They sat down on a settee in front of the hearth, Mara, her legs curled up underneath her skirt, turned sideways, facing him.

He puffed on his slim cigar. "When will you be going back to Bisbee?"

"I plan to return on December eighth."

"Do you still want me to accompany you?"

"By all means."

"You are an extremely direct woman. I like that; it's refreshing."

"You're pretty direct yourself, Wyatt."

"Yep, I am." He stubbed out his cigar in a brass ashtray on the coffee table and slid across the couch toward her. "Fact is, I'm gonna come to the point right now."

A muscle twitched at the side of one eye as he reached for her. She felt a fluttering in her stomach. Her arms slid over his shoulders and her hands clasped the back of his neck, her fingers stroking the curly hair at his nape. He cradled her in his powerful arms as if she were a child and bent her back against the armrest.

Mara's legs uncoiled, and she stretched out full length beside him on the wide couch. His hands slid underneath the loose skirt of the caftan and worked their way slowly and tantalizingly up her thighs, over the fullness of her hips, all the way up to her breasts. She sat up so that he could pull it over her head and off. She wore the single undergarment that she found comfortable and practical, a silk teddy, without even a corselet to support her ripe breasts.

The firelight played over her half-naked body, casting provocative shadows over her bare shoulders and limbs. The heat of the flames fanned the fire in her loins. "Hurry, my darling," she urged him. "I want you so very badly."

She watched him undress, boldly and eagerly. She adored his hard, lean, muscular male physique, very much like Gordon's form but with less flesh around the middle. Gordon's sedentary existence of the past few years was exacting a noticeable toll; affluence had its drawbacks. A tremor coursed through her from head to toe as he removed the last of his clothing and knelt naked beside her. His hard masculinity was imposing, thrusting out and up at a sheer urgent angle from his taut belly.

Mara began to remove her chemise, but he stopped her. "Let me do it, my love."

He slipped the straps down over her shoulders, exposing her magnificent breasts; the nipples were as hard and turgid as his member. He buried his face between, smothering the soft, perfumed valley with kisses. She pressed her hands on either side of her soft mounds in order to cradle his head more securely and pleasurably.

What she was experiencing was pure, unadulterated lust. She did not love Wyatt Earp in the deep, tender way she cared for Gordon.

Gordon . . . The very thought of him threatened to subdue her ardor. Guilt and conscience contested the animal hunger of the flesh. Fragmented passages of the marriage service flashed across her mind: *love, honor, cherish . . . to have and to hold . . . forsaking all others . . . till death do us part.*

No amount of speculation or anticipation could have realized the emotions that were assailing her at this time. "Assailing" was descriptive; she was powerless in the grasp of violent, primitive feelings that manipulated her as if she were a puppet on a string. It was one thing to contemplate how it would be to make love with a man other than Gordon; she was certain she was not the only married woman who entertained such forbidden licentious daydreams. Now, on the verge of the *fait accompli,* Mara was overwhelmed by wild passions such as she had never enjoyed before.

"Do it now," she begged him, pushing his hands off her tingling breasts and planting them on either side of her body. He moved between her trembling thighs, and she engulfed him with octopus tenacity, her arms locked tightly about his neck, her heels pressing urgently into the small of his back, pulling him into her.

She cried out in pleasure as he entered her with a single clean thrust worthy of a master swordsman. Time was endless as the two of them passed over the frontier of everyday human consciousness into a world where desire and gratification obscured all else.

She regained her senses long after the final sweet, soul-rending paroxysm had subsided, leaving her body wrung out and at peace with the world. She raised herself on an elbow and studied his strong profile silhouetted darkly against the dancing flames in the hearth.

His voice was soft: "Was it good for you?"

"Indescribably delicious. And you?"

"The very best. I've never known a woman like you before."

She laughed. "Marion says all cats are black in the dark."

"Not so." He reached down, fumbling with his clothing on the floor, and found a cheroot. He stood up and walked to the fire to light it with a flaming twig. She admired his long, straight legs, lean hips, and broad back. Soon the heat in her loins and belly was rekindling.

"Come here, please," she asked him.

He turned and went back to the couch. "What is it?"

"There's something I want to find out." Her hands played brazenly over his body, caressing, coddling, fondling until he was fully aroused. She smiled lovingly at the hard evidence of his want for her. "Care to have another go at it, ducks?" she asked, in parody of Marion Murphy.

"Don't mind if I do, ducks," he replied, giving her a playful slap on her bare bottom.

Once again she opened herself to him the way a flower opens to the bright light of the sun. His radiance was so blinding that she shut her eyes and let herself be caught up and whirled away in the vortex of their earthshaking passion.

CHAPTER FIFTEEN

It was an unusually brisk day with atypical low-hanging dark clouds over the Bisbee district. It suited the European immigrants who were homesick for the cold, dark, wintry days that were customary during the Christmas season in their native lands.

Gwen Tate hummed carols while she prepared a batch of cookies for the oven, while Olga, the family's stout Danish cook, sat at the table, pudgy arms folded across her ample bosom, watching her with disapproval. She kept telling her mistress that a lady's place was in the parlor, *not* in the kitchen, but to no avail. In Gwen's words:

"I wasn't born into the slothful life, like some I could name, nor am I given to putting on airs, like some others who try to forget they scrubbed floors, washed windows, and slaved over a stove like the rest of us low-class biddies."

Gwen never did become accustomed to having other people cook, wash, sew, and keep house for the family.

In the midst of her baking, Dylan came into the kitchen and helped himself to a hot sweet from a pan already out of the oven and cooling. "Mmmm . . . delicious. Nobody can bake butter cookies like you, Mum. He stooped and kissed her cheek streaked with flour.

Gwen beamed and cast her eyes self-consciously at Olga, who was puffing up with indignation.

"You look bright and bushy-tailed this morning, son," she told him.

He grinned and ran a hand through his curly mop, kinky from a recent washing. "Bushy-headed, at least. Say, isn't this weather fine? Makes me want to write a poem about Wales."

"Well, it's hardly Welsh weather, but it will have to do. Where are you off to?"

"The Goldwater-Castenada store to do some Christmas shopping. Can I get you anything?"

She replied in Welsh so that Olga would not understand. "Joe said he was expecting a shipment of tippets from Scotland. He promised to put aside one of the shawls for me, a present for Olga. See if they've come in."

"I will indeed." He put on his Stetson and headed for the door.

"Put on a sweater; it's chilly," she called after him.

"Wool shirt's plenty warm," he said, and went out the door.

She looked out the window and was overcome with bittersweet emotion as she watched him cross the yard, hands in the pockets of his denim trousers, his hair blowing wildly in the wind. Secretly, Dylan was Gwen's favorite, not because she loved him better than her other children but because he was the most vulnerable—not strong in character and purpose, like the others; although, as Drew kept pointing out with misgiving, Emlyn and Gilbert seemed to be faltering in those attributes in recent years.

"Let their women pull them around by the nose," he would grumble. "Should never have married above them in class. You'll see, their progeny will inherit the thin blood of the Baxters and the Mintons. It always works that way."

"Nonsense," Gwen scoffed. "Millicent's father was a war hero."

"Ha! Maybe so, but he was quick enough to resign his commission soon as he got a fancy job offer from those eastern bankers. And now that wife of Emlyn's is trying to make him a bootlicker as well, not that she's any the worse than Jayne. Can you imagine Gilbert as an investment broker? That lad's more at home with a pick in his hands and calluses on his butt. I'm gonna make him an offer he can't refuse—put him in charge of our research and development division down in South America."

"Jayne go to South America? You must be mad, Drew. That's no place for a woman, that terrible jungle."

Drew cackled and slapped the table. "Not for a hothouse flower like her, but for the *right* woman. Well, maybe it'll open his eyes and make him seek out the right woman, one who's not scared to get her fingernails dirty and who's up to screwing on a blanket on the good earth if the passion tells her to."

"You're disgraceful, Drew Tate! I won't listen to another word!"

She refused to listen to his views on Dylan, too: *a weak sister . . . a pansy . . . sits down when he pees. You're a dear, sweet boy and I love you dearly,* she said silently as Dylan disappeared around the corner of the house and headed down the hill into town.

The atmosphere that day was full of goodwill and cheer on Main Street: people exchanging greetings as they passed on the street; shop windows decorated with greenery and some with cactuses and scrub pines adorned with colored ornaments and candles.

The Goldwater-Castenada dry-goods-and-notions store was teeming with shoppers when Dylan entered. He received a hearty handshake from Joe Goldwater.

"How are your mama and papa, son?"

"Just fine, Joe, and your family?"

"We got more Christmas spirit than the gentiles, let me tell you. I told the kids that maybe Santa Claus will come down our chimney this year. It's getting harder and harder for them being the only kids who don't get presents. Say, I haven't seen that beautiful sister of yours in a long time. Not sick, is she?"

"No, Mara's been visiting someone in Tombstone."

Joe slapped his head and feigned shock. "Ach! Don't tell me, please; I can guess. It's that harlot woman, Marion Murphy."

Dylan grinned. "That 'harlot' woman is fast becoming the most famous female in the territory."

"*Infamous,* you mean!"

"There are more multimillionaires who have asked her to marry them than there are spikes on a cactus."

Suddenly there was a commotion—loud, excited voices from the back room. Goldwater frowned. " 'Scuse me, son. Something is sure stirring up old Pete back there." He walked back down the aisle toward the rear of the store.

Simultaneously, two men who had been browsing at a table of sale items near the front entrance drew Colt .45 six-guns and leveled them at the patrons. "Just stay where you are and keep quiet and nobody will get hurt," one of them snarled. A woman screamed and ran down the aisle after Joe Goldwater.

"Shit! She'll wake up the dead!" the taller of the two bandits said, and put a bullet squarely in her back.

"You damned fool!" his partner cursed. "That's gonna wake up the whole town!" He strode to the front door in time to see a passer-by who was about to enter the store turn back and bolt down the street. Without hesitation, the robber stepped out of the store and gunned down the man before he had covered ten paces.

In the back room, three of the gang had slipped

into the store by the rear entrance and covered Goldwater and his bookkeeper, Pete Dall, with their guns.
"Open the safe or we'll kill you! Pronto!"

"Do as he says, Pete," Goldwater snapped.

With trembling fingers Dall twirled the dials and
flipped the handle. The gang leader kicked him aside
brutally.

"All right, you coyotes, empty it!"

The contents of the safe were dumped into two pil-
lowcases, and the robbers started to leave by way of
the front entrance; but, before they stepped through
the curtain dividing the store from the back room, the
leader glanced at a door on one side of the room.
"What's in there?"

"Dry-goods storeroom," Goldwater answered quickly.

"We'll see about that." The man strode to the door
and flung it open. Inside, a small, wizened man, José
Castenada, was huddled in his bed; he was recovering
from a bout of dysentery.

"Dry goods, eh?" The robber walked to the bed and
pointed the revolver at Castenada. "What you hiding
in here, spik? Come on, hand it over or I'll blow you
clear back to Mexico City."

Whimpering in fear, Goldwater's partner reached
under his pillow and produced a fair-sized sack of gold
nuggets, his life's savings.

The robber grinned. "Now, that's better, you fucking
greaser." He slapped the sick man on the side of the
head, knocking him out of bed to the floor. "Okay,
let's get moving, men."

They walked into the main store, where even more
violent drama was about to transpire. Alerted by the
sound of gunfire, Deputy Sheriff D. T. Smith, who was
alone in the jail down the street, buckled on his pistol
belt, grabbed a rifle from the gun rack, and ran out

into the road. Panicky pedestrians were scattering like sheep seeking shelter.

"It's the Goldwater store!" someone shouted to him. Unfortunately, no one thought to warn Smith that there was a five-man gang holding up the store. Fearlessly Smith advanced on the scene of the action, his rifle held at the ready.

Inside the store, one of the thieves took his Colt in both hands, braced his arms on the door jamb, and drew a bead on the lawman. With a single shot he found the bull's-eye. Smith never knew what hit him.

Meanwhile, throughout the robbery and shootings, Dylan Tate had been standing immobilized along with the other customers. He was filled with outraged horror at the brutal way the bandits had gunned down three helpless victims. When the one who was guarding the door had his back turned, Dylan saw his opportunity. At the instant the shot that killed Sheriff Smith rang out, Dylan leaped at the other bandit, wrenched the six-gun from his grasp, and punched him on the side of the head. Caught off guard, the man staggered and went down on his knees.

Dylan stepped back and pointed the weapon at the other man as he whirled around. "Drop it or you're a dead man!" he yelled.

All of the bravado washed out of the killer now that he was on the wrong end of a gun. He let the pistol slip from his fingers to the floor. "Don't kill me," he whined. "I won't give you trouble."

Tragically, Dylan had not reckoned with the three in the back room. Stealthily they moved down the aisle in his direction, guns at the ready; and they had no intention of affording Dylan the generous opportunity he had given their crony, to drop his weapon. Cold-bloodedly the leader squeezed off two shots into the young man's back. Dylan Tate died instantly.

With their loot in hand, the holdup men dashed

from the store to their horses, tethered in a side alley. In a parting gesture of defiance and contempt for the decent residents of Bisbee, the five galloped the length of town to the end of Mule Pass Gulch, firing indiscriminately into the buildings on either side of the street.

The echoes of the gunshots were still bouncing off the surrounding hills when the stagecoach from Tombstone arrived.

"What the devil's going on here?" Wyatt demanded of the depot clerk as he leaped to the ground.

"Big holdup down at the Goldwater-Castenada store. The varmints murdered four people in cold blood, including a woman!"

The ex-marshal's face turned crimson with anger. "Dirty scum! Has anyone gone after 'em?"

"A deputy's on his way to the county seat at Tombstone to notify the district sheriff. Here Deputy Billy Daniels is forming a posse." He pointed to the mob congregating around a building farther along Main Street. "Everybody and his brother is volunteering."

Mara got out of the coach and joined Wyatt. "What is it?"

He repeated what the depot clerk had told him. She was horrified. "How terrible! And so close to Christmas! They're a pack of wild beasts!"

Wyatt snorted. "Don't insult our animal friends, Mara; they kill only for food and self-preservation."

She observed him with curiosity. He kept staring down the street at the growing mob of irate townsmen who were eager to avenge the senseless killing of four of their own. His expression was inscrutable, except for the eyes—cold as ice, yet burning with submerged fire. When he looked back at her, she felt as if she were staring down the smoking barrels of twin six-guns.

"Will it never stop?" he muttered. In bitter frustration, he took off his hat and slammed it hard against his thigh. "Damn the bastards anyway!"

She touched his arm. "Come with me, Wyatt. I must see if Joe Goldwater is all right. He's an old family friend."

They hurried along Main Street to the Goldwater-Castenada store. A contingent of Union troops, camped on the outskirts of town, had arrived to lend assistance to the meager police force; they had cordoned off the area until the dead bodies were removed. The lieutenant in charge recognized Mara; he had been an aide to Millicent's father, Colonel Baxter. He touched the peak of his cap:

"Mrs. Ewing, are you all right, ma'am?"

She resisted the impulse to correct him: Mrs. *Tate.* "I'm fine, George. We just returned on the stage from Tombstone. What a hideous welcome. May I speak with Mr. Goldwater, please?"

The request flustered him. He averted his eyes from hers and kicked up dirt with the toe of his boot, then took a deep breath and looked up. "Ma'am, I don't think you ought to go in there; it's not a pretty sight."

"I don't intend to gape, lieutenant. I just want to make certain that Joe Goldwater isn't injured."

"Mr. Goldwater is fine, ma'am. I——"

"Then I intend to see him." She brushed past him and went to the front entrance of the store. It was a stark moment that would be forever etched in her mind. When she entered, Joe Goldwater was down on his knees beside a body, weeping and wringing his hands.

"Such a good boy. So young. Why? Why? Why?" he lamented.

It was her brother Dylan, sprawled on his back with his arms and legs outspread. Ironically, in death he looked more serene than he had ever appeared in life.

"Oh, my God! It can't be! Dylan!" She pressed her knuckles hard against her mouth to keep from screaming. She swayed and would have fallen if Wyatt had not hurried up behind her and grabbed her arms.

"What is it, Mara? Do you know him?"

"He's . . . he's my brother!" She turned to him and buried her face in his chest.

Joe Goldwater got up and walked unsteadily to her. He placed a gnarled hand on her shoulder. "Mara, *liebchen,* I know what you feel. I loved that boy like a son. So sensitive, so much feeling. Do you know, Dylan once thrashed a trio of hoodlums single-handed because they called me a Christ killer?"

"He hated violence," she wailed.

"I know, but he tried to disarm these killers, because it outraged his sense of righteousness and decency, what they were doing. He was a hero, Mara."

She regained control of herself and wiped her eyes with a handkerchief. "Joe . . . do you know who they were?"

He shrugged. "Two of them looked vaguely familiar. I don't know. So many faces passing through Bisbee these days. Cowboy hats, beards, they all look alike."

Wyatt Earp drew himself up to his full six feet three inches. "Well, talking about 'em ain't doing no good. I'm gonna join up with one of the posses."

Mara was startled. "But you said you'd never use a gun again."

"I know what I said, but any man who'd turn his back on an outrage like this one, let them rattlesnakes go, would lose his right to call himself a man. I'll see you by and by, Mara." He patted her back and looked across her at Joe Goldwater. "Mr. Goldwater, my guns have been packed away for the past year. Do you have a Colt .45 I can buy?"

"Do I have a Colt .45? I have the best line of firearms you can find in this state, Mr.—what did you say your name is?"

"Wyatt Earp."

The old man's eyes bulged. "Wyatt Earp? *The* Wyatt Earp, the famous U.S. marshal?"

Wyatt tugged at one corner of his mustache; flattery embarrassed him. "I guess that's me, sir."

Joe Goldwater grabbed his hand in both of his and wrung it vigorously. "Marshal Earp, you are a living legend in this territory, and outside of it as well. This is a memorable pleasure, sir, to shake hands with the fastest gun in the West."

"There are some would challenge that statement, sir."

"Ach! Too many did challenge it and they all paid the price. Come along, Mr. Earp, you can have any one of my guns you want and it's on the house." He led Wyatt to a large table at the rear of the store, where a variety of handguns were neatly laid out in rows. "Just got a shipment of brand-new guns from the East, real beauties, some of them with pearl handles."

Wyatt smiled and shook his head. "No thanks; I prefer my guns secondhand. New guns and new holsters slow you up. Got to break 'em in right." He picked up one tarnished veteran that had the trigger wired back tight against the guard. He grimaced. "Bet the former owner of this little trick is pushing up the daisies for sure. Never saw a fanner who could hit the side of a barn."

He faked a draw and, with the pistol held tight to his hip, fanned the hammer five times in succession with his left hand. Shaking his head, he put it down and inspected and discarded four more. Some of them had no triggers at all—truly sophisticated fanners.

Eventually he settled on a pair of well-worn .45-caliber Colts with fine hair triggers, and selected a pistol belt and two holsters with leather as soft and pliable as chamois. It required at least five minutes until he had the belt properly adjusted to afford the precise degree of "drag." Securing the pistols in the holsters, he made a half-dozen quick draws to see that they cleared the leather smoothly.

"That should do it. Now I'll take a box of ammunition, Mr. Goldwater."

"At your service."

The owner produced a box of shells, and Wyatt levered five shells into each gun, leaving one chamber empty for the hammer to rest on safely. Any experienced gunfighter had far too much respect for the tools of his trade to risk the loss of a kneecap or a foot because of an accidental discharge. He snapped the cylinders shut with a deft flick of his wrist and let the six-guns drop lightly into the holsters. "I'll see you all later."

"Not so fast, ducks," Mara said, blocking his way. "You'll have to wait for me to hurry home and change."

"Change?"

"Why, of course. I can't very well go riding off into the hills in this outfit, now, can I?"

"What the devil are you talking about?"

"I'm coming with you." Her expression and her voice were hard as granite. "The bastards murdered my brother, and I want to be there when they're strung up, Wyatt."

"Now, Mara, be sensible."

Their eyes locked. "Mr. Earp, I am joining a posse whether or not you like it. Besides, you'll need a horse, and I have two beauties. Come along."

He started to protest once more, but Joe Goldwater laid a hand on his arm. "Better do as she says, Mr. Earp. That little lady is a Tate, and the Tates always get their own way in the end."

CHAPTER SIXTEEN

Wyatt and Mara rode with Deputy Bill Daniels's posse, heading into the Chiricahua Mountains, where some friendly Indians reported they had spotted five horsemen several hours earlier.

Mara looked like a boy in her buckskin shirt and trousers with her long hair tucked up underneath her Stetson. She was armed with a Spencer repeating rifle sheathed in a leather saddle boot. Wyatt Earp had substituted a mackinaw for his suit jacket but had retained his shiny black boots, black trousers, and black flat-topped hat. Their mounts were two powerful stallions, a chestnut and a skewbald.

The trail of the outlaws was not hard to follow. At one point it stopped dead at the brink of a sheer cliff.

Deputy Daniels dismounted, removed his hat, and scratched his head. "What the devil! Looks like they disappeared into thin air!"

Wyatt and Mara joined him at the top of the bluff, which overlooked an expanse of barren plains land. "I think not." Wyatt pointed down to the rocks at the base of the cliff. "There are their horses."

Mara was appalled. "You mean they deliberately killed their horses? I can't believe it!"

"Old outlaw trick. Evidently the poor beasts were run ragged, and when they could no longer continue, the bastards rode them over the cliff, hoping we'd overlook their carcasses so far down." He turned to the deputy. "Daniels, must be a ranch somewhere close. They wouldn't have done this if they didn't know where they could get fresh horses."

"Yep, down that gulch to the left, it winds down to the valley floor. The West place lies around a bend. Big spread."

"Let's go; we're catching up to them, that's for sure."

Daniels led the posse down the gulch to where the West ranch house and outbuildings were located. Cows grazed leisurely in a meadow behind the barn; otherwise there was no sign of life. A spiral of smoke curled into the air from one of the house's chimneys.

The posse members dismounted and left their horses in a grove of trees. With guns at the ready, they approached the house cautiously. The first harbinger of tragedy was a dead shepherd dog lying near the horse corral; it had been shot through the head. The corral was empty, and the open gate swung creakingly in the light wind.

"They're gone," Daniels said.

Wyatt looked grim. "And I wonder what they've left behind inside. Maybe you'd better stay out here, Mara."

"Nonsense!" she snapped irritably. "I wish you would stop treating me like a child. I can stomach anything you men can, and I can shoot better than most of you."

"As you say." He watched her with covert admiration.

Now, there is a woman a man could spend a lifetime with and not get bored with or tired of—one spirited filly.

Two hours earlier Bob West, his wife Irma, and his seventeen-year-old daughter Maureen had been sitting at the kitchen table taking a break from their chores, eating home-baked bread and freshly churned butter.

"Howdy, folks," a voice called from the open doorway. "See we're just in time for lunch."

The Wests looked up startled but not apprehensive. Except for the hostile Apaches, most of the inhabitants of the district were friendly and neighborly, and so were travelers passing through.

Irma West, a rotund woman with a pleasantly homely face, rose and bustled to the door, all hospitality. "Land sakes, boys, come on in. You're more than welcome to share our humble fare with us."

"Mighty kind of you, ma'am. The big fellow, with a bushy red beard and a wicked scar over his left eye, tipped his ten-gallon hat and came into the kitchen. He was followed by four other men, all of them heavily bearded, smelling of sweat and horses, and generally disheveled.

Bob West experienced a twinge of apprehension now as he scrutinized the group. They were bristling with guns and knives. "You fellers prospectors?" he inquired.

Their redheaded leader smiled, and there were snickers from the others. "You might say so," he drawled. "We're lookin' for gold."

West blinked uncertainly. "You're looking in the wrong place, mister. You should be over in the Superstition Mountains."

"Oh, we've done right well up this way." He and his cronies laughed at their private joke.

"Please sit down," Irma urged. "I'll brew up a pot of coffee, and we've got plenty of bread and fresh butter and some fruit bread I done baked this morning. Maureen, come give me a hand, child."

The leader winked at one of his henchmen as they took places at the big table. "Child—you hear that, Tex? Quite a child, now, ain't she?"

Maureen West was a voluptuous girl whose obvious physical charms not even her plain gingham dress could conceal. Blonde, blue-eyed, with a pretty round face and china-doll features, Maureen was nubile in every sense of the word; and she was not oblivious of the interest she was provoking in the five strangers. She liked the young one they called Dan, and when she served his plate, she let her right breast press firmly against his shoulder. In the valley where the Wests lived, eligible men were a rare commodity. Maureen had never known a man in the biblical sense, but she sorely yearned to terminate that frustrating condition.

She played the coquette all the while the men were eating and drinking, bending low over the table so that they could look down into her cleavage, flaunting her hips in a saucy fashion. In her naïveté, the young woman did not realize that she was baiting the lions in their dens.

When they were finished eating, Red Sample whispered to Dan Kelly, "That little bitch has got me horny as hell. How about you, old bud?"

"Stiff as a ramrod."

"Then I say we have a little dessert." He rose, wiped his mouth on his sleeve, and walked over to Maureen. "Come on, honey chile, you made it plain to us that your little bun is hot. Now, you show us to a nice soft bed and we'll cool it off for you."

The girl was stunned, paralyzed, speechless; her pale-blue eyes were round with terror as she comprehended what his intent was. He seized her wrist roughly, and that galvanized her into action. She tried to pull away from him screaming and howling like a wounded animal.

"You cut that out!" Bob West said. "Don't appreciate that kind of joking around. My girl Maureen is a good girl."

Red laughed. *Good?* My guess is she's going to be *terrific.*"

"Let her go, you sonovabitch!" Bob charged at Sample. He had covered no more than three steps when one of the killers felled him from behind with a cruel blow on the head with the butt of a six-gun.

Irma West clapped her hands to her face and cried out in horror, "You've killed Paw! Please have mercy! Don't hurt my baby!" She fell to her knees, hands clasped as if in prayer, and implored them: "Take anything you want, but please don't touch her. She's a virgin."

"Hot damn!" Red flipped his hat across the room and began to unbuckle his gun belt. "I don't believe I've ever had a virgin in all my life. Dan, you and Tex tie up these two while me and the boys escort this little lady to the bedroom. Here's how we'll work it. Naturally I get firsts. The rest of you can draw straws to determine place-and-show positions." He snickered. "There'll still be plenty in the kitty for you suckers who finish out of the money."

" 'Kitty'—oh, that's rich, Red."

They all commenced laughing uproariously.

Red Sample dragged the hysterical, struggling girl out of the kitchen and down the hall to the first bedroom he came to, followed by Dan Dowd and Bill Delaney. Dan Kelly and Tex Howard proceeded to tie up the unconscious father and the faint mother with clothesline.

"Please don't hurt me!" the girl begged as Red pinned her down on the bed.

"Tie her ankles to the footposts," he ordered.

It required all of his strength to contain her, so desperate was she to get away. She did manage to free one hand and raked her nails across his face from forehead to chin. Blood oozed out of the five parallel furrows.

"You lousy bitch!" He backhanded her in the face, splitting her lip and nose. Now her blood splattered over the front of his shirt and hands. The blow stunned her, making it possible for him to tie her wrists to the headposts.

Red stepped back and looked down at her. She lay spread-eagled and helpless, staring up at him with the fearful eyes of a wounded doe. Her gingham skirt was bunched up about her round thighs, and the killer's lustful gaze traveled up her slender legs.

"Lordy, will you look at them gams," he said in a voice rasping with desire. Dan and Bill were grinning like slavering wolves closing in for the kill.

"Hurry up, Red," Dan whined. He rubbed the lump in his trousers. "I don't wanna lose it here in my britches."

Red walked to the side of the bed, hooked the fingers of one hand inside the bodice of her dress, and ripped it clean down to the waist. Similarly he tore off her shirtwaist, exposing her full breasts. She whimpered and writhed in agony as he cruelly tweaked one pink nipple and then the other between his callused thumb and forefinger.

"Love them titties!" Bill moaned.

Methodically Red stripped off her skirt and her white cotton underdrawers. At this final humiliation, the girl began to sob like a child: "Mama! Papa! Help me! Please, won't someone help me?"

"I think I'll help myself first, darlin'." Red unbuttoned his pants and let them drop to his ankles. He wore no underwear. Maureen could not tolerate the sight of his aroused masculinity. She had heard what men were like, and at times it had titillated her imagination not unpleasantly; but in her wildest dreams she had never pictured anything as gross as the harsh reality. She closed her eyes and turned her head away on the pillow.

Wasting no time, Red clambered between her wide-spread thighs and attacked her without mercy. "Damn!" he cursed. "Like going up against a stone wall."

Relentlessly he persisted, and all the while her screams reverberated through the farmhouse.

Dan Kelly and Tex Howard, coming up the hall from the kitchen, stopped dead in their tracks and cringed in empathy.

"God! Never heard anything like it in my life," Kelly said in awe. "Not even when they cut off my paw's leg with a wood saw."

By the time they reached the bedroom, Red Sample had accomplished his nefarious purpose and collapsed on the girl, who, mercifully, had fainted from the ordeal.

"C'mon, it's my turn," Bill Delaney complained, and grabbed Red by the feet and dragged him off the foot of the bed.

"Leggo, you bastard!" Red kicked his tormentor in the groin and sat up.

Delaney squealed like a stuck pig and doubled up. "What you go and do that for? Damn near broke it off!"

Dan Dowd giggled. "While you're gettin' your wind back, I'll take your turn." He dropped his pants and started to get on top of the girl; but, as he gazed at the bloody, brutalized form on the bed, the lust drained out of him. He shook his head in disbelief. "Looks like a side of fresh-slaughtered lamb. Think I'll pass." He buttoned his trousers and walked out of the room.

The other men were not so finicky, and before they were done with her, Maureen West had been raped and sodomized twelve times.

At last Red Sample called a halt to the carnage: "We'd better get the hell out of here before they catch up with us."

They went out into the front yard and opened the corral. Red chose the best five horses and let the remainder run loose. The loot from the robbery was stashed in his saddlebag. He dug his spurs into the belly of the roan gelding, and they rode off from the ravished farm in a cloud of Arizona dust.

Less than an hour later, Deputy Daniels's posse approached the farmhouse. With Daniels and Wyatt Earp in the lead, they filed up the front steps and through the open doorway. They found Bob West and his wife in the kitchen, bound to chairs with lengths of clothesline. Both were in a state of shock and could not reply to questions their rescuers posed.

At last the stricken man managed to whisper, Maureen . . . please . . . bedroom."

Wyatt strode down the hall, gun drawn, with Mara right behind him. The hideous scene that confronted them in the daughter's bedroom caused Mara to sway and clutch at the door jamb for support.

"Oh, my God!" It was almost too much to bear, and she covered her face with her hands.

"Jesus!" Wyatt muttered. "Never saw anything worse than this in my life. Not even the Apaches . . ." He shook his head in disbelief and holstered his Colt. "Let's cut her loose, boys."

Daniels and another posse member assisted him in freeing Maureen, who lay immobile like a bloody rag doll with blank shoe-button eyes staring unseeingly at the ceiling.

Mara took charge now. "All right, you men clear out of here and let me take care of her. Wyatt, see if you can find sheets—anything that we can tear up into bandages—and boil some water." She stroked the girl's head. "There, there, ducks, it's over, and everything will be all right from now on."

A half-hour later she joined Wyatt and the other men in the big kitchen. They were drinking coffee from tin mugs.

"How is she, Mara?" Wyatt asked.

"Alive and clean, but she'll be in a state of shock

for a long time." She bit her underlip. "Maybe she'll never recover from the nightmare she's been through."

Wyatt's big hands clenched and unclenched, as if he were strangling someone. "When we catch up with them murdering coyotes, they're going to pay and pay and *pay!*"

"We'll string 'em up!" a man vowed.

"No, we won't; hanging is too good for 'em," Wyatt said. "First we'll thrash the bejabbers out of 'em and then we'll take 'em back to stand trial."

There were dissenting grumbles. "Why waste time and money on a trial?"

"Because their suffering should be prolonged. You know how it is being locked up in a small jail cell, thinking day and night how it's going to feel when the executioner puts that noose around your neck, knowing there's no hope? Oh, yes, boys, I've seen a hassle of killers sweating out the hangman. Near the end you can see death in their eyes. Snapping their necks is only one small part of their punishment." Wyatt looked to Mara. "How are the old man and woman?"

"Resting, but we can't leave them alone here. Someone has to take care of them."

"I guess you're elected," Wyatt said.

"I guess so," she said with reluctance. "I want to be there when you get them so badly it hurts, but this situation has to take precedence. Good luck, boys. You'd better get back on the trail."

"We'll stop by for you after we capture them," he promised.

She stood on the front porch and watched the posse ride to the west, watched until the thunder of the horses' hooves was only a faint echo.

The trail was easy to follow over the flatland, but when they reached the foothills of the mountains, it was no longer clearly defined in the rocky terrain and thick underbrush trampled by hordes of wildlife every which way. They traced it painstakingly down a gorge that branched out in three tributaries at the far end.

"Now what?" Daniels scratched his head. He looked at John Heith, who owned a saloon in Brewery Gulch. "You were an army tracker, John. How does it look to you?"

Heith, a ruddy-faced, balding man who enjoyed sampling his own wares, dismounted and walked back and forth, inspecting the approaches to the three separate ravines. Several times he got down on his knees and ran his hands over the loose soil and stones. Finally he stood up and indicated the left branch. "They took this way; no doubt about it."

Wyatt Earp wore a puzzled frown. "You sure about that?"

"Positive." Heith mounted again and slapped the reins on his stallion's neck. "Giddyap."

Wyatt started to speak, then thought better of it; but his cold blue eyes were fixed on the stout saloon-keeper's red neck. He thought about what the girl had said, most of it hysterical gibberish; but there were lucid spaces. She knew their names: Bill, Red, two men named Dan, and . . . oh, yes, one last name—Tex Howard.

Wyatt said it aloud: "Tex Howard."

Heith hunched down in the saddle.

"Sound familiar to any of you boys—Tex Howard?"

The men were silent, and Wyatt shrugged. About ten minutes later, a short, wiry man exclaimed, "Tex Howard! By golly, now I remember. Say Heith, he used to hang out in your place, right?"

"Don't recollect," Heith mumbled.

Then a resident of Tombstone spoke up: "Sure you do, John. In fact, you two were together at the Oriental saloon last week."

"You got me mixed up with somebody else," the saloonkeeper said heatedly. "I haven't been in Tombstone in months."

"I saw you with my own eyes, John."

All eyes were riveted on Heith now.

Wyatt reined in his horse and held up a hand: "Halt! Something is mighty wrong here." He dismounted and walked back and forth, twenty paces up the trail and back down again, his keen eyes inspecting every square inch of ground. Finally he walked back and grabbed Heath's horse by the bridle. "This bastard has been leading us on a wild-goose chase. No horses been down this ravine lately."

"What about it, John?" Daniels snapped.

Heith's beefy face was crimson, and there was fear in his eyes and in his voice: "It's a damned lie! Earp, you go to hell! You ain't a marshal anymore. Mind your own business!"

In reply, the ex-lawman grabbed Heith's leg and dragged him off his horse. Clutching him by his neck bandanna, Wyatt ripped the barrel of a six-gun once over each of the man's cheeks. The front sight tore ragged gashes on his face.

"Jesus!" he howled, and covered the wounds with his hands. "Don't pistol-whip me, Earp! Please! Stop him, you guys. He's a killer!"

"And you need to be killed, Heith," Daniels said coldly. "What about it? You gonna talk, or does Mr. Earp continue with his interrogation?"

"I'll talk! I'll tell you everything; just don't let him hurt me again!"

Wyatt shoved him down in the dust with contempt. "So talk."

"Red Sample and Tex Howard, they planned it all. Then there was Dan Dowd, Bill Delaney, and Dan Kelly."

"And you."

"I cased the Goldwater store for 'em. Told 'em how to gain entry at the back and where they could stash their getaway horses."

"Where are they going to hole up?"

"Across the border in Mexico—Sonora, Deming, Nogales. Howard and Sample got a whorehouse in Clifton."

Daniels removed his hat and wiped his brow. "Well, now that we have them placed, no need to rush things, boys. They'll be sitting ducks."

The words were prophetic. By the end of January all five killers had been captured, tried, and sentenced to death on March 8, 1884.

Because he had not been present at the actual crime, John Heith received a relatively light sentence of twenty years in Yuma prison. The outraged citizens of Bisbee were not about to let him off so easily, however. One morning in February a mob descended on the jail and demanded that the sheriff hand over Heith. He scarcely looked up from his newspaper and coffee:

"Key's on the hook. He's in the last cell."

Pleading and crying, the prisoner was dragged out of his cell and hauled to Toughnut Street. There a rope was strung over the crossarm of a telegraph pole and the noose secured around Heith's thick neck. Still babbling, he was hauled into the air, and the rope was fastened around a steel spike in the pole. The body hung there all that day as a warning to any others who might be contemplating further crime against the rich little hamlet.

On the morning of the execution, the sheriff and his deputies marched the condemned men out into the prison courtyard, where the gallows was surrounded by a festive crowd. Five identical nooses hung from the crossbeam.

As the handkerchief was tied around Dowd's eyes,

he commented, "It's damned hot up here. Get on with it."

Tex Howard chuckled. "Damn it, man, it's gonna be a helluva lot hotter where you're going!"

As the traps were sprung, Mara Tate turned away and took Wyatt Earp's arm. "Let's go. I wanted to see them get their necks snapped, and I'm glad I was present."

He smiled and squeezed her arm. "I keep saying it, but it's the truth: You are quite a woman, Mara Ewing Tate."

Back at the house, she looked in on Mara the second, who was napping, then joined Wyatt in the parlor. "Help yourself to a drink and let me have a large sherry."

He lifted his eyebrows. "Large? Guess you want to take the edge off the hanging."

"It's not that; it's this." She showed him the telegram:

DARLING I'LL BE HOME THE SECOND WEEK IN MARCH STOP CAN'T WAIT TO HOLD MY DAUGHTER IN MY ARMS STOP CAN'T WAIT TO HOLD YOU IN MY ARMS STOP ALL OF MY LOVE STOP GORDON

He sighed and let the message fall to the ground. "I suppose this is my cue to hit the road. Just as well. I've been here too long as it is."

She went to him and put her arms around his neck. "This has been one of the happiest times of my life, Wyatt. I'll never forget you."

"Nor I you, my darling."

They kissed tenderly without passion. Desire was quenched in both of them by a sense of imminent loss and sadness. Then, without warning, Mara's vision blurred and the room appeared to tilt at a sharp angle. She clutched at Wyatt to keep from falling.

"What's wrong?" he asked in concern. "You're so pale. Here, sip your sherry." Supporting her with one arm, he picked up her glass and put it to her mouth.

"I . . . I . . . can't swallow. Can't see. Numb all over."

"You feel faint?"

"No . . . it's different. I feel sort of . . . disembodied. Yes, that's it . . . as if my body is being torn apart, as if a part of me is going to die . . . my soul. I . . . I . . ." Her eyes closed and she went limp in his arms.

MARA
THE
SECOND

CHAPTER ONE

Yes, that's it . . . as if my body is being torn apart, as if a part of me is going to die . . . my soul. I . . . I . . .

Fiedler glanced at the clock on the wall. Mara had been under for just over two hours; it was enough for one day. Gently he advised her: "You've done very well, Mara, but you must be very tired. No more questions. I want you to wake up now. I will count to five and——"

"No!" Her face was contorted by emotions he could not fathom, and her head wagged from side to side in negative insistence. "I want to stay here. I *am* the first Mara."

He patted her hand; it was cold and clammy. To his dismay, her pulse rate began to fall. The digital display on the electronic monitor attached to her left arm flashed 28, 26, 25, 24 . . . He turned to the enamel-topped table behind him and picked up a sterilized syringe from the starched towel. No time to enlist the nurse's help. Working quickly and calmly, he removed the IV needle from her right arm and injected Adrenalin into her vein. He spoke to her slowly and authoritatively: "Mara, you will listen to me and do exactly as I tell you. Do you understand?"

She did not reply, and the disapproving, resentful frown remained fixed on her face.

"I am going to begin the count, Mara, and when I reach five, you *will* awaken."

To his relief, the pulse rate commenced climbing: 28, 30, 32, 36, 40. . . .

He exhaled loudly. She would be all right now. "Listen to me, Mara: One . . . two . . . three . . . four . . . *five*. Wake up, Mara!" He snapped his fingers close to her ear.

Her expression was relaxed once more, her brow smooth; a hint of a smile played around her mouth. Her eyelids began to flutter, then fully opened, and she stared blankly at the ceiling.

"Mara?"

Her head turned on the pillow and she looked at him. Gradually recognition replaced the emptiness. "Max?" Her voice was faint.

"Yes, I am Max, and you are Mara the third —Mara Rodgers Tate."

She was perplexed. "Mara Rodgers Tate? No, I am Mara Ewing Tate. I . . ." She came around slowly. "I . . . I'm so confused." She lifted a hand and brushed a lock of hair back off her forehead.

"Of course you're confused. This has been an extremely trying experience for you."

"Mara Rodgers Tate . . . Yes, I'm still half asleep. It was the dream. I had the most incredible dream that I was Mara Ewing Tate, my own grandmother. It was so real."

"They frequently seem more real than reality itself. 'Till their own dreams at length deceive 'em, And oft repeating, they believe 'em'—Matthew Prior, I believe. . . . Here, let me help you sit up."

As she swung her legs off the side of the cot and leaned forward, he had a tantalizing glimpse of her full breasts beneath the loose smock. His face burned.

Max, what is this with you all of a sudden, playing the voyeur schoolboy again. It's getting hard. Come on now, Max, stop this nonsense!

Mara tilted her head to one side and regarded him

with curiosity. "Max, what are you thinking? I am receiving disturbing vibrations from you. Has it got anything to do with what happened while I was in a trance? What *did* happen? What did I say?" She looked at the recorder on the table, still activated. "May I hear the recording of what I said?"

"I don't think that would be advisable, not now, anyway—not until I have a chance to listen to the tapes again and evaluate them."

She nodded. "If you say so. You're the doctor."

"I *am* the shrink," he said solemnly.

She laughed. "You *are* the nut. . . . Max, please hand me my purse; I'd like a cigarette."

"Not in my office," he said. "That's a no-no, off limits."

"Don't be such a tyrant," she said with some irritability. Mara Tate was not accustomed to denial.

"I'm sorry, but that's the rule."

"Rule." She slipped off the cot. "Okay, make yourself scarce while I dress."

"The female body is no novelty to these old peepers." He leered at her.

"All the same to me." She began to untie the ribbons holding the smock closed.

"I'm on my way." He whirled around and walked out of the room.

When she came back into his office, he was sitting behind his desk reading mail. He looked up and removed his glasses. "You look chipper and fit again."

"I feel marvelous, only ravenous. Can I buy you lunch?"

He gave it some thought. "All right. . . . Yes, I'd like that; it will give us a chance to discuss some details pertinent to this morning's session."

"How about we go to my place? There'll be more privacy there, and my cook Hilde is a gem of a chef."

He grinned boyishly. "Will you be showing me your

etchings? I am but a simple country lad and easily led astray."

Her finely tweezed eyebrows lifted. "Wait until you see my bedroom. Many a lad, country and city, has gone astray after they see my boudoir gadgetry."

Now his eyebrows lifted. "Boudoir gadgetry? That has a lascivious ring to it."

"I'll save it as a surprise. Let's go."

When they stepped out of the elevator, she took his hand and swung it lightly as they walked. Fiedler literally swelled up with pride, conscious that he was the object of numerous envious glares from other males. He could read their thoughts:

What's a dumpy little schmuck like him doing with that gorgeous hunk of woman?

He tickled her palm with his index finger. "Does this mean we're going steady?"

She threw back her head and laughed—a hearty laugh—thoroughly unselfconscious that she was inviting public attention. Fiedler had never met a woman who possessed more self-confidence and poise than Mara Tate. His heart was soaring with a joy he had not experienced since his first serious crush, when the object of his affection had consented to wear his class ring.

Deliberately he concentrated on his wife Ruth—dear, sweet, faithful Ruth, mother of his children, she who had toiled in a sweatshop to help him complete his internship at Bellevue. He wanted to experience guilt for his infidelity—infidelity was still infidelity even if it was only in the mind—but there was not one whit of remorse in him.

Mara Tate was strong on precognition; he had come to respect it in the short period he had known her. She looked him directly in the eye and asked, "What is your wife like, Max?"

The betraying blush again, the stammer: "My wife

. . . yes . . . her name is——" Damn it! His mind was
blank for an instant. He gulped. "Her name is Ruth."
He recovered in time to turn it into one of his defensive comic routines: "Let's see . . . five-three in her
stockinged feet, hundred and eighteen pounds; black
hair, brown eyes, pug nose; size thirty-four B cup;
good legs; has a mole on her left tush."

"Dr. Fiedler, you are outrageous." She thrust two
fingers between her front teeth and let go with a shrill
whistle worthy of an Arizona cowhand. "Learned that
summer at Glammorgab."

He stared at her. "Glamm—whatever. What in hell
is that?"

"The Tate family estate. Comes from the Welsh
town of the same name where my grandmother was
born. You must visit sometime."

"I'll stop in to say hello when I'm passing through.
Do you spend much time there?"

"Not anymore. My home base is New York, the
Tate building."

He opened the cab door for her, admiring the swell
of her backside in the tight skirt as she bent to enter.
I haven't been so horny since my wedding night!

Fiedler was duly impressed by her penthouse apartment, especially the rooftop garden with its variety
of plants and shrubs imported from Arizona. He
turned up the collar of his topcoat against the brisk
autumn wind. "How do they thrive in this damnable
climate after being pampered by all that Arizona sun?"

Mara smiled. "Tough and adaptable, like everything
else cultivated in Arizona—and that includes the
women."

"Amen. But you see before you a hothouse daisy,
so let's go inside and thaw out."

Francine Watkins was courteous to Fiedler, if a
trifle distant. Fiedler sensed it and understood: Mara's
black maid-companion was overprotective of her mis-

tress and friend. She handed Mara a list of people who had been trying to contact her by phone. "Sara says the ones with the asterisks get top priority."

"Thanks, I'll get to them right off. You will excuse me for about a quarter of an hour, won't you, Max? Why don't you go into the library and look through some of the family tomes?"

"Good idea."

"Francine, bring Dr. Fiedler a drink and tell Hilde to prepare us a couple of platters of cold seafood—lobster, clams, crab meat, and shrimp."

"My God, that's a gourmet feast!" Fiedler exclaimed. "My usual style is Chock-Full-o'-Nuts."

The maid led him to the small, cozy study. "Here you are, doctor. That shelf against the wall behind the desk, those books are all about the Tates."

"Thanks, Francine."

"What will you have to drink?"

"A Pepsi." It was automatic. "No, make it a Scotch on the rocks; I'm chilled to the bone."

He took three volumes down from the top shelf and seated himself at the desk; then, thumbing through the index of each, he chose one that presented extensive coverage of the era Mara had described under hypnosis that morning.

Described? Or lived through again? Mara the first? Mara the third?

Cool it, Fiedler. Don't lose your scientific objectivity, or you'll start believing that she is a reincarnation!

"Christ, maybe I *am* starting to believe it!" he said aloud.

There are more things in heaven and earth, Horatio, Than are dreamt of in your philosophy. . . .

This particular Tate chronicle had been authored by Professor Orville Kellerman, chairman of the Department of History at the University of Arizona, on commission from the Tate Foundation. It was to the family's credit that it had opted for candor and honesty and had given Professor Kellerman carte blanche in his assignment, which he had researched thoroughly and recorded faithfully, even those episodes that reflected unfavorably on certain members of the clan.

The period from 1885 through 1900 was a time of entrenchment for the Tates. In the short span of nine years, they had literally gone from rags to riches more extravagant than Drew Tate's wildest dreams, their empire founded on a slab of copper-carbonate ore accidentally dislodged by Mara the first that fateful day in Tombstone Canyon. The next fifteen years saw the expansion of their copper empire and the consolidation of Tate International Industries, a series of acquisitions of sister companies in which copper was the common bond and linked by vertical mergers.

Here were the first indications, too, of the breakdown of the once close-knit family. The Emlyn Tates moved to Philadelphia, where Emlyn accepted a position from his father-in-law and, by the turn of the century, was installed as president of the Baxter Savings and Loan Bank. Millicent bore him three children, a son, William, and two daughters, Shirley and Grace.

Allan Tate married Maria Beaver, sold his shares in the family company, and invested in a large California vineyard, an orange grove, and real estate in an obscure area in Los Angeles that would one day become world-famous as Hollywood, the motion-picture capital of the globe. Maria gave birth to a son, the handsomest of all the Tate children.

Drew Tate did persuade Gilbert to remain with TII as chief of exploration and research of all Tate mining interests in South America. Gilbert sired a pair of twins, Preston and Samantha.

By 1900, Arizona was one of the world's leading producers of copper in the world, as well as one of the nation's foremost producers of gold and silver, mere by-products of copper mining. But, as Drew had predicted years earlier, the high-grade copper ore was all but depleted by then. Nevertheless, his foresight in searching for a method to profitably extract copper from low-grade ore was close to success, due to the combined efforts of two bright young engineers named L. D. Ricketts and J. C. Jackling, who were to refine open-pit mining to an art.

Great mining enterprises were springing up throughout the territory, and there was increasing clamor from the legislature at the capital, Phoenix, for statehood. To name the more influential and richest producers of copper, the Arizona Copper Company and Detroit Copper Company in the Clifton and Morenci district; the Copper Queen and the Calumet and Arizona, in addition to the Copper King, at Bisbee; the Old Dominion Mining and Smelting Company in the Globe district; the United Verde at Jerome—together their owners constituted one of the most powerful congressional blocs in Washington, D.C.

Drew and Gwen, both hardy and in their seventies, were becoming addicted to world travel. Drew, for a number of years, had been delegating more and more executive authority to Gordon Ewing and to Mara, who took an active and forceful role in the management of the company's far-flung investments.

Mara the second, at seventeen, was attending the University of Arizona at Tucson, and was regarded as the belle of Arizona high society, whose ranks kept swelling with the increasing affluence of the population.

"Spitting image of your mum," her doting grandfather would boast. The resemblance was uncanny but for one feature: Mara's daughter had green eyes flecked with specks of gold that appeared to swirl and sparkle when the direct sunlight shone on her face.

Life was good for the Tates—"a horn of plenty,"

as Gwen described their infinite good fortune. Then, without warning, as is so often the case, fate displayed its fickleness in the form of inflicting a double tragedy upon the family.

Fiedler looked up from the book as Mara entered the study. "I'm sorry; my phone calls took far longer than I had anticipated."

"Has it been long?" He glanced at his watch. "How about that? I've been reading over an hour. It seemed like minutes. Fascinating history. The Tates were quite a tribe at that."

"Tribe? You make them sound primitive."

"They did possess certain primitive instincts. Self-preservation, the instinct for survival—they're the blood and bones of success."

"We can chat over lunch. Francine says it's on the table."

They ate at a small table in the alcove of a huge bay window overlooking the park.

"What a magnificent view," he commented.

"I can't wait to get back to the apartment after a day of being cooped up in an office. New York gives me claustrophobia, even the streets. I always have the sensation that the skyscrapers are going to crash down on the teeming mobs. High up here, it's more like the wide-open spaces of Arizona. . . . So, do you approve of the Tates?"

"I admire them very much. Of course, I've barely scratched the surface. Incidentally, may I take a few of the volumes back to my office with me?"

She was apprehensive and defensive. "I'd prefer that they remain in my study, Max. I hope you understand. It's nothing personal. Once you step out of here into that jungle, God only knows what could happen to you. Muggers. You could be hit by a bus or suffer a heart attack."

"That's all right," he said, pacifying her. "I understand perfectly"—although he did not understand. Underneath the hard shell of this hugely successful woman business executive was a shadowy area of vulnerability that would have to be explored. He was not altogether displeased by the protest that, in reading the books here, he must inevitably see a good deal more of Mara Tate, maybe even get to see the inner sanctum she had alluded to earlier—her bedroom.

"What you said before in the study, how fast the time passed while you were reading—it was like that for me when I was hypnotized. You said only two hours; yet for me it seemed like years. I'm serious. I was living years of experiences that Mara . . . that I . . ." She faltered.

"No, not *you;* Mara Ewing Tate. You imagined you were she, that's all."

She put down her fork and stared at her plate in bafflement. "I don't know. It was so real, and yet you claim it all happened within two hours."

"Albert Einstein, in a lecture at Princeton, offered a simplistic definition of his theory of relativity to a group of freshmen. He told them: 'You sit here listening to an old man ramble on about higher mathematics, and every minute seems to take an eternity to pass, while tonight some of you will be sitting in a parked car on lovers' lane embracing a soft, pretty, fragrant young woman, and two hours will seem to pass in the wink of an eye.' Do you grasp what he meant?"

Mara laughed. "To be sure, and that's what happened to me?"

"Yes; it was a highly pleasurable experience re-enacting all those stories you had heard from your mother and grandmother and had read about in all those Tate chronicles, but to continue: Einstein's theory of relativity can be applied on still another plane. According to Einstein, if we were aboard a spaceship traveling through space at extraordinary speed, as the ship approached the speed of light, time would, literally, slow down. For example, at ninety-three thousand miles per second—half the speed of light— our clocks would slow down fifteen minutes in one hour. At one hundred sixty-three thousand miles per second—seven-eighths the speed of light—the clock would slow down by a full half-hour."

"That's incomprehensible to me."

"It's been proven by two different methods. First a team of California scientists shot a stream of mesons —infinitesimal particles—through a mile-long tunnel and measured their life-spans. As their velocities approached the speed of light, the life-spans of the mesons doubled, tripled, and quadrupled. Merely a reverse way of demonstrating that for these particles, time did indeed slow down as they accelerated to super velocities. Since then, atomic clocks have been put into space aboard satellites, and these super-accurate instruments show minute but definite lapses at high velocities."

"Fascinating, but what does it have to do with me?"

He swallowed a tender shrimp and licked butter off his fingers. "I'm leading up to the Fiedler theory of relativity. There is no computer on earth, no matter how sophisticated, that can ever exceed the scope of the human brain. Oh, they tabulate facts and numbers at lightning speed, but I'm fairly certain that if the full capabilities of the human brain were exploited, it could match and even surpass the performance of the computer. Even a genius like Einstein utilized only a small fraction of his potential brainpower, somewhere around one-eighth.

"Now, my point is, operating at super velocities, the thought processes also slow down time. In other words, Mara, a lifetime of information stored up in your memory bank can be reviewed in seconds, minutes, certainly in two hours. Do you see the connection?"

"Yes, I think so, and it's very intriguing. I can hardly wait until our next session, Max. When will you put me under again?"

He sat back in the chair and rubbed his chin thoughtfully; he had reservations about repeating the experiment too soon. "I think we should wait a while before I regress you again. It's a highly traumatic experience, a hazardous strain both to the mind and to the body. Let's continue with conventional therapy for a few weeks."

Her lips were a thin, stubborn slash of crimson, her eyes went from gray to deep blue, and her voice was sharp. "That's absurd! I told you from the start, Max, that I do *not* need a shrink. My head is all together, and I have no intention of lying on your couch babbling on about my frustrations and my sex life like some Westchester matron. For your information, my sex life is just *great*. I have never been repressed about *anything*. What I want I go after, what I think I say, and I always do exactly what I want to do!"

Max wiped his mouth with the linen napkin and stood up. His smile was tight and his voice too even: "I admire your candor, Mara, and if that's the way you feel, there's nothing I can do to change your mind; but I have no intention of permitting you to prescribe for your own case. That's like the old saw that a lawyer who handles his own case has a fool for a client."

Mara stood up, fists clenched at her sides. "Damn you, Max, you can be terribly exasperating!"

He met her glare without blinking. "And right now I find *you* 'terribly exasperating,' Miss Tate. I repeat —no more parlor games until I decide."

"It was *not* a parlor game; you said that yourself. Oh, Max!" For a fleeting instant he thought she was going to break into tears, but it was a deception. She lit a cigarette and turned, facing the window. "I'm not accustomed to taking orders."

"Neither am I, not when somebody tries to tell me how to conduct myself professionally. You know, those Westchester matrons you hold in such contempt, they're really very nice women, and the ones who come to me need help desperately and are very grateful to me for helping them through the bad times and tight spots in life. I can't—I *won't* waste time on a spoiled female like you who wants to run my show. Good-by, Miss Tate. I'll put a bill in the mail." He nodded curtly and spun on his heel. "I'll see myself to the door."

He was halfway across the sunken living room when she came after him. "Max, please don't walk out on me."

He kept on walking, and climbed the short flight up to the foyer.

"Max!" It was the tone of desperation he was waiting for. "Max, don't leave me. I need your help. I *do!* I promise, we'll do it your way—the couch, the whole shtick. Christ, why is it you make me feel like I'm not a liberated woman?"

He descended the steps, walked back to her, and took her hands in his. "Nobody is totally liberated —not women, not men, not you, not me. We all depend on each other; we all need each other to lean on when the going gets rough. Like John Donne said, no man is an island."

She embraced him and buried her face in the angle of his neck and shoulder. "It feels good to lean on you, Max."

He patted her back.

CHAPTER TWO

As in any other endeavor that Mara Tate undertook, she embarked on analysis with enthusiasm and made a major effort to divulge to Fiedler her innermost thoughts and feelings. On some occasions her candor discomfited him, as when she detailed every love affair she'd ever had, going back to her thirteenth birthday, when she was seduced by the young groom hired to care for the palomino pony her father had given her on that occasion.

"Seduced by" was not quite apt, for it was the lusty adolescent girl who had done the seducing.

"It was absolutely shameless the way I planned it. After the party, I went out to the barn to look at my wonderful present, only before I went, I took off my panties. I patted and spoke to Prince for a time and then I pretended that I had left some trinket up in the hayloft; my girl friends and I used to hold hen parties up there when we wanted to talk about boys and sex in total privacy.

"Anyway, I asked George to hold the ladder for me." She laughed and tugged at her earlobe. "In the modern vernacular, that lad *really* turned me on. He was big and blond with blue eyes, and his muscles had muscles"—her eyes gleamed mischievously, knowing that she was embarrassing Fiedler—"namely that big muscle in his pants."

Fiedler coughed and reached for his water glass. She was sitting across the desk from him in a low leather chair with her legs crossed above the knee,

affording Fiedler a generous view of her long, shapely, silken limbs.

"Am I boring you, doctor?"

" 'Titillating' is the word. Proceed, Miss Tate."

"What a hussy I was. I climbed up that straight ladder while poor George stood at the bottom, looking up my skirt. From the way his eyes were bulging and his face was fire red, I knew he must be getting quite an eyeful. Up in the loft, I pretended to be searching around; then I called for him to come up and help me. The poor dear; he had one hand in his pocket, holding it down, but not with much success.

"One way or another, we got into a tickling match, and there we were rolling about in the hay so very innocently——"

Fiedler cleared his throat: "I'll *bet*."

"Then, quite by accident, I grabbed him *there* and . . . and"—she grinned—"the rest is history. Or would you prefer for me to be more explicit?"

"That won't be necessary; I am fully cognizant of the physiological composition of the male and female genitalia and how they complement each other."

After that, there was a succession of men in her life, culminating in her current dual relationship with Lewis O'Toole, her chief accountant, and Robert Hunter, head of the legal firm that represented Tate International Industries.

It pained Fiedler to know that she would go home this night and make love with one of those men while he and Ruth sat propped up in bed, she reading the latest romantic potboiler, he trying to concentrate on the latest copy of the *Journal of Psychiatry* while, at the same time, conjuring up lurid fantasies of Mara and O'Toole, or Mara and Hunter—possibly all three —doing the two-backed beast on her royal couch.

He averted his gaze from her mouth-watering legs

and forced it back to his note pad. "Yet you've never had any inclination to be married?"

"Oh, I was tempted a few times, but good reason prevailed. You see, I look upon marriage as a very serious commitment. If I ever did marry, I'd want the whole nut—a cozy cottage in the country with a white picket fence around it, and me and the kids waiting at the gate at sunset for my beloved to return from his labors."

Fiedler leaned back in the swivel chair and roared with merriment. "Oh, Jesus Christ! Mara Tate in a bargain-basement frock with a white apron, baking bread and changing diapers! Oh, Lord!" He was almost weeping. "I can easier see Jack Kennedy as a shoe salesman."

The light of nostalgia illuminated her expression. "As a matter of fact, Jack Kennedy would make a damn good shoe salesman. He'd make a good whatever he set his mind to. I'm like that, too. If I chose to become a wife and a mother, I'd be damn good at it."

"I believe you would." He seized the opportunity to press a point she was constantly avoiding, the one facet of her life she was reluctant to confide in him: "Why won't you tell me about President Kennedy? Was he something special to you?"

Her smile was distant, not meant for him. "Was he special to me? Jack is special to all of his friends. He is a special person."

"I don't mean that kind of special. Did he—does he —occupy a special place in your affections?"

"Of course. I was in love with him; I still am. . . . Look, Max, I regard marriage as a very serious commitment, as I said before, and not just from a personal standpoint. I take other people's marriages just as seriously as I would take my own. In case I neglected to mention it, I have never fooled around with a married man. I don't covet my sisters' property. Jack

Kennedy and every other married man I know are off limits."

Fiedler's brief relationship with Mara Tate had set him off on an ego trip, one he envisioned would have a specific destination. Where the meandering route would lead was still vague. If he lucked out, it might be a rainbow ending in a pot of gold.

I'm a married man—lock, stock, and barrel married. I am also off limits with Mara Tate!

The rainbow vanished; the expanding balloon of ego exploded.

I'm just a funny little baggy-pants comedian full of pathos, like Chaplin.

"Want to tell me what's bugging you, Max?" she inquired with cunning insight.

He removed his glasses and snapped off the tape recorder. "Nothing—just weary. I think we'll wrap it up for today. How about you? You been sleeping better lately?"

She removed her cigarette case from her purse. "I thought we were wrapping it up for today."

"We are; it's a friendly query—and put those cigarettes away."

"Damned tyrant!" she said, but obeyed. "I'll sleep a lot better when this messy business with Coppertone Cookware is settled."

"I read in *The Times* that the case goes to court next week. Will it be bad?"

"It couldn't be worse. You know, it isn't just Coppertone we have to contend with. The SEC and the Justice Department have been breathing hot on my dear cousin Sean's heels for years. Up till now he's been lucky—luck and the fact that I've always been around to bail him out of the jams he's gotten himself into."

"You bailed him out?"

"Paid off his gambling debts, you might say. Not

the Vegas kind, though he's probably lost a bundle at the crap table over the years. Sean is always making deals on anticipated profits from previous deals. Sometimes he'll be juggling five balls in the air at the same time."

"Why did you allow him to get away with it? I mean, you're the main honcho at TII."

"Oh, they were all private deals to begin with. He knows that his position at Tate is gratuitous. He's a Tate, and the Tates have always taken care of their own; it's part of the tradition."

"Only this time you've gone to bat for him once too often."

"It looks that way. The prosecutor is going to dredge up all of Sean's past misadventures, and the whole shebang is going to fall before the domino theory. Damn! If I can't have a cigarette, how about a drink?"

"Scotch and water, right?" He pressed the intercom button and spoke to his secretary: "Darling, would you scare up some refreshments for me and Miss Tate? Scotch and water, a double, and a Pepsi for me."

"God, how inconsiderate can I get? I keep forgetting I'm not your only patient." She made a move to stand up, but he waved her down.

"Relax . . . I got a cancellation for the next hour." He did not mention that he could have filled the gap easily but preferred to let her time run over into the next session. "What's the worst that can happen? I'm not up on legal high jinks."

"Well, the court can find us guilty of perjury, filing false reports with the SEC and falsifying reports to TII stockholders, then remove me and Sean and his assistant Harvey Sayer, of Coppertone, from office and appoint a receiver to oversee the management of the firm. That would be a major disaster, not for me personally but for the company. It's like a girl getting married by proxy to a serviceman. She's a wife in name only, and he's the head of a household, only he's clear across the Atlantic serving in Europe."

The secretary brought in the drinks. "Thanks, dear," Fiedler said with a wink. "Listen, who is my last patient this afternoon?"

"Sally Watkins, four o'clock."

"Thanks again."

When she was gone, he asked Mara, "Is it legal for the prosecutor to raise allegations against your cousin out of the past? You said that up till now he's always been able to keep his nose clean."

"You're confusing it with criminal law. It is illegal to cite a defendant's past record to incriminate him on new charges; but this is different." She lifted her glass. "Cheers."

"Prosit." He drained his glass. "Is there any one thing they can pin on him aside from his finagling the deal with Coppertone?"

"I'm afraid so. Five years ago Sean came to me with a very good deal—I mean a true find. There was this small manufacturing company, Cilento Copper Parts, owned by two elderly partners. They were running scared because bigger companies were forcing them out of business, and they wanted to sell out and retire to Florida.

"Sean negotiated the price—$1,350,000. It was a buy for TII and more than fair to the partners. We signed the contracts and everybody was happy. No more than a month had gone by when TII was approached by one of the giants in the industry, United Brass Works, with an offer to buy Cilento from us for $2,500,000."

Fiedler whistled. "A profit of $1,150,000. That was quite a coup Sean pulled off, I'd say."

"It looked that way to me, too—at first. Then it came out that Sean was moonlighting as an agent for small firms like Cilento that wanted to sell out, and when the deal was closed, he'd receive a finder's fee."

"Sounds legitimate."

"Oh, it was legit all right, but now hear this: It turned out that while he was representing Cilento and his partner, he had contacted United Brass and had received a confirmed offer from them to buy Cilento out for $2 million."

"Oh, shit!" Fiedler winced. "I've seen penny-ante chiselers on Delancey Street who worked that game, but Tate Industries?"

"You got it. Before it was over, Cilento and his partner got themselves a slick lawyer and filed a suit against Sean and TII for complicity to commit fraud. We settled it out of court for $500,000, but TII was smeared across every financial page in the nation. The real point is that I would have authorized Sean to top United's offer in the first place if he had leveled with me—Cilento Copper has earned us excess profits of $7 million to date—but no, Sean can never take the straight approach to anything; he's got to be devious. All of his schemes are convoluted. Now, can you imagine a smart prosecutor passing up an opportunity to introduce the Cilento case into the court record when we go to trial?"

"No, truthfully I can't. Jesus Christ! With a cousin like Sean Tate, who needs enemies?"

"I've had it with him this time, no matter what the outcome." She finished her Scotch and stood up. "I've got to get back to the office, Max. Thanks for everything. Do you know, you are a living doll—a sweet, generous, understanding man. If you weren't already married, I just might break down and grab you off." She came around the desk, put an arm around his neck, and kissed him on the lips lightly.

Fiedler wracked his mind for a flip riposte but could

do no better than: "By way of coincidence, my wife has booked passage on *Titanic Two* next week."

She gave it a polite chuckle and patted his cheek. "Incidentally, you are invited to a small social gathering at my apartment next Friday. You must bring Ruth; I'd like to meet her and compare notes about you."

Shit! I'm going to blush again!

"That's great; I'll ask her. She has a lot of club work on Fridays, but I'm sure she'll make an exception to meet the renowned Mara Tate."

"Flattery will get you everywhere. I'll see you again on Wednesday, same time."

She departed, and Fiedler stood behind his desk in brooding silence.

If you weren't already married . . ."

"If only I weren't," he said wistfully.

Ruth Fiedler was a plain, nice-looking woman of thirty with short dark hair and bangs, a sharp nose, and skin that showed traces of adolescent acne. Her figure was good, if a little overweight.

Fiedler first introduced the topic of Mara Tate's party while they were preparing for bed.

"I wouldn't miss it for the world," she slurped through a mouthful of foamy toothpaste. She rinsed her mouth and came back into the bedroom, where Fiedler was reading a pamphlet on preoperative hypnosis. "Is she very sexy?" she asked casually as she slipped her shorty nightgown over her head. "I've seen her picture in the papers; she's quite a doll."

"Hmmmm . . . her pictures flatter her; she's photogenic."

"Is she sexy?"

"If you like the type, I guess so."

"Do you like the type?" She sat cross-legged on the bed beside him.

"She's very attractive."

"You've got the hots for her, don't you, Max?"

Play it cool, Max, very, very cool. Can't afford to muff this play.

"I raped her this afternoon in the examining room," he said, and leered up her gown. "I feel like a gynecologist. Nice view."

"Dirty old man." She arranged her limbs in a more modest posture.

"As Groucho used to say, Baby, if you make it hard for me, I'm going to hold it against you. So what are we waiting for?" He tossed the pamphlet into the air and cast off the covers.

The very last thing Fiedler felt like doing this night, when his mind was full of Mara Tate, was to make love to his wife; but, considering what tack the conversation was taking, he deemed it prudent to make the amorous overture.

Their lovemaking had all the spontaneity and spark of a cold knish. He had the bizarre sensation that the two of them were a pair of windup toys, motivated by internal springs that simulated the motions of flesh-and-blood arms, legs, fingers, and sexual parts.

He lay on top of her for a while after they were done, knowing she relished post-sexual intimacy.

"Was it good for you?" she asked.

"What?" he said absently, imagining how it would be after he and Mara had completed a glorious mutual orgasm.

"Was it good?"

"Oh, my God, couldn't you tell? My toes are still curled up. How about you?"

"Nice. I liked it. I always like it, even when I don't come."

Nice—Mara would never define a sexual encounter so blandly.

He rolled off her and sat up. "I'm going to the

bathroom." He padded into the john and urinated. Washing his hands, he studied his face in the mirror: typical Joe Blow who achieved his adulterous designs only in daydreams.

"What'll I wear to the party?" she called to him.

"Your diaphragm; that's paramount. These high-society parties usually end up in mass orgies."

"It wouldn't surprise me in the least. And don't think I can't guess who you'd head for at the first drop of a pair of panties: Mara Tate."

" 'Bushwa,' as they used to say in the colonial service."

He stole another glance at his mirror image. There was decided satanic cast to his mien.

CHAPTER THREE

Mara Tate's party was semiformal. The women wore, for the most part, cocktail dresses. The men wore jackets and ties, although there were several ad-agency types sporting velour shirts with ascots, and one turtleneck sweater.

Ruth looked homey and all-American in a prairie-plaid flannel dress; the frill-top blouse had pearl buttons and a shirred shoulder yoke; the skirt was billowy with a deep hemline flounce.

Mara Tate dominated the distaff finery, as she always did. Her Indian-silk sapphire-blue gown glowed like a jewel. It was lined with magenta tulle and had a trapunto-stitched top that tied at one shoulder; the other shoulder was boldly bared. She greeted them warmly in the foyer:

"Ruth, I've been looking forward to meeting you. I suppose your husband has told you I'm infatuated with him?"

Ruth shrugged. "I'm used to it; it's his occupational hazard."

"Yes indeed," he intoned solemnly, touching the knot of his knitted tie. "I'm such a forceful father figure, all the ladies yearn to have me bounce them on my knee and pat their chubby bottoms."

Mara's eyes, more blue than gray tonight, sparkled like sunlight glinting on the sea. "Ahh, then I have something to look forward to. Come along and I'll introduce you. Francine, bring a tray of drinks over here, please."

True to form, as soon as it became known that Fiedler was a psychiatrist, a clique formed around him. He was accustomed to it and fielded the barrage of lay questions diplomatically and politely, careful to make his replies as simplistic as possible. Fortified with two long Scotch and sodas, he warmed to his task, not without a growing feeling of self-importance.

"You're the life of the party," Mara told him during one respite, when he'd headed for the bathroom.

"You'll get my bill in the morning," he joked.

"When do I get my pat on the bottom?"

Automatically he looked around the room for his wife.

Mara laughed. "Don't worry; Ruth can't hear me. As a matter of fact, she's enthralled by Randall Harvey, the author."

"Oh, yes, I've heard her mention the name often. Randall Harvey—imagine that."

She looked at her diamond-studded wristwatch. "Ten o'clock. He should be here shortly."

"Who?"

She winked. "It's my surprise of the evening, so you'll have to wait."

"Ten o'clock?" He feigned surprise. "What, it's already past my bedtime."

"You'll wake up when *he* arrives."

Fiedler excused himself and found the john.

No more than a quarter of an hour later, he was conversing with TII vice-president Jean Castle and Mara's secretary, Sara Cohen—bright, articulate women in their late thirties, with short, mannish haircuts and wearing simple but elegant gowns; assertive women yet feminine—when the doorbell chimes sounded.

"I'm investing heavily in oil and steel and the auto industry, doctor," Jean said. "After Kennedy is inaugurated, the market is going to take off like that well-known bird."

"I'm chicken," Fiedler admitted. "Municipal bonds and public utilities are my speed."

The two business-shrewd ladies observed him with a certain condescension. "Well," said Sarah Cohen, "different strokes for different folks."

"Did I hear my name being bandied about?" said a voice from behind him.

It was a damned familiar voice: brawd Bawston vowels; shades of Harvard, Back Bay, and Hyannis Port. The hair at the back of Fiedler's neck bristled. He turned and looked into the smiling Irish eyes of John Fitzgerald Kennedy, took in the famous roguish smile —of all the Kennedy men, best typified by Jack—the hallmark shock of thick red hair shared by the clan.

Mara was holding possessively to his left arm. "Dr. Fiedler, I would like to present the next president of the United States, John Kennedy."

"A distinct pleasure, Dr. Fiedler." Kennedy patted her hand on his arm. "Take good care of our girl here. She says you rate on a plateau above Sigmund Freud." The president-elect's handshake was firm but not intimidating.

Fiedler favored him with his impish grin. "Mara says you rate on a plateau above George Washington. This is not only a distinct pleasure for me, sir, but a distinct shock as well. Never in my wildest dreams . . ." He shook his head and left it unfinished.

They all laughed, and Kennedy greeted Castle and Cohen: "Jean . . . Sara." He gave each of them a light kiss on the cheek and squeezed their hands.

Fiedler mused, *He certainly is familiar with this Tate crowd. I wonder* . . . He looked around to see if he could identify the secret-service men who constantly dogged the footsteps of presidents, former presidents, and presidents-elect, but he saw no one other than the invited guests. He had to ask about it: "Mr. President" —he halted—"what does one call the president-elect?"

Kennedy smiled again; in fact, the smile was perpetual. "Why not try 'Jack'?"

"I'll stick with 'Mr. Kennedy.' Sir, would it be impertinent of me to inquire how you got here tonight? I mean, where are the watchdogs?"

"Threw 'em off the scent. I like to do that. It drives 'em crazy." Kennedy winked at him. "With a pair of dark glasses and a fedora. In a hat I'm practically anonymous; it comes in handy."

"He's absolutely mad," Mara said.

"To be frank, Dr. Fiedler," the president-elect continued, "it wouldn't faze me to travel by bus or subway. It is my firm conviction that anyone who sincerely wants to assassinate the president of the United States, or any other world leader, can accomplish the deed if he is sufficiently dedicated. Every time the president rides through a crowd, he's in jeopardy. You can't station a guard in every one of the thousand windows overlooking the motorcade."

"That is eminently fatalistic," Fiedler said, "and also very realistic."

Mara interrupted: "Will you excuse us? I want Jack to meet some people." And she whisked him away.

"This has really been a night to remember," Fiedler said in genuine awe. "Look at my wife; she's absolutely petrified."

"He's a real doll," Sara observed, stars in her eyes.

"You both look like schoolgirls," Fiedler said with amusement.

"He has that effect," Jean admitted. "What is that new word that is bandied about—'charisma'?"

"Whatever it means, he's got it," Fiedler conceded. Across the room, Jack Kennedy and Mara were conversing with TII president Wendell Holmes and attorney Bob Hunter. Kennedy was speaking:

"Dad told me to alert you that the Justice Department is not shooting from the hip in this case; they're taking dead aim. They've got more ammunition than Coppertone and that Cilento fiasco. Their investigators are burning the midnight oil on the Harlan Electronics transaction with Diamond Industries Limited."

Mara frowned. "That's ridiculous, another gaffe on the part of cousin Sean. But Diamond Industries came away with a tidy profit."

"At whose expense?" Holmes reminded her. "TII picked up the check."

The trouble had evolved from Sean Tate's personal acquisition of a small electronics firm. With the help of a "creative bookkeeper," the record of sales and earnings had been falsified to Diamond Industries, which was interested in purchasing the company from the new owner. As a result of the manipulation, Diamond had paid $1 million for a property that was worth no more than $750,000. To save Sean's hide, TII had offered Diamond $1,250,000 for Harlan, and the offer was accepted.

"That's not the way it is at all, Wendell," she objected. "We paid Diamond $1,250,000 for a property they had already paid Sean $1 million for. That million went back into the coffers of TII, so the difference amounted to $250,000. In other words, TII acquired a property worth $750,000 for the sum of $250,000. I'd call that a very shrewd and legit deal, wouldn't you?"

"It's the way it was accomplished, Mara," her chief attorney said, "the sleight-of-hand technique of one Sean Tate that has had the feds frothing at the mouth for years." He grimaced. "Did I say 'sleight of hand'? Change that to 'damn-right clumsy'!"

A bevy of tittering women descended on Kennedy, terminating the conversation. Mara excused herself and looked around for Fiedler. He was talking to a tall, svelte black woman wearing a form-clinging white satin sheath and a matching turban coiled about her rather elongated head. She had a classic Abyssinian profile. Her name was Marsha Simpkins, and she was the owner and president of a chain of cosmetic stores that catered primarily to women of color. She and Fiedler were obviously hitting it off splendidly.

She smiled at Mara's approach. "Darling, where did you find this man? He's positively delightful! I've half a mind to waste my shrink and convert to Dr. Fiedler's therapy group."

Mara's eyes widened. "Do you do group therapy, Max? I didn't know that."

"Sure; it's highly beneficial for certain patients—not for everyone, though."

Her smile was strained. "I could never discuss my innermost personal problems and thoughts with total strangers."

Marsha hugged her. "It's a gas, gal. You really ought to try it." She rolled her eyes so that the whites showed prominently. "The things you *hear*—raunchier than a Kathleen Windsor novel!"

"Voyeur," Mara chided her fondly. "Listen, you two, dinner is about to be served. Buffet, but I can promise that Hilde has outdone herself."

Ruth Fiedler joined them. Still dazed from the shock of meeting John Fitzgerald Kennedy, she said to Mara, "This is like a fairy tale. I feel like Cinderella at the royal ball meeting Prince Charming."

"And in another hour and a half you'll go up in smoke and end up back at the kitchen of your wicked stepmother, clad in rags and sweeping up ashes," Fiedler said. He was much amused by her air of girlish innocence. Normally, Ruth was a pretty cool lady. Well, who could blame her? This was not exactly your run-of-the-mill coffee klatch.

Linking arms with Mara and his wife, he strode into the dining room, head held high and proud.

CHAPTER FOUR

The first day in court the tone was set for what was to come in the weeks and months ahead. It was plain to Mara Tate and TII's legal staff, headed by Robert Hunter, that the federal government, through its advocates in the SEC and the attorney general's office and a powerful congressional bloc headed by Montana's senior senator, Mark Manning, was conducting a personal vendetta against Tate International Industries.

Mara's business association, as well as her familial ties, with Sean Tate was exploited by the federal prosecutor at every opportunity. When she took the witness chair, she knew she was in for a bad time at his opening question:

"Miss Tate, what does the name 'Cilento Copper Parts' mean to you?"

"Tate International Industries purchased the company back in 1955."

"Is it true that by that transaction you and your cousin and then general manager, Sean Tate, conspired to defraud the owners of Cilento Copper Parts, Mr. Nicholas Cilento and Mr. Harry Cohen, out of more than $1 million—$1,150,000, to be exact?"

"That is not true."

The prosecutor, Leonard Dillon, a short, swaggering man with a Clarence Darrow complex, picked up a document from the prosecution table and stalked over to the witness box. He almost touched Mara's nose with it:

"Miss Tate, I have here in my hand a deposition signed by Mr. George Heller, executive vice-president of the United Brass Works, that prior to the sale of Cilento Copper Parts to Tate International Industries, he and Sean Tate, who *allegedly was acting in the capacity of sales agent for Cilento Copper,* had reached a tentative agreement for the purchase of Cilento by United Brass for the sum of $2 million! At least two weeks before TII purchased Cilento Copper for only $1,350,000! *Is that not in fact true?"*

"Yes, it is true, but I can explain——"

"Not now you can't. Miss Tate, just answer the question with a simple yes or no. If you have a point to make, it can be made when your attorney redirects."

Mara compressed her lips, and two bright splotches tinted her cheeks.

Don't lose your cool, Mara, my girl.

"And is it not also true, Miss Tate, that within one month after TII purchased Cilento Copper, your company turned around and sold it to United Brass for $2,500,000, at a net profit of $1,150,000?"

"Yes, it is true." Mara crossed her legs and tugged down the hem of her wool-knit flannel skirt.

She had never felt so helpless, so impotent, in her life. Even if the prosecutor had permitted her to do so, how could she logically defend herself or TII against the allegation? How could she explain: *Yes, I knew that Sean was wheeling and dealing, but not until it was too late to do anything about it. No, Cilento and Cohen were not cheated; they had received a fair price for a business that had been going downhill for three years. Sean was right about one thing: They were too old and unsophisticated to manage their firm in the accelerated tempo of the fifties, and too frightened to make a good deal on their own. If they had dealt outright with United Brass, they would have ended up with less than TII paid them.*

Yes, Sean was double-dealing with them and with me, but what he did was not so vile and unethical an act as the prosecutor would suggest. Big business is an unmerciful crucible. You take the heat and come out stronger for the experience, or you end up on the slag heap, dead ashes. There are no Marquis of Queensbury rules to go by.

The prosecutor's voice intruded on her thoughts: "Miss Tate, in March of this past year, Coppertone Cookware, a subsidiary of Tate International Industries, purchased a firm titled Harlan Electronics, is that not so?"

"Yes, it did." Her eyes impaled Sean Tate sitting at the defense table with Harvey Sayer, who was mopping his forehead with a sodden handkerchief. Her cousin looked down guiltily.

"TII paid $1,200,000 for the acquisition, is that correct?"

"It is."

"What was the real worth of Harlan Electronics when TII purchased it?"

"In my estimation, it was worth precisely what TII paid for it."

"Really?" His smile was saturnine. "The board of examiners for the Securities and Exchange Commission say differently." He held up a fact sheet. "Their appraisal lists the net worth of Harlan Electronics at the time of purchase as being not in excess of $750,000, some half-million dollars less than TII paid for it— *$500,000 of your stockbrokers' money.*"

"May I remind you that the Tate family is the largest single stockholder."

"And may I remind you not to inject gratuitous comments outside the scope of this examination." He crossed his arms and looked her squarely in the eye. "Now then, in my understanding, it was Sean Tate who made the original acquisition of Harlan Electronics—that is, before TII purchased it from Diamond Industries."

"Yes, it was his personal property and he sold the company to Diamond Industries."

"For $1 million?"

"Yes, and Diamond Industries netted a profit of $200,000 on the deal."

"Not exactly a handsome profit, but they were very, very grateful to make any profit at all, particularly after their accountants discovered that Sean Tate had falsified the records of sales and earnings in his prospectus to Diamond Industries."

"Objection!" Bob Hunter leaped to his feet. "The prosecutor is presuming facts not in evidence!"

"Objection sustained," the judge ruled. "Strike the prosecutor's remarks from the record, commencing with 'Not exactly a handsome profit.' "

The prosecutor nodded and turned back to Mara. "You stated before that Harlan Electronics was Mr. Tate's 'personal property'?"

Mara's antennae picked up something ominous in the question; it was reflected in her wary reply: "Well, yes . . . that is what Mr. Tate told me."

"I hate to abuse your naïveté, Miss Tate, but in fact Mr. Tate owned only 2,000 shares of Harlan Electronics. The majority stockholder, the possessor of 20,000 shares of Harlan Electronics as of January first of this year was—according to the records of the Securities and Exchange Commission—one Vito Mosconi, Mr. Sean Tate's brother-in-law. . . . You may step down, Miss Tate. No further questions at this time."

His proclamation created a mild furor in the courtroom. Barbara Tate, Sean's wife, was the daughter of one and the sister of the other of two of the most notorious Mafia-family figures on the East Coast: Bruno Mosconi and his son Vito.

Mara was stunned by the revelation. It was bad enough that the proud Tate name had to be linked to the Mafia by marriage; but to have a Tate-Mosconi business alliance brandished before the public eye was unspeakable!

"Miss Tate," the judge said softly, "you may step down."

Her eyes swiveled in his direction, glazed over with shock; all of the vibrant color was drained out of them. "I . . . Yes, I'm sorry." She swayed as she walked back to the defense table, and Bob Hunter got up and same around to assist her.

"Mara, are you all right?"

She shook her head. "I'm fine." She glared at Sean before she sat down. "You stinking son of a bitch!" she whispered. "But you're going to get what's due you, Sean. Wait until your scummy father-in-law and brother-in-law find themselves on the front page again because of you. You'll be better off in jail!"

Sean slumped down in his chair, a beaten, frightened man; his face was chalk white. He winced visibly as Harvey Sayer was called to take the witness stand.

Sayer's testimony was a disaster, and it irrevocably doomed not only himself but his codefendants as well. The prosecutor dogged him without mercy.

"Mr. Sayer, in April of this year, Coppertone Cookware paid the legal firm of Blandings and Olson the sum of $90,000. What was the money paid for?"

"Legal services, naturally."

"Legal services?" His voice rang with sarcasm. "The truth is, Mr. Sayer, Blandings and Olson performed no such legal services last April. In fact, it has not performed any services for Coppertone whatsoever to the present date."

Sayer's collar was wilted by perspiration. His hands were clenched in a death grip on the witness-box rail in front of him. "It was an advance," he said lamely.

"An advance? Well, well, well. Mr. Sayer, on the same day that Coppertone's check for $90,000 cleared, did John Blandings, the senior member of the firm, deliver to you and to Mr. Sean Tate two checks, each in the amount of $25,000?"

Sayer could no longer control his trembling. The judge leaned over and spoke to him: "Are you feeling ill, Mr. Sayer?"

He shook his head. "No, I'm all right, Your Honor."

"Then please answer the question."

Sayer licked his parched lips. "That transaction had nothing to do with the advance we paid Blandings and Olson. John Blandings was repaying personal loans that Mr. Tate and I had tendered to him six months earlier to see him through a stock-market crisis."

"I see. . . . To your knowledge, had Miss Mara Tate contributed to this alleged loan to John Blandings?"

"Not to my knowledge."

The prosecutor looked back at the defense table and glared at Mara. "Then how do you account for the fact that a check for the identical sum of $25,000, and signed by John Blandings, was also delivered to Mara Tate at the offices of Tate International Industries on the same day that you and Mr. Tate received your checks?"

Sayer was thoroughly demoralized. He looked at Sean Tate in a desperate plea for help, but he would get no help from that totally vanquished man.

"I . . . I . . . It's too involved. You had better ask Miss Tate."

"I intend to do just that. . . . Just one more question, Mr. Sayer: To be accurate, should not the title of the law firm of Blandings and Olson really be *Sayer,* Blandings, and Olson? Isn't it true that you, sir, are the silent partner of John Blandings and Andrew Olson?"

Sayer's mouth opened, but nothing came out.

"Mr. Sayer, I must remind you that you are under oath. Please answer the question."

Sayer rested his elbows on the rail and covered his face with his hands. "Yes." His muffled reply was barely audible.

"That will be all, Mr. Sayer."

Hunter put Mara back on the witness stand, and although she was cool and composed, nothing she said could overcome the sordid picture that the prosecutor had put together out of Sayer's testimony. Her explanation that the $25,000 check she had received from Blandings and Olson, and two subsequent checks for the same amount, were repayments for the $75,000 she had loaned to Sean to aid him in acquiring Harlan Electronics—or so she had believed at the time—evoked skepticism from both the prosecutor and the judge.

After the session was over, Mara confided to Hunter, "Bob, if I were the judge, I wouldn't believe a damned thing that I testified to. Sean to Harvey to Mara—we're that old shifty double-play combo."

"Let's not jump to conclusions," he temporized. "I thought *you* came across with great sincerity."

They got a temporary reprieve when Judge Quentin Bascomb withheld his ruling on the SEC's motion for him to appoint a receiver to safeguard the interests of TII shareholders until the outcome of an impending federal grand jury investigation into the activities of the management of that firm.

On the day that Harvey Sayer received his subpoena to testify before the grand jury in Manhattan, he shot himself in the head and died in the operating room.

To Fiedler's dismay, Mara discontinued her therapy sessions. "Just temporarily, Max darling, until this awful mess is over and done with."

He took her hand in his hands. "Mara, now of all times you *need* therapy. Look at the way you're running your health into the ground. You're smoking what, two, three packs a day?"

"Four."

He slapped his forehead. *"Gott im Himmel!* And the booze—you must kill a fifth of Scotch a day."

"At least." She stood up, indicating that their interview was finished. "Max, I'm sorry; I've got to do it my own way. But I promise I will come back to you." She made a dramatic Garbo-like gesture and cast an arm across her eyes. Her voice was husky: "I *vill* come back to you, my beloved; but now I vant to be alone."

Testifying before the grand jury, Mara had to face her interrogators without benefit of counsel. It was an unsettling, lonely experience even for an honest man or woman. For days afterward, her reveries were haunted by vignettes of the events of that ordeal:

"This so-called $90,000 advance that Coppertone Cookware paid to Blandings and Olson—is it customary to pay out such a large sum of money in *advance* of services to be performed?"

"No, it is not," Mara replied. "Let me try to explain something to you. Yes, the sum of $90,000 seems exorbitant taken out of context; yet, in the annual budget of a diverse and large corporation such as Tate International Industries, it constitutes a rather insignificant sum. What I'm driving at is that I, as chairwoman of the board of directors of TII, cannot be expected to personally approve and scrutinize every transaction of company management. I have a score of responsible executives who have the authority to approve payments of that size, including Sean Tate, the president of Coppertone Cookware."

"Now, about the $90,000 'advance' that Coppertone Cookware paid to the law firm of Blandings and Olson . . . Subsequently Sean Tate, the late Harvey Sayer, and *you,* Miss Tate, received kickbacks of $25,000 apiece."

Mara was choking on her suppressed rage. "They were *not* kickbacks—not in my case, at least. I keep repeating that Blandings and Olson were acting as intermediaries, as counsels for Sean Tate, and the three $25,000 checks they sent to me constituted repayment for a $75,000 loan I had made to Mr. Tate the year before."

"Hmmm . . . Miss Tate, you have a reputation for being a businesswoman of exceptional acumen. Do you expect this panel to believe that the chairwoman of the board of TII would loan a colleague the sum of $75,000 for an indefinite period and *interest free?*"

"Sean Tate happens to be family. Yes, I don't charge interest to family members."

"How magnanimous of you, Miss Tate. This entire matter appears to be obfuscated by 'personal loans.' " Sean Tate and Harvey Sayer made personal loans to John Blandings. You made a personal loan to Sean Tate. I would say that what we are dealing with here is a game of musical loans."

The jurors applauded the snide joke with muffled laughter.

"Come on now, Miss Tate, surely you don't expect any reasonable man or woman to swallow all of these elaborately contrived coincidences?"

The grand jury did not accept any of her explanations, and she, along with Sean Tate, was indicted on seven counts—five counts of perjury, and two counts charging that they had filed false and misleading information in TII's annual report to the SEC.

Later that month, two stockholders of Coppertone Cookware and TII shares filed suit against Sean Tate and Mara Tate for recovery of $5 million for the companies, which, allegedly, Sean and Mara had "conspired to divert, along with other substantial funds and assets," to their own personal use. Federal Judge Norman Lewis ruled in the plaintiffs' favor, and Mara and Sean

Tate were ordered to reimburse the company treasury out of their own personal assets.

The dominoes were beginning to fall.

In a concurrent decision, Judge Bascomb, who was holding in abeyance his decision in the case of the SEC against Mara and Sean Tate, now decided in favor of the SEC, and he appointed a receiver to oversee the management of Tate International Industries.

The following day, Mara arrived at Max Fiedler's office without an appointment.

"I'm full up, Mara; you should have phoned." Reading the anguish in her eyes, he softened. "Tell you what: I'll cancel a luncheon date and see you from noon to two o'clock; that's my next appointment."

"I appreciate that, Max."

He had never seen her so wan and pale. All of the color and vibrancy he associated with Mara Tate were missing; she looked like a washed-out water color. It was his custom to make some comment about her appearance, but on this occasion, he limited comment to her attire, which consisted of a herringbone blazer over a silk shirt and a pencil-slim wool-knit skirt. "You must tell my wife who your dressmaker is. You look very, very chic. Then again, don't you always."

She smiled. "Nice try, Max, but I look like hell and you know it. I'll read my *Times* while I'm waiting."

"If you want anything—coffee, tea, or me—just tell Nancy."

"I'll wait for you."

It was over an hour before Nancy announced, "Dr. Fiedler will see you now, Miss Tate."

She entered his inner sanctum, as she always thought of it, and sat down in the comfortable leather chair across the desk from Fiedler.

He began, "I am not about to ask you how things

are going, because I've read all the papers. Cheap shot, the whole business."

"No, Max, the courts went along on the assumption that you can tell a person by the company he or she keeps. In this instance, I've been 'keeping company' with my cousin Sean and his parasite, Harvey Sayer, for far too long. I've been careless, indigent, smug, and self-satisfied—so much so, I didn't see the forest for the trees. I accept the judgment, and I'll take my medicine like a brave little girl. God, what it would be like to be a little girl again!"

The innocuous statement struck bad vibes with Fiedler. He steered the conversation away from nostalgic reminiscence. "That's one helluva stiff judgment, $5 million. I mean, I'd have to break open my piggy bank to make them shekels."

"The money is the least part of it. It won't break the bank, and that includes Sean's share as well. He hasn't got a pot to piss in anymore. . . . It's TII, Max. I feel as though someone decapitated me. The company has been my whole life; it's been the whole life of every Tate worth his or her salt, going back to Drew."

"There's more to life than money and work."

"Screw the money!"

"Work, then. 'All work and no play makes Jack a dull boy.'"

"My name isn't Jack, and I get all the playtime I require, more than most gals. Work is Adrenalin to me. The worst of it is that damned receiver the court appointed. Receivership is the kiss of death. Receivers have no imagination and they don't give a damn. They look upon a company with total detachment. They sit on their hands and mark time so as not to rock the boat, so that nobody can accuse *them* of mismanagement. No, Max, I'm afraid that this is the old ball game. The best thing I can do now is to resign

—permanently. Maybe I'll go back to Glammorgab."
She winked at him. "Want to be my shrink in residence,
Max?"

"I'll take it under advisement. . . . Anything special
you want to talk about today, aside from TII and the
case?"

She closed her eyes and leaned back in the chair.
"You know what really hurts, Max? Sean. I know the
kind of man he is—a liar, a cheat, a chiseler—but,
still and all, he's a Tate. It's a disgrace that a Tate
could let happen to him all that's happened to Sean.
I remember him as a young man, a college kid—him
and my other cousin, Brian Tate, Jr."

"The junior senator from Arizona?"

"Yes. The irony is that the family thought it would
be Sean who would make a name for himself. He was
the clever one—quick, charming, graduated *magna
cum laude*. He didn't have to end up like this. Do you
know that some of his moves at TII were close to
brilliant? Even the Coppertone Cookware fiasco. He
was getting the company back on its feet; the books
prove it. The damned fool! He steals pennies when he
could be earning hard bucks with half of the effort
and ability and aggravation. Why, Max . . . why?"

"There's a black sheep in every family; it's obliga-
tory."

She frowned. "Black sheep . . . damn! Sean isn't
the only one, either. My great grandfather, Drew Tate,
used to say that too much money thins the bloodline
and breeds decadence."

"Another way of putting it: 'Power corrupts, and
absolute power corrupts absolutely.'"

"Lord Acton . . . only it's 'Power *tends* to corrupt.'
Yes, money and power, they're readily interchange-
able. . . . Well, I guess the Tates have just about played
out the skein: Sean and I drummed out of the corps in
disgrace; the rest of the tribe scattered around the

world with the lotus eaters. For the most part, they're a ne'er-do-well lot:

"Cousin Larry—he's descended from Aunt Samantha, the daughter of Gilbert Tate—is a second-rate Hollywood producer." She smiled. "He's a real bastard, and I do mean *real;* Samantha got knocked up by a wastrel named Floyd Channing. . . . Then there's Samantha's twin brother, Preston, who was killed in World War One. Preston is Sean's father.

"Brian and Brian Jr., the senator, they're descended from Allan Tate. And, of course, there's Brian Jr.'s sister, Doris; she's married to a Texas oilman and has two kids in their teens. We rarely see the Lee Barons.

"Cousin Jean, Jane, and Carl all live in Europe. Carl is married to a Greek shipping heiress. Shirley Wilson, Emlyn Tate's middle daughter, is their mother. Her sister Grace married a Mormon missionary; they live in Salt Lake City and have a gaggle of kids I never saw. The Slocums don't approve of the rest of the wicked Tate clan. William was Emlyn's only son."

"General 'Buzz' Tate?" Fiedler inquired.

"That's Uncle Buzz. He was a big hero in both world wars and retired as a major general—Medal of Honor, the works."

"I'd say they constitute an illustrious family tree."

"No, they've all gone soft, except for Brian Jr. and me."

When she had first begun to speak about the family, Fiedler was toying with a novel desk ornament a patient had given him: a series of eight steel balls suspended from a chrome bar on thin wires and swinging freely within their frame stand. It was called a perpetual-motion machine—a misnomer, for it had to be properly activated; however, when it was, it could sustain motion for an extraordinary length of time. The ball on either end had to be swung out and up to the full extent of its wire and then released so that it would swing down and strike the next ball squarely. This ball, in turn, would transmit the energy to the next ball, and so on down the line to the last ball, which would be struck out and up into the air almost as high as the initial ball had been lifted. The cycle would be repeated until all of the original energy expended had been dissipated. It was fascinating to observe, and after a time the effect was mesmeric.

All during her discourse, Mara's eyes involuntarily followed the motion of the eight balls, back and forth, back and forth. Her expression was impassive, and gradually a desultory quality invaded her voice.

"You're getting very sleepy," Fiedler said; it was a command, not a question.

"I am tired suddenly."

"That's good. Relax. Let yourself float. Pretend you are a big balloon and that you are lifting out of the chair and drifting lazily toward the ceiling."

"How nice to be a balloon, floating on the balmy summer air currents."

"Yes, pretend we're in Florida." Outside his window, the thermometer affixed to the frame registered 20°. "I've heard rumors that Senator Tate entertains aspirations to be president one day."

"That may well be. He's a protégé of Jack Kennedy's, and he stands to be appointed to a cabinet post after the inauguration."

"There now, Mara," he went on in a coaxing, soothing tone, "you are released from your corporeal self. Up, up, up and away you go. Close your eyes and let yourself go."

She obeyed, and a serene, almost angelic expression softened her features, hard and tensed for so many weeks. The perpetual-motion machine was wearing down inexorably—*clack . . . clack . . . clack . . . clack . . . clack*—till at last the balls were still, trembling ever so slightly on their frail strands.

Mara's head slipped forward, and Fiedler looked pleased. He *was* pleased, and with good reason: He had succeeded in putting her into a trance without sodium pentothal. The next object was to deepen the state.

He stood up, walked around the desk, and bent over her. The lounge chair was adjustable, and he tilted it back so that she was in a reclining position. He snapped on the tape recorder on his desk, drew up a small stool, and sat down beside her, then took her hand and stroked the long, slender fingers.

"You have just drifted out of the window, Mara, and are floating up into the bright-blue sky. See all the fleecy clouds?"

"Oh, yes!" she said with enthusiasm. "They're so lovely."

He spoke softly and in a monotone, elevating her to exalted heights from which the world below was no more significant than a blue-green ball seen from astronomical regions of the universe.

"You are in another dimension now, Mara, another world, another time . . . another you."

Outside the window, the sound of a carillon playing "Silent Night" drifted up from the street.

"In less than a week it will be Christmas, Mara."

"I love Christmas, even more than my birthday."

"Tell me about a Christmas you loved the most."

CHAPTER FIVE

Mara Tate 'the second fell in love with Samuel Rodgers, Jr., at first sight. Her father, Gordon Ewing, now president of Tate International Industries, had made the acquaintance of Samuel Rodgers, Sr., during his travels in Europe. The Rodgers family had sizable investments in sugar both in Cuba and in the Hawaiian Islands; they had incurred heavy losses in their Cuban investments after the onset of the revolution in 1895.

From their home in England, the Rodgers family had crossed the Atlantic and were presently journeying across the United States to spend the Christmas holiday with their daughter and son-in-law, who operated a sugar-refining plant in San Francisco.

At Tucson they disembarked from the Southern Pacific Railroad and traveled overland by coach to Bisbee to spend a few days with the Ewings. They arrived on December 15, 1897.

It was just after noon, and Mara and her cousin Samantha were up in her boudoir stretched out on a bearskin rug before a blazing fire. Outside, it was a cold, bleak day, and the north wind whistled and creaked beneath the eaves.

Mara drew up her knees close to her chest and wrapped her arms around her legs. "I just love it up here on days like this. It's so . . . so cozy. I feel good all over."

Samantha, not quite a year younger than her cousin, reacted with a feline smile. There was definitely something catlike about the girl: the way her dark, straight hair was smoothed sleekly back, revealing her widow's peak; and the slant of her green eyes—a paler green than Mara's but a product of the same family genes.

"It would be a lot cozier if we had a couple of boys to snuggle up with us."

"Oh, Sammy!" Mara said, laughing. "Is that all you ever think about—boys?"

Samantha, lying on her stomach with her cheek resting on one forearm, stretched out her other hand and tickled the underside of one of Mara's thighs.

Mara started and pushed the hand away. "What do you think you're doing?"

Samantha smirked. "Suppose it had been that handsome Johnny Starr at school who tickled you like that instead of me? You'd swoon!" She rolled her eyes and flung her hands into the air. "Oh, Johnny, do it again —*please.*"

Mara blushed fire-red. "I'd slap his face, that's for sure."

"Maybe, but you'd be thinking 'Do it again.' "

"Oh, stop acting like a silly girl."

"I like being silly. Besides, why are you blushing if it's not true?"

"Because you are so outrageous. Your mother should hear you saying such things."

"Ha!" Samantha snorted. "My dear mother doesn't give a damn what I say or do. That's why she packs me off every chance she gets. If it isn't to school, it's to relatives. 'Samantha, dear, how would you like to visit Uncle Gordon and Aunt Mara and your grandpa and grandma for Christmas? You and Cousin Mara get along so famously, and there's nothing for you to do here in New York City,' " she said, in perfect mimicry of her mother, Jayne Minton Tate.

"Well, we do get along, Sammy," Mara said in a subdued voice. "And I just love having you here for

the holidays, really I do. Everybody does—honestly."
She crawled over on her hands and knees to where
Samantha was lying and put an arm around her thin
shoulders.

Samantha turned her head and looked up at Mara;
tears were glistening in her eyes. "Thanks, coz. There
isn't anyone in the world I love more than I love you."

The two cousins embraced in awkward silence.

Mara felt terrible for Samantha. Her mother had
endured three years in South America with her husband, Gilbert Tate, and then had returned to her
parents' town house in New York City with her twin
children, ostensibly for a summer vacation; but she
had never returned, and after ten years' absence, she
and Gilbert might just as well be divorced.

"These people who are visiting you from England,
what are they like?" Samantha suddenly asked.

"I don't know. They're visiting their daughter in
San Francisco, who is having a baby, and another child,
a son named Samuel Jr."

Samantha perked up. "Another 'Sammy' in the
house—how cozy. How old is he?"

"Twenty—too old for you, my girl."

"Why so? I think a man should be older than a
woman. He should have experience so that he can
break her in properly to sex."

Mara slapped her head and whooped with laughter.
"There she goes again! What do you know about sex?"

Samantha sat up and crossed her legs Indian fashion.
Her smile was foxy. "You'd be surprised, my dear.
Would you believe it if I told you that last semester
at school I actually did *it* with a boy from the prep
school down the road?"

Mara was shocked. "I don't believe you for a
minute."

"Then don't, but I did; I swear it. Let me tell you

in precise detail what happened, and then you'll believe me."

And she did. And with every sentence, Mara's eyes grew rounder and her mouth gaped wider and wider. Her face was flushed with excitement, her heart beat faster, and the kindling heat in her loins was not unpleasant at all. She squirmed restlessly on the fur rug as Samantha came to the climax of her tale:

"For the first time it felt very good, even if we didn't exactly make it work the way it should." She pressed a hand over her mouth and giggled. "He got so crazy, like he couldn't wait, poor boy, and silly thing that I am, I thought he had peed on my belly."

Mara grimaced. "It sounds dreadfully messy to me."

A knock on the door made them both leap up guiltily.

"Come in," Mara called out.

The door opened, and Maggie the maid poked her head into the room. "Miss Mara and Miss Samantha, the madam says you should both come down and meet the guests. They got here a little while ago."

"Is he good-looking, Maggie?" Samantha asked.

"Is who good-looking?" It dawned on her and she grinned. "Oh, you mean the young gentleman. Yes, he's quite good-looking: tall, slim—maybe too thin at that—wavy black hair, brown eyes, and his nose is a trifle too large. Matter of fact, he looks a bit like President Lincoln did when he was a youth—I saw photos—only better-looking."

"Sounds ripe to me, coz." Samantha ran to the bureau and examined herself in the mirror. I'd better change this frock; it makes me look too young. What will you wear, Mara?"

"My riding breeches, of course. I don't intend to give up my daily exercise just because some strange boy has descended upon us."

"Good, then I won't have any competition. I think

I'll wear my country-plaid shirtwaist dress. You know the one; it's got puff sleeves, buttoned cuffs, and a buttoned bodice."

"The brown-and-cream dress, yes, it's very chic. Are you going to wear a crinoline under it?"

"No, it doesn't require one; the skirt is shirred and the lightly stiffened cummerbund gives it plenty of flair. . . . Do you have a teddy I can borrow, something really frothy and wicked?"

"You are positively mad!" Mara hooted. "He's not going to see your underclothing!"

Samantha's cat-eyes gleamed. "A smart girl always prepares for the unexpected."

Mara laughed and threw her arms around her cousin. "You certainly brighten life up for me, Sammy. I wish you didn't have to leave ever."

Ten minutes later Mara went tripping down the sweeping circular staircase, clad in riding boots, breeches, and a plaid woolen shirt. Her long black hair was braided across the top of her head. She went directly to the parlor, where her mother and father and the newcomers were sipping sherry and eating tea sandwiches.

Her mother appraised her disapprovingly. "Mara, you're not going riding today when we have visitors?"

"I won't be more than an hour, Mother, I promise."

Gordon Ewing introduced the Rodgerses. "My daughter, Mara, namesake of her mother . . . Mara, this is Mr. and Mrs. Rodgers and their son, Samuel Jr."

"How do you do?" She made a somewhat awkward curtsy. She did not see the son at first because he was standing off to one side admiring a painting of a section of Grand Canyon. When she did notice him, a chill ran along her spine.

He was gorgeous! Unlike so many young men of the burgeoning Arizona high society, who affected the dandy fashion in imitation of their eastern cousins

—pretty, foppish boys with slicked-back hair, pencil-thin mustaches, and lacquered fingernails—Sam Rodgers, Jr., was clean-shaven, had wavy black hair, as Maggie had said, and a profile that could have been carved out of Arizona granite. His teeth were slightly crooked, and there was a wide space between the top front incisors.

"Hello there, Mara," he said in a voice that had the resonance of a bass-organ pipe.

"He-hello," she stammered, feeling the blood rise in her swanlike neck.

"She's positively lovely, Mrs. Ewing," Mrs. Rodgers offered.

"So much like her beautiful mother," the elder Rodgers said. "You must be very proud of her, Gordon."

"I am indeed, although you are not seeing her in her most elegant plumage. Mara, child, you look like a stableboy. He put one arm around his daughter's waist and the other around his wife's. "Peas in a pod, her grandfather calls them." He winked at the other man. "Of course, that was before my dear wife put on weight."

"Gordon Ewing!" his wife said, feigning outrage. "Imagine you complaining about my weight! Just look at that paunch of yours." She slapped his stomach with the back of her hand.

Everyone laughed, and the couple exchanged an affectionate hug. They didn't look their age. Perhaps they had added a few pounds, but their figures were still fine, if a bit more stolid and settled than when they first met.

"Well, if you are going riding, hop to it," Gordon said. "Supper will be a half-hour early tonight."

Mara looked uncertain, perplexed. She walked to a window and looked out across the rolling plain behind the house. Tangled balls of tumbleweed skittered across the windswept terrain like great bouncing rubber balls. Abruptly she turned back to the others and, somewhat self-consciously, announced, "I do think I can forego my riding for one day. It's not a particularly pleasant day for it."

Her mother's dark eyes gleamed with feminine intuition as she looked from Mara to Sam Jr. and back to Mara. "Perhaps Sam would care to ride with you tomorrow, dear. You can show him the countryside."

Sam was enthused. "I say, that would be marvelous."

Mara excused herself. "I must go up and bathe and dress." She curtsied again and left the room.

She found Samantha crouching on the staircase, suppressing her giggling with both hands. Mara lifted an eyebrow. "Eavesdropping again, are you?"

"I just had a peek into the parlor." She clasped her hands over her bosom and sighed. "He's positively a dream. And don't you love his British accent?"

"He's all right." Mara shrugged and stomped up the stairs, with Samantha at her heels.

"All right! Oh, no, my dear cousin, you can't fool me. You are infatuated with him. It stuck out all over you."

Mara stopped and looked back at her, aghast. "Oh, it did, did it? Stop teasing me, Sam."

"Oh, not to him it didn't—men are such naïve creatures—but I'll wager your mother noticed it; his mother, too."

They went up to Mara's room and made preparations for a grand entrance before supper, timing their descent to coincide with Sam's presence in the downstairs front hall, where Gordon was showing the Rodgers men the huge crystal chandelier in the center of the cathedral ceiling.

"Had it shipped all the way from Copenhagen," he was saying.

The three men lapsed into silence at sight of the

two beautiful young girls as they came down the staircase with mincing, demure steps. Their long skirts concealed their feet, and they seemed to float from the second floor to the marble foyer floor.

Samantha was wearing her country-plaid shirtwaist gown. Her hair, worn loose, was gathered up gently in a chignon snood festooned with semiprecious gems.

Mara wore a wispy gown of superfine pima cotton, an old-English flower print with a rounded shoulder yoke, long, billowy, push-up sleeves, and a two-tiered skirt nipped in by a cummerbund. Her hair was a high Grecian swirl, "a confection," as young Sam termed it, held in place by elegant combs and barrettes. The one year's seniority she held over her cousin was never more apparent than when they were attired in formal dress.

The object of their mutual affection, Sam Jr., treated Mara like a woman; but, to Samantha's chagrin and sorrow, he regarded her as the "kid cousin." "He even patted me on the head like a child!" she complained bitterly later.

Business and politics dominated the conversation at dinner that night.

"When we were in New York, we met a friend of yours, Gordon," Samuel Rodgers said, "a William Andrews Clark."

Gordon grinned. "Andy Clark, that old horse thief. The United Verde mine at Jerome. Did you ever hear how he pulled off that deal? Phelps-Dodge designated Dr. James Douglas as their agent to buy the property from Eugene Jerome. Jim, frugal Scotsman that he is, submitted an offer of $30,000. Jerome said he wouldn't take less than $300,000. When Douglas related what had happened to Phelps-Dodge, they told him to grab it for $300,000—it was worth ten times that at least—but he was too late. Andy Clark, of Butte, Montana, had closed the deal for the asking price only a few hours before. He's quite an operator, that Andy. They say he keeps the left side of the ledger in Jerome—as part of the contract, they named the city after him—and the right side of the ledger in New York."

"The left hand doesn't know what the right hand is doing," Rodgers observed.

"And neither does anyone else. You know, there's been talk now for several years about levying a bullion tax on all the mines in Arizona and Montana. Every time it comes up, Clark sends his superintendent to the Jerome bank and he makes an exorbitant withdrawal. Andy tugs at his red beard and winks. 'Gotta go to Phoenix and buy me some mules and jackasses,' he says. A few days later he comes back minus the money and without any livestock. Coincidentally, the tax bill dies in the committee within the week. There's a standing joke that it's the 'mule legislature.' Andy brags that they are the best legislators money can buy."

The men laughed uproariously, but the ladies didn't think it was amusing at all. "That's how unscrupulous characters like Clark get away with murder," Gordon's wife chided. "Everyone laughs at his chicanery. He's becoming a folk hero."

"His time will come," Gordon assured her. "As soon as the territory achieves statehood, the federal government will put the wraps on Andy and all the others like him."

"Is that an imminent possibility?" Rodgers wanted to know.

"Five, ten years at the most, but it's inevitable. Speaking of the federal government, what is Washington doing about protecting American investments in Cuba?"

"War fever is building day by day, particularly after the disparaging remarks the Spanish minister made about President McKinley. Mind you, this situation has far more ominous implications for the United States than it does for England. That canal you chaps are planning to build across the isthmus—the strategic importance of Cuba is unmistakable."

"Yes, a hostile government in Cuba could pose a serious threat to the canal in the event of war," Gordon said. "It would seem that the United States must do everything possible to ensure that such a threat is removed."

"War with Spain?" his wife asked.

"I'm afraid so."

She shuddered. "I'm glad I don't have a son. If he took after his father, he'd be the first to enlist."

"If the United States declares war on Spain, I for one will enlist," young Sam declared.

"Don't talk nonsense," his mother snapped. "You're a British subject."

"That's true, but father's investments in Cuban sugar are in jeopardy the same as the Americans'."

"By Jove, you're right, son." His father clapped him on the shoulder. "Bully for you! I'd join up myself if they'd have me."

"Old fool," his wife said.

After the meal, the ladies retired to the parlor, where the maid served them coffee and cordials, and the men went off to Gordon's study for brandy and cigars. Young Sam chose to remain with the women despite his father's frown of disapproval.

When he had finished his coffee, Sam stood up and walked over to the oil painting of the Grand Canyon.

"It fascinates you, doesn't it?" Mara said.

"It's one of the wonders of the world," he said, with awe in his voice. "I recently read a book about the Grand Canyon—the diaries of a fellow named John Wesley Powell."

"Yes, he was the first to navigate the entire length of the canyon."

Sam's eyes gleamed. "What sport. Do you know I'm

considered an excellent yachtsman over in England? My first year at Oxford I won first prize rowing a one-man shell."

"Why don't you come back this summer and take a boat through the Grand Canyon?"

"Yes indeed." Samantha nudged Mara with an elbow. "My dear cousin would be delighted if you'd visit her next summer," she said, then added: "So you could see the canyon, *of course*."

"I just might take you up on that," he said with enthusiasm.

"And I'll be your copilot on the boat," Mara said.

Samantha giggled. "Listen to the silly girl."

"It's not silly at all. Do you agree, Sam?"

He shifted from one foot to the other. "Well . . . I don't think boating through the Grand Canyon is exactly a feminine pastime."

Mara stamped her foot. "I'll have you know that a Mrs. Edward Ayres navigated the Grand Canyon almost twenty years ago! I'm just as competent as you are, Sam Rodgers, and don't you ever forget it! I can do anything a man can do. If we go to war with Cuba, maybe *I'll* enlist!"

"Don't be angry with me," Sam remonstrated. "I stand corrected."

"I'm not angry!" she said in pique.

"Yes you are; I can tell by the way those golden flecks in your eyes begin to swirl like the bubbles in mineral water."

Mara blushed. "It's too bad if you don't like my eyes."

"To the contrary, you have beautiful eyes, and I'd be honored to have you accompany me on a boat trip through the Grand Canyon."

Later that night, after Mara and Samantha had gone to bed, Samantha teased her cousin: " 'To the contrary, you have beautiful eyes,' " she gushed in a broad imitation of Sam's English accent.

"Oh, shut up and go to sleep, brat!"

"I'll wager you'll be dreaming of Sam tonight," she said slyly. "You and Sam sailing along the Colorado River." She tittered. "Better still, you and Sam in bed together!"

Mara was glad for the darkness, because she could feel herself blushing. "You should have your mouth washed out with soap, Samantha Tate!"

"Just the same, you wouldn't mind if Sam were to climb into bed with you, coz."

"Stop it! I won't hear another word. I'm covering my ears."

"Good night, dear cousin Mara. Remember, sweet dreams."

"I hope you have a violent nightmare."

The girlish chatter subsided, and Mara swiftly felt herself drifting into the warm, pleasant, lethargic state that precedes sleep—so drowsy, half asleep, balanced on the borderline between consciousness and unconsciousness, the mind relaxed, vulnerable to suggestion.

Just the same, you wouldn't mind if Sam were to climb into the sack with you, coz.

The seven days that the Rodgerses spent at the Ewing home before departing for San Francisco were among the happiest and most memorable days in the life of Mara the second. She and Sam spent the better part of each morning touring the countryside on horseback. They visited the site of the old Copper King mine up Tombstone Canyon, a rambling complex of low, flat buildings, mills, and heavy mining machinery. The din was so loud they had to shout to communicate.

"It never stops, night and day," she yelled.

Sam grimaced and covered his ears with his hands. "I'd go mad if I had to listen to it constantly."

She laughed. "My grandfather says it's the music he likes to hear—the stamping machines pounding out copper and gold and silver—better than any brass band."

"Gold and silver?"

"By-products along with the copper. Still, Arizona ranks with the leading gold and silver producers in the world, even though it's the copper that is king."

"I'd like to have a go at looking for gold."

" 'Prospecting,' not 'looking for,' " she corrected him. "If you want to be an Arizonan, you'll have to learn to talk like one."

Sam reached out and tousled her hair. "Precocious brat."

"Do you know how the Tates first discovered the Copper King? My father was chasing my mother up this very gulch, and when she slipped, she dislodged this outcropping that was rich in copper carbonate."

"Chasing your mother? I say, that's a novel way to *prospect* for gold—chasing young women about in the wilderness." He looked at her squarely. "By the way, did he accomplish his purpose? With your mother, I mean."

She gave him a saucy sidelong glance. "I would surmise he did. After all, I am here as living testimony that his mission was accomplished—ultimately, in any case."

Sam threw back his leonine head and laughed at the sky. "Your mother should hear you."

She slapped her horse's rump and took off at a gallop, yelling back to him, "You can chase me. Maybe lightning will strike twice."

She led him up a winding trail to the top of the tallest mountain in the area. From a mesa on top, there was a breathtaking view of the rugged, beautiful —often grotesquely beautiful—landscape for miles around.

"What a grandiose panorama," Sam said, with the humility mortal man invariably feels when confronted with eternal grandeur.

"It's hard to believe that all of this land was once covered by the sea. Layer upon layer of clam shells became the limestone that is the bedrock of the territory."

Sam contemplated it in reverent silence: the rocky spires, deep valleys, caves, waterfalls, and infinite expanses of sand and rock adorned by gigantic monuments sculpted by the hand of God.

They ate a picnic lunch under a tree while the horses grazed nearby.

"Too bad you have to leave so soon," she told him. "There is so much you haven't seen—the cave homes of the ancient cliff dwellers; the Petrified Forest; Montezuma Castle, a genuine castle constructed in the middle of a hundred-fifty-foot cliffside. Oh yes, and the White Dove, an old Spanish mission, so dazzlingly beautiful it makes one want to cry. The dome is a miracle of architecture, and, in a way, the monks who supervised the work did effect a miracle of sorts with respect to the dome. What they did was to fill the mission with sand right to the top; then they had the workers shape a mold of the dome out of wet sand and pour the mortar on top of it. Once it had set, the Indian workers had to shovel out all of the sand; it must have taken them weeks, maybe months."

"They must have been very amiable chaps, the Indians, to put up with all of that backbreaking work."

Mara grinned over her sandwich. "There's where the miracle comes in. The monks had laced the sand with gold coins at night when the workers weren't around. So, when it came time to remove the sand, they divulged what they had done. You can imagine the enthusiasm of those Indians after that."

Sam laughed. "White man's chicanery again. Pity the noble savages."

Before they started back, he took a small package wrapped in white tissue paper out of his saddlebag. "I want you to have this as a memento of me. We'll be leaving tomorrow morning, you know. It's not a Christmas gift, just a remembrance."

She squealed with delight. "Oh, Sam, how thoughtful of you!" She untied and opened it with eager fingers and held the object up to the light. It was a round glass paperweight filled with water and particles of a white substance that resembled snowflakes. Inside the globe were two small porcelain figurines, a boy and a girl, holding hands.

Sam took it from her. "Here, see? You turn it upside down like this, then right side up again, and we have a snowstorm enveloping our two lovers."

"How novel. How lovely." She took it back and studied the microcosm within the globe. "Two lovers."

The spectacle hypnotized her, and she experienced an odd sensation. If she concentrated with sufficient intensity, it would be possible for her to project the spirit, the soul—whatever one chose to label that intangible twin of the corporeal self—inside the globe. She would be that girl, Sam that boy—lovers frolicking in the snow.

"Oh, Sam, I'm going to miss you so much. Thank you!" She reached up, put a hand at the back of his head, drew down his face close to hers, and kissed him softly on the lips; then she broke away and walked briskly to her horse.

"It's time we were starting home." She mounted, careful to keep her eyes to the front; it wouldn't do to let him know that she was crying.

CHAPTER SIX

Gordon Ewing came down to breakfast on the morning of February 16, 1898, to find a special edition of the Tombstone *Epitaph* folded alongside his plate.

"It was delivered on the early-morning coach," the maid informed him.

When he opened it, the headline leaped off the page at him, bright red letters an inch high: BATTLESHIP MAINE SUNK IN HAVANA HARBOR! ! ! "Sneaky bastards!" he cursed as his wife entered the dining room.

"Whatever is it, Gordon?"

"The Spanish have sunk one of our battlewagons off Cuba—Two hundred sixty men lost."

"How horrible!"

He slammed the paper down. "This means war; no way out of it now."

After two months of futile negotiations, the war fever of the indignant American public, encouraged and inflamed by certain irresponsible newspapers—namely, the yellow journals of publisher William Randolph Hearst—raged to such a pitch that Congress and the executive branch were compelled to take drastic action.

President McKinley demanded that Spain withdraw from Cuba, an ultimatum that no nation could accede to and retain its honor and prestige, wherefore on April 24 Spain declared war on the United States.

In no section of the country was patriotism more

zealous than in the four remaining western territories: Arizona, New Mexico, Oklahoma, and the Indian Territory. Prospectors, cowboys, even the college-bred scions of Arizona high society flocked to hastily formed enlistment stations.

In the early part of May, Mara received a visit from her old friend Marion Murphy, retired from the oldest profession and the reigning queen of Phoenix's social whirl.

"Marion, you look marvelous," Mara said, embracing her.

"You too, ducks. How are things with you?"

"Couldn't be better."

They made small talk for a half-hour or so over tea and sandwiches; then Marion divulged the purpose of her visit:

"They say there's a shortage of nurses in the army. I intend to form a corps right here in Arizona and volunteer for combat service. Back in the early days, women like us, we got plenty of experience attending to the sick and the wounded, the casualties from Indian warfare and barroom shoot-outs. Can I count you in, Mara?"

"You certainly can. How do we start?"

"I still hold leases on my old cathouses at the other end of Mule Pass Gulch. I'm going to clear out one of them and turn it into an enlistment center and training school for nurses. Tomorrow I've got a carload of instruction manuals and two genuine nurses coming down from the capital to get the operation under way."

Young Mara burst into the room, clad in a grimy riding habit. "Aunt Marion, what a wonderful surprise!" She rushed over to Marion and hugged her.

Marion kissed her and patted her derriere. "My, we're getting to be a big girl, aren't we?" She eyed the girl's burgeoning breasts straining against the wool of her sweater. "You look divine, ducks, but you smell like a mountain goat."

"I should; the new gelding took a spill in the sheep meadow and I landed in a pile of manure. I'm off to have a bath; but first, what is this about an enlistment center?"

Marion outlined her plans for forming a nursing corps to serve in the Spanish-American War.

"What a marvelous idea!" she exclaimed. "I want to join along with Mother, of course."

"I'm afraid not, darling," her mother said. "You are much too young to enlist."

The daughter's green eyes flashed with defiance, and the golden flecks swirled dazzlingly. "I am not! I may be fifteen, but inside I feel much older."

"*Look* older as well," Marion conceded.

"Marion, don't encourage her."

It required no one's encouragement, for Mara the second, blessed—or cursed—with her mother's obstinacy, tenacity, and iron will, would not be diverted from her purpose.

Her mother finally gave in to a lame compromise. "Well, you can take instruction at the center with us, but as far as serving in a combat zone, that is out of the question. Your father and I won't have it, not for an instant."

That evening at dinner, Gordon informed them, "Most of our boys are competing to get into the First United States Cavalry. They'll make good horse soldiers, being used to riding and outdoor life. 'Rough Riders' or 'Teddy's Terrors,' as they are colorfully called, will be training at San Antonio, Texas."

"Teddy's Terrors?" His wife was puzzled.

"Theodore Roosevelt, our former assistant secretary of the navy. He's resigned to organize the regiment."

Marion beamed. "Good old Teddy. Met him a few

years back when he was hunting mountain goats out here."

Gordon lifted an eyebrow at her. "Was it a social or a professional association?"

His wife scolded him. "Gordon, what a terrible joke, and in front of your daughter, no less."

"Oh, Mother," Mara said in exasperation, "I am practically a grown woman, and I do know about the facts of life. And I know what the men who visit Aunt Marion's bordellos go there for."

"Mara, another word out of you and you will go to your room!"

Gordon and Marion were chuckling behind their napkins. Gordon winked at the ex-madam and said to his wife, "After all, my dear, she *is* your daughter."

"A chip off the old block, as me old mum used to say," Marion agreed.

"To get back to Teddy Roosevelt," Gordon said; "he's a man of enormous vitality and charm, just what our cavalry shock troops need to whip them into fighting shape. He's even attracted a following of Ivy League young men from back east. The Denver *Post* ran a headline: 'Dudes Are All Right; Curled Darlings of Society Join Teddy's Terrors.' And another journal observed: 'The New York swells who enlisted in the First Regiment of the U.S. Volunteer Cavalry had to leave their valets at home.' The editorial writer went on to say, 'There is local fear that the simple manners and customs of the New Mexico cowboy may be contaminated and his morals contaminated by contact with these New York slickers.' Isn't that amusing?"

All of them laughed, with the exception of young Mara. "I hope the Rodgerses returned to England before this war business broke out."

"Oh?" said her mother, and they all stared at Mara.

"What I mean is, you recall what young Sam said about enlisting if war broke out?"

"I daresay his headstrong statement was just that—youth blowing off steam."

"I don't think so, Father. Sam meant precisely what he said. If he is still in the United States, he'll be among the first to join up."

She was unusually silent for the remainder of the meal, and when it was over, she excused herself and went up to her bedroom, where, though it was still early, she climbed into bed. Sleep eluded her, however. Her head was spinning with thoughts of Sam Rodgers and war and becoming a nurse. Young she might be, but Mara was determined to be the best nurse in the training program.

Her arms were folded loosely across her chest. Idly she brought up her hands and cupped her breasts, massaged them ever so gently, her body warming pleasurably and her nipples rising stiffly against her palms.

She shut her eyes and conjured up an image of herself and Sam in bed together, naked flesh pressed against naked flesh. Her heartbeat quickened, and her entire body was bathed in an aura of teasing erotic lassitude. Dear God, how she desired the hard male flesh of Sam Rodgers! Never in her life had she seen a man sexually aroused. (True there had been several dirty little boys at school who had exposed themselves to her and other girls, but they didn't count.) She strained to visualize Sam kneeling over her, turgid with lust for her soft body. It was *his* hands on her breasts. Mara moaned and began to rotate her bare buttocks against the sheet. Her nerve endings were so sensitive that sheet, covers—anything that came into contact with her flesh—felt searing hot. She was consumed with passion.

Mara wondered whether there were places such as Marion had introduced to Bisbee, houses of ill repute, which catered to a female clientele. If so, she would have been sorely tempted to patronize the establishment, so urgent was her need.

The following week the supplies and the two trained nurses arrived at Bisbee from Phoenix. The house designated by Marion as their training headquarters had been stripped of the more frivolous appointments necessitated by the profession of its previous tenants: lewd paintings and murals; French bidets; and the whips and chains and other bizarre devices preferred by certain unconventional clients.

Marion addressed the volunteers, who numbered a dozen girls between the ages of fifteen and twenty-five, not counting the elder Mara and the nurses from Phoenix.

"Our textbook will be the *United States Army Manual of Field Medicine,* issued by the surgeon general's office. I expect each and every one of you —and that includes Mrs. Ewing and myself—to read a chapter each night after classes are over and to be prepared the following session to answer questions posed to you by Miss Joan Hagen and Miss Cecile Dumas, our nursing instructors.

"This course will consist of four weeks' basic training, after which our group will be assigned by the surgeon general to a medical and nursing team attached to a military unit.

"One more thing before we commence: Miss Hagen and Miss Dumas will require living quarters during their stay in Bisbee. I would put them up at my home here, but there are extenuating circumstances that prevent such an arrangement." She cleared her throat self-consciously.

Mara the first concealed a smile with her hand. She was aware that for the past week a prominent U.S. senator had taken up residence in Marion's fashionable villa on the outskirts of Bisbee, one of a dozen palatial homes she owned. His face and name were almost as well known as President McKinley's, and it was essential that his anonymity be preserved.

Mara spoke up: "Marion, I would consider it a privilege to have the two young ladies stay with our family. We have ample living space, and I am sure that they and my daughter Mara will enjoy one another's company."

The young women were obviously pleased. Joan Hagen was a pleasant-looking, slightly plump girl of twenty-three, whose jolly round face was distinguished by pretty blue eyes and bright freckles across her cheeks and the bridge of her nose.

Cecile Dumas was a striking brunette with classic features, intense black eyes, high cheekbones, and jet-black hair cut to near-boyish length, with bangs curling down over her high forehead. She was tall and willowy, with small breasts, curvaceous hips and buttocks, and long, slender legs. Her parents were French immigrants who had settled in Phoenix, and Cecile, who had been eight when they arrived in America, still retained a charming hint of her native tongue. She was twenty years old.

In the first lesson, which lasted two hours, Joan and Cecile demonstrated elementary first aid: how to apply a tourniquet and a pressure bandage to stop bleeding; the various methods and antiseptics employed to disinfect wounds, bed clothing, and other paraphernalia; techniques of isolation of patients suspected of carrying infectious diseases; and, to the mortification of the more sensitive young women, a candid lecture on how to deal with venereal disease.

"And that goes for every one of you girls here, too," Marion interjected. "You are going to be subjected to a good deal of attention from the young soldiers you meet. They are lonely men away from home and family, frightened of the uncertainty ahead of them, and they will be starved for comfort and affection. Also, they will outnumber you females more than a hundred to one. So you see, pretty young women like yourselves will be a commodity more sought after than even food or drink. . . . Now, as me old mum used to tell me, 'Marion, if you can't be good, at least be careful.' Do I make myself clear? If you're going to indulge in hanky-panky, when it's done, be sure to douche with a strong mixture of vinegar and water, with a dash of iodine mixed in for good measure."

All of the Bisbee volunteers, with the exception of young Mara, were blushing furiously and giggling out of embarrassment, their eyes fixed shyly on the floor.

Mara, her face furrowed in concentration, was scribbling away industriously in her notebook: "Vinegar . . . water . . . dash of iodine," she murmured, and wet her lips with her tongue.

Later, when they were walking home, Mara, Joan, and Cecile, the French girl observed, "Mara, you and your beautiful mama are not like the other American women I have met. If sex is mentioned, they become outraged or else they faint with shame. They like to pretend it does not exist, fornication between men and women, that it's something to be done guiltily in the dark. There was a young bride, a nurse, I met in St. Francis Hospital, where I worked for a time. I asked her how she liked her sex life with her new husband. At first she was so shocked that she couldn't even speak. When she found her voice, she said, 'When we have sex, I close my eyes, think of the American flag and hum "The Star-Spangled Banner." ' *Mon Dieu*"— Cecile slapped her forehead in mystification—"the poor deprived things do not know what they are missing, eh, Joanie?" She nudged her friend in the ribs with an elbow.

Joan Hagen was mildly flustered. "Is that all you ever think of, Cecile?"

Cecile shrugged. "We French females are born with the instinct for sex, just as we are born with the instinct to eat and drink and breathe. It is a necessity of life, no?"

"Hardly a necessity of life," Joan demurred.

"You are a hypocrite, my friend. I know what you and that handsome young intern were doing every night back in the linen room—adding to the dirty linen!" She laughed boisterously.

Mara compressed her lips and said with determination, "I for one cannot wait to experience sex. It must be marvelous if two people love each other."

"Love . . . what is love?" Cecile philosophized. "Is it in the heart or in the head or in the loins exclusively?"

"Some of all three," Mara offered.

By the time they reached the Ewing homestead, situated on top of one of the highest hills surrounding Bisbee, Joan and Cecile were exhausted.

"Mon Dieu," Cecile gasped, "you do this every *day?"*

"Not every day; sometimes I ride a horse. But the exercise will do you both good. Do you know that Bisbee is no doubt the only city in the country where there is no postal delivery? All the dwellings are built on such steep hillsides, no sensible man would accept the job."

She showed them to their living quarters—a spacious L-shaped room with two single beds and a dressing area. "The bath is at the end of the hall," she said.

The Phoenix girls were traveling light, one suitcase apiece. "Where we will be going, we won't be needing any feminine fripperies," Cecile said. "The army will issue us our nurses' uniforms."

She cast her cashmere shawl over a chair back, removed her starched shirtwaist, and stepped out of her town skirt, tight-fitted and trimmed with a flounce of wool. She was not the least self-conscious about undressing in front of her companions. When she removed her petticoat, Mara's eyes widened. Cecile's sole undergarment was a sheer peach chemise trimmed with gauzy lace. The dark-thatched V of her groin was visible under the diaphanous material.

"No feminine fripperies?" Mara mused. "My dear Cecile, if you arrive at an army post wearing provocative underclothes like that, you may well be raped by the whole regiment!"

"Oo-la-la!" The French girl clapped her hands together gleefully. "I can hardly wait."

Joan Hagen shook her head indulgently. "Mara, she's really not as bad as she pretends. I've seen more than one doctor at St. Francis get his face slapped for mistaking our little Frenchy's antics."

Cecile sniffed. "Only because they didn't say please."

Mara laughed. "You are incorrigible, Cecile."

Supper that evening was an informal affair. Mara and her mother, out of deference to the nurses from Phoenix, who had a limited wardrobe, wore plain town gowns. Joan wore a modest gray tailored suit with a wasp waist accentuated by a boned corset. Cecile, however, sported a long-sleeved white satin blouse with a plunging neckline, and a bell skirt trimmed with flounces, lawn ruffles, and lace frills.

"She's charming," Gordon commented to his wife in an aside before they sat down.

"She certainly outshines the rest of us tonight. I expected the poor child to appear in sackcloth and ashes, from the way she spoke earlier.

Cecile proved to be a scintillating conversationalist as well as a charmer, and her knowledge of French industry and commerce astonished Gordon.

"You wouldn't happen to be related to Pierre Dumas of Paris?" he inquired.

"To be sure, Monsieur Ewing. He is my uncle, my father's brother."

"That is amazing. Pierre and I were very close friends when I first went to Europe. How is the old roué these days?"

"We received a letter from him last week. Uncle Pierre is a staunch supporter of the United States in this conflict with Spain. It was at his urging that my brother Louis enlisted in the service; and I left my nursing position at St. Francis for the same cause." She extended an arm straight into the air in a salute: *"Vive l'Amerique!"*

Gordon beamed. "I'll drink to that." He sipped his wine. "By the way, how do you think our California *vin blanc* compares with the French wine?"

"I am no connoisseur, Monsieur Ewing, but for myself I like it very much." She lifted her glass in a toast: "To the ultimate victory of the United States and the downfall of Spain. *A toute force,* may it overcome!"

"Le Commencement de la fin," Gordon said, tapping her glass with his own.

Mara exchanged a look of vexation with her daughter. "How nice you have this opportunity to brush up on your French, Gordon," she said archly.

He sensed her meaning and said brusquely, "Yes indeed; I must be terribly rusty."

"Not at all, sir," Cecile objected. "Your accent is *magnifique*. You might have been native-born."

"Well, thank you, my dear." He touched the ascot at his throat self-consciously and cleared his throat. Then, changing the subject, he addressed his daughter: "Speaking of the war, I had a cablegram from Sam Rodgers today regarding his investments in South America. He intends to visit Gilbert down in Buenos Aires next month. He informed me that his son remained in San Francisco with his sister's family and that now he has enlisted in the American army. It would seem I misjudged that lad's backbone and determination."

His daughter clasped a hand to her throat; she experienced the frightening sensation that her heart was fluttering in her chest like a terrified bird. "When? Where is he? What kind of service?"

"Samuel didn't say, but my guess would be cavalry. Young Sam was an accomplished equestrian back in London, rode in all the fashionable events."

"Oh, dear," his daughter said faintly, and for the remainder of the meal she was subdued and contributed little to the conversation.

Sleep did not come easily to Mara that night. The muted chimes of the grandfather clock in the lower hall tolled eleven, then midnight, and finally one. She twisted and turned and squirmed; cast off the covers because she was too hot; minutes later, shivered from cold and pulled them back over her tormented body.

Sam Rodgers—he was the cause of her restlessness. *Sam! Sam! Sam!* she cried out silently as she conjured up images of his long, lithe, muscular body, his granite profile, as craggy and indomitable as the stone testimonials carved out of the Arizona terrain by centuries of wind and rain and glacial snow and ice. Tears oozed out of her closed eyelids as she summoned up that glorious instant when her lips had caressed his.

Sam, I love you!

She started at the unexpected sound, a gentle rapping at her door, fracturing the dead silence of the night. She sat upright. Her vocal cords were tight, and it was difficult to speak: "Yes? Who is it?"

"It is I, Cecile. May I come in?"

"Cecile? Yes . . . come in, Cecile."

The door opened with a gentle creaking, and the French girl entered the room on soundless bare feet. She was encompassed within a penumbra of yellow candlelight cast by the pewter holder she carried in her right hand.

Closing the door silently and leaning back against it, she said, "I'm sorry to trouble you, Mara, but I can't sleep. I'm so high-strung, I feel as if I'm about to crawl out of my skin. It must be the strangeness of these new surroundings."

Mara sighed. "That's all right, Cecile. I feel the same way, and these are not unfamiliar surroundings to me. It must be the excitement of our new venture. I've never been away from my family in my entire life, and shortly the two of us will be crossing a new frontier, going into the unknown—God only knows our destination. . . . Do come in and sit down." She patted the bed and glanced at the fireplace aglow with dying embers. "If you'd like, we can put another log on the hearth."

"Oh, I *would* like that, Mara. I have such an urgent need to be close to another human being. You're right. I feel so alone away from my family in Phoenix. It's strange. I've known you for only one day, but I feel closer to you than I do to my old friend Joan."

"I'm flattered, Cecile; I like you, too. And I like Joan."

"Of course. It's just that I feel that you and I share . . . I don't know how to define it."

"I understand. I think the word is 'empathy.' " She got out of bed and walked over to the fireplace, where she removed the fire screen and laid a dry log on the cherry-red embers. There was a crackle, a puff of smoke, and the wood ignited in a shower of sparks.

"There, that feels wonderful." She sat down cross-legged on the thick fur rug before the hearth and wrapped the heavy flannel nightgown tightly about her body.

Cecile came toward her, gliding like a wraith across the thick carpet, her breasts and hips undulating sensuously. Her perfect teeth, framed in the fragile oval of her Latin face, gleamed like pink pearls. She emerged from the shadows into the rosy perimeter of the firelight, a vision of loveliness in a billowy black-silk nightgown with a frosting of lace and ribbon beading.

Mara was mildly surprised that she would don such frivolous nightwear under the particular circumstances; Cecile was a nurse going off to war, not a giddy bride on her honeymoon. Still, Mara respected everyone's right to say, act, and dress as one pleased, so long as his or her behavior did not infringe on the civil rights of other people.

"Fire feels good. This nightgown was not intended to provide much warmth." Her smile was subtly suggestive as she went to the hearth and turned her back on the flames, her arms folded underneath her small but perfect breasts. "Ah, that feels better."

"Your gown is very lovely," Mara said, "but you should have worn a robe over it. Now, my old flannel Mother Hubbard nightdress would keep me warm in a winter gale."

Cecile thrust her arms high over her head and stretched like a cat, her back arched and her bosom straining at the silk mesh. She stood with her legs spread wide apart, so that her flawless figure was vividly silhouetted through the sheer fabric against the backdrop of the bright flames behind her.

Mara began to feel uneasy. The French girl's behavior was—though the rational part of her mind rejected the conclusion, instinctively she knew it was the right one—brazenly flirtatious. Mara was familiar with the term "homosexual," but it was just a term in a dictionary; she had never encountered a member of either sex whose physical desire was directed at members of the same sex. She resisted the urge to cringe away when Cecile came over and sat down facing her with her long legs drawn up under her haunches.

Cecile smiled. "That feels better now." She examined Mara's nightgown. "What you're wearing may be warm, but think of how you'd feel if a handsome young gentleman should enter your room unexpectedly?"

Mara met her gaze unblinkingly. "That would hardly be the kind of thing a young 'gentleman' would do unless he was invited. And, in any event, if he didn't like my nightgown, he could damn well go to hell!"

"Bravo!" Cecile laughed and clapped her hands. "No matter; the issue would be strictly academic. Under such circumstances, your nightgown would not remain on for more than a few minutes. Your eyes would meet—*le regard rouge*—and the matter would be promptly decided." She became serious. "What you said this afternoon about looking forward to experiencing sex—you were jesting, yes?"

"No, it is the truth," Mara admitted without hesitation. "I am a virgin."

Cecile was incredulous. She tilted her head to one side and put a hand to her cheek. "A virgin! I lost my virginity at the age of eleven."

"You are more precocious than I am."

Cecile sidled across the thick rug until her knees were almost touching Mara's; the motion caused her nightgown to slip up over her legs, baring them to midthigh. Mara looked up quickly, fixing her attention on the pert tip of Cecile's nose. She was annoyed with herself for being so discomfited:

Stop behaving like a ninny! Cecile is a coquette; it's in her blood. She is like an actress on stage, and she must perform both to men and to women. Your trepidations are a sign of your emotional immaturity! She regards you as a friend, nothing more. What is wrong with two women feeling and displaying affection for each other?

On numerous occasions, she had seen some of the roughest cowboys and miners hug and kiss an old comrade whom they had not encountered in months or years. As for the men in her family, they had always been generous in showing their love for one another.

Reassured, she steered the conversation back to Cecile's and Joan's purpose in being in Bisbee. "All we girls—my mother, too—feel so fortunate to have the benefit of your experience. Even after one lesson, I'm more confident about my decision to enlist in army nursing."

"Thank you, *ma chère,* and Joan and I are fortunate to have such charming girls as pupils." She winked. "I think you will be the teacher's pet."

Mara's face and neck turned scarlet. "I'm sure the older girls will prove to be much more competent than I," she mumbled in confusion. "What will our curriculum be tomorrow?"

"How to relieve nervous tension."

"Nervous tension?"

"Yes. Fear, apprehension, and tension contribute to the pain a soldier feels when he's been wounded. Frequently they are responsible for most of the pain. At this minute you are suffering from tension, pain; I can see it by the way you are holding your head to one side and so stiffly."

Mara was flustered at the girl's insight. The tautness in her neck muscles radiated up one side of her head to the crown and down into her spine. "It's been a long, hard day and I am very tired, that's all."

Suddenly Cecile was all professionalism: "See here, young lady, I *am* the nurse," she said sternly. "Now, you do as you're told, or you'll never get to sleep tonight. Lie down flat and roll over on your stomach. Come along; don't dawdle."

It is difficult for most people, particularly the young and impressionable, to disregard the tone of accustomed authority. So it was that, with some misgiving, Mara stretched out prone on the carpet with her hands on either side of her head. She tensed as Cecile straddled her hips and placed her hands on her shoulders, her thumbs pressing into the taut cords at the base of her neck.

"Now, doesn't this feel good?" The nurse began to knead her shoulder and back muscles with firm, strong fingers, and her thumbs dug deeper into Mara's soft flesh.

"Yes . . . yes, it's very relaxing." Under the persistent ministrations of Cecile, the tension gradually went out to her cords and muscles. The heat from the fire toasted her right side and her face. The combination of massage and warmth was a narcotic, and her body lapsed into a blissful lassitude. Soon she was as limp as a rag doll. Her eyelids grew heavy—heavier, heavier, until at last they closed.

In a dream state, her mind succumbed to her flesh, and sexual fantasies ran rampant inside her head, a montage of erotic imagery: she and Sam on a bed of soft grass, their naked limbs entwined, bodies undulating, writhing in lascivious ecstasy; Sam kissing her lips, her throat, her breasts, her heaving belly, her thighs. "Oh, that feels so wonderful," she murmured, and rotated her hips against the soft pile of the rug.

Something alien intruded on her semiconscious state of wanton pleasure. Cecile was sitting astride her now, her buttocks working rhythmically against Mara's. She felt a hand reaching back and lifting the hem of her nightgown, warm, teasing fingers stroking the backs of her thighs and the half-moons of her bottom, then inserting themselves between her thighs.

Mara gasped as the shock jolted her back to reality. She tried to unseat Cecile, but the French girl was too strong and firmly entrenched. "Cecile, what are you doing? Stop it at once!"

The girl's soft laughter was close to her right ear; she could feel her hot breath. "*Ma cherie,* do not fight it. Enjoy! Enjoy! This is the *joie de vivre.* If there is no other purpose in life but this exquisite experience, that would be enough."

Mara tried to rear up as the probing fingers found their mark. "Oh! No, no, no! Please *stop!*"

All of her willpower, her strength, was being undermined by an invisible force. She could only whimper when Cecile rolled her over on her back and hiked the nightgown all the way up over her breasts. Her head rolled from side to side in torment as Cecile kissed her breasts, her pink tongue coaxing the nipples to swell and become rigid.

"This isn't right!" she wailed as those lips worked their way downward, tarrying at her navel to tongue-tease the sensitive cleft.

"You are not enjoying it, *cherie?*"

"No, no, *no!*" she lied. "We musn't!"

We mustn't—the crack in the dike; an acknowledgment of participation.

"Why mustn't we?"

"Because it isn't right; it isn't *natural.*"

"Then why does it feel so wonderful? Our bodies are divine instruments created by God. So long as we do not try to deceive ourselves and betray our natural emotions, we will flower to the full human potential that He intended for us, His children. The passion we are experiencing is as near as we can come to a divine bliss in this our present life. Blood and flesh and bone, our complex nervous system, our miraculous brain— the *body,* it is the barometer of the soul. If it feels *good,* it is *right.*"

If it feels good, it is right—the phrase struck a responsive chord; some dim thing out of the past. The past? Or was it the future? The future? It was outlandish!

Darkness closed over Mara. It was as if she and Cecile were dissolving into the nothingness of eternity.

"Mara, what did you say?"

"If it feels good, it is right. You said that once about hypnosis."

"Not exactly. I said that if it works, then it is good, something along that order. . . . Do you feel good now?"

"Yes, but I don't want to feel good, not like this; it isn't right."

"Whatever you are imagining, it has upset you very much. Now, I want you to push it out of your mind. The thought is fading. You will forget it."

"Yes . . . I will forget it."

"I think perhaps this is enough for the session. I want to bring you back here to the present."

"No, not yet—not with this unpleasantness washing about in my mind like dirty bilge water."

"Dirty bilge water? What a quaint simile. Never mind. . . . Now you must pass on to a more satisfying time. Can you do that, Mara? Can you move on?"

"I . . . I think so. I want to. . . . There—I can almost see it, feel it now."

"What is that?"

"When Sam and I were reunited."

CHAPTER SEVEN

The First United States Volunteer Cavalry Regiment was assembled in May 1898 at San Antonio, Texas. The old all-blue cavalry uniform had been replaced by khaki riding breeches and shirt; but the Rough Riders still wore the dashing blue shirt with a red bandanna knotted around the neck.

The first week was devoted to introducing the troopers to their new mounts, primarily unbroken mustangs; it was a debacle. "The Rough Riders are well named," wrote a reporter in the San Antonio *Bulletin,* "because they are truly getting a 'rough ride.' Yesterday, troopers were flying through the air like Roman-candle balls at a Fourth of July picnic." Eventually, however, persistence prevailed, and by the time the regiment was due to entrain for the port of embarkation at Tampa, Florida, at the end of May, the horses were subdued into reasonable obedience.

At Tampa the regiment was confronted by total chaos—near anarchy. The city and its outskirts were literally overflowing with soldiers, more than twice as many as there were transports in the harbor to contain them.

"What do we do now, Colonel Roosevelt?" the regimental adjutant asked in desperation.

Roosevelt, red-faced and fuming mad, shouted at him in a rasping voice that was described as sounding "like a buzz saw cutting through a pine knot." "Damn it, captain, we'll just confiscate one of those transports! As I see it, it's every man for himself."

The mission was accomplished with a minimum of casualties, all on the side of the military police guarding the transports. Nine days later, as the convoy was approaching the south coast of Cuba, Colonel Roosevelt gave his troopers a final briefing:

"Admiral Dewey has decisively defeated the Spanish fleet at Manila in the Philippines. Their Cuban fleet at Santiago is effectively bottled up. We will land below Santiago harbor in four hours and join up with the division under the command of General Joe Wheeler."

Wheeler, an ex-Confederate cavalryman, committed the most celebrated gaffe of the war when, in the heat of action, he cursed the enemy for being "Goddamned Yankees."

Witnessing the landings from the bridge of a navy cruiser were a group of nurses attached to the First Regiment, among them Mara, Cecile, and Joan; Mara's mother had been assigned to a base hospital in Florida with most of the older volunteers.

Mara was aghast when the horses were all stampeded overboard to make it through the heavy surf to land on their own. "How cruel!" she exclaimed.

"Never you mind, miss," a young lieutenant assured her. "The beasts stand a better chance of getting ashore safely than if they were in boats."

His statement seemed to be borne out as, within a few minutes after the first boatloads of soldiers were put over the sides of the transports, two of the landing craft capsized.

Mara turned away. "I don't want to watch it."

"If you don't have the stomach to watch men die, then you shouldn't be over here, Mara," Cecile told her.

"I suppose you're right."

The nurses remained aboard ship until the following morning, and that night they stood at the rail until midnight observing the spectacular pyrotechnic display in the eastern sky, accompanied by the muffled thunder of artillery.

"That would be San Juan Hill," Lieutenant Walker deduced. He had taken a fancy to Mara.

"He follows you around like a dog after a bitch in heat," Cecile had once teased her.

"What a revolting metaphor," Mara had replied.

"*Cherie,* we are all animals at heart."

"San Juan Hill is the key to capturing Santiago," the lieutenant went on. "It is the most heavily defended position on the island."

After the landings, Wheeler's division pushed straight ahead into the jungle and made contact with the Spanish defenders. The advance units, consisting of nearly 1,000 men, engaged in a fierce fire fight with the Spaniards in which 52 men were wounded and 16 killed.

These were the first casualties to arrive at the field hospital where Mara and her sister nurses were assigned. Initially the stench of blood and sweat, excrement and urine, and gangrene were nauseating. With the exception of Cecile and Joan, the two seasoned veterans, the rest of the girls vomited two and three times a day. Within the week, however, Mara wrote to her mother: "The smells become as familiar and unobtrusive as the scent of honeysuckle and roses out on the veranda back home."

The horrific sights of war were not as easy to dismiss: arms and legs hanging by threads of skin; eyes gouged out; entrails spilling out on the stretchers like tangled spaghetti.

During one operation, a field surgeon amputated a soldier's left arm and handed it to Mara. "Dump it in the blood bucket," he instructed.

While she was walking across the tent to the bucket, the fingers on the hand of the severed limb underwent a muscular reflex and tightened on Mara's arm. She screamed and almost fainted.

Cecile came up behind her and grabbed her shoulders. "Steady, *cherie,* it is only a muscular spasm."

One week after they had landed and pushed inland, the Rough Riders were entrenched in a half-circle around the base of San Juan Hill. Colonel Roosevelt briefed his officers on the impending offensive scheduled for the next morning:

"Here we have the first line of defense." He sketched with his pointer on a situation map pinned on the wall of the command tent. "These earthworks are manned by veteran Spanish infantry armed with the most modern Mauser rifles. . . . Now, up here at the summit, there is a barbed-wire fence. At this point the soundest strategy, in my estimation, will be to dismount and advance through the wire on foot."

"Begging your pardon, sir," interjected a young second lieutenant with a British accent. "In my opinion, it would be prudent to leave the horses behind and do battle like mounted infantry."

Roosevelt removed his glasses and squinted at the young upstart. "And what is your reasoning, lieutenant?"

"On horseback the men will be far more vulnerable targets for those sharpshooters than if they hug the ground like infantry."

A wide, toothy grin spread over the regimental commander's face. "By God, I think you have something there, Lieutenant Rodgers"—the smile faded—"but I deem it only proper that I, as your leader, will lead the charge on horseback. . . . All right, gentlemen, meeting adjourned. We'd all better get some shut-eye so that we'll be full of piss and vinegar for the big fight tomorrow."

Once inside his bedroll, Sam Rodgers tossed and turned restlessly, wide awake. His brain was a merry-go-round of recollections, all of them about Mara Ewing: how his heart had skipped a beat the first time he laid eyes on her; riding with her across the Arizona wilderness, the heat radiating through his body each time his hand touched her hand, his knee brushed against her knee; the magic of her kiss the last day they had spent together on the bluff.

Less than ten miles away, Mara lay sleepless on her hard cot in the nurses' tent. Clutched in her hands, close to her bosom, was the glass paperweight Sam had given her. Even though it was dark, she could vividly picture the miniature scene within the globe, the snow swirling around the boy and girl locked in warm embrace.

"Oh, to be so close to you, Sam, my darling," she whispered. "I would give anything to see you again."

The troopers of the First Regiment crouched tensely in the brush at the foot of San Juan Hill, along with the black Ninth Cavalry on their right flank. Colonel Roosevelt rode his horse back and forth along the thin khaki line, shouting encouragement and praise at his untried Rough Riders:

"We'll not only push 'em off this hill; we'll push 'em clear back into the ocean!"

H-hour arrived, and with a flourish of his cavalry saber, Teddy issued the order to his Terrors: *"Charge!"*

The battle cry went up from 500 eager throats in unison as the men of the First and the Ninth surged up the slopes of San Juan Hill.

"Let's get 'em, men!" yelled Lieutenant Sam Rodgers, leading the way for A Troop.

Within minutes the summit of the hill was obscured in smoke as the Spanish defenders poured volley after volley into the ranks of the Americans. A trooper just behind Rodgers stumbled and fell. The lieutenant turned and kneeled beside him.

"Perkins, are you all right?" Then he saw the gaping hole in the back of the lad's head and knew that Perkins would be answering no more questions in this life. He leaped up and ran forward again, taking his place at the point of the advance.

Halfway up, visibility was reduced to no more than ten feet. Orange and red flares sporadically lit up the white screen, the muzzle bursts of cannon and exploding shells tearing up the grassy slope. Men were falling all around Rodgers like flies. A bullet zipped off his cavalry hat, and he forged ahead bareheaded.

He saw the dim outline of a horse through the haze twenty yards ahead. As he drew closer, he saw that it was Colonel Roosevelt's mount. The colonel was clipping his way through a tangle of barbed wire.

"Lieutenant Rodgers," he said as Sam reached him, "bully! Here, lend a hand."

Working feverishly, they cleared a gap through the barricade, and the troopers of the First poured through it, their voices lifted in a victory cry. Then they were face to face with the enemy. A Spaniard charged at Rodgers with fixed bayonet aimed at his gut, the lieutenant dropped him with two rounds from his service pistol. A score of isolated hand-to-hand encounters were taking place all around him. He saw the colonel decapitate one enemy with a swath of his saber.

Soon the balance began to tip in favor of the Rough Riders. The ground on both sides of the earthworks was littered with dead and wounded, predominantly Spaniards. The enemy ranks shattered all at once, and the defenders flung away their weapons and retreated in disorder.

"*Charge!*" Roosevelt bawled. "Don't give 'em any respite!"

Lieutenant Rodgers started in pursuit when, without warning, he was slammed backward and off his feet as if a giant fist had struck him squarely in the chest. He lay on his back, stunned and gasping for air. The last thing he remembered was a circle of anxious faces hovering over him; then darkness closed in—merciful oblivion.

The next thing he was aware of was the sound of voices, dim and unintelligible, as if they were calling to him from a great distance out of the blackness of the deep night. Gradually they were drawing closer, and the blackness was no longer so intense but tinged with a rosy glow like the first light of dawn.

"Lieutenant, can you hear me?"—a coarse male voice.

"I think he's regaining consciousness, doctor"—a sweet, gentle, feminine voice, vaguely familiar.

"All right, nurse, there's nothing further I can do here. I'm confident that he'll make it. You watch him carefully for the next hour and let me know immediately if there's any change for the worse."

"Yes, sir."

Rodgers felt a hand on his, so soft, so warm, so female.

"Sam, can you hear me?"

He was startled. How could she know his name? His identification tags, of course. But "Sam," not "lieutenant"? Unconventionally familiar, he thought.

"Sam, speak to me." She was pressing his hand with an intimate urgency, stroking his forehead. It was preposterous, but then she was *kissing* his hand.

He opened his eyes slowly and stared directly into the eyes of this mystery woman. Her face was fuzzy at first, haloed in the film that lay over his eyes. He blinked several times until his vision cleared, and realized he was lying on a cot in a hospital tent and the woman was a nurse. Her uniform and cap were rumpled and stained with blood and mud, but her face was the loveliest vision he had ever beheld. His mind was playing tricks on him; she looked so much like his beloved Mara.

"Sam, darling." She smiled, and tears streamed down her cheeks and fell on his bared arm. "You're alive and you're going to get well."

His mouth flew open in astonishment. "No, it *can't* be." His voice was weak.

"But it is. I'm Mara."

"No, it's a dream, or else I'm dead and you are an angel—my special angel."

She laughed softly. "I'll be your angel if you insist, but I am a flesh-and-blood angel. Here, feel." She took his hand and pressed it to her lips.

"I love you, Mara."

"I love you, Sam."

"Will you marry me?"

"Don't you think I'm too young?"

"Are you?"

"You be the judge." She took his hand and slipped it inside the bodice of her uniform. He cupped her breast, firm as a fresh peach. Her nipple swelled against his palm.

"You are definitely not too young. Still, your parents must give their consent. As soon as I'm discharged from the cavalry, I'll visit Arizona and ask for your hand."

She removed his hand from inside her blouse, and not an instant too soon, for the tent flap parted and an officer entered the aid station. His rasping voice identified him even before Sam recognized the face:

"Lieutenant Rodgers?"

"Colonel Roosevelt . . ." He tried to sit up.

"As you were, lieutenant. How is he, nurse?"

"He's just fine, sir." Her smile was radiant, and its significance was not lost on the colonel.

"And that pleases you, miss."

"I could do cartwheels, I'm so pleased."

Roosevelt cackled. "I'd like to see that. Say, Rodgers, how do you rate such an exquisitely beautiful nurse?"

"I'm a lucky man." He reached for her hand and squeezed it.

The blue eyes twinkled behind the steel-rimmed spectacles. "I would tend to agree—*extremely* lucky. I have the feeling that you two were acquainted before the war."

"Yes, sir. We met while Sam and his parents were traveling through Arizona."

Roosevelt cocked his head to one side, studying her curiously. "You look familiar, nurse. Have we met before?"

"No, but I think you may have met my mother, Mara Ewing."

"Mara Ewing? The Tates?"

"Yes, sir."

"Your father is Gordon Ewing. You're Drew Tate's granddaughter."

"And proud of it."

"As well you should be. Well, well, well, it is a small world at that. When you see them, tell them that Teddy sends his fondest regards."

"Thank you, colonel, I will." Slyly she added, "I think perhaps we have another mutual friend in Arizona—Marion Murphy."

He was stricken. His cheeks were beet red, and a coughing fit seized him. "Ahhhrhmmm . . . Did you say Marion Murphy?"

"Yes, sir. Can I fetch you a glass of water?"

"No, thank you, I'm fine. . . . Marion Murphy— yes, the name rings a bell. I believe we met casually at some social function in Denver or Phoenix."

"Oh? I had the impression that you were intimate friends." She placed a subtle emphasis on "intimate."

"Well, you have the wrong impression." He wagged a finger at her. "Young lady, I have the feeling that my leg is being pulled."

She was the picture of innocence. "Colonel Roosevelt, I don't know what you mean."

"Don't you, now." He patted Sam's leg. "Lieutenant, you had better watch your step with this wily vixen."

"You can depend on it, sir. Did we win the battle, Colonel Roosevelt?"

"Handily, my boy. Santiago is ours, and the Spanish fleet in the harbor is doomed." His expression was sober. "At precious cost, though. Ninety of our boys were killed or badly wounded. The division casualties numbered almost four hundred."

"Damn! I can't wait to get back into action."

"By the time you're on your feet again, lieutenant, the war will be over. All the boys will be home before next Thanksgiving. Tomorrow the wounded will be transported back to the States, to the regimental rest-and-recreation center at Montauk Point, on Long Island."

Mara and Sam looked at each other in dismay. He clutched her hand. "But I don't want to leave Cuba," he protested.

"Can't say I blame you, boy, but we all have to make sacrifices in wartime." He winked at Mara. "I just came from headquarters. The general is asking for nursing volunteers to service the hospital at Montauk. Know anyone who may be interested in applying, Miss Ewing?"

"I'm on my way!" she shouted, and bolted out of the tent.

"On the double, nurse!" he yelled after her. "Looks like you've got yourself a nurse, Lieutenant Rodgers."

"And hopefully a wife."

"Congratulations. You've got yourself a real handful of woman there."

"She is that, sir." His palm still tingled from the thrust of her nipple. "A handful indeed."

CHAPTER EIGHT

The war ended in August 1898. Under the terms of the Treaty of Paris, signed on December 10, Spain freed Cuba, which came under U.S. tutelage; ceded Puerto Rico and Guam to the United States; and surrendered the Philippine Islands to the United States for $20 million.

Gordon Ewing laid the morning paper down beside his plate and observed, "Tate Industries could have paid more than that. The days of the Spanish Empire are gone forever. From now on, Spain will become a second-rate power." He and his wife exchanged understanding looks as their daughter strolled into the dining room, absorbed in the letter she was reading. She walked straight into a chair.

"Oops! Pardon me."

"You've been reading Sam's letter over and over since it arrived this morning."

Mara blushed. "He's such a fascinating writer. When he describes the Christmas season in Yorkshire, you can almost smell the holly and plum pudding."

After his discharge from the First Regiment, Sam Rodgers had returned to the family estate in England to convalesce.

"When does he expect to be visiting America again?"

"In the early spring. He is going to accept a position with one of his father's refineries in San Francisco, at least until we're married."

The Ewings had given their consent to the union of their daughter with Samuel Rodgers, Jr., on the condition that the couple wait until Mara turned seventeen.

After Gordon had left for the office, the elder Mara had a serious conversation with her daughter. "I hope you won't be leaving Arizona after you and Sam are married."

"I hadn't thought about it, Mother. I suppose it's my duty to go where my husband wishes to settle."

"Your first duty is to the Tates," her mother said incisively. "You and I, my dear, we're very much alike; we take a fierce pride in our heritage, the Tate traditions. Your grandfather, your father, and I, we have built an empire from a single vein of gold discovered by accident in Tombstone Canyon. Tate International Industries has spread throughout the world: Europe, Africa, South America, Hawaii, the Far East; our investments span the globe.

"Your grandfather's days are numbered. Then there will be only your father and me; and we're not getting any younger, either. The two of us would like you to give us your vow that you will carry on after we are gone."

Young Mara rubbed her throat. The implied responsibility was enormous, overwhelming to a girl who was not yet seventeen years old. "You expect me to become the head of Tate Industries? What about Uncle Gilbert and Uncle Emlyn and Uncle Allan?"

Her mother's lips were compressed into a thin line; her dark eyes flashed. "In my estimation, your uncles have betrayed the family and all that the name Tate stands for in this country, this world. I hate to sound fatuous, but one must face reality: The Tates are as close to an American royal family as there can be in a democratic society; along with such other luminaries as the Rockefellers, the Vanderbilts, and the Astors.

"Along with money and power, there is responsibility—*noblesse oblige*. Emlyn and Gilbert and Allan, I'm sad to say, are incapable of wearing the mantle of nobility; neither are their children. Emlyn has become a fat, complacent banker. His son Buzz wants to pursue a military career. His two daughters, sweet girls, are mindless creatures born to give birth and serve God and their husbands."

Her nose wrinkled in distaste. "Gilbert is perfectly content to oversee his little feudal empire in South America and service the girls in his harem. Your twin cousins Preston and Samantha are spoiled darlings of New York's foppish social whirl.

"Allan, he comes the closest to being worthy of the Tate tradition. If the family hadn't driven him away because of his alliance with the half-breed Mexican whore he married, he might have gone on to become the head of the empire. As it is now, he's built a respectable empire of his own in California. His son Brian—he's a true Tate—has the responsibility to serve as a worthy heir to his father's holdings.

"And that leaves us, Mara—your father, me, and you. You will become the heir apparent to Tate International Industries. If Sam Rodgers is half the man I give him credit for being, he will understand and support you in this vast endeavor, just as your father has supported me all of these years."

Mara was awed. "You make it sound so . . . so . . . I can't describe it—as if I had taken a nun's vow of chastity to become the bride of the Lord, as my friend Cecile expressed it. Her parents wanted her to take the veil." She suppressed the urge to laugh; the idea of Cecile Dumas practicing chastity was hilarious.

Her mother smiled. "I daresay that a vow of chastity will not be necessary. If it had, I . . . well, never mind."

Young Mara understood. She was not oblivious of the way her mother and father looked at each other, touched each other; how often they went to bed long before she did. Someday it would be like that with her and Sam.

Oh, my darling, how I yearn for your touch, your caress, your kiss. It is physical agony not to have you here beside me.

She took a deep breath and declared, "I can do it, Mother. I won't let you down. I won't let the family down. I will do my damnedest to be deserving of the name Tate."

Her mother embraced her. "Bless you, my love. You are every inch a Tate."

Early in May the following year, Samuel Rodgers, Jr., stepped off a train at Phoenix, Arizona, on his way to Bisbee. The night before he was due to arrive, Mara did not sleep a wink. Her mind was crammed with thoughts of Sam and herself together, holding hands like the lovers in the paperweight, entwined in passionate embrace in bed, their naked bodies feverish with lust. At this last thought, she bounded out of bed and went out onto the balcony overlooking the garden.

What you need, my girl, is a cold bath, or else you'll end up doing what nice young ladies are not supposed to do!

From dawn till nearly dusk she waited impatiently, pacing about the house and the garden, nagging at her mother, her father, the servants, even her pet dog, Nugget, a small Scottish border collie. "What can be keeping him? He should have been here hours ago. Oh, he exasperates me so!" She stamped a foot in frustration.

Gordon chuckled and lit his pipe with a stick from the fireplace. "How can you blame Sam? It's the Southern Pacific Railroad you should be castigating."

At five o'clock the vigil ended. At the first rap of the knocker on the big front door, Mara screeched and bolted down the hall. She skidded six feet across the polished marble floor and slammed hard into the oaken portal.

Ignoring the pain in her shoulder, she yanked the door wide open and flung herself into his arms. "My darling, my sweetheart, if I'd had to wait a minute longer for you, I would have perished." She snuggled into his arms and closed her eyes, with her face pressed against his chest. "I can hear your heart beating; it says 'love, love, love.' Oh, Sam! Was it a bad trip? You look tired. Have you lost weight? Are you certain you were fit enough to travel?"

Sam laughed and hugged her. "How you rattle on! I feel fine, fit, and I have not lost weight. Say, can I come in?"

"Of course. Leave your luggage on the porch. Father's valet, Fulton, will take it up to your room. Come along now and see Mother and Father."

Gordon and his wife had tactfully remained in the parlor so that the young couple could have their reunion in privacy.

Now they gave their future son-in-law a warm welcome, Mara kissing his cheek. "How is your mother and father, Sam?"

"Perfectly fine. They send their love."

Gordon gripped his hand and held on to it. "We're all very proud of you, son, what you did for the United States in the war."

"I did it for freedom, sir. I believe Mr. Edmund Burke said it in Parliament: 'All that is required for the triumph of evil is for good men to remain silent and do nothing.' "

"A highly commendable sentiment, Sam, one none of us should ever forget."

The maid served sherry and tea with biscuits and jam, and the conversation ranged from family and friends to the past war with Spain and the economic futures of the two English-speaking powers of the world, England and the United States.

"I see continued prosperity ahead for both of our

great nations," Gordon forecast. "Copper, gold, silver, oil, wheat, livestock—our national product will double, triple in the next decade. Arizona is the leading producer of copper in the United States, and between them, Jackling, Ricketts, and Joralman just about have the problems of open-pit mining solved. A number of big operations are already under way: Bisbee, Globe, Morenci, Ajo, Bagdad, Tucson. Yes, sir, Sam, the future looks bright all the way to the horizon.

"And look at England; she's at the pinnacle of her glory. 'The sun never sets on the British Empire'—a proud statement. Africa, India, Canada, Australia, the Far East—a veritable bottomless horn of plenty."

Sam Rodgers took a somewhat more conservative view. " 'Pinnacle of her glory'—that may be more apt than you intended, sir. From a pinnacle, there is no way to go except down. . . . Quite frankly, I see the next decade, two decades, as confronting England with the most crucial and critical issues in all of her history. We are on the verge of war in South Africa; we've been plagued with mutinies and dissension in India for the past fifty years; and there is the expansionist policies of Germany to contend with in the immediate future."

"Germany? Why, I thought that Germany and England were bound together by bonds of blood?"

Sam's laugh was harsh. "You mean because Queen Victoria is Kaiser Wilhelm's aunt? Mr. Ewing, it's common knowledge that he has nothing but contempt for both Queen Victoria and England."

Mara chided her husband: "I wish you would stop embroiling all of us in politics. Mara and I would much prefer to speak of more optimistic topics."

"Yes, such as my wedding plans," the girl added.

The men laughed, and Gordon threw up his hands. "My boy, I for one could not be happier than to have you as our newest member of the family; but, to be honest, I am not the least interested in your so-called wedding plans. That has such an ominous sound to it —'plans'—rather as if the ladies are plotting a military campaign."

His wife gave him a haughty glance. "Capturing a husband is no mean feat these days; it requires a concentrated application of female wiles."

"There you have it, Sam, straight from the horse's mouth. Better retreat while we're ahead. What say we go to the study and have a nip of something more formidable than sherry?"

"Oh no you don't, Father!" Mara grabbed hold of his arm and Sam's arm and held fast. "You are not going to steal Sam away from me so soon after his arrival. Now, I want the two of you to sit down and listen to *my* wedding plan*ssss,*" she said with a sinister sibilancy.

"I'm all for that, darling," Sam said, "but there is something I'd like to discuss first. . . . Last time I visited here, I expressed my intention of navigating the Colorado River in a boat. I've been busy making preparations for the venture. As a matter of fact, I stopped over in Denver for a week, contacting several veteran boatmen who have made the voyage. Chap named Hall made the first trip down the gorge with Major John Wesley Powell. I commissioned him to construct a boat for me."

The two Maras were astonished. "You can't be serious, Sam?" said the mother.

"Oh, he's serious, all right, Mother. Once he makes up his mind about something, he's like a mule."

He hugged her around the waist. "I made up my mind to marry you, didn't I?"

She reached up and patted his cheek. "Quite the contrary; *I* made up my mind to marry you. And as your future wife, I say to you what Ruth said to

Naomi in the Bible: "Whither thou goest, I goest.' So there; it's settled!"

"Out of the question," her father said.

"Quite," Sam echoed.

"So it's settled, then," Mara said breezily. "I wonder what I shall wear and take with me."

The two men stared at her, speechless, then looked to each other helplessly.

"The boat is big enough for two?" Gordon asked with resignation.

"Yes, I suppose so. It will be an eighteen-foot boat, double-ribbed and divided into three watertight compartments, built of light pine for easy maneuverability and portage. I estimated on carrying along two hundred and fifty pounds of supplies and equipment; I'll have to raise that to four hundred now. We'll have to skimp, but we can't risk any more weight."

The gold flecks in Mara's green eyes were swirling like bubbles in champagne; she was intoxicated at the anticipation of such high adventure. "Remember, Mother, how you used to read me tales about the Grand Canyon when I was small?"

"How could I forget? Do you know, Sam, when I was a child in Wales, and my father Drew was first planning to emigrate, I devoured every book and paper and magazine I could lay my hands on that furnished information and lore about the Arizona Territory. The Grand Canyon was my grand obsession." Her eyes misted over in reminiscence. "The idea of a torrent of water carving a mile-deep gorge, five hundred miles long, out of solid rock flabbergasts the imagination."

"I share your obsession, Mrs. Ewing. Just think of it: The Colorado River actually drops one mile in its journey through the Great Unknown. That's what the ancient Pueblo Indians called it—the Great Unknown."

"Where will your journey commence?" Gordon wanted to know.

"From the same point that Major Powell started out —Green River, Wyoming. We'll cruise down the Green River to the head of the Colorado, and then it's into the canyon."

"I can hardly wait!" Mara said, clapping her hands.

That evening the men and the women dressed for the formal acceptance of Samuel Rodgers, Jr., into the family. Mother and daughter made their entrance together in the parlor, where Sam and Gordon were sipping sherry. They put down their tulip crystal glasses and stood up smartly.

"You both look incredibly beautiful," Gordon murmured. He walked over to them and kissed each lightly on a cheek.

His wife was stunning in a black-satin slipper skirt that billowed into a deep flounce, and a coordinated white-satin blouse, which had a flaring collar framing the V neck, and full sleeves with buttoned cuffs.

Mara was a fantasy of sapphire and jade, a brilliant contrast of blue skirt and quilted jacket, open in front to reveal the seductive, low-cut green camisole underneath. There was a wicked invitation in her eyes as she sashayed over to her fiancé and took him by the hand. "Do I pass muster, sir?"

"You are ravishing," he said, unable to take his gaze off the upper hemispheres of her breasts peeping over the top of the camisole.

She leaned close to him and whispered, "I wish you would—ravish me, I mean."

He flushed scarlet, looking fearfully in the direction of her parents.

"It's all right; they didn't hear." Her smile was teasing. "And even if they had, Mum and Da would understand. They were young themselves once."

"Not all that long ago," Sam demurred. "If I had

met your lovely mother before I met you, and if she were single, I would have proposed on the spot."

Mara sniffed. "Hmmph! So mother rates higher than I do, is that it? Cecile was right: All men are fickle beasts." She held out her arm to him. "Would you care to escort me into the dining room?"

"I think I'd prefer to escort your mother," Sam said archly.

She stamped her feet in mock anger while her mother and father laughed appreciatively. "Well, I like *that* —my own mother taking the spotlight away from me!"

Her mother came over to Sam and offered him her arm. "I'd be honored to have such a handsome gentleman escort me, but no more honored than I will be to have him for my son-in-law."

"Amen," said Gordon, and took his daughter's arm. "Allow me, my dear."

And the proud and happy foursome paraded into the dining hall, where the long table covered with a snow-white Irish-linen tablecloth glittered with highly polished silver and crystal tableware in the glow from the massive chandelier overhead festooned with scores of candles.

CHAPTER NINE

After a long and arduous journey by rail and coach, Sam and Mara arrived at Green River, Wyoming, in the last week of May, accompanied by her parents and a small coterie of close friends from Bisbee who wanted to give the young adventurers a rousing send-off. There was still a week of preparation ahead of them before they could embark.

Andy Hall, the carpenter who had built the boat, displayed his creation with justifiable pride. "Ain't she a beauty, Mr. Rodgers?"

Sam ran his hand over the varnished and highly polished oak gunwale with admiration. "A beauty and then some," he said.

"And she rides like a dream. I've had her in white water five times this past week, and she's as much at home as an otter in the water. Changed the rudder and steering stem twice until I got one that felt as natural as if it had been born on the boat. What will you name her, sir? I can stencil it on this afternoon."

Sam smiled at his beloved. "What else? *Mara the Second*."

She kissed him. "Thank you, love; I am honored."

"And so am I," echoed her mother, "even if I am only the namesake."

"No, that isn't right." Sam rubbed his chin as an afterthought hit him. "Tell you what, Andy; make that simply the *Mara*. These two gorgeous ladies merit equal billing."

His bride-to-be was grateful for his thought. She

put an arm around her mother's waist. "That's only right. Mother and I were cut from the same cloth, as Grandma Tate always says."

"The same cloth," Sam repeated. For no explicable reason, the phrase fostered an eerie sensation within him, a vague disquiet. Standing there together, clad almost identically in plain brown traveling gowns and brown bonnets, they could have been twin sisters. He imagined that he was gazing on the two halves of a stereoscopic slide and that when it was inserted into a lens guide, the two of them would merge into a single three-dimensional image.

"What's wrong, dear?" Mara called to him.

"Nothing, darling, nothing at all; I was just thinking about the *Mara*."

The Mara—in a sense, what he told her was the gospel truth.

For the next three days Sam and Mara spent four to six hours a day aboard the boat while Andy Hall instructed them in the intricacies of rivermanship. "One thing never to forget, Mr. Rodgers: You heading down a chute into the rapids, don't let 'er yaw. Sturdy and level as she is, she'll broach for sure in the fearsome white water of the Colorado."

The night before they embarked, the provisions and equipment were loaded aboard the *Mara* and secured with heavy rope. Andy Hall slept in a sleeping bag on the boat to guard against pilferage.

After a pleasant dinner at the hotel where the Ewings were staying, Sam and Mara went to bed early. They slept soundly and awoke at dawn, fresh and eager to get started. They dressed in heavy work shirts and moleskin trousers, and wore knee-length watertight leather boots. Mara's long hair was braided across the top of her head. With her stocking cap pulled low over her forehead, she might have been a slender, delicate-featured boy.

Gordon, his wife, and Andy Hall stood on the Green River landing in the blue early light and waved to them as the *Mara* put her nose out into the channel. Behind them were a handful of friends and curious townspeople.

"Be careful of snakes and don't catch cold!" Mara's mother shouted.

"And be sure and write us every day!" Gordon jested.

Sam sat in the stern with his hand steady and sure on the stem. Mara looked back at the diminishing figures on the dock until they vanished in the morning mist over the placid surface of the river; then she retrieved a thick leather-bound diary from a knapsack and inscribed the first entry in it:

June 1, 1899

We sailed from Green River landing at 6:30 A.M. to a reception that was somewhat less tumultous than the send-off accorded John Wesley Powell.

The succeeding entries for the next three days were similarly mundane. In fact, on the afternoon of the third day, Mara recorded merely:

Ditto, ditto, ditto.

The Green River was bounded by rolling hills and virgin greenery on both sides, soothing but unspectacular scenery. On the afternoon of June 4, however, they reached the head of the mighty Colorado and cruised into the first major canyon, and the monotonous serenity was dramatically shattered. Sheer bluffs towered over them to a height of a thousand feet on both sides of the river, and abruptly the air, moments before so balmy and enervating, turned cold, clammy, almost ominous, recalling to Mara the fairy tales she had read as a child about the Black Forest of Germany, which was inhabited by witches, demons, and evil spirits.

Gordon pointed to a sand spit jutting out into the water on the port side. "There's a good campsite for tonight. Lots of dried brush for firewood, too." He eased the rudder right and called out to Mara, "Give me some paddle on the starboard. There we go."

While their supper of dried meat and potatoes and vegetables was simmering over the cookfire, Mara took out her sketch pad. "Major Powell named this Flaming Gorge," she said.

The rays of the setting sun slanting on the iridescent stone on the eastern bluff and reflecting across to the western wall filled the canyon with fire. "I can understand why," Sam observed. "God, isn't it magnificent?"

They ate their stew along with pan biscuits and steaming coffee, conversing animatedly and speculating about the adventures that lay ahead of them in the Great Unknown.

"Oh, Sam," she said with excitement," our first night in the Grand Canyon! We should have brought along a bottle of champagne to celebrate."

"Make believe the coffee is champagne."

"Ugh!" She wrinkled up her nose. "Your coffee tastes like tar."

He winked. "Good; it will stick to your insides, so you won't upchuck when we hit white water tomorrow."

"Anything you can endure I can endure, too." Her green eyes brightened as a fading sunbeam slashed across her face. "I know one thing we can do to celebrate our first night."

Her emphasis on "first night" did not escape him, and his pulse accelerated. There were times in the course of their relationship when their mutual desire for each other was almost impossible to bridle. On those occasions when they could no longer bank the fire in their flesh and blood, they would bring each other to sweet release by means of kisses and lusty caresses. Sam had never violated Mara's virginity, but it was not for lack of willingness on her part. On this special night she was determined to be seduced, or vice-versa.

When it was time to climb into their bedrolls, Mara kneeled down beside Sam and put her arms around his neck. "Tonight I am going to sleep with you." She clapped a hand across his mouth as he began to protest. "No, don't say anything; just do as I ask. I want you to make love to me, darling. I've waited so long —too long. Now my yearning for you is unbearable. You feel that way, too; don't deny it. Now, let's undress and get on with it."

Without shyness, she unbuttoned the front of her shirt and slipped out of it. Crossing her arms, she grasped the hem of her woolen undervest and pulled it over her head. Her breasts swung free.

Sam gazed at her adoringly, the flames of desire licking up his thighs and searing his loins, radiating out through his whole body. "You're beautiful," he whispered.

"Touch me." She took his hands and gently guided them to her breasts, ripe and firm. His fingers tingled as they closed tenderly over the soft, creamy globes. Her nipples grew hard against his trembling, sweating palms.

Her hands were fumbling with his belt buckle and then the buttons on his fly. Now they trembled as nervously as his as she sought the hard, bursting thrust of his manhood. Sam let out a long sigh as her soft, loving fingers encircled his throbbing staff.

"Let's not tarry, my sweet," she said, "it's getting chilly. I want to be beside you in the bedroll."

They cast off their remaining clothing with impatient abandon and crawled into the fleece-lined sleeping bag, pulling the warm folds tightly around their nude bodies glued together, mouth to mouth, chest to bosom, belly to belly, thigh to thigh.

She broke off the kiss to gasp for air, the sweet taste of his exploring tongue still fresh in her mouth. She laughed—a loud, wild, rapturous laughter. "Isn't this gloriously wicked, making love out here in the open? Not like being together in an inhibiting bedroom where you have to suppress your passion for fear that someone down the hall might hear you and know what you're doing."

She was intoxicated by the intensity of her passion. She threw her arms wide and began to shout, "I hope everyone out there can hear me! I am madly, immodestly, uncontrollably in love with Sam Rodgers. I want his body, his hard male flesh, to penetrate my body so very deeply, to the very core of my womanly soul. Sam, my lover, do it to me *now;* I won't deny myself another instant longer!"

She lay flat on her back with her thighs spread wide to receive him. As he mounted her, her hands and feet dug ardently into his back and buttocks, drawing him into her yearning, quivering, lubricious flesh with lusty vigor.

"The irresistible force meets the unyielding resistance," she quipped as he attempted to penetrate the bastion of her maidenhood. She gritted her teeth and grunted, "Harder! You must push harder, darling."

"I don't want to hurt you, sweetheart."

"I don't give a damn! Hurt me! It can't be anything like the torture I have endured waiting for you to consummate our love. Push!"

And she urged him on with all the strength of her arms and legs. She winced as the barrier broke and he lunged into her. The sharp pain was quickly dispelled by the waves of pleasure and delight that engulfed her with his every stroke. She matched her rhythm to his own, and they quickened the pace, soaring to the summit faster than either one of them wanted to, trying desperately to prolong the wanton euphoria.

"There's always tomorrow," he said to her as they basked in the aftermath of the act of love, naked limbs entwined, their hands still caressing each other lovingly.

"Tomorrow?" Mara pretended to be indignant. "There is always later on tonight!"

"Hussy!" He slapped her behind.

"*Your* hussy, my love—my beautiful, wonderful stallion. You *are* my stallion, my stud." And her skillful fingers were determined to demonstrate the soundness of her brash claim.

All through that night they slept the serene sleep of innocents, enfolded in each other's arms. Dawn was nonexistent in the abyss. The rosy glow of the rising sun shimmered high up on the bluffs and crept slowly downward, until the canyon was once again ablaze with fire.

The warmth on her eyelids woke Mara. Her memory sluggish from her deep slumber, she started at sight of the naked form beside her; but, as his hand stroked the curve of her hip, it all came back to her, and a smile of total contentment and fulfillment spread over her face. "Oh, Sam, my darling," she murmured. She bent to kiss him on the lips and cupped his chin in her hand.

His eyes fluttered and opened, his expression as blank as her own had been at first awakening. Tender recognition followed, and he put an arm around her neck and pulled her down to nestle in his matted chest. He kissed the top of her head. "My love; my wife . . ."

"My loving husband . . ."

There was no need for any further affirmation of the place each occupied in the other's heart.

He patted her rump. "Time we were on our way; it must be well past eight o'clock, from the looks of things." He sat up and looked through his clothing, piled beside the bedroll, for his timepiece. Finding it, he exclaimed, "It's almost nine! Come on, rise and shine!"

They bathed in the icy water of the Colorado. Sam looked at Mara as she was toweling herself. "You have the skin tone of an Indian maiden. Must be the cold water and the reflection of the light in this gorge."

Mara laughed. "Well, I am not an Indian, and I am *certainly* not a maiden, for which I give God profound thanks. It's really been a bore waiting all these years to be deflowered. . . . I can't wait for you to light the fire."

"No time for a fire this morning; we've got to make up the time we lost."

"Time lost because of my wicked, seductive wiles," she said. "Would you rather have back the time I cost you?"

Sam's laughter echoed back and forth off the canyon walls. "You are a wicked wench, Mara Ewing."

"Mara Tate," she said in all earnestness.

Sam's brow puckered; he was uncertain whether or not she was joking. "Mara *Tate* Ewing."

"Both my mother and I think it's more practical to retain our identities with the family. Tate International Industries—the Tate name carries with it commanding respect and authority; it makes good business sense, that's all." She tried to dismiss it. "After all, as the bard said, 'What's in a name?' Don't you agree?" She averted her face from his curious and somewhat puzzled expression.

"To be sure," he mumbled.

"You do understand, darling?"

"I suppose so." He turned away abruptly and began to pack the gear into the bedroll.

Truth was, he did not understand at all, and the episode left a sour taste in his mouth that lingered until well past midday. At last he was able to rationalize his perturbation with Mara:

We all have our quirks and eccentricities, and even the most devoted lovers must learn to accept the shortcomings of the other partner. No doubt she has misgivings about some of my idiosyncracies.

A burdensome weight was lifted from his mind.

"Well, old sourpuss, that's the first time I've seen you smile since we left the campsite this morning," she chided.

"Preoccupied with what lies ahead of us. Tomorrow we encounter our first big test—rapids."

She clambered back to the stern and sat down beside him on the broad seat. Kissing his cheek, she said, "I have every confidence in you to overcome the most dire pitfalls we will face in the days and weeks ahead." She snuggled her head into the crook of his brawny shoulder. "I feel so safe with you, darling—as if nothing can ever harm me so long as you are at my side."

"I'll do my best to be worthy of your trust, my sweet."

"What time will we stop for lunch? Quite frankly, beef jerky and hardtack and cold water are not my idea of a satisfying breakfast."

"Soon as we come upon a suitable site. Have you noticed how dark it's becoming the deeper we travel into the gorge?"

Mara gazed upward, squinting against the bright-blue sky. Until now she had been oblivious of the gradual transformation that had been taking place as the bluffs towered ever higher and the gap between them at the top seemed to close like the jaws of a giant vise, relentlessly diminishing the expanse of visible sky and limiting the access of sunlight filtering down to the canyon floor. From this point on, they would travel in perpetual shadow.

Mara shivered and folded her arms across her body. "Perhaps this is the mythological river Styx in the underworld, and it will lead us into the twilight world of the dead."

Sam laughed. "I don't believe Major Powell mentioned anything of that sort in his journals." He shook his head. "You have a vivid imagination, dear. When we're out of here, you should write a book: *The Adventures of Mara Ewing in the Underworld.* Sounds smashing."

He watched her covertly, waiting for her to correct him: Mara Ewing *Tate.*

Mara sensed intuitively why he had said it, and the unspoken challenge he was posing to her—*What will it be when we're man and wife? Mara Ewing Rodgers or Mara Rodgers Tate?*—but she put it out of her thoughts and gazed around at the majestic bluffs reaching up into the heavens. "Seven million years ago the Colorado River was flowing along the surface —seven million years carving this gigantic gorge out of the rock. Almost the whole history of the earth can be read in the strata of the canyon walls."

"Yes, it's amazing. See, there's the lavender-brown layer of Tapeats sandstone, over that the green stone of the Cambrian period, then the pale purple of the Devonian, the vermilion of the Redwall, and, above it, the brighter red stone and the buff-colored Cocino sandstone. Ah, see that layer of creamy gray? That's from the Kaibab period. What a geologist's paradise!"

"Sam, up ahead on the right bank, that nice sandy beach."

"Perfect; we'll stop over for lunch. Hard paddle on the starboard side."

The smooth water held constant for the remainder of that day, and they were free to marvel at the scenic wonders along the route: brilliant multicolored rock formations and fossils; exotic plant and animal life; the ruins of a Pueblo village perched high on the rocky walls; magnificent trees growing horizontally out of seemingly sheer rock; an ancient Havasupai community.

"It's overwhelming," Mara said. "Impossible to imagine that this wilderness was once inhabited; but why?"

"Protection from wild animals and hostile human tribes."

Deep in the bowels of the earth now, darkness closed in in early afternoon. In the premature twilight they beached the boat and bathed before supper. Observing Mara standing naked in ankle-deep water, Sam remarked, "The wonders of the Grand Canyon cannot compare with the wonder of you, my darling. Woman is truly God's classic work of art. You look like a statue carved out of flawless ivory."

"Sam, you're embarrassing me." Coyly she covered her *mons Veneris* with one hand and shielded her breasts with the other arm.

"I am quite insatiable for you, you wench, and you know it."

As he came toward her, she noted, with rising excitement, the quick arousal of his manhood. She closed her eyes and moaned with pleasure as he compressed it full length along her quivering belly. They made wild, passionate love on a blanket while a flock of birds circled overhead, filling the air with their song. Afterward, Sam put on his shirt and trousers while Mara crawled into the bedroll and curled up in languid, feline contentment.

"I should get up and help you with supper," she said half-heartedly.

"No, you stay put tonight. I shall light the fire and prepare the 'vittles,' as you Arizonans so colorfully phrase it."

It was the most eerie and disquieting feeling Mara had ever experienced, lying in the bedroll in Stygian darkness, watching the sunlight playing brilliant color rhapsodies on the upper terraces of the bluffs thousands of feet above them. The blue sky had been reduced to a thin ribbon separating the north and south ridges of the canyon. She shuddered uneasily and cuddled up as close to Sam as she could.

"Hey, are you trying to crawl inside of me?" he said.

"Why shouldn't I?" she joked. "You've been crawling into me for the past two days."

"Lewd wench." He slapped her bare bottom.

"Seriously, Sam, I wish you'd keep the fire going all night. I'm scared."

"Darling, if I sit up all night and tend the fire, I won't have strength left tomorrow to shoot the rapids."

"Shoot the rapids?" she said. "You certainly are picking up our American slang. I guess you'll make a fair-dinkum digger at that."

" 'Fair dinkum'? Wherever did you pick up that?"

"Read a novel about Australia—*Blaze of Passion*—very exciting and romantic."

"I don't care to read about romance; I prefer to practice it."

"I intend to get all the practice I can," she told him solemnly. "I want to become perfect at it."

"You're perfect just the way you are."

"Speaking of which, you certainly are an accomplished lover. How many other girls have you gone to bed with before me?" She clamped a hand over his mouth. "No, I don't want to know!"

Sam laughed. "Somewhat less than a thousand, love."

"Ohhhhh . . ." she caterwauled. "You lascivious beast, you! Don't touch me, you carnal glutton!"

"Shhhh . . . listen. What do you hear?"

She strained her ears and held her breath. Over the gentle rush of the river, there floated a constant distant thunder. "An oncoming storm?" she asked.

"No; that's a waterfall. Tomorrow we will get our baptism of fire. Now, go to sleep and stop playing with my whachamacallit."

She turned over and fitted her body into his; they meshed like stacked spoons. In a state of euphoric bliss, she quickly drifted off into sleep.

Sam lay awake for a good while longer, anticipating the trials and dangers that awaited them downriver. In this land of the Great Unknown, a broken leg or arm or a bout of pneumonia could easily mean one's death warrant.

CHAPTER TEN

On June 6 we are approaching our first rapids, Mara wrote in her journal. It would be the last entry she would be able to write aboard the boat for two harrowing days.

"Hold on!" Sam shouted above the roar of water rushing over rock. The *Mara* leaped forward like a racehorse breaking out of the starting gate and plunged into a steep, boiling chute. Sam's powerful fingers gripped the stem—rudder right, rudder left, rudder straight; left, right, left, right, left—as he maneuvered the boat artfully through a maze of sawtooth rocks. The muscles in his forearms and biceps quivered from the strain. Then, in a sudden spurt, they were through, and the *Mara* skidded across calm water like a planing surfboard.

Mara smiled and thought her face would crack with the aftermath of nervous tension. "That wasn't so bad," she said gamely.

"You're right," Sam said ruefully. "The worst is yet to come. You've read Powell's diaries."

For the next two days the *Mara* raced down a watery incline imperiled by sharp rocks and huge boulders on all sides—down, down, ever deeper into the river gorge. The days grew shorter; twilight now descended at high noon. The last twelve hours were pure hell. Sam had all he could do to exert control over the speeding boat, which was leaping and bucking like a wild stallion through the white frothy water.

Unexpectedly, they glided out onto a small lake as unruffled as a mirror surface. At the far side of the lagoon the water tumbled over the edge of a thunderous waterfall. Sam steered the *Mara* to the most hospitable-looking bank and beached her.

"This calls for a reconnoiter," he said. He took Mara's hand and helped her out of the boat. They walked down the shoreline to the edge of the waterfall and gazed down to the foot of the falls, where the river spilled into an angry witch's cauldron. The roar, reverberating off the canyon walls, was deafening.

Mara covered her ears and screamed, "Powell said it was like being inside a bass drum."

"An understatement," Sam yelled back. "This portage is going to take all day. Let's get started."

First all the supplies and equipment had to be unloaded and lowered on lines to the beach at the foot of the waterfall. The big problem was the boat itself.

"It's lucky Andy made her out of pine," Sam said as he and Mara dragged and pushed the slim craft across the wet sand to the edge.

Even more lucky was Sam's foresight in including a small block and tackle among his equipment. He was able to rig it up to a stout tree near the edge, and slowly and laboriously the *Mara* was eased over the precipice and lowered gently to the floor below.

Finally he lowered Mara on a stout line and shinned down the rope after her. He gazed upward at the tree to which the rope was tied. "I hate to leave good line behind, but we don't have much choice."

Night was upon them, so they made camp about a half-mile farther downriver to get away from the shattering cacophony of the falls.

This has to be the worst of it, Mara wrote in her journal just before she collapsed into an exhausted stupor. There was no lovemaking that night.

Next day the going was fairly smooth for a few hours until they rounded a bend and were sucked into a narrow, curving channel that headed straight for a gigantic boulder forty feet wide and equally high, with a sharply jutting prow like that of an ocean liner. Where the onrushing river broke against the sharp extremity, a twenty-foot wave of water was thrown up on each side of the boulder, obscuring the channel on both flanks.

Making a blind guess, Sam gave the *Mara* hard right rudder, and she lurched to the right and plunged into a wall of water at sickening speed. All control was lost now as she was caught in a vortex at the rear of the boulder and sent spinning, half submerged, like a leaf sucked down a drainpipe.

Sam and Mara held onto metal handholds set into the gunwale on both sides of the boat and prayed as the *Mara* careened pell-mell down the churning waterway.

They were stunned and barely realized it when they were safely through the gauntlet and found themselves once again on another placid stretch of water. A veritable Garden of Paradise—white sandy beaches on either shore, with pine trees growing in clusters back from the banks to the canyon walls, the air aromatic with the spice of their needles.

They beached the boat, unloaded the waterlogged supplies to dry, and bailed out the *Mara.* Last of all they hung up their clothing on tree branches and crawled into their communal bedroll. They cuddled close together for warmth but without ardor. They were too fatigued even to eat supper. Although it was only three o'clock in the afternoon, they slept the sleep of the dead until dawn the following morning.

"I don't know how much more of this we can take —you, I, the boat," Sam said as Mara boiled water for coffee the next blue-gray morning.

"I'm one big ache from head to foot," she said.

Sam's mouth compressed grimly. "Well, there's no

turning back. All we can do is grit our teeth and pray."

Their confidence was slowly restored as progress that morning and all afternoon was smooth, fast, and uneventful.

"Maybe we are through the worst of it," Sam said as they set up camp for the night.

A hot, rib-sticking meal of boiled beef, potatoes, and vegetables elated their spirits, and, as a special treat, Sam opened a bottle of brandy he had tucked away for just such an occasion.

Both were giggling like children and eager to make love as they crawled naked into the bedroll. They coupled quickly and started all over again, this time dallying in erotic foreplay for more than a half-hour. Sam lavished kisses all over her body.

Mara writhed in near-unbearable pleasure as his tongue teased her navel; whimpered as his mouth glided down her belly and his hands spread her thighs wide. "Oh, my darling," she cried out in ecstasy, "don't stop! *Please* don't stop. Here, swing your leg across me; I want to adore you with my lips."

He did, and with trembling fingers she guided his hard, pulsing flesh to her ravenous mouth.

When they had finished, lying limp and satiated in each other's arms, she whispered, "It keeps getting better all the time. One time it will be too much to endure, and I will expire of terminal love."

"Don't do that, love. I'll try and be more temperate in the future."

"Don't you dare!" She tickled his ribs, and they kissed and lay still, waiting for blissful sleep.

The next day was even better than the first, and their good fortune stretched over the course of the next four days. They were confident and jubilant and celebrated with brandy each night.

On June 23 Sam observed, "Have you noticed the canyon walls are narrowing?"

"Yes, and the highest yet. We must be at the lowest point of the gorge."

They were in fact so far down, the rims of the walls on each side seemed almost to touch high up in the fleecy clouds, leaving only a strip of sky sandwiched between them.

The canyon became even more narrow with each passing day, and the river flowed commensurately faster. Thousands of years of rock slides were piled up along the banks and obstructing the channel, creating the most treacherous obstacle course they had yet encountered. Whirlpools and cross tides whiplashed the boat from one canyon wall to the other and buffeted her against half-submerged rocks. Sam screamed at Mara to lie down in the bottom of the boat.

He was battling the tiller with both hands, but it was an impossible task. It was a wonder to him that the frail pine craft could survive such brutal punishment. No sooner were they miraculously past the labyrinth than the *Mara* shot down a steep, sinuous chute. The thunder of a waterfall loomed up louder and louder as they descended upon it with breakneck speed.

"Paddle for shore!" Sam shouted, and leaned hard against the stem.

With maddening inertia, the boat inched toward the nearest bank. They were only a half-mile from the brink and certain death. Mara was kneeling amidships, paddling with all of her strength. Sam let go of the tiller and grabbed an oar to help.

When he could see the water was waist deep, he leaped out and yelled to Mara to do the same. Only a massive surge of adrenaline gave them the physical strength to wade ashore, dragging the boat along as they went.

"We're going to make it!" Sam shouted. "Hang on, ducks!"

The snaggletoothed rim of the falls was just thirty yards away. And then it happened:

Mara slipped on a slimy flat rock, and her wet hands slid the length of the gunwale to the prow. She tried for a more secure hold just as a wave crashed over her. Screaming with terror, she was ripped from the boat and catapulted toward the brink.

Sam on the port side had secure footing in ankle-deep water now. With a herculean effort, he lifted the boat and hurled it onto the bank. Paralyzed with fear, he watched his beloved swept right over the edge; but providence was with her. There was a big round boulder directly in her path, and with her legs spread wide, she managed to straddle it.

"Hold on!" Sam shouted. He grabbed an oar and raced down the narrow strip of sand until he came abreast of her. He waded out as far as he dared and extended the oar. "Grab on and I'll pull you ashore. Make certain you have a good grip."

Before they left Green River, Andy Hall had treated the oars with resin and pine tar, and this precaution saved Mara's life. Clamping the rock as tightly as she could with her knees, she let go with her hands and grabbed at the oar. When she was confident that she had a firm grip, she kicked at the rock and propelled herself toward the bank. That momentum and Sam's mighty tug brought her safely to shore.

The two of them looked at each other mutely. He embraced her; she was as limp as a rag doll. He kissed her cold, unresponsive lips and lowered her gently to the ground. They lay there silently for almost an hour; at last they fell asleep, still clutching at each other.

The next two weeks were a living hell—rapids and falls one upon the other in maddening succession, each one seemingly worse than the one before.

One day they made only two miles. As they huddled around the campfire that night, Mara said, "I'm frightened, Sam. There's an aura of evil about the canyon. I keep feeling there's an unseen monster out there in the dark waiting to destroy us."

"Poppycock!" Sam scoffed at her premonitions, but inwardly his apprehensions were as real as her own. An eerie howling wind screamed through the gorge soon after midnight, shaking and bending the pine trees on the sandy peninsula where they had made camp. The banshee wail intensified.

Mara sat upright in the bedroll and woke Sam. "Something awful is going to happen; I know it!"

"Easy, easy, love. The wind can't harm us. Lie back and relax." He put his arms around her and pulled her down beside him again.

Almost as if in defiance of his dismissal, the angry heavens hurled down thunderbolt after thunderbolt into the canyon, blinding blue splashes of dazzling fire exploding all around their retreat, followed by torrents of rain. Their campfire was shielded by layer upon layer of thickly interlaced pine branches, but the gods were not to be denied their vengeance. A twister swept down the river like a small tornado, sucking water, leaves, and light stones up into its spinning vortex. It descended on the peninsula, uprooting trees and sending their supplies scattering in all directions. Then, before it sped on, it picked up the campfire and cast flaming coals and faggots into the trees and over their beached boat, which they had wisely stashed in a small gully, remnant of a dried-up mountain stream, out of reach of the raging river and wind.

Wind and rain ceased as abruptly as they had erupted.

"The boat! We must save the boat!" Sam shouted.

The wet wood was smoldering in a dozen different places, so hot were the embers. Together they doused the incipient blazes with water and wet sand and beat out the last stubborn coals with burlap sacks. They spent the rest of the night scavenging for their supplies and utensils, strewn all over the peninsula. It was dawn before they had everything packed up and secured in the boat.

As bone-weary as they were, they pushed on. Every moment lost was a threat. If they were to survive, they had to escape from the canyon before their food and strength were expended.

The light seemed brighter that morning. "I do believe the walls are getting lower," Sam said.

"They are," Mara exulted. "See that ribbon of bright-blue sky? It's getting wider."

After the ordeal of the previous night, Mother Nature repented and favored them with fair, warm weather and smooth sailing. They made good time for the next week. The wild water ended and the *Mara* glided over serene water as the canyon widened dramatically and then was joined by two small tributaries.

Sam got out his charts. "Yes, I recognize this place from Powell's notes."

"Are we almost out?" she asked anxiously.

"Not quite, but at least the worst is over."

That remark proved to be overly optimistic, because the very next day they plunged into more rapids and had to portage six times in a span of twenty-four hours.

It was the last week in July when, once again, the walls closed in on them; it became so narrow that the river filled the canyon from bluff to bluff, and there were no banks at all on which they could make camp. For two straight days they were confined to the boat, with only brief respites of restless sleep on the hard boards.

Then, on August 8, there was a miracle; at least it seemed one to Sam and Mara. Suddenly they broke through the narrow passage and emerged into an enormous grotto Mara described in wonder as "a celestial cathedral." She quoted from Powell's journal: " 'We are inside God's own cathedral. . . . Today I walked along a natural pavement cut into one wall of the canyon as smooth as polished marble.' "

It was a scenic wonder such as neither of them had ever witnessed before and would not witness again, even in a region of the country where Nature had created a surfeit of grandiose monuments. Here were soaring arches, spires, walls smooth as glass and veined with orange, red, green, blue, yellow—all the hues of the rainbow and then some. The only sounds were the rush of the river and the squealing of giant bats. Thousands of feet above them, the walls appeared to curve inward to form a nave where misty clouds floated around like gray ghosts.

"This is really it," Sam said in awe: "*the* grandest part of *the* Grand Canyon, rock bottom, where it is one mile to the surface."

They camped there that night, and next morning they walked along the "pavement" Powell had boasted of. Afterward they ate a meager breakfast—provisions were dwindling—and resumed their fantastic journey.

Conditions were steadily improving, however, and by mid-August the canyon widened appreciably every day, the sheer walls beginning to slope away on each side, opening up a wide expanse of blue sky and allowing the sun to penetrate into the gorge.

Mara stood up in the boat and threw her arms wide open to embrace the glorious heavens. "Oh, thank you, God! I was beginning to think we'd never see the sun again."

Sam put his arms around her and hugged her to him. "It's not quite done with us yet, sweet. Powell says there is one last nightmare to overcome before we're home free."

His prediction was borne out the next day when

the current accelerated as the canyon walls began to narrow once again. Sam and Mara bailed feverishly, hour after hour, to keep pace with the water oozing in through the leaky seams. The *Mara* was picked up on the crest of a huge wave that formed where the gorge became a narrow defile—a water gutter, in effect—lifted high, and sent spinning like a top down a serpentine course that terminated in a hazardous whirlpool filling a basin at the foot of the chute. It seemed to Mara that the Grand Canyon was bound to destroy them. Then, in a dramatic turnabout, the *Mara* was hurled through a narrow breach in the rock and they were scaling across calm waters in a broad open valley with low grassy hills on either side reaching all the way to the horizon.

"We're through!" Sam shouted.

He and Mara embraced, almost tipping over the boat in their excitement and fervor. With tears of joy and gratitude flowing down their cheeks, they turned and gazed backward at the granite bluffs of the Grand Canyon towering majestically through the morning mist.

"Major Powell said it best," Mara told him: " 'So long as there are human beings of vision, courage, and determination who refuse to falter in the face of adversity, nothing in this universe can forever remain the Great Unknown.' "

MARA
THE
THIRD

CHAPTER ONE

"And so you married Sam Rodgers the following fall?"

"Yes, right after my seventeenth birthday."

"And Sam went into the family business?"

"Yes, and my ambitions for him were more than realized. Sam became indispensable to Tate International Industries. In the first decade of the twentieth century, TII's mining holdings led the United States in copper production, and in my lifetime, it never relinquished that leadership in any year."

"Entering a new century must be an exciting experience. . . . What did I say? Why the pained expression suddenly?"

"Actually, it was more a traumatic experience, for the Tates at least—no, for the whole world, for that matter. It heralded an era of dramatic, radical change —socially, politically, sociologically, and psychologically. I suppose it really began with the death of Queen Victoria. Her reign had covered the better part of the nineteenth century. She was regarded as an institution, a symbol of stability and security, a veritable Rock of Gibraltar."

"A universal mother figure."

"You could say that. In any event, her demise seemed to unsettle some intangible social balance, a human understanding and unity that affected millions the world over. That small span of ten years saw a succession of explosive events that were felt around the globe."

"Such as? My history is faulty."

"In 1903 two events occurred that would forever after alter the lives of all generations to come: Henry Ford began the Ford Motor Company, and the Wright brothers made their historic flight at Kitty Hawk. Virtually overnight the world would shrink, and the enforced intimacy that the automobile and airplane would foster among peoples and nations would spread hostility and chaos throughout the twentieth century. There was a sort of biblical destiny to be played out, the tragic inevitability of the Greek theater.

"Man and his wondrous machines . . . My grandfather Drew predicted that in time it would be the machines that ran the men who devised them—Mary Shelley's Frankenstein monster. Time proved him right. By way of example, there was the fiery destruction of the excursion steamer the General Slocum *at Hell's Gate in 1904, with the loss of over a thousand lives. That was the year of the Russo-Japanese War.*

"Disaster followed disaster. In 1906 there was the dreadful San Francisco fire and earthquake. . . . There were positive events, though. If I recall correctly, it was in 1907 that the United States issued its first challenge to England's naval supremacy with an unparalleled round-the-world cruise made by the U.S. fleet. And a year later Robert E. Peary became the first human being to set foot on the North Pole.

"Petty affectations, children vying for honors on the athletic field . . . When King Edward died in 1910, just nine years after ascending the throne, it was an omen to all of humanity. Edward burned himself out prematurely by his excesses in the same manner that the modern technological world seems hell-bent on self-destruction. That was also the year Drew and Gwen Tate died. She went first of pneumonia and he followed soon after, from grief. But they lived a long and fruitful life, more than eighty years of it. There should have been no regrets on the family's part, and there

weren't, really, but we loved them both so dearly. The loss of love leaves an empty space that can be forgotten in time but never refilled.

"Oh, God, I am going to cry! I can't help it. So many heart-wrenching calamities, one on top of the other—a world war that came near to fulfilling Drew's prophecy; mankind cannibalized by his machines, his bombs, his machine guns, his cannon, his tanks, his aircraft, driving him to the brink of Armageddon."

"You passed over something that occurred in the year 1912, before the war."

"Deliberately so; it is too painful to think about."

"For Mara Rodgers Tate. Now, what I want you to do is to count backward with me from one hundred to one very slowly, and as we count, you will travel back in time, one year at a time. Are you ready?"

"Yes."

"Let us commence: One hundred . . . ninety-nine . . . You will no longer be Mara Rodgers Tate. When you reach the count of fifty, you will be Mara Ewing Tate. Is that understood? Good. Proceed: Ninety-eight . . . ninety-seven . . ."

" 'Mara Rodgers Tate'—it's positively humiliating," Sam growled as he examined the signature his wife had affixed to a company contract.

Just before they left Arizona for an extended vacation in Europe, Gordon Ewing and his wife Mara, heiress to the Tate empire, had assigned their power of attorney to their daughter.

"Stop being chauvinistic, Sam," she chided. "Without the name Tate, I would lose the considerable authority I hold over my peers in the business world. I realize you prefer to think of me as Mrs. Samuel Rodgers, Jr. Well, you go right ahead; I have no objection. In my intimate personal life I am quite content to be your chattel," she teased.

"Confound it, Mara, I don't appreciate being the butt of your jokes!"

She went over to him and put her arms around his neck, pressing her body tightly against him. "Do you know you're cute when you pout, Sam?"

"There you go again," he said in exasperation. "I ought to turn you over my knee and paddle your bottom."

She stood on tiptoe and kissed the hard angle of his jawbone just below the ear, then ran the tip of her tongue all the way down to the dimple in his chin. "I wouldn't object to that little game, either. Why don't I close the bedroom door and we'll discuss it at greater length? Speaking of greater length . . ." She reached a hand between them and fondled him. "Yes, I can tell you're not averse to joining me in an afternoon siesta."

Sam laughed softly and grasped her buttocks with both hands. "There'll not be much 'siesting' done, I'll wager. Just let me lock that contract in the wall safe." He walked to her writing desk and picked up the paper she had signed. "I'll be right back. You can start without me."

Her laughter followed him down the hall as he proceeded to the library.

When he returned, she was stretched out on the satin-quilted counterpane, nude. He stood over her, contemplating her languid, seductive posture with rising ardor. Thirteen years of marriage had not dulled his desire for the one and only woman in his life. Like a lush and exotic garden, she had grown more luxuriant with the passing years. Her breasts, like firm young fruits the first time he had caressed them, were still firm but fuller; and while at sixteen Mara had a flat belly and slim hips, her figure shapely but boyishly slender, at twenty-nine her charms were voluptuous.

"You remind me of a Rubens nude," he told her as he removed his clothing.

"I am *not* a Rubens nude; they are fat and sloppy."
The subject triggered a painful recollection, and her
expression mirrored it.

"What is it, love?" he asked as he lay down beside
her.

"I was just remembering what Dr. Fawcett said to
me the last time I had an examination: 'Mrs. Rodgers,
with a marvelous figure such as you possess, you
should have ten children.' "

"Did he, now?" Sam said very softly, his sexual
desire waning. It was the one thorn nettling what was
an otherwise idyllic marriage—Mara's inability to con-
ceive a child. He gathered her into his arms and kissed
her forehead and her closed eyelids tenderly. "We
could always adopt, you know, my dear; it's done
everywhere. Did you know that the Paxtons—he's the
head of our London office—have adopted twins?"

"No!" she said adamantly, and her green eyes narrowed with feline defiance. "I want a child of my own,
made out of our own flesh and blood, Sam, and I will
never give up trying." She coaxed his flagging member
with both hands. "Of course, that requires some cooperation on your part. Come along, darling, purge
your mind of unpleasantries and let's have another go
at it."

That night, their daughter's letter caught up with the
Gordon Ewings in London at the Savoy Hotel one week
before they were to accompany Colonel John Jacob
Astor and his wife on the maiden voyage of the pride
of the British White Star Line, heralded as "the greatest
ship on the seas"—the *Titanic.*

Gordon was sitting at the breakfast table in their
luxury suite reading the London *Times,* only half listening as Mara read their daughter's letter to him: " 'I am
determined to bear Sam's child if it takes fifty years.
I will never abandon hope, and I promise you that one

day you will live to see me suckle my own *baby at my breast. . . .'*"

Gordon chuckled and shook his head. "Oh, she's a Tate, no doubt about it—stubborn as English bulldogs. Fifty years indeed! Poor Sam; I hope he has a strong back."

"Gordon Ewing, what a naughty thing to say."

"I enjoy being naughty and so do you, and I daresay the lechery runs in the family. Seriously, there is one thing even the Tates can't have their say in: the will of God."

Mara's dark eyes glowed. "That may be true, Gordon, but God, of all the beings in his universe, certainly has the prerogative to change his mind."

He took her hand in his hands. "Would it be so terrible if we weren't to become grandparents?"

"I think it would be catastrophic. What will happen to Tate International Industries when you and I are gone?"

"You do have brothers and nephews and nieces."

"Don't be ridiculous, Gordon! Emlyn, Allan, Gilbert, and their silly wives and children, all any of them are good for now is to clip coupons and squander their stock dividends and bank-interest checks."

"Isn't that a bit arrogant and unfair, my dear?"

"It is the truth and you know it better than anyone else, Gordon. Mara and I, we are fortunate having men like you and Samuel." She clasped her hands together. "I pray to God that our daughter will bless us with a granddaughter."

Gordon frowned and pushed his plate aside. "A granddaughter? What about a grandson?"

She averted his questioning gaze. "Well, of course, the gender is not important, just so long as there is a legitimate Tate to carry on the business."

His expression was faintly reprimanding. "The 'business'? Don't you mean the 'dynasty'?"

"Don't be sarcastic, Gordon."

"Hmmmm . . . I suggest we forget the Tates and the business and all the rest of the somber realities of life and devote our exclusive attentions and energies to enjoying this gala event we are privileged to be a part of: the maiden voyage of the *Titanic*."

CHAPTER TWO

Mara was entranced by her first glimpse of the elegant entrance hall on the main deck of the *Titanic,* appointed in polished teak and mahogany and carpeted with ankle-deep Persian rugs. The spacious room was dominated by a sweeping staircase leading up to the mezzanine, encircled by a Roman colonnade.

Equally as impressive was the grand recreational salon, bedecked with classical wall tapestries and crystal chandeliers and furnished with plush lounges, easy chairs, and writing desks overlooked by broad windows with leaded glass. A roaring fire crackled merrily in the enormous fireplace; on the wall above it, a grandmother clock chirped away the final minutes before sailing time.

The ocean liner's mighty whistle reverberated throughout the ship, and a steward poked his head into the cabin of the John Jacob Astors, where the last of the guests at an elaborate farewell party were toasting the travelers with French champagne.

"All ashore who's going ashore!" he announced.

"Anyone care to go on deck?" Astor inquired. He was a handsome man with dark hair and a military bearing, fashionably attired in a navy-blue pinstripe suit with a dashing ascot at his throat. His wife was a raven-haired beauty, the toast of New York and London society. Her high, large bosom was displayed to good advantage by a daringly low-cut velvet gown with a lace insert over her cleavage that played to advantage rather than concealed her natural charms.

"I don't think so, dear," she replied. "Southampton is not my favorite port of embarkation."

The 2,307 passenger list numbered many of the most illustrious men and women of wealth and world-wide prestige in American and British high society. Present in the Astors' lavish suite at the *Titanic*'s sailing were Gordon and Mara Ewing; Major Archibald Butt; billionaire Isidor Straus; Benjamin Guggenheim; F. D. Millet; William T. Snead; Bruce Ismay, the general director of the White Star Line; the ship's renowned architect and builder, Thomas Andrews; and many of the great men's ladies. Conversation was animated and excited, if a bit mundane for Mara's taste.

"Like a bunch of silly children setting off on a picnic," she whispered to her husband.

He patted her arm. "It *is* a picnic of sorts. You don't have to pay attention; just smile and nod your head."

"Don't you simply adore Captain Smith?" gushed a skinny blonde woman wearing an ostrich-plume hat. "He reminds me of old St. Nick with those white whiskers."

"More of a graying walrus," commented her escort.

"Did you know this is his last voyage?" interjected Astor.

"A fitting tribute to one of our finest skippers," said White Star's Ismay. "Thirty-eight years' service and never a mishap."

"Tell us about your marvelous ship, Mr. Ismay," Mrs. Astor pleaded.

"My dear lady, Mr. Andrews is the man to pose your question to. After all, the *Titanic* is his brainchild, a monument to progress."

"Is it really unsinkable, Mr. Andrews?" asked a stunning brunette who had languidly draped herself over the back of the architect's chair.

"Short of an act of God, yes, I would say the

Titanic is unsinkable," Andrews said with pride. He never tired of talking about his creation.

The ship was something to be proud of. A 46,328 Leviathan, she was 882.5 feet long and 92 feet wide and comfortably accommodated her 2,223 passengers and crewmen. Belowdecks her holds were partitioned off into a series of watertight compartments, all of which could be sealed off in the event of a mishap, so that only that portion of the ship that was affected by a hypothetical accident would take on water.

Andrews held up a hand for silence, almost with reverence, and announced, "We're under way. Do you hear the humming of her engines? Two sets that function independently—four-cylinder reciprocating engines."

Mara was troubled. "Mr. Andrews, how many lifeboats does the *Titanic* have?"

He seemed shocked. "Lifeboats, madam? Well, of course, the *Titanic*'s are merely window dressing—lends her a shipshape appearance, if you will excuse the pun. Actually, there are only twenty lifeboats."

"And what is their total capacity?"

Andrews rubbed his chin, displeased with her persistence. "Oh, I'd say up to twelve hundred."

"But there are more than twenty-two hundred people aboard."

His attitude became surly now. "Madam, you shouldn't trouble your pretty head with such fantasies. The *Titanic,* I repeat, is unsinkable."

"Short of an act of God, I know," Mara said with sarcasm. "That is what they said about the *Titan.*"

"The *Titan?*" several of the guests said in unison. The discussion between Mara and Andrews was drawing an audience.

"Yes, from the novel of the same name, by Morgan Robertson, published just before the turn of the century. It's about this ocean liner, *Titan*—allegedly unsinkable—embarking on its maiden voyage with more than two thousand wealthy passengers. It was eight hundred feet long and displaced forty-five thousand tons, and it too carried only twenty-odd lifeboats for 'cosmetic appearance.' It sailed from England in mid-April and struck an iceberg in the North Atlantic, and nearly all the passengers and crew were lost."

A murmur of discontent and apprehension circulated through the throng around her.

"My word, Mrs. Rodgers, what are you trying to do—scare us out of our wits?" Colonel Astor said, with a clear note of chagrin in his voice.

"I won't listen to another word of this drivel," one stout matron stated haughtily. She looked at Mara sternly through her lorgnette. "Fiction, indeed!"

Later, when they were back in their own quarters, even Gordon was critical of Mara's impulsive behavior: "It was not very tactful of you, my dear, putting the damper on a festive party the way you did."

"I'm sorry about spoiling Colonel Astor's party, but I think it's highly irresponsible of the White Star Line to send a new ship to sea with insufficient lifeboats."

That evening they were among the honored guests at the captain's table. It was a gala occasion, and both the passengers and the ship's officers were "dressed to the nines," as Mara's Welsh mother would have put it. Captain Smith himself was resplendent in his dress whites glittering with gold braid. The gold insignia of the White Star Line on the peak of his cap, placed beside his plate, flashed in the light from the crystal chandeliers.

The dining hall was a rainbow of color as couples twirled around the dance floor, polished to mirror brilliance, to the band's medley of Strauss waltzes, the men looking stiff in their black tuxedoes, starched shirts, and white ties, the women preening like peacocks in their elegant ball gowns of silk and brocade.

Mrs. Astor wore a tartan that recalled a muted old tapestry. Mara wore a gown of lime Lyons silk trimmed with white lace and green ribbon a shade darker than the dress and puff sleeves. Her silk stockings were striped in gold and apricot, and on her feet were delicate patent-leather boots with silver toe-caps and tassels.

The dialog at virtually every table in the vast hall was about the *Titanic* and this historic voyage they, the passengers, were privileged to be a part of. Mrs. Astor, still perturbed by the story Mara had narrated at the bon voyage party in their suite, was obsessed by the threat of icebergs.

Captain Smith, a jovial, portly man, laughed and patted her arm. "My dear madam, while it is true that this unusually mild winter we have been through has caused an excessive number of icebergs to break off from the polar ice caps and drift south with the Labrador current, on orders from the home office, our navigators have charted a course for the *Titanic* far to the south of the closest iceberg."

Just as politely and patiently, he replied to scores of queries addressed to him by other passengers: "Yes, we are capable of making better than thirty knots, but, as is the case with all new White Star ships, we are holding to a steady speed of twenty, give or take a knot according to the currents."

"When will we get to New York?"

"We are due to arrive off the Grand Banks on Sunday night, which means——" He was interrupted as the purser came over to the table and bent to whisper in his ear. Captain Smith nodded and apologized to his guests: "If you will excuse me, I am wanted on the bridge. Duty before pleasure." He rose and put his cap under one arm, bowing to his guests. "You have honored me by your presence at my table, especially the lovely ladies. So, until we meet again . . ."

"Have a look for an iceberg while you're up there, captain!" one wag shouted after him, and everyone at the table had a good laugh, except for Mara.

Later, a psychologist asked Mara to dance. He was a tall, wiry man, with close-cropped steel-gray hair and a Vandyke beard. "I understand you are an admirer of the novelist Morgan Robertson, Mrs. Ewing."

Mara smiled. "Oh, you've heard about this afternoon? Now you are pulling my leg, is that it?"

"On the contrary. In my profession we are studiously reticent about ridiculing the philosophies and beliefs of others. Tell me, have you ever heard of 'promnesia'?"

"I can't say that I have, doctor."

"It means 'a memory of the future.' "

"Memory of the future? How quaint."

"Yes, and there're some who believe that what is commonly referred to as 'premonition' is, in reality, the ability to look into the future."

A cold chill ran up Mara's spine. She was suddenly somber. "Let us hope, doctor, that Morgan Robertson was not inspired by promnesia when he sat down to write the novel *Titan*. . . . Do you mind if we sit down? I have a blinding headache."

She still suffered from the throbbing in her temples when she and Gordon had turned in for the night. She snuggled close to him in the big double bed, pressing a cheek to his chest. "Gordon, make love to me; I want to be close to you."

"I'd be delighted." He chuckled. "This may be a famous first. What better way to christen a new ocean liner than to make love on her the first night out? By Jove, I wonder how many of the others have the same idea. John Jacob possibly; *she* looks like she enjoys a good roll in the hay."

"Don't be lewd, Gordon." She slipped out of her

satin nightgown and straddled his hips. "I feel like being in charge tonight."

"By all means."

She encouraged him to full tumescence with her hands and deftly effected penetration. Her contractions commenced before his own, and by the time he was ready, she was already building to her second orgasm. "That was magnificent," she sighed afterward. "I am thoroughly satiated."

He pinched her buttocks. "A perfect ending to a perfect day and an omen of a perfect voyage all the way to New York, that writer chap be damned!"

Mara smiled. "Yes, and what a ninny I am to make such a big issue of it." She fell asleep in a state of peace and contentment.

The next day dawned with the sun brilliant in a cloudless azure sky and the ocean calm as an Irish loch. "It's almost balmy," Mara observed to Mrs. Astor as they lay in deck chairs having midmorning brunch—tea and cakes or bouillon and salt crackers— while their husbands played shuffleboard.

"No iceberg could exist in such weather," Mrs. Astor said; but Mara detected a residual of anxiety in her manner.

The day after that was even better; Mara was too warm even to wrap herself in a blanket while she sunned herself. In fact, for five days the *Titanic* knifed through calm seas, and the meteorological reports received from Canada over the radio forecast clement weather all the way to New York.

They arrived off the Grand Banks Sunday night, April 14, and set a course southwest for New York. First-Officer Murdock stopped on his way to the bridge to check with the radio operator on duty, John Phillips:

"Anything to report, Mr. Phillips?"

"Nothing significant, sir. . . . Oh, there have been

a rash of sightings of ice up north, but the nearest one to us that I can ascertain is over two hundred miles away."

Murdock smiled. "That's of no concern. Good night, Phillips." He strode briskly down the deck to the bridge, whistling a happy cockney tune.

When he entered the wheelhouse, he was surprised to see Mr. and Mrs. Ewing dressed in formal wear, she with a sable coat draped over her shoulders. "Good evening," he said. "Come to see how the other half lives, righto?"

"Lieutenant Lightoller was kind enough to invite us to come up and see how you chaps manage a monster like the *Titanic*."

Murdock laughed. "It's all done with mirrors. Seriously, though, with all the gyros and sophisticated navigational equipment we have, she practically sails herself." He turned to the second officer. "How is it going, Lightoller?"

"Water's like a mirror, sir—too placid for my taste."

"You would rather be sailing through high seas?" Mara asked curiously.

"Not high seas, ma'am, but *active* seas. You see, the ocean is to a sailor what the lay of the land is to a geologist. There's much to be learned from the way the sea moves; it's like a living, breathing thing. You can read the waves. If there's anything out there in the night, we can judge approximately what it is and where it lies by studying the backwash of the breakers. The lookouts can spot it miles off, but not tonight; it's like a pond."

"Icebergs—is that what you're referring to?" Mara said. A frown creased her brow. "But I understand the closest we'll come to an iceberg is over two hundred miles."

Gordon put his arm around her. "I couldn't help

observing that the lookouts have been doubled tonight; why so if you don't anticipate danger?"

The two officers exchanged a smug look, and Murdock explained in a slightly condescending tone, "The thing is, Mr. Ewing, at sea one has to anticipate the unexpected, especially on a night like this when there is no moon and still water."

"But the stars are brilliant. By Jove, they appear to come down right into the water!"

There were clusters of glittering stars lying in a 360° sweep of the horizon. One had the illusion that the *Titanic* was the hub of a gigantic wheel, the spokes of which were the slivers of light the stars sent knifing across the smooth surface of the water to converge on the ship. It made for hazardous visual distortion.

" 'Phosphorescent stagnation' is what we call it," Murdock said.

"Well, I'll be off to bed," Lightoller said. He tipped his cap to Mara and Gordon. "Night, Mrs. Ewing, Mr. Ewing. Sleep well."

Mara and Gordon remained on deck, so fascinated were they by naval procedure: the intent concentration of the helmsman; Murdock and the other officers in the wheelhouse poring obsessively over their charts. Time passed quickly, and it was almost midnight when she noted with a start the clock on the wall. "Gracious, Gordon, I'm afraid we've overstayed our welcome up here."

"Right. Let's go down to the main lounge for a nightcap and then we'll retire."

"It's been a pleasure to have you on the bridge, Mr. Ewing," Murdock said. "I'm sorry I couldn't give you more time."

"You've been simply marvelous, lieutenant," Mara said, smiling.

He left the wheelhouse with them. "Think I'll finish my watch up front at the rail; better visibility without the lights in the wheelhouse." He walked forward and took up a post high above the gentle sea.

There was a glare emanating from a hatch far down the deck. Murdock cupped his hands to his mouth and shouted, "You down there, shut the fore-scuttle hatch; it's fogging my vision!"

Mara and Gordon were halfway down the companionway to the main deck when the Klaxon din of the bell in the crow's nest sounded the alarm. Three times the bell tolled.

Gordon had done his nautical homework thoroughly since they had boarded the *Titanic*. He gripped Mara's arm and muttered, "Jesus, there's an object dead ahead! Come along; let's go back up to the bridge and see what's happening."

They turned and started back up the steps, arriving at the wheelhouse just as Murdock shoved the telegraphs communicating with the engine rooms to full stop and then yelled at the wheelman, "Hard-a-starboard!"

He rushed out of the wheelhouse and stood at the rail, his knuckles clenched white on the ice-crusted steel bar. Gordon and Mara joined him, and the three of them stared in silent horror at the terrifying apparition straight ahead—a vast mountain of ice towering over the *Titanic* no more than a quarter of a mile away and closing the distance rapidly. The ship was sliding off to port but not nearly fast enough.

"Damn, damn, damn!" Murdock cursed softly. Too late he realized that he should not have ordered the engines stopped; the inertia of the water on the ship's hull was dragging her back and leaving her at the mercy of the iceberg.

For a fleeting instant it appeared as if they would escape unscathed or, at worst, with only minor damage as ship and berg closed, the *Titanic*'s starboard side sliding and bumping along the wall of ice with a screeching sound like fingernails scraping across a black-board, only magnified a thousand times. As the ship cruised past the iceberg, Mara and Gordon emitted a long-drawn sigh of relief.

"We made it," Mara said in a tremulous voice.

The decks were coated with fragments of ice that had showered down on the ship during the short con-frontation, but the ship was otherwise sturdy and intact—or so it seemed to everyone, with the exception of the *Titanic*'s designer, Thomas Andrews. He had rushed up to the bridge at the sound of the first alarm, and when the rending screeching commenced, he buried his face in his hands and began to sob quietly to himself in the certain knowledge that his pride and joy was doomed.

His worst fears were borne out when he and Mur-dock and the ship's carpenter rushed belowdecks to appraise the damage. Upon impact with the liner, a sharp shelf of ice far below the waterline had ripped into the steel hull and, with the efficiency of a can opener, cut a jagged gash down her starboard side for more than 250 feet. Although her watertight compart-ments were secured as soon as the accident occurred, the damage was far too extensive for this safety fea-ture to furnish anything more than a temporary re-prieve.

"Ten compartments taking on water fast," the car-penter reported to Captain Smith, who, white-faced and grim, had joined the inspection party. "Water level is already fifteen feet above keel level; no way to stop it from reaching the boilers, and then——" He did not have to complete the statement, not even for Gordon and Mara, who were hovering on the sidelines, trying to remain inconspicuous.

Captain Smith, in a state of shock, nodded and spoke

in a calm, matter-of-fact voice: "Murdock, order all hands on deck and prepare to launch lifeboats. Ship's officers and the men in the boiler rooms are to remain at their posts for the time being."

Carefully coached stewards made the rounds of the cabins, smiles frozen on their faces, and spread the word: "Please report to your lifeboat stations and bring your life preservers with you. It's merely a precaution until minor repairs are completed and we get under way again. Won't take more than an hour or two."

The passengers were not unduly alarmed as the mass exodus onto the boat decks commenced. In fact, a party atmosphere prevailed as flasks of spirits were passed among the cliques around the boats. They were a ragtag bunch clad in a variety of outlandish costumes: some women with fur coats thrown on over their nightgowns, others with their hair done up in curlers and their faces smeared with cold cream; men in evening dress or in heavy turtleneck sweaters with ski caps and earmuffs; even one shapely nude, as could be discerned when her ankle-length mink fell open briefly.

Mara and her husband kept themselves apart from their frivolous shipmates. She kept staring up at the boats being readied by the crew.

"Just as it was in *Titan*," she said; "only twenty boats. When they are filled, there will still be fifteen hundred people left aboard the *Titanic*."

Gordon put an arm around her and pulled her against him. "Steady, old girl. We've come through a lot of hard times in our lives; we'll see this through as well." He kissed the top of her head and closed his eyes, holding back the tears.

In the radio room, Captain Smith was frantically exhorting the telegrapher,

"Faster, Phillips, faster! Don't let up for an instant!"

The operator's fingers were a blur on the key as he tapped out one S.O.S. after another:

> CQD MGY (TITANIC)
> URGENTLY REQUEST HELP AT ONCE
> WE HAVE STRUCK AN ICEBERG
> IN POSITION 41 46 N50 14w

Sea traffic was teeming in the Atlantic that peaceful night, but, of them all, only a few acknowledged the distress call from the *Titanic*. It was an era when the entire world was afflicted with complacency, a malaise that resulted in carelessness and indifference. Aboard many of the ships close enough to lend assistance, the radio officers had closed up shop for the night. One such operator, on the *California*, stood on the bridge with his captain and watched the spectacular display of aerial pyrotechnics no more than six miles off—the red-and-white emergency flares sent up by the *Titanic*:

"Jolly good show, eh what, captain?"

"By Jove, that must be quite a party!"

Quite a party indeed. With tears streaming down his cheeks, Phillips kept his futile vigil at the telegraph key.

> S.O.S. S.O.S. TITANIC SINKING BY THE BOW
> WOMEN AND CHILDREN BEING LOADED INTO
> LIFEBOATS FOR THE LOVE OF GOD
> SEND ASSISTANCE

There was one ship whose conscientious radio operators never left their posts unmanned. Aboard the old Cunard ocean liner *Carpathia*, Captain Arthur Rostron was rudely awakened in the middle of the night. He sat up groggily and rubbed his eyes:

"What is it, Sparks?"

"It's the *Titanic,* sir; she's sinking."

"Good God!" Fully alert now, Captain Rostron leaped out of his bunk and dressed hastily. "How far away is she?"

The telegrapher gave the *Titanic*'s position.

"That's about an hour's time if we make full speed." He rushed up to the bridge and gave the order to the chief engineer: "Push her to the limit!"

Within minutes the old *Carpathia* was making twenty-five knots, faster than Rostron or any other of her skippers had ever dared to push her. As she drew closer to the doomed super liner, the *Carpathia* entered the ice floe that had done in the unsinkable queen of the seas. In a brilliant display of seamanship and daring that won the admiration of his officers, as well as a place in the annals of seafaring fame, Rostron weaved his ship through a tortuous maze of ice, never once slackening her speed.

At 2:00 A.M. Phillips sent out his final dispatch:

S.O.S. S.O.S. TO ALL SHIPS FROM TITANIC
ENGINE ROOM FLOODED TO THE BOILERS
WE ARE LOST

On deck and belowdecks scores of heartrending dramas were being played out. The ship's band on the stern deck was playing a medley of inspirational and nostalgic songs: "Londonderry Air"; "Nearer My God to Thee"; "Crossing the Bar."

Major Archibald Butt patrolled the decks, singing at the top of his lungs, his revolver drawn. Not all the men were as valiant; some cowards dressed up in women's clothing and tried to smuggle themselves into the lifeboats with the women and children. Butt accosted at least a dozen of them. Hurling them roughly back onto the deck, he would shove his gun under their noses: "Try that again and I'll blow your bloody head off!"

One of those he overlooked, who leaped aboard a lifeboat being lowered from a lower deck, was Bruce Ismay, the general director of the White Star Line. "God forgive me," he cried, "but I don't want to die!" Later he would regret that he had not perished like a man, for forever after he would live in infamous disgrace, a leper among his peers.

A father with tears streaming down his face handed his two infant sons to a woman in one of the boats, along with a note. "Please see that my wife is notified. She's in Paris at this address."

Mrs. Astor was one of the last to board a lifeboat.

"You too, sir. There's room for one more," the loading officer whispered.

Colonel Astor looked around and spotted a fat woman wringing her hands and wailing. "What about that lady?" he inquired.

The officer sneered. "She's cheap steerage trash. Hurry it up, sir!"

Astor summoned his old friend Archibald Butt. "Major, hold your gun on this scoundrel and don't let this boat be lowered until I have that poor woman aboard!"

He accomplished his purpose, kissed his wife one last time, and backed off as the boat was swung over the side of the badly listing ship, one of 1,517 passengers, mostly men, who remained staunch as their wives and children pulled away from the *Titanic* into the ice field.

When it was Mara's turn to board the last boat, she held back and took her husband's arm possessively. "No thank you; my place is here with my husband."

"For God's sake," he implored her, "I won't hear of it! You will get into that boat, and that is an order, madam!"

She threw back her head and laughed. "You should know better than to try to order me around, Gordon." Her eyes glistened as she looked into his. "Besides, you don't think you're going to get away from me that easily, do you? You and I, we shall be together until the end of time."

Colonel Astor cleared his throat. "Ewing . . . what say we go down to the salon and have a farewell drink together, you and I and Mrs. Ewing?"

Mara took him by the arm and walked between them along the deck. "That's a marvelous idea, Colonel Astor." She sang along with the band as it played "Rule Britannia."

In the salon, millionaires and cabin boys clinked glasses and linked arms in a display of courage and camaraderie that caused a lump to form in Mara's throat. The three of them walked to the bar and helped themselves to champagne from one of the countless bottles littering the gleaming mahogany counter. As they lifted the crystal goblets, a great shudder ran through the giant liner as a series of violent explosions traveled her full length.

"Her death rattle," said Astor. "Here's to a gallant old girl. It's no disgrace to die with a queen."

They drank quickly, and Gordon wrapped his arms around his wife and kissed her tenderly. "My darling, I love you more at this moment than I have ever loved you before, if that's possible."

"I love you as much, my one and only love."

They were kissing when the *Titanic* rose up at the stern until she was almost perpendicular in the water, then, with a mighty roar like that of an express train plunging out of control down a steep grade, nose-dived into the depths of the Atlantic.

"A giant whale diving," someone in one of the lifeboats muttered.

Not long afterward a hysterical cheer went up from 700 throats simultaneously as the survivors saw the *Carpathia* steaming toward them through the ice with her rockets lighting up the sky, heralding her arrival. The ordeal was over.

CHAPTER THREE

She lapsed into total silence, her head hanging limply to one side and her eyes closed. Her expression reflected the peace and serenity of death. Her red lips were moist and slightly parted. Fiedler was entranced by her beauty.

Unable to resist an impulse, he rose from his seat, bent over her—so close his mouth was inches from hers and he could detect a faintly spicy aroma to her breath, as though she had been eating apples and cinnamon—and kissed her. It was a tender kiss, without passion; even so, he came to his senses with a sense of shock and self-loathing, recoiling from her so forcefully that he knocked over the stool behind him.

My God; what kind of a turd are you, molesting a female patient while she's under a trance? You could lose your license for doing a thing like that! You deserve to lose it, schmuck!

He took out a handkerchief and mopped his perspiring forehead. His hands were trembling, and his voice was tremulous as he addressed her: "Mara . . . it's time to return to the present. Can you hear me, Mara?"

Her face clouded over again, and her voice in reply was flat and toneless: "I can hear you. . . . Who are you? Am I in the hereafter?"

"No, you are very much alive."

"But I thought I . . . I was drowning."

"No, it is Mara Ewing who died aboard the *Titanic* —Mara Ewing *Tate,* if you prefer."

She frowned. "Then who am I? I am Mara. Mara Rodgers?"

"Yes, but not Mara the second; you are the third Mara. . . . Now, do as I tell you. You are going to come forward from 1912 to 1930, 1940, 1950. . . . Count with me: 1951, 1952, 1953 . . ."

She obeyed: "1958, 1959, 1960——"

"Stop there. It is 1960 and you are lying on a couch in my office. Do you know who I am, Mara?"

Her eyelids began to flutter. ". . . I think so. You are, you are . . . yes . . . Max, Max Fiedler!" She responded like a child pleased with herself for spelling a word correctly in a school spelling bee.

"I am, and you, Mara, will shortly awaken feeling refreshed, optimistic, full of the Yuletide spirit that this date deserves. It is December twenty-first, 1960. . . . Now, I will count from one to five, and when I reach five, you will open your eyes and be fully awake. Here we go: One . . . two . . . three . . . four . . . *five!*"

She opened her eyes, smiled, and held out a hand to him. "Max . . . dear Max. Why do I feel so good? I had a terrible dream. I shouldn't feel this good."

"Of course you should. You know, dreams, even nightmares, serve a vital cathartic purpose. They pump out the"—he chose the metaphor purposefully—"bilge water, so to speak."

She shuddered. *"Bilge water*—that was in my dream. The water was rising in the ship's hull too fast for the pumps to keep pace with it."

"Yes, but it was only a dream, and now you are awake and safe and sound without a care in the world."

She took a while to digest what he had said, then shook her head slowly. "No, Max, it was more than a dream; it actually *happened.*"

"But not to you, Mara; it happened to your grandmother, the first Mara. It was she who died in the shipwreck of the *Titanic.*"

"Then how is it that I know exactly what happened, in precise detail—intimate moments that died with her?"

"Did they die? Many of the women who survived the disaster were intimate friends of your grandparents, including Mrs. John Jacob Astor. There is a book in your family library containing scores of accounts of what transpired in those final hours before the *Titanic* went down, memoirs that describe in obsessive detail what the survivors thought and felt and saw. Excellent therapy for them. As for what occurred after the last boat was lowered from the ship, a person with your imagination, deep personal concern and love for your grandparents, and the desire to know what their last minutes were like, why, it is only natural that you project, theorize what could have happened."

Fiedler sensed the conflict that was raging within her. There was a part of her that wanted desperately to accept his rational, logical deductions at the same time another part of her, deep and hard to reach, wanted to believe that she was the reincarnation of her beloved ancestor.

She was regarding him with such intensity that he became self-conscious. He laughed dryly and touched the knot of his tie. "What's wrong? Did I spill ketchup on my tie, or is my fly open?"

"Max . . . come sit beside me." She patted the leather cushion next to her.

"My pleasure." He sat down and took one of her hands between his. "Let's pack it in for today and go Christmas shopping; it's the twenty-first and I ain't bought a single gift yet."

"Do you and Ruth celebrate Christmas?"

"Are you kidding? My oldest kid sings in the Christmas-pageant choir every year."

Her eyes held his like magnets. He sat stock-still, not breathing, as she put her hands on his shoulders and then slowly reached around to the nape of his neck. "Max—my dear Max—what would I do without you? You've become indispensable to me."

"Par for the course. It happens all the time—if therapy is successful, that is. Come to think of it, I make a pretty convincing father figure"—he patted his paunch—"pleasingly plump, gray at the temples, and everyone says I've got a kindly face. That's as positive as they can get."

"I don't see you as a father figure at all. I think you are a very attractive man. . . . Yes, Max darling, I am attracted to you the way a woman is attracted to a desirable male."

Sweet Jesus! Please, nurse, come in and break this up!

Mara raised herself to a sitting position, her face so near to his that it was a blur. Her eyes merged into a single Cyclopean orb. She wore a small, funny, teasing smile. "Do you know what else I dreamed, Max?"

He swallowed with difficulty. "No."

"I dreamed you kissed me."

His physical and mental faculties were paralyzed by abject mortification. His tongue was glued to the roof of his mouth.

"Like in the fairy tale, Max. I was Sleeping Beauty, doomed by a sorceress to sleep for all eternity unless the one prince in the world who was destined to be my true love came along and kissed my lips." She angled her head to one side so that their noses would not collide and kissed him—chastely at first, then with mounting ardor. Her arms embraced him tightly, pulling his body against hers.

Fiedler was acutely conscious of her breasts, firm against his chest, but he was impassive and rigid, resisting her with all of his willpower. As the kiss lingered on, however, his flesh and blood overcame the restraints of conscience and inhibition.

Damn! I'm getting a hard-on! And it's going to be a doozy!

Their lips parted briefly. "I want you to touch me, Max. Here, like this." She took one of his hands and placed it on her knee. He glanced down and saw that her skirt was pulled back high on her thighs. To his surprise, she wore stockings and a garter belt.

The inanity slipped out before he could suppress it: "I thought all females were born with panty hose these days."

"I despise panty hose," she said; "they make a woman look like a stuffed rag doll. . . . I'm old-fashioned and feminine. I like silk stockings, no nylons, and frilly garter belts and undies."

"Amen!" he said, verging on euphoria. "You're my kind of woman."

"That's what I've been trying to tell you." She moved his hand up along her thigh. He felt warm, bare flesh above the top of the stocking and had the heady sensation that he would melt into a pool of liquid butter, like the tigers in the children's fable *Little Black Sambo*.

"That feels so good, Max. You have a nice touch —tender, loving, not harsh and demanding." She moved his hand higher.

Fiedler started and let out a muffled protest as his fingers encountered the silken crotch of her panties, the warm, soft, idyllic nest of her womanhood. "Jesus, Joseph, and Mary! This has got to stop!"

"Says who? We're both consenting adults."

Fiedler let out a yelp as she brazenly reached down and tested his unmanageable erection. Mara snickered.

"I would say your mood is way, way beyond mere 'consent,' Max darling. You're as horny for me as I am for you; admit it."

"Horny shmorny, that is not the issue. Remember,

you said married men were off limits. Believe me, I am very much married; just ask my wife."

Her smile was wicked. "So, I'm a woman with the prerogative to change my mind, and I just changed it." She moved his hand down her thigh again. "You're getting me far too worked up, darling. I might end up raping you on your own shrink couch."

Fiedler let out a long sigh of relief. "This is definitely not the time or the place for hanky-panky."

"My place tonight." She swung her legs off to the far side of the couch.

"No!"

"Why not?"

"My wife!"

She shrugged. "You're a big boy, Max; you don't have to meet a curfew. You told me once, you have to go out a lot at night to help desperate patients." She smiled that tantalizing smile again. "I am very, very desperate, Max." She patted his still rigid penis. "And so are you."

"This is absurd!"

"What's absurd about a man and a woman going to bed together? It happens every night, and morning, and afternoon. It's the universal pastime, sweet love. Are all psychiatrists as naïve as you? Anyway, I think it's cute." She stood up and arranged her skirt. "All right, I'll see you tonight at my apartment. What would you like to have for dinner?"

"I'll take potluck," he said, realizing as he said it that he was committing himself to attending the rendezvous.

At five-thirty, after his last patients had left, Fiedler phoned his wife: "Ruth, I won't be home for supper tonight. I've got a consultation at Bellevue."

"You're a liar, Max, and a bad one at that. You're going to see your rich *shiksa* girl friend."

"That is the most ridiculous thing I've ever heard, Ruth."

"There, you're talking pompous. You always do that when you lie. Good night, and give her my worst." She hung up the phone.

Fiedler sat there stunned, mouth agape, staring at the dead phone in his hand, which sounded as if it had a bee inside the earpiece.

Do I really do that? talk pompous when I'm lying? Maybe she *should have been the shrink.*

Shaking his head, he hung up. Well, he would not be a liar. What would he do? He would go to Mara's apartment and explain to her that the entire situation was absurd. He was a married man with a family that he loved, and he would not jeopardize his relationship with his wife under any circumstances.

There you go, Max, talking pompous again!

He sent home the staff, locked the office door, and took a shower in the bathroom. He always kept a spare set of underwear and socks in the office, along with a blue serge suit, in case of emergencies like this one.

" 'Emergencies'?" he said out loud. "That is a euphemism if ever I heard one, Max."

It was seven-thirty when he arrived at Mara's penthouse apartment, feeling like an adolescent calling on his first big crush. He smoothed back his hair, straightened his tie, sucked in his gut, and pushed the button.

Francine Watkins opened the door. She was wearing a pastel-blue tailored suit over a dark-blue blouse. She smiled. "Hi there, Dr. Fiedler. How are you tonight?"

"Greetings, Francine. I feel full of the Yuletide spirit. How about you?"

"I feel great. Come on in and get out of your coat and into a dry martini."

"I think I just may have a stronger libation tonight." What was it they called it—*courage in a bottle*. He descended the steps from the foyer into the living room and got the shock of his life: Tate Industries' chief accountant, Lewis O'Toole, was sitting on the divan with Mara.

She rose, face wreathed in smiles, and came over to him. "Max, I thought you were going to stand me up." She kissed him wetly on the lips. "Oh, you're cold as ice. Francine, mix the good doctor a drink."

"One martini coming up," Francine called as she went to the bar.

"Martini?" Mara's fine eyebrows arched quizzically. In a low voice she said, "Building up your nerve, eh, doc?"

He brayed like a jackass to cover his embarrassment, praying that O'Toole hadn't heard the remark. She grabbed his arm possessively and led him over to the divan.

O'Toole wore a perpetual supercilious smirk, so it was difficult to read his thoughts. He stood up and offered his hand: "Good evening, doctor."

Fiedler shook hands, looking from one to the other of them nervously. "Hi, Mr. O'Toole. . . . Say, if I'm interrupting something, I'll go into the library and catch up on my reading."

"Not at all, Max," she said. "Lewis is my last pipeline to TII—my spy, you might say. He's bringing me up to date on what's happening."

"Nothing bad, I trust."

"No; as a matter of fact, the company seems to be doing very well without me," she said ruefully.

"That, love, is the primary goal of every top executive, or at least it should be," O'Toole said: "creating a smooth, efficient, well-oiled machine that can function without a watchdog."

Francine brought over Fiedler's martini. She was wearing her coat and hat. "Mara, the doctor's head is in the cooler. Hilde's gone, and she said to tell you that the quiche is in the microwave oven on warm and the salad is in the icebox. I've got to run, too. Good night, all."

O'Toole looked at his wristwatch. "Say, I've got to be going myself; it's almost eight."

"I'll see you to the door."

O'Toole shook hands again with Fiedler. "Happy Chanukah, Dr. Fiedler."

Fiedler overlooked the hint of snobbery in his tone. "You should have a good one, too, Mr. O'Toole," he said in a broad Yiddish dialect.

He watched them walk across the room with a lascivious smile. Mara looked breathtaking in a crimson housecoat, a deep-cowled flow of velour falling to the floor, form-clinging with a subtle flare that defined the flawless buttocks and thighs underneath it with every step. Her hair was tied at the back with red ribbon in a ponytail that fell almost to the small of her back.

She kissed O'Toole lightly on the cheek and bid him good night. Clasping her hands behind her back like a child, she came toward Fiedler with a little prancing step. It was an endearing gesture, and at that moment he loved Mara Tate Rodgers more than he loved anything else on earth.

"Rodgers Tate," he corrected himself.

"What did you say?" she asked.

"Nothing; I was just thinking out loud."

"I've had a one-track mind ever since we parted this afternoon, Max. Do you want to eat first or after?"

His face was on fire. "Spoken like a true executive —forthright and direct."

"I like the way you blush. You remind me of a Kewpie doll; no, more like a Hummel."

"Which illustrates the point I am about to make. What in the hell is a matzo ball like me doing in a situation like this, having candlelight dinner with a gorgeous, rich, socialite Wasp lady as a prelude to indulging in lechery and debauchery in her boudoir? Jesus Christ, I *need* this!" He downed the martini in a single gulp.

Mara put her arms around his neck and pressed her lips to the throbbing artery in his throat. She murmured, "Stop running yourself down, Max. You're brilliant, witty, kind, compassionate, and ———"

"Gorgeous, too. Me and Gable—people are always mistaking us for twins."

"You're very special to me."

"Mr. Nice Guy, that's me."

"What's wrong with being nice?"

He succumbed to a cheap impulse: "I bet you don't say that to O'Toole—lean, leonine, lithe, Hathaway-shirt-type O'Toole. He's always looking down his long, aristocratic nose at me. I keep expecting him to hand me his jacket and say 'Shorten the cuffs, Max, and sponge and press.' "

Mara laughed and hugged him tighter. "That's unfair. *You* are the one who is prejudiced. As a matter of fact, Lewis has a great deal of respect for you."

"I'll bet."

"I don't want to talk about Lewis or anyone or anything to do with TII. Come with me, darling."

She took his hand and led him down the hallway and into her bedroom. When she pressed a mercury switch, the room was suffused with pale-green light emanating from concealed fixtures behind the broad ceiling molding.

"What's your sexiest color?" she asked. "Green, blue, red, orange—you name it." To demonstrate, she twirled the dial, and the green faded into pastel blue, dark blue, purple, one overlapping the other from one end of the spectrum to the other.

"I'll opt for red." His gaze wandered around the luxurious room, lavishly appointed yet feminine and tasteful. The electronic headboard intrigued him. "It's something out of Buck Rogers and the Twenty-fifth Century."

"Strictly functional—phone service, music, TV, food, and drink. Would you like some caviar and champagne? It's in the icebox. Press that red button."

"No thanks; I'll settle for some good music."

She stood hipshot, with one hand on her side and the index finger of her other hand pressed against her pursed lips. "Let me see. . . . What type of music arouses the savage beast in you, Max?"

"Chopin, the études."

"You got it, buddy." She slid aside a wood panel at one side of the console, revealing a selection directory similar to the readout on a commercial jukebox. She pressed one of the numerous buttons and, almost instantly, melodious, fiery piano enveloped them from the four walls.

Fiedler winced. "Could we keep it down? I feel like I'm inside a woofer."

She reduced it to a pleasing level in the background and sat down on the bed. "No more stalling, Max; you've committed yourself." Not at all self-conscious, she unfastened her gown and stripped it off her shoulders.

As he had suspected, she was naked underneath it. For a time all he could do was stare at her, devouring her with ardent eyes. She was all any man could hope for in a woman, and more. When she reached behind her head to untie the ribbon holding her hair, her breasts thrust out and upward, the nipples alluringly upturned.

Slowly she lay back on the coverlet, letting her hair fan out over the pillow; then, smiling, she held out her arms to him. "Make love to me, darling. I want you very badly—desperately."

Fiedler had never felt so inept and clumsy, not even

on his wedding night. His fingers fumbled futilely at buttons and his zipper. One arm became entangled in the sleeve of his T-shirt, and stepping out of his shorts, he stumbled and fell to his knees.

Mara was delighted. Her laughter was hearty, earthy. "Oh, Max, you are adorable. Come to me, you bumbling shrink."

He lay down beside her and placed one hand on a breast as he bent to kiss her; and—miraculously, it seemed to him—all of his anxiety and uncertainty dissipated. He had dreaded the possibility that he might be impotent, confronted by this exquisite, exciting female, who, since he had first looked at her, represented to him the absolute epitome of womanhood, an ethereal being to be idolized upon a pedestal.

But now beside him, naked breast to breast, loin to loin, thigh to thigh, she was reality—hot flesh and blood, responding to every subtle tender touch of his fingers on her nipples, her belly, her thighs, whimpering with ecstasy as he stroked her clitoris, writhing and begging; "Max, darling, fuck me! I can't wait any longer!"

Her hands tugged at him so urgently that he had to caution her: "Honeybun, if you keep that up, you'll tear it out at the roots." Crazy with desire himself, he slipped between her trembling thighs and went into her cautiously, letting her hands guide him. He moaned as she coddled his hard testicles with one hand after full penetration.

Her contractions began before his and endured, it seemed, timelessly. In a landmark experience that he would cherish until his dying day, Max achieved two orgasms, back to back, without any intermission.

"Was I any good?" he asked afterward as she snuggled into his arms, purring like a satisfied kitten.

"The best—four times good for me. How about you?"

"Four times!" He rolled his eyes at the ceiling in wonder. "What a woman! Twice for me, and it makes me feel like a genuine stud."

"My very own stud." She caressed his limp and somewhat tender manhood.

A small frown of discontent puckered his forehead. A Johnny-come-lately in her private stable of studs, he thought.

Knock it off, Max! Stop agonizing like you just found out that the girl you gave your frat pin to wasn't a virgin.

Even Ruth had candidly told him he had not been the first man she'd slept with.

Don't blow it. You are Cinderella at the ball with the lovely princess in your arms; so enjoy, because midnight will come as surely as the sun will rise tomorrow morning, and you'll be back at the couch sweeping the sooty ashes off the hearth of the human psyche.

CHAPTER FOUR

Mara fell into a deep sleep. She looked so peaceful and angelic that Fiedler did not have the heart to wake her. His watch read ten-minutes-to-nine. It was early. As long as he got home before midnight, he could handle his wife's accusations.

To hell with you, Ruth!

Defensive bravado masking guilt.

Doctor, heal thyself!

He was ravenously hungry. Putting on his clothes and socks and shoes, he left the bedroom quietly and found his way to the kitchen. He saw the quiche through the glass door of the microwave oven but decided to leave it until she woke up. Opening the icebox, he reconnoitered for leftovers. His mouth watered at the sight of half a roast chicken under a plastic bell. He took it out, poured himself a glass of skimmed milk, and, carrying both, walked down the hall and into the den. He put them down on the green desk blotter, turned on the three-way light switch to high, and stood for a time at the window, looking out over the city.

At night New York was a fairy-tale city, the grimy and sordid aspects concealed by the veil of darkness; the stark, steel, skeletal skyscrapers, subdued by night, ornamented by the lights glowing in hundreds of thousands of windows and the tower beacons flashing like stars atop a forest of giant Christmas trees.

A gust of wind pelted the window with sleet and played a dirge around the corners of the roof and the shivering shrubbery in Mara's terrace garden. He drew the blinds, walked to the bookcase, and took down the latest volume of Tate history he had been perusing.

Chewing on a cold chicken leg, he leaned back in the leather desk chair and began reading where he had left off last time: an era extending from 1910 through the present. It was dull, mundane reading for the most part. Odd, he reflected, how the excitement and adventure of the narrative declined commensurately as the Tates attained ever higher goals and financial gain and social status.

Old Drew Tate was right: As the bloodline got thinner, so did the meat of their story become emaciated.

Preston, the father of Sean Tate, was the most colorful member of the family in their middle period. He was a confirmed playboy who devoted his short life to whiskey, women, and high-stakes poker games. As much as a million dollars changed hands frequently at card games celebrated at the Gilbert Tates' Cape Cod estate, where their wayward son took up residence with his family.

Shortly after World War I began, broke and heavily in debt, Preston fled to Canada and joined the Canadian army. He was killed at Verdun in 1916.

It was during that period—1912, to be exact—that Arizona "came of age"; that is, when William Howard Taft proclaimed the territory to be the forty-eighth state of the United States. That was also the year when a speculator named "Rawhide" Jimmy Douglas invested half a million dollars in an unprofitable mine called the Little Daisy and subsequently struck the richest copper lode ever mined in the world.

Arizona was deeply involved, because of its proximity, with the Mexican revolution of 1916 when Pancho Villa's rebels threatened Sonora and Nogales. The Arizona National Guard dispelled Villa's army with flair and dispatch. Two years later, during the undeclared war with Mexico, Arizona militiamen shot and killed a band of Mexican smugglers at Nogales. In the short, violent conflict, thirty-two American troops were killed in the battle of Nogales, as well as eighty Mexican soldiers and the mayor of Sonora. It was a decisive American victory, and the Mexicans sued for an armistice.

By 1920 the price of copper had fallen to twelve cents a pound, and by 1925 the government stopped buying it altogether. The decline of what was commonly referred to as "the Arizona franchise" posed no hardship for the rich copper barons who had pioneered metal mining in the old territory, families like the Tates and the Douglases and the Turners. Even lesser tycoons prospered, William Andrews Clark, selling out his holdings to Phelps-Dodge for $21 million!

By 1950 the Tate mines throughout Arizona had produced no less than $200 million in copper, gold, and silver, not to mention the enormous profits from their ever-expanding conglomerate, Tate International Industries.

Undoubtedly the most dramatic and exciting event that occurred within the Tate family in the early part of the new century was the birth of a baby girl to Sam Rodgers and his wife Mara on October 20, 1921, after twenty-one years of infertile marriage.

As she nursed her child at her breast hours after the birth, the mother, looking more radiant than she had in years, boasted to her husband, "Just before she died, I wrote my mother and vowed that you and I would produce an heir even if it required fifty years to accomplish the feat."

Sam chuckled. "That would have been an accomplishment indeed—I mean, if we had had to wait fifty years." Slyly he asked her, "Well, inasmuch as it's a girl, what shall we name her?"

"Mara, of course," she replied, without any hesitancy or false modesty. "It's a tradition, Sam; you know that."

"Suppose it had been a boy?"

"No, there was no chance of that. My mother came to me in a dream early in my pregnancy and assured me: 'It will be a girl, darling, never fret; and she will be born on the same day as you and I—October twentieth."

When the doctor made his next visit, Sam consulted him about his disconcerting conversations with Mara: "This business about her mother speaking to her from beyond the grave—you don't think it's her mind, do you?"

The doctor laughed and slapped Sam's shoulder. "Mr. Rodgers, a short period of postpartum neurosis is not uncommon, particularly in older women giving birth to their first child. It will pass, never fear."

Fiedler bolted upright in the chair, dropping his chicken leg and nearly upsetting his glass of milk as a voice intoned from behind his chair: "Yes, I was born on October twentieth, just as Grandmother Mara predicted. . . . Excuse me for reading over your shoulder; I know it isn't polite."

"Mara!" He spun about in the swivel chair and confronted her. "You're damned right! I almost shit in my pants. I thought it was——" He contained it.

But she guessed and goaded him: "Do you believe in ghosts, Max?"

He grinned and shut the book. "Go to hell, Miss Rodgers."

"Tate."

"You are what we on Delancey Street used to call 'a real pisser.' Come here, wench," he said, grabbing her and pulling her down on his lap. He kissed her neck and slipped a hand inside the crimson robe, caressing her breasts.

"Keep that up and it's back to bed," she said, patting his cheek.

He withdrew his hand and playfully slapped her backside. "No more hanky-panky. Let's go into the kitchen and eat that quiche."

She frowned at the stack of chicken bones on the plate. "You mean to say you're still hungry after all this?"

"Just an appetizer. Come on, let's go."

"Whatever you say, my lord and master, only you go into the dining room and sit down. I enjoy waiting on my men; it's that old-fashioned Welsh background."

"I don't much care for being *one* of your *men*."

Mara laughed. "Jealous, eh? Don't be. I think I'm in love with you, Max, and, like Horton the elephant, 'I meant what I said and I said what I meant, an elephant's faithful one hundred percent.' What do you feel about me, Max? Honestly. I know I'm a good lay, but what else?" She stood close to him and put her hands on his shoulders. Her keen blue-gray eyes bored into his.

Fiedler rested his hands on the flare of her hips. "I love you, Mara Tate, more than I've ever loved anyone in my life, and that's the truth."

She kissed him on the mouth. "I believe you, Max Fiedler." She pressed her cheek against his. "What will you tell Ruth?"

"Ruth?" It came as a jolt to him. Ruth and the children had been eclipsed by his grand passion. Now the eclipse was over. He shut his eyes and there they were, as vivid and real as if the three of them were standing in the doorway, their expressions severe and admonishing—Ruth, Leslie, and David.

"Your wife, Ruth. What will you tell her? When?"

"I don't know. Let me think."

Without a word, Mara withdrew to the kitchen, and a short while later they had consumed, in silence, the quiche, a wilted salad, and coffee as good as his favorite brew at Chock Full o' Nuts.

Fiedler knew she was waiting for the answer to her question. He wiped his mouth and put down his fork. "This is insane."

"Insane?"

"You and me. I mean, I'm not in your league; I'm not even minor league. If I wasn't your psychiatrist, if you weren't so damned grateful and dependent on me, you wouldn't know that I was alive."

"Don't start that 'father-image' bullshit again, Max. You may be the world's greatest shrink since Sigmund, but you have a blind spot when it comes to love. It's wonderful, it's inexplicable, and it's mysterious. It's the one human occupation that cannot be defined by logic, where two and two do not necessarily add up to four. I don't give a damn why I love you, Max; I don't want to know, even if you could give me an explanation. I love you and you love me, and that's all that matters. So, when will you tell your wife?"

Fiedler stammered, "Y-yes, tell her. I . . . I . . ay-yi-yi, I don't even know *what* to tell her! It's not enough to say, 'Hey, by the way, Mara Tate and me, we have this thing going for us, sooooo, what I'm gonna do is chuck the whole nut—you, the kids, my practice. Mara and me, we're going to set up this clinic, like the one Dr. Schweitzer had in Africa, only it's going to be in the Middle East. Maybe a good shrink could defuse the age-old powder keg."

"Okay, kiddo, you want a clinic? You got it."

Fiedler rolled his eyes, endeavoring to look coy. "Oh, goody, I always wanted to be a kept man; but you really don't have to buy my favors, darling."

Suddenly the smile was wiped off her face and she turned deathly pale. She swayed in the chair and gripped the edge of the table for support, upsetting a glass of water. "Max!" It was a frightening plea.

"Mara, what's wrong?" He leaped up and hurried around the table to her side. "Are you ill?"

"I . . . I don't know. Dizzy. Feel strange." She put a hand over her eyes. "I heard a voice calling to me."

"It's only the wind, Mara. Listen to it howling around the terrace."

"Wind? No, it was my mother."

He was relieved to observe that the color was returning to her face and her trembling had subsided.

She looked up at him and smiled weakly. "It's all right now. I'm sorry. Let's have a coffee and brandy in front of the fire."

"You go in and sit down," he told her. "I'll serve you."

She squeezed his hand. "No, I'm fine, *really* I am. Come along." When they were settled on the loveseat in front of the fireplace, she asked him, "Max . . . do you think I'm crazy?"

He shrugged. "We're all a little crazy, to use your word. I prefer 'mental quirks.' "

"This thing you do to me when I'm under hypnosis —age regression, time regression—you put me through the paces, but you don't truly believe that what I say and do is genuine, that I *do* go back in time."

"Mara, it's a form of therapy," he said evasively, "and a highly effective form of treatment—in your case at any rate."

"Max, I *do* go back. I am three different people in three different times. I am leading three different lives simultaneously in three different dimensions. You remember what you told me about Einstein's theory of relativity? I've been reading everything I can lay my hands on about the subject, some of it wild and speculative, far, far out in space. Do you know what I believe, Max? I believe that human existence is an infinite motion-picture film. The frames pass over the projection lens and the story unfolds, but what takes place in the past is not obliterated; it exists forever, is still there recorded on the film. If one desires to revive a given episode, the projector can be switched into reverse. You and I together, we've discovered a way to reverse the process in real life. I'm the perfect subject. What do spiritualists call it? I'm a born 'contact' with the world hereafter." She clutched his hands so hard, it hurt him.

He spoke to her gently: "Mara, you have this preoccupation with your ancestors. Your mother and your grandmother, they were strong, dominant women. They made an indelible impression on you. You identify very strongly with them. That's perfectly natural, but——"

"Max, it's more than that and you know it! The three of us, the three Maras, were all born on the same day!"

"Yes, that is unusual, but not as much so as you like to make out. Think about it; there are billions of people in this world and only 365 days in a year. Granted the odds against grandmother, mother, and daughter being born on the same day are astronomical, just as are the odds against twin sisters giving birth on the same day; yet there are countless cases of it occurring in the record books. . . . Do you know what the odds are, in a bridge game, of being dealt thirteen cards of the same suit? The computer tells us it's 158,753,389,899 to one; yet it has happened, and more than once!

"I could quote you impossible odds that have been defied, a list as long as my arm. Your case is no different. There's nothing supernatural about the three Maras being born on the same day; it's all in the throw of the dice, nothing more. . . . As I was saying, this preoccupation of yours with Tates dead and past, you must not let it become a consuming obsession. You have got to keep your perspective."

She wasn't listening to him. "Max, I want you to put me under again, tonight—*now.*"

"Absolutely not. It's out of the question." Fiedler was becoming annoyed, on the verge of losing his patience.

What about your perspective, doctor? A man of medicine who gets angry with a sick patient?

You're right. I should remove myself from the case. In loving her, I have violated the Hippocratic oath. My emotional involvement challenges my objectivity and credibility as a physician.

And now Mara was challenging him. Her eyes were defiant, there was an indomitable thrust to her chin, and her tone was adamant: "If you won't put me in a trance, I'll do it myself. I can, you know, Max. I've practiced at it."

Frightened and disconcerted, he gripped her arms: "Mara, you mustn't do that; it can be extremely dangerous! Hypnosis in the wrong hands can be as lethal as a loaded gun in a child's."

"You're intimating that I am an irresponsible child?"

"It's a metaphor."

"Fuck you, Max!" She pulled away from him and stood up. "I'm going into the bedroom, with or without you." She strode off purposefully.

"Mara, wait!" He punched the cushion in frustration. "Shit!"

CHAPTER FIVE

Fiedler had no choice, really; he had to cooperate with Mara, because it would be the lesser of two evils. She lay down on the bed with her hands folded across her abdomen and her eyes fixed on the ceiling.

It was remarkable how receptive she had become to hypnotic suggestion over the course of her therapy. He could put her under in less than sixty seconds, and within another ninety seconds, he was able to reduce her to a level of deep trance such as he never achieved with any other subject.

"Tonight I am going to let you dictate the direction this session will take. Suppose you concentrate on some unforgettable date, one that brought you either pleasure or pain; it makes no difference."

There was a lengthy silence, and it took him a while before he saw that tears were running down her face from underneath her closed eyelids.

"Why don't you talk about it, Mara? Don't keep it bottled up inside you. Can you tell me what the date is?"

"I will never forget it—December ninth, 1956."

He took her pulse; it was twenty-eight beats per minute. She had reached the critical plateau.

It had been a last-minute decision to book a charter flight from San Juan, Puerto Rico, to Miami rather than fly directly to New York, as they originally intended.

"I want to see for myself if Sean is making as much

progress on that condominium deal as he professes he is," Sam told his wife as they and forty-five other passengers boarded the DC-3.

"You don't have much faith in my young cousin, do you, Sam?" she said, tongue in cheek.

"I daresay I do not. Sean Tate is a liar and a charlatan. He's devious, two-faced, and thoroughly unscrupulous."

Mara smiled and put her hand on top of his. "I could not have phrased it better myself. I can't wait to see his expression when we arrive on the doorstep unannounced. Barbara's, too."

"Yes, Barbara. I don't like a TII executive marrying into a mob family. The Mosconis, in my estimation, are one of the most ruthless of their breed."

"Nor I, and especially a Tate. It appalls me, too, that Sean is so friendly with them."

"Thick as thieves, I believe the expression is, my dear."

A pretty stewardess walked down the aisle, cautioning the passengers, "Please fasten your seat belts. "Please put out your cigarettes and pipes and cigars. The No Smoking sign is on."

The sturdy airplane strained at the brakes like a thoroughbred racehorse poised to break out of the starting gate.

"Best damned plane ever made," Sam said. "Rather be aboard a DC-3 than any other commercial carrier. She's the workhorse of the U.S. air fleet."

They took off into a bright, cloudless sky and headed west for Florida. Not long after, the monotonous drone of the twin engines lulled Mara into a light slumber. Both hale and hearty in their seventies, Sam and Mara indulged themselves more and more frequently with morning and afternoon naps, and now Sam, too, dozed intermittently while he waded through the Sunday *New York Times*.

"It says here that Ike will be taking the oath of office in a private ceremony on January twentieth because it falls on a Sunday; then on Monday he'll repeat the oath in a public inaugural ceremony on the east portico of the White House," he said, noticing that Mara was awake. "I only wish he was a Democrat. I like the guy personally."

"I think Mamie is a darling, too," she said groggily, glancing out the window. "Oh, look, Sam, it's clouding up."

He hunched down and peered across her. "Hmmmm . . . odd-looking stuff, isn't it."

"Yes; it almost has a phosphorescent hue."

As the DC-3 proceeded east, the queer fog became thicker. Other passengers were commenting on the strange phenomenon, some of them rather apprehensively.

The captain's voice came over the intercom: "Ladies and gentlemen, we are about to increase our altitude to twenty thousand feet to climb above this unexpected weather disturbance. Please fasten your seat belts."

The DC-3 began to climb at a steep angle that did not seem warranted by the captain's casual announcement; then there followed a succession of bizarre events: The reading lamps above the passenger seats started blinking on and off, as did the No Smoking and Fasten Seat Belts indicators over the door leading into the cockpit, followed by a most alarming exchange between the plane's crew blaring over the intercom:

"Jesus Christ, I never saw anything like this! That damned fog is on fire!"

"Saint Elmo's fire! Look at it jumping all over the wings and the fuselage!"

Mara and Sam could not believe their eyes. The entire aircraft was enveloped by flickering balls of pale-blue fire.

A stewardess ran down the aisle and into the cockpit. "Shut off that damned speaker, captain; you're scaring the passengers to death!"

"It *is* off."

"No, it's not!"

"My God, the radio system has gone wacky; I can't turn it off!"

"That's not the only thing is wacky, Jack!" the copilot said. "My compasses are spinning like tops; both the gyro and the magnetic compasses are out!"

"Larry, contact the tower at Havana and ask 'em what's going on here. Maybe the military is testing another A-bomb."

The copilot did immediately: "This is Britannia flight 654 San Juan to Miami calling Havana. . . . Tower, please come in; this is an emergency!"

The response from Havana was prompt but barely intelligible, owing to static: "Acknowledge flight 654 . . . Havana calling 654 . . . come in. What is your emergency?"

"All of our instruments are behaving erratically. There must be a short circuit in the electrical system."

"That wouldn't affect the magnetic compasses!" the navigator shouted.

From the tower in Havana: "Flight 654 . . . what is your position?"

"Our last position before the instruments failed, about ten minutes ago, was longitude seventy-four degrees west and latitude twenty-two degrees north."

"Flight 654, that should put you approximately off the coast of Sagua la Grande. How is your visibility?"

"Negative. I can't see more than a foot beyond the windshield because of dense fog."

"Dense fog?" The operator at Havana sounded puzzled. "That's funny. There are a dozen flights in your area, and all but you are reporting bright skies and unlimited visibility."

"Damn, we're out of it!" the pilot said jubilantly.

And the passengers breathed a communal sigh of relief as the plane broke out of the overcast and into the clear weather.

Mara gripped Sam's arm. "Sam, have you ever seen a sky like this? It's green instead of blue, and the sunlight is orange."

A woman in the rear began to scream: "Do you know what's happening? We're in the Bermuda Triangle!"

Two stewardesses raced back and tried to calm her down: "It's all right, madam. We'll be through this in a few minutes. It's a freak weather phenomenon, very common in this area."

Mara tried to recall a magazine article she had read about the notorious Bermuda Triangle, an area off the coast of the southeastern United States marked off by a hypothetical triangle, one side extending from Bermuda to southern Florida, a second from Florida east to Puerto Rico, and a third from Puerto Rico back to Bermuda. Within this triangle, over the years, there had occurred scores of fatalities among planes and ships in which no wreckage or survivors had ever been discovered. They had, in fact, vanished without a trace. Conjecture was rampant among laymen and experts alike. Was it caused by aberrant atmospheric phenomena? or a magnetic anomaly? Or was a diabolical supernatural force at work in the damnable Bermuda Triangle?

The Havana tower came in once more: "Flight 654 . . . you should be able to reach Miami by dead reckoning if you can see the sun again."

"You won't believe this," the captain said tremulously. "I don't believe it myself, and I am looking at it. There are two suns in the sky, one on the port side, the other on the starboard. It's like a mirror image."

"Steady, sir. That's probably just what it is—an illusion caused by atmospheric distortion. Iy my years in this part of the ocean, I've seen and heard some wild and improbable things."

"I know . . . the Bermuda Triangle."

"Coincidence. I'll tell you what to——" The rest of it was erased by violent static, and then the radio went dead.

"What do we do now?" asked the copilot.

"I'm going to take her down again."

"Back into the damnable fog?"

"Hopefully below it. We've got to find some landmark to go by. Here goes." Into the intercom, which for some inexplicable reason had not suffered the malfunction that was afflicting all the other electronic equipment and instruments, he said, "Ladies and gentlemen, if you have removed your seat belts, please put them on again. We are going down in an endeavor to get below the fog."

The DC-3 plunged back into the opaque cloud, descending at a gradual angle, the copilot calling off the diminishing altitude: "Fifteen thousand . . . thirteen . . . ten . . . eight . . ."

At 6,000 feet they broke into the clear, or so they believed. Then the navigator shouted excitedly: "Christ, it's all around us! We're in the eye!"

It was an apt description. The plane was in the center of what seemed to be a hurricane, except that there was no wind and no rain.

"Some kind of freak of nature," the pilot observed. "Stay cool, men."

Mara clutched Sam's hand. "Look down there at the water, the current."

Crewmen and passengers were wonder-struck at the curiosity taking place on the surface of the ocean. The violent turbulence, which was churning up froth and whitecaps as far as the eye could see, made it easy to chart the direction of the current. It was flowing clockwise around the perimeter of the eye in decreasing circles, like water flowing out of a sink and down a drain.

The DC-3 was almost · halfway across when they saw it—a gigantic maelstrom. Sink and drain were no longer similes. The vast whirlpool was sucking millions of gallons of water per second down into its bottomless maw.

"My God, this is out of a science-fiction movie!" said the pilot in awe.

"We're still losing altitude," the copilot warned. "Put her nose up again."

"Sonovabitch!" The captain was pulling back on the wheel as hard as he could, but the ship would not respond and kept losing altitude. "We're caught in some kind of magnetic field! I've lost control. . . . Ladies and gentlemen, prepare for an emergency landing. The stewardesses have instructed you in this emergency procedure. Now, don't panic. We can stay afloat for some time once we are on the surface. There are life preservers and inflatable boats—— What the hell! Who am I kidding?" He sat in his seat, hands still locked on the useless controls, his gaze fixed on the giant vortex looming up closer and closer.

Back in the cabin, the passengers were still. They were hypnotized and in a state of shock.

"We are being pulled down into the very core," Mara whispered to Sam. "Good-by, my darling."

He put an arm around her shoulders and kissed her cheek. "Better close your eyes. Don't look at it, love."

Then it was over.

CHAPTER SIX

When she came out of it, Mara had the wild, desperate expression of a terrified animal. Her fingers clawed into the satin quilt; her eyes rolled from side to side; and an unintelligible, whimpering gibberish emanated from her slack, drooling mouth.

Fiedler reached for her hand, but she yanked it away from him and cringed back against the headboard. "Darling, it's all right."

"The plane?"

"There is no plane; it was all in your imagination. You're here with me in your apartment, in your own bed. Look around. Does this look like a plane?"

Her gaze traveled around the room, assimilating all of its familiar appointments: bed, electronic appliances, vanity, chaise longue, the oil paintings of her mother and grandmother on one wall. The tension went out of her body, and she exhaled a sigh of relief.

"All in your imagination, Mara, none of it real."

She compressed her lips and looked at him intently. Her voice was weak but full of conviction: "Oh, it was real, Max, and nothing you can say or do will change my mind. I was in that plane crash that killed my mother and father"—her words caught in her throat—"only it wasn't a crash, not the kind of accident due to malfunction or human error. None of those aboard had any chance whatsoever. You keep insisting that I have this total recall of all that I've heard and read about the Tates, but don't you see, Max, in this instance your rational theory doesn't

377

stand up to the facts? No one ever knew what happened aboard the DC-3 that disappeared—yes, disappeared, not crashed—inside the Bermuda Triangle. There were no survivors, no witnesses to describe what took place in the fatal hour before the plane lost contact with the tower at Havana."

"Plenty of speculation, though, in the papers at the time. The last radio bulletins from the plane have been distorted beyond all common sense and reason. The alleged supernatural forces of evil that pervade that area of the Atlantic make much better copy than your everyday mundane aircraft disaster. Remember, dear, you spent a month down there right after it happened, going over every square mile of ocean around the projected crash site with a fine-tooth comb. You lived, breathed, and slept with only one thing on your mind—the Bermuda Triangle. I've told you before, Mara, you are an extremely imaginative woman."

"Perhaps you're right, Max." She sat up abruptly and brushed back her hair with her hands. "Max, you've been a dear, and I will love you always." She held his face between her hands and kissed him on the mouth.

Fiedler was mildly disturbed. It was not like Mara Tate to surrender to the will of an adversary or accept the other's viewpoint so docilely. "What's up, doc?" he quipped. "You looking to straighten me out with a sucker punch, is that it?"

Her smile was pasteboard. "Don't be silly. The truth is, I'm exhausted. Tonight has been exceptionally emotional for me, in more ways than one." She stroked his thigh.

Fiedler grinned foolishly. "Well . . . it has for me, too. Okay, I'll go and let you sleep. Promise me you'll phone me first thing in the morning, soon as you wake up?"

"I promise."

He kissed her again and stood up. "Don't even shower. Don't even change. Here, I'll cover you with the quilt. Timing is everything in life, including being an essential of sound and healthy slumber."

She smiled as he tucked the quilt around her sides and up to her throat. "I feel comfy cozy. Wish you were in here with me."

"Me too, but believe me, I do not intend to make this a one-night stand. Good night and sweet dreams."

"You too."

Just before he left the room, he stopped and studied the two family matriarchs immortalized in oil. Their eyes seemed to follow him as he walked to the bedroom door. His feelings were so vivid and real that the hair bristled at his nape. He hurried out into the hallway and shut the door behind him—gratefully.

Max, you are teetering on the edge yourself!

The scene with his wife Ruth that night was bitter but not loud and sordid. She was waiting in the darkened living room, smoking a cigarette, when he let himself in. He did not see her until light exploded out of the blackness.

"Jesus!" He was startled. "What are you doing up at this hour?"

"What were you doing out, as if I didn't know?" The hard set of her jaw muscles and her contemptuous glare alerted him that this was combat, unconditional warfare.

"I tried to tell you I had an emergency."

"A consultation at Bellevue?" she said with rank sarcasm.

"All right, so I had a session with Mara Tate. I know how you feel about her, so I lied. I'm sorry; it was childish of me."

She walked over to him. "What you and the rich

shiksa were doing was anything but childish, or maybe I'm wrong; maybe you were 'playing doctor.' "

He tried to rally a modicum of righteous indignation. "What a cheap thing to say; it's not worthy of you, Ruth."

"You fucking hypocrite. "You reek of the bitch—musk and that five-hundred-dollar-an-ounce Frog perfume she bathes in! Was she as good as you expected, Max?" She confronted him, arms folded underneath her heavy breasts, a disdainful smile on her face.

He threw up his hands in abject defeat. "I should have known better than to think you would be sane and reasonable about this."

"I should be sane and reasonable with a husband and the father of my children who commits adultery? a physician who screws his patient? Max, they ought to take away your shingle and your couch. You're a disgrace to your profession."

It was a telling blow because it pierced so near to the heart. He hung his head and did not reply.

The hell of it is, she's right. I am *a disgrace to my profession. I am a spineless, self-indulgent shit!*

"Do you want me to leave?" he asked tonelessly, not looking at her.

Her voice softened. "That's a silly question, Max. We've been through far too much together to condemn you for one lousy mistake, even it it's broken a part of my heart—an 'emotional infarction,' you might say. Too many bad times and too many good times together, not to mention two wonderful kids whom you adore—I know that—and who adore you." She inhaled a deep, sobbing breath. "No, Max, I'm willing to forget this terrible night if . . . if I have your word that you will not see Mara Tate again, not even as a patient."

"Ruth . . ." He could only stare at her in amazement —amazement not because of her unexpected magnanimous and forgiving gesture but because of his adamant unwillingness to accept her generosity, her absolution. As they said in romantic novels, Mara Tate was a sickness in his blood, a sickness that he cherished the way some ailing folk cherish those of their infirmities that have become as much a vital part of their existence and being as healthy body and brain tissue.

"What will it be, Max?"

He was not up to any further sparring that night. "Look, let's talk about it in the morning. We're both tired and overwrought. Matters like this require cool heads to settle."

"No, Max; as far as I am concerned, it is now or never. I stated my conditions for settling things once and for all. They are simple conditions and eminently fair and reasonable, you have to admit. "Forget Mara Tate and I'll forget about tonight; so help me, I will never bring it up again as long as we both shall live."

"You don't know what you're saying," he mumbled, knowing how weak and ineffectual it sounded. "I think I'd better sleep at the office tonight. I'll phone you tomorrow."

"You needn't bother," she said, in a voice on the verge of breaking.

He rushed out of the apartment with his hands covering his ears so that he would not hear her anguished wailing.

Fiedler slept on the foldaway couch in his office. "Slept" was wishful thinking; he lay awake staring at the spokes of light that slanted across his ceiling at five-second intervals when a distant rooftop beacon swept across his venetian blinds. He lay awake agonizing over the scene with Ruth and his fears for Mara until the beacon's light was dimmed with the intrusion of dawn.

He dozed then, how long he did not know; it seemed like mere seconds when the shrill ring of the telephone assailed him like a dagger piercing his eardrums. He bounded off the couch and staggered over to the desk. It rang again, and just as he picked it up, he looked at the clock on the wall: ten minutes after seven. An icy hand clenched his racing heart.

"Hello?" he said hoarsely.

"Hello, Dr. Fiedler; this is Francine Watkins."

"Francine! What is it?"

"Is Miss Tate with you?"

"With me? What are you talking about?"

"I thought . . ." She hesitated. "Well, you were with her last night. I thought——"

"Do you mean that Mara is not at her apartment?"

"No, that's where I am. I just got back from a friend's place downtown. We had a Christmas party. Her bed's unmade, but she's not in the apartment."

"That's impossible; she was sleeping like a baby when I left her, shortly before one." He grimaced. What a stupid, self-incriminating thing to say, admitting that Mara was in bed when he left the apartment —left her *bedroom*.

Francine did not pick up on it; she was too distraught. "What should I do, doctor?"

"Get on the phone. Call TII. Call all of her close friends and business associates: Sean Tate, Lewis O'Toole, Jean Castle—— Oh, hell, Francine, you know who to call better than I do. Look, I'm on my way over right now. If we can't get any leads on her, there's only one thing left to do: call in the police. Good-by." As soon as he'd hung up, he phoned Leslie Tompkins.

Fiedler and Tompkins arrived at Mara's apartment within five minutes of each other. When they walked into the living room, Francine was pacing the floor, smoking a cigarette.

"I'm scared to hell," she muttered, jamming her hands deep into the pockets of her shaggy sweater.

"Francine, did you check her closets, her wardrobe?" Fiedler asked. "Is there anything missing?"

"Yes; right after I phoned you, I found her big suitcase gone, and plenty of clothes to fill it."

Fiedler gripped Tompkins's arm. "That's a good sign; at least we know she didn't wander out of here in a daze or a demoralized state. She's thinking practically, rationally—well, somewhat rationally. We can be fairly confident she's not standing on the Brooklyn Bridge contemplating suicide."

"I wish I could be as sure as you, Max," her internist declared.

"She took money, too," Francine said. "Her wall safe is open, and her checkbook and credit cards are gone."

"Another bright note," Fiedler said, brightening considerably now. "Well, our course is clear. I'll phone the police."

Within a half-hour, two plainclothesmen from the Missing Persons Bureau—Sergeant Cocoran and his partner, Detective Levy—arrived at the apartment, and they all sat down around the coffee table in the living room. Francine served them coffee and pastry while Fiedler did his best to describe the chronology of events that had led up to the mysterious disappearance of Mara Tate the third.

"You're sure she had no health problems?"

"She was physically sound as a dollar," Tompkins said. "Mentally . . ." He looked to Fiedler.

"Yes, Dr. Fiedler"—Cocoran seized on Tompkins's uncertainty—"was she mentally unsound? Of course she must have been, or she would not have been a patient of yours to begin with."

"Sergeant," Fiedler replied heatedly, "as a psychiatrist, I do not acknowledge the validity of such terms as 'mentally unsound' or 'crazy'; you know what I'm saying? Miss Tate had problems, yes. I mean, her professional responsibilities were enough to tax the emotional, mental, and physical limits of any top-ten management executives in the United States, male or female. Yes, she was feeling the strain of command. Every one of us has his or her own personal crises to contend with at times in our lives. That is why she was taking therapy with me."

"Exactly what was her state of mind last night when you saw her?"

"She was in high spirits."

"And yet, after supper, you felt obliged to have a therapy session with her? here in her own apartment?" The sergeant and the detective exchanged a brief glance and impaled Fiedler with cold, challenging stares. "Isn't it rather unorthodox, doctor, to engage in psychoanalysis in a patient's own home? You said this was a social occasion."

Fiedler prayed to God that he was not betraying his true feelings. He felt Tompkins's eyes on him, too; doubtless the internist was just as curious as the police-men about the previous night's tête-à-tête.

"Engage in psychoanalysis," Cocoran had said; *engage in sexual intercourse* is what Fiedler was think-ing.

"You are quite accurate, sergeant," he answered promptly. "It happened right after we had eaten supper. We were having coffee in front of the fireplace when, unexpectedly, she asked me to put her in a trance state."

"A trance state?"

"Yes, it's an accepted form of therapy in which the patient is put into a trance either by conventional hypnosis or by an injection of sodium pentothal or some other drug. While he is in this condition, the analyst 'takes him back in time,' to employ a layman's term, enabling him to remember events in his past life that have been lying dormant in the subconscious mind for years—in many cases, painful things his conscious mind has deliberately blocked out. In reconstructing such occasions under hypnosis, the analyst frequently can assist the patient in dealing with his present problems."

"Yeah, we had to attend a lecture at N.Y.U. last year about that, didn't we, Levy?"

"Something like it."

Neither could conceal his skepticism, his patronizing air.

"Go on, Dr. Fiedler," Cocoran said. "Why did you agree to do something that you believed to be professionally unethical?"

"Unethical?" Fiedler bridled. "Don't you go putting words in my mouth, sergeant. Unorthodox, perhaps, unusual, but damn well *not* unethical. The fact is, the only reason I agreed to this session last night was because Miss Tate threatened to experiment with self-hypnosis after I departed. As her analyst, I couldn't risk that. She had become quite proficient in self-hypnosis; and, in my professional opinion, it can be very dangerous to practice without a control present."

The policemen were contemplating him as if he were an alien species from outer space, every shrink joke they had ever heard no doubt running through their minds.

Fiedler got in a quick zinger. "I know what you're thinking, fellers: 'You don't have to be crazy to become a shrink, but it sure helps.' I understand."

It found its mark, and both men shifted their feet and avoided his defiant gaze.

Cocoran cleared his throat. "All right, so you went through with it," he said, adding: "In her bedroom."

"That's right—at Miss Tate's request."

"Did she undress before she got into bed?"

Slimy, salacious sonovabitch! Stay cool, Max!

"Miss Tate did not get into bed; she lay down on top of the bed, and she was wearing the same hostess gown she had on when I arrived and she was entertaining her accountant, Mr. Lewis O'Toole." He turned to Francine, who was hovering in the background. "Francine, did she take that gown along with her?"

"No, sir, it's still on the bed where she left it."

Detective Levy rubbed a heavy jaw, blue with stubble. "The way it looks to me, Russ, she was in big trouble with the law and couldn't stand the gaff. Like most of 'em, she takes it on the lam. Right now, I'll bet she's on an airliner winging her way to Cuba or Bermuda or the Biminis."

"That's sheer nonsense!" Dr. Tompkins snapped irritably. "Mara Tate is not some cheap embezzler; she is one of the most respected citizens in the United States, a close and trusted friend of President-elect Kennedy. I assure you she is not 'on the lam,' Detective Levy!"

"He's right, Harry," Cocoran said slowly; "but something very, very serious caused her to run away, and if anyone's capable of making an educated guess at what triggered her action, it's Dr. Fiedler, in my book. What about it, doc? Did this trance you put her into last night produce any clues that can help us?"

Fiedler stood up abruptly. "I think I'm beginning to get an inkling of what was on her mind when she decided to leave New York. You probably don't recall, sergeant, but back in 1956 Miss Tate's father and mother were killed in an air crash on a flight from Puerto Rico to Florida."

"It almost drove her into a nervous breakdown," Tompkins chimed in. "The Tates, this branch of the family, were a fiercely close-knit group. Long after the C.A.B., the navy, and the coast guard had given up the search for survivors, Mara kept on looking in her own private plane; she's a qualified pilot, among her many other accomplishments. It went on for days, weeks."

"That's where you should start looking for her, sergeant," Fiedler said, his excitement mounting. "I'll stake my reputation that she's headed south for Florida and then——" He decided to keep his rampant imagination to himself: *Miami, Cuba, Puerto Rico*— all of the foreboding expanses of land and water contained within the Bermuda Triangle.

CHAPTER SEVEN

It was two days later before the all-points bulletin issued by the New York police seeking the whereabouts of Mara Rodgers Tate produced results. Sergeant Cocoran notified Max Fiedler at his office in the middle of a therapy session. The analyst's secretary had orders to put through any call regarding Mara Tate, no matter whom he was seeing or what he was doing, a procedure he had never before enacted since beginning his practice.

He took the phone call in the small lavatory: "Anything new, sarge?"

"Got a real strong lead. Found out she was the woman called herself Mary Rogers who took a flight to Miami the morning after you saw her—a stewardess identified her photo—but she threw us off the scent by chartering a small plane to fly her back to Jacksonville. She was identified up there, too, using the same name, the day after. It took another day to trace what she did after that. Had to canvass every two-bit airport in the area; the waterfront, too. Finally, an old salt who runs a small marina at Green Cove Springs gave us the final clue: Mara Tate, alias Mary Rodgers, rented a fishing boat from him day before yesterday —sixteen-footer powered by twin Chrysler engines. Said she wanted to hook a marlin. The marina owner's son-in-law was hired to go out with her.

"Now comes the weird part, doc. Ten miles out of port she pulls a revolver and orders the young guy overboard in an inflatable dinghy. Can you imagine that?"

"I can imagine," Fiedler said under his breath. "So then what happened?"

"Nothing so far. Coast guard and navy have been alerted. There'll be a comprehensive air and sea search for the boat. Don't worry; they'll find her pretty quick."

"That's wonderful, sergeant," Fiedler said with numb lips. "Let me know if there are any new developments. . . . And thanks a million for letting me know."

"You bet, doc. So long."

Fiedler hung up and stared thoughtfully at the wall instrument for a while as he sat slumped over on the closed toilet lid. At length he stood up and walked back to his office and his impatient patient.

"Mrs. Weatherby . . . I'm terribly sorry, but we're going to have to reschedule you for another day. I've just received some very tragic news. Death in the family—my Aunt Jessica," he lied. "Please forgive me."

The stylish matron left in a huff, and Fiedler sat down behind his desk and picked up the microphone of his recorder. He cleared his throat and began to speak:

> Dear Ruth,
>   This is the most difficult task I have ever forced myself to do in my entire life. No, I do not have to "force myself." I have no control over my behavior. I am compelled by a power far beyond my own capacity to force any direction or decision as to my destiny.
>   As a psychoanalyst and psychiatrist, I have dedicated all of my adult life to fighting the shibboleths of superstition, ignorance, prejudice, and irrational fear. No longer do we burn witches or drive wooden stakes through werewolves' hearts or confine human beings in filthy, sadistic asylums

of doom, like Bedlam, for the crime of demoniac possession. I am the personification of "the man of reason"; I was, that is.

I hereby abdicate that title. In subjecting Mara Tate to the "rites" of age regression, I have unwittingly rendered myself vulnerable to that same irreversible power. In short, I have become a man possessed by the past. I realize none of this will make any sense to you, any more than it makes any sense to that part of me that affixed that plaque on my office door: "Dr. Maximilian S. Fiedler."

During the past four days, I have subjected myself to intensive and probing self-analysis. Do I love you, Ruth, and my children? The answer is overwhelmingly affirmative. I love you dearly. I adore my children. I will love the three of you unreservedly until the day I die. Mara Tate— what do I feel for her? Mara and I are cloned by a force, a power—an alchemic agent—that has no definition in our philosophy, not of this world and understanding. My Russian grandmother would have had a no-nonsense explanation for my condition: I have been inhabited by a dybbuk. I cannot advance a more valid thesis.

My legal affairs are all in order, and I have satisfied myself that you and the children will be more than adequately provided for over the next twenty years. Our attorney, Joe Anderson, is honest as well as brilliant, and genuinely concerned about the family's future welfare.

This is becoming unbearably painful for me, and I must curb the craving to ramble on and rationalize my actions, which, as I declared earlier, are inexcusable, inexplicable, and can never be justified by the criteria that you and I have known and accepted since our birth.

> *In parting, I ask you for one gift. Please kiss the children for me and tell them that I will love them through all eternity, as I will always love you.*
>
> *Good-by, Ruth, my darling wife*
>
> *Max*

Fiedler switched off the tape recorder and buried his head in his arms on the cold glass desk-top. After a while he sat up wearily, removed the cassette from the recorder, and locked it in the top drawer of his desk. He looked at the wall clock; it was almost time for his next appointment. He picked up the desk phone and pushed the button for the outer office: "Honey . . . you can send Mrs. Lacey in as soon as she gets here."

The tempo of his existence never varied for the next four days. He saw patients from ten in the morning to five-thirty in the afternoon. On Sunday he spent the day in bed in the hotel room he had rented, reading *The New York Times*. He was strangely at peace with the world.

He phoned Ruth religiously every day to inquire about her and the children.

She was curiously placid, almost apologetic: "I'm sorry about her, Max. Maybe you were telling the truth after all. She must have been desperately overwrought that night you saw her. I mean, the very next morning——"

"It's all right, Ruth. How could you know?"

"I should have trusted you, Max. Can you ever forgive me?"

"Nothing to forgive, Ruth; it's over and done with."

"Max . . . the children miss you. I told them you were in Chicago testifying at a big trial. Max . . . I miss you. When are you coming home?"

It was not an easy question for a proud woman like Ruth Fiedler to ask of a husband. Max knew that in her mind it was tantamount to groveling. His eyes filled up and his voice was thick: "Ruth, we'll settle the whole mess very soon; I give you my word. I'm working on something very, very big, and I've got to give it my full attention."

"Another patient like *her*. *Gott im himmel!* Max . . . you've been working too hard for too long. The strain is breaking you apart; it's breaking *me* apart." Suddenly the tone of her voice changed, brightened: "Max, darling, why don't you take some time off and we'll go away—Hawaii, the Virgin Islands, Europe—just the two of us. My parents will jump at the opportunity to take care of the kids. Please, Max, for me!"

Despising himself for his duplicity and cowardice, he told her, "I'll think about it, honest to God. Just give me a few more days."

"Whatever you say, Max—a few more days; but, dear God, say you will. It will do the two of us a world of good." Her laughter was brittle. "Just like a second honeymoon, right?"

"Right. . . . Look, Ruth, I have to go now. They're expecting me at Bellevue."

"All right, Max." She laughed nervously, close to hysteria. "Look, if we don't see you, happy New Year."

"Yeah . . . same to you and the kids." He hung up the phone and fell back on the bed in a state of total exhaustion. "Happy New Year!" he muttered scornfully. He picked up *The Times* and scanned the headline for the last time:

NAVY AND COAST GUARD ABANDON SEARCH FOR COPPER HEIRESS MARA TATE!

Mara even rated bigger typeface than Castro. Rumors out of Washington, D.C., had it that the United States was about to break off diplomatic relations with Cuba within the week.

Fiedler sat up, reached for the phone, and dialed the front desk: "This is Dr. Max Fiedler in room 711. I would like to get on the earliest flight to Havana, Cuba. Thanks. Oh, and make up my bill."

It might be sticky for an American to gain admission to Cuba in these critical times; but, if he had to, Fiedler would throw his weight around. Six months earlier he had treated the wife of a highly placed Cuban official in their United Nations mission: short-term therapy and highly successful. In accomplishing her cure, he had earned the undying gratitude of the Cuban minister.

He made a mental note to mail the cassette to Ruth. It was time.

EPILOGUE

Max Fiedler was at peace with himself and with the world as he ambled along the white beach at Sagua la Grande on the north coast of Cuba. He wore a red-and-white-striped polo shirt, white denim trousers cut off jaggedly at the knees, and white sneakers. Slung over his shoulder was a seaman's bag.

Soon he approached a run-down marina with a rickety pier extending about fifty feet into the ocean. Moored to it were half a dozen boats of various sizes and designs.

A fat man in baggy pants and a colorful shirt waddled out of the building. "Good morning, *señor*. Can I be of service to you?"

"Yes, I'd like to rent a boat for the day." He pointed to a trim little launch about twelve feet in length. It had no cabin, but a sun awning, supported by four bamboo poles at the corners, was strung above the cockpit.

The proprietor's eyes narrowed. "You have no fishing gear?"

"No, I'm strictly a sightseer."

"Sightseer . . . an American sightseer . . . hmmmm."

Fiedler could guess what he was thinking. Havana and other vacation havens on the tropical island had, not long before, been teeming with American tourists. However, deteriorating relations between Fidel Castro's revolutionary government and the United States, culminating in the nationalization and seizure of all Cuban banks and industrial companies by the rebels, and the retaliatory sugar embargo against Cuba by the United States, had created a hostile environment that virtually curtailed all tourist trade.

Fiedler assured him: "I am a member of the United States Trade Commission negotiating for an equitable settlement of the differences between our two great nations. Only last evening I had dinner with Che Guevera."

"Ahhhh, *señor,* please forgive me." His round face was a beaming sun. "We will all pray for your success. Cuba and America, they have always been traditional comrades. Side by side the American soldiers fought with us to liberate Cuba from the Spanish." He offered his hand, and Fiedler wrung it warmly.

"And now about the boat?"

"It is yours. . . . Do you know how to operate such a craft?"

Fiedler grinned. "I was an ensign in the United States Navy during the Korean War. I know a good deal about boats, big and small." It was the truth.

Fifteen minutes later, the *Fiesta* was putt-putting out of the picturesque little harbor into the open sea. The engine could use a tune-up and general overhaul, he mused, but she was otherwise sound and seaworthy —although the latter consideration was merely academic, as the sea undulated in soft swells that glittered with quicksilver slashes of sunlight.

When the coastline of Cuba disappeared over the horizon, Fiedler headed the boat's prow into the northeasterly gentle breeze and fixed the tiller. Opening his sea bag, he removed a sextant, a relic of his naval service, and a set of charts, and took a fix on the sun, recording his position: longitude 74° west; latitude 22° north. His destination was a point somewhere within a radius of ten miles of the last reported location of the DC-3 that had vanished in the Bermuda

Triangle on December 9, 1956, with Mara Tate's parents aboard.

Twice during the past week, Mara had visited him in fitful dreams:

Come to me, Max. I want you so desperately. I love you, Max. I am waiting. . . .

Her voice had trailed off with the winter winds wailing around the cornice outside his hotel-room window, recalling him to wakefulness.

You are surely going mad, Max, his rational self would plead with him. *Stop all this demonology before it's too late.* But the alien Fiedler was indomitable.

Time passed and he shot the sun again—none too soon; a film was passing across it, giving it the appearance of a dull copper coin. The wind grew stronger, churning up whitecaps. His heart beat accelerated as the overcast deepened until the sun was obscured altogether and the ceiling was descending onto the sea, the fog eerily phosphorescent.

Fiedler ignored the tiller now, was oblivious that the engine had stalled. He lay back on the cushions and reveled in the warm lassitude that was permeating his limbs. Blue blobs of Saint Elmo's fire danced around the boat's gunwales.

Suddenly he became aware of a distant roaring and sat upright. The *Fiesta* was drifting out of the fog into the magic circle of the eye, just as it had been described on tape by Mara when she was in deep trance.

Mara the first? Mara the second? Mara the third? Which one? Or were all three one?

It was of no consequence. Greenish sky overhead. Orange sun. *Two suns!*

He experienced not one twinge of fear, merely intense excitement and anticipation.

The boat was drifting faster now—faster and faster toward the core of the eye—the roaring building in crescendo, enveloping him in deafening quadraphonic sound. Then he was over the lip and hurtling down and around the sides of the maelstrom, around and around and down and down. It took his breath away, reminding him of the first time he had dared to ride the Cyclone at Coney Island as a boy. This was a supersonic roller coaster, but there was no danger of his falling out of the boat; centrifugal force pinned him fast against the boards.

Mustering all of his strength, he managed to pull himself partially up against the side so that he could peer over the gunwale. It was as near as he had come to fear or panic: The whirlpool was a bottomless black hole. It rang a responsive chord, but enlightenment eluded him.

And then every hair, short and long, fine and coarse, on every square inch of his body stood up, thousands of minute antennae, as her voice reverberated through the length of the diminishing cone like an echo rebounding from one mountain to another:

Max, you have come to me!
Max, you have come to me!
Max, you have come to me!

And he was through the barrier.

FOUR SIZZLING HISTORICAL ROMANCES BY STEPHANIE BLAKE